Also by LEX LANDER

Another Day, Another Jackal
End as an Assassin – André Warner, Manhunter Vol I

I KILL

LEX LANDER

Kaybec Publishing

First Published in 2016 by

Kaybec Publishing
441 Avenue President
Kennedy Suite 1003
Montreal
Québec H3A 0A4

ISBN: 978-0-9949981-4-9

Lex Lander. I Kill

I

Clair

One

Though my nightmares only come with the dark, they do not come from sleep. I view them in a state of wakefulness, through wide open eyes. It makes no difference whether I go to bed alone or with company, whether the room is lit or in darkness, whether I am at home or in some faraway place. An irresistible impulse rolls me onto my back, compels me to gaze ceiling-wards, to confront over and over the lifelike holograms that scroll across the plaster expanse, richly-coloured and so tangible I can smell them, taste them, even reach out and touch them.

They never vary, these nightmares. The images begin with the Italian girl. A glorious fifteen, maybe sixteen years old, hair falling to her waist in a golden cape; on the threshold of serious beauty. Across the paved *piazza* she runs, her gait slightly knock-kneed, her shadow bounding ahead, sharp-etched in the harsh Sicilian sunlight, into the arms of Luigi Pavan, her father. The man I have been hired to kill.

'*Papa! Papa!*' she cries, followed by a gush of Italian that is clearly a question, unintelligible to me, but faithfully lodged forever in my subconscious. '*Chi è quest'uomo? Cio che egli vuole?*' And her papa hugs her, keeping her back turned towards me as he murmurs in her ear, regarding me without blinking.

The gun is already in my fist. A Beretta PX4 Storm, the 17-round magazine version, coupled to a sound suppressor.

Slide racked, awaiting only the command from my curled forefinger. The timing is impeccable – would be impeccable were it not for the presence of the girl. The girl is not part of the plan. Nor is backing out. I am in too deep, my identity revealed, as it always is at the moment of execution. The next step must be forward.

The *piazza* is deserted. From a nearby tangle of bougainvillea the lazy drone of a bee pursuing its life's work. The windows of the encircling buildings are blind, shuttered against the furnace of the afternoon sun. Only the liquid outpourings of Pavarotti trickling through a gap in the shutters on the top floor of Pavan's *taverna* bear testimony to the presence of other humanity. Yet he is not cowed, this big, near-blond Italian who hails from Torino. A man with a taste for Ferraris and a mistress for every day of the week, funded by trade in heroin, crack, and worse. A man whom no laws can touch. Not a man to admire or respect, except perhaps for his guts in looking his executioner in the eye as his life is about to be ended.

At this point, in my spectral vision as in the reality, it becomes apparent to me why he holds my gaze so unflinchingly. Not after all in defiance, not in some last great show of bravado, but to distract. To gain time. As one hand caresses his daughter, the other is out of sight, up to no good …

I jump up, kicking the plastic chair clear while simultaneously extending my gun arm to sight on his head.

'Let the girl go, Pavan!' I yell. I don't speak Italian but his English is good enough to get my drift.

His response is an unintelligible snarl. As the startled girl twists round in his arms to face me, his weapon comes into the open – a snub-barrelled revolver with a shrouded hammer. I stay cool, confident in my ability to take him out without harming his daughter even as her presence, shielding all but his head, makes me hesitate, almost fatally. In the micro-second that separates intent from implementation he pumps two fast shots at me, the first parting my hair, the second smashing into my shoulder, sending me stumbling.

Somehow I keep my balance, converting the stumble to a dive. As my belly meets the ground and a third bullet ricochets off the paving somewhere behind me, overlaying a squeal from Pavan's daughter, I am already lining up the Beretta on his head. A single shot would be enough. But at the very instant the hammer comes down he clasps the girl to him, effectively protecting his head with hers. Maybe he still hopes to deter me and simply underestimates my speed, or maybe he is prepared to sacrifice his flesh and blood to save himself, or just maybe it's really no more than a reflex.

The girl's eyes widen. They are a bluish grey, I notice. In that fragment of a moment her pretty, immature features, contorted more by surprise than fear, are stored in my mind like a saved image on a digital camera. Her mouth pops open to form the beginnings of a squeal that is sheared off when the soft-nosed bullet ploughs into her temple, a fraction below the hairline. The top of her skull bursts into fragments, spraying bright blood and brain and chips of bone over the table and over me. Even lying on my bed, knowing full well that the scene is no more than a re-enactment of history, I flinch as the slender body in its blue T-shirt and yellow biker shorts seems to deflate like a punctured ball, beauty and life instantly flying from it.

The bullet that kills her does not spare Pavan. On exit it slices along his jaw, gouging a groove all the way back to his ear, tearing away the lobe. More blood sprays. The revolver slips from his grasp, but he has lost all interest in it. Sinking to his knees, he holds his mutilated daughter at arm's length, shaking her, and sobbing *'Bambina mia!'* over and over, his voice made incoherent by his shattered jaw. Gore dribbles from his mouth onto her T-shirt. All that beauty, all that perfection, gone in the flicker of an eyelid.

Back on my feet, shaken by the consequences of my shot, I am barely aware of the throb of my wounded shoulder. The revulsion, the remorse, these emotions do not hit me yet. The adrenaline still courses, instincts still fire on all cylinders, and above all I remain bent on honouring my precious contract. I circle the table. Pavan pays me no heed. Moaning volubly, he lowers his daughter gently to the ground. He seems to have forgotten I am here, and why. Behind me, on the far side of the *piazza*, a shout, male, is followed by a shriek, female. Members of his family. Pavan's unsilenced shots have alerted them, negating the value of my own weapon's sound suppressor.

Pavarotti is coming to a crescendo, the last rousing bars making the very air shimmer. It seems poetic somehow to finish the job as the tenor's mighty voice soars to its climax amidst the final crash and thump of the orchestra.

'Here it comes,' I say softly to Pavan. 'With love from the brothers.'

Hunched over his daughter's body, he does not react. About killing *him* I have no compunction at all. I blow a hole in the back of his head from a range of two inches and he subsides soundlessly on top of his daughter, in a pose that borders on obscene.

More shouts, then shots as I sprint for the unmarked stolen Fiat with the false plates. The shooting is wild, panicky. Glass shatters. I am moving too fast for them to draw a bead on me. No time to pause and regret the death of the girl, terrible though it is. Self-preservation, finely honed from years of evading pursuit, expels me from that place. As I start the engine the left rear window explodes inwards, scattering

4

baubles of glass over my head and shoulders. Another shot goes nowhere. Then I am accelerating away, hurling the Fiat into a bend that instantly screens me from view.

It is not until the late evening of that day that emotions crowd out the physical stresses of the getaway. When I am safely across the water in Valetta, ensconced in the corner of the bar at the very old but ordinary Castille Hotel, my shoulder wound dressed (it's no more than a groove in the skin), cuddling a glass of Cheval Blanc, Malta's unique home grown wine. Only then, with the pressure easing, does the enormity of my crime descend on me, like a black thundercloud. My eyes moisten. There, in public and for the first time in my adult life, I let tears flow, and if anyone notices I don't care. Through a decade of contract killing I have never harmed an innocent person, far less a child. My track record is pure, my professionalism absolute. Until this day. Albeit that I have achieved the result I have been paid for, it is a bungled job and there is no getting away from the fact.

As I gradually regain control over my dolour I make an effort to quash the "if only" recriminations. It will be a passing phase. A good night's sleep will heal the wound, and put the incident behind me. Life, for me at any rate, will go on. But there I am wrong. The remorse does not diminish after a good night's sleep because sleep itself is denied me and indeed is to become a luxury. Days pass and become weeks, weeks become months, and still that young girl's lovely face lives on in my mind. If anything the balloon of my conscience swells in size and intensity, heated by the roaring fires of guilt. It becomes my ever-present companion. It squats on my shoulders like a vengeful imp, riding me, pricking me, and giving me no peace.

*

After that experience I retired from my deadly profession to heal the wounds of my mind and plan a new beginning. It was a route I had gone down before and the outcome this time around was no different. No obvious new beginnings presented themselves, and I sank gradually into depression. To lubricate the passage of the empty hours and blot out the guilty memories I took up the balm of liquor. Additional anaesthetic was provided by a plethora of sex, whenever and with whomsoever I could get it, paid or unpaid. Not because my sex drive had suddenly escalated; if anything the opposite was true. The sex was incidental, the object was to avoid spending nights alone. I wasn't particular, nor was I proud. When to my disappointment even regular doses of booze and bimbos failed to keep the door closed on the past, I stepped up the booze and began to dabble in so-called recreational drugs. For a while these placebos worked, by deadening my senses without noticeably impairing my sexual prowess.

In this pathetic, pitiful manner, so help me God, I whiled away a summer and two winters. Now, as another spring got under way, I sensed the approach of the proverbial moment of truth. A coming to an intersection in my road to nowheresville, where I would be presented with a choice between two alternative routes: carry on down the one I was travelling, surely a dead end, or take the fork in search of the fabled sunlit uplands, if I knew where they were. The prospect was daunting. And if my instincts were right, and that choice would shortly have to be made, was I still capable of rousing myself to make it?

*

Behind me the girl stirred, muttered drowsily. After our lovemaking, no matter what the hour, she always slept the sleep of the exhausted. And always awakened bursting with renewed desire and energy and the need for a cigarette. Name of Simone, from Grenoble. Dropped-out student doing a summer stint as waitress at the Hotel Mercure, down in Andorra-la-Vella, the diminutive capital city of Andorra the country, where I had made my home these past two years. Just nineteen years old – Simone, not the city. Put another way, half my age. She didn't mind, why should I? A female body, with all the necessary trappings, was all I required. She served a purpose.

'André?' A lazy, pouting drawl from the rumpled bed.

'You awake?' I said, turning from the window.

She was not only awake but sitting up. Her breasts were shaped like isosceles cones, perfectly symmetrical. She stretched and made them quiver, doing wicked things to me. Simone, my teenage playmate. Simone of the sandy hair, brown eyes, sensuous lips, magnolia skin, spotted here and there with moles. When we had sex, did she lie back and think of France, I wondered?

'You know,' she said, 'when you stand with the sun behind you, your hair looks like a little field of corn.' She made a V of her arms and a pout of her lips. 'Come back to bed, chéri.'

I'm a sucker for the unclothed female form, so I obeyed the summons. My sex drive remained reliable, regardless of my state of mind and sobriety. But as we lunged and plunged away at each other, she with her thighs back under her armpits – the girl was double-jointed, I swear – I saw as always another face, with blonde hair and wide blue-grey eyes, heard anew the cries of 'Papa! Papa!' dinning away inside my head, endlessly, endlessly, endlessly …

Around nine am, just as I was stepping under the shower, my cell phone chirruped. Fuming gently, I wrapped a towel around my waist and went into the bedroom, leaving a spoor of damp footprints. The rumpled bed was empty, my play-mate long gone to serve at tables.

'André Warner?' It was Giorgy, business associate and maker of calls at inconvenient times. 'Good morning, my friend, how are you?' he breezed on, without waiting for an acknowledgement. His greetings were consistently breezy and never more so than when he caught me pants down.

'I was in the shower,' I grumbled, in no mood for his pleasantries.

'You are always in the shower. What is it that makes you so dirty?'

'The jobs I did for you maybe?' I quipped sourly.

Giorgy – full name Giorgio du Poletti – was a Sicilian who worked for an organization he referred to as the Syndicate. Maybe a euphemism for the Mafia, though I didn't think so. He was a tall, slim, elegant man with silver-streaked hair and an infinite supply of Savile Row suits. A man I had known on and off for six years. A man who, until my retirement, had provided me with regular employment killing the enemies of his masters.

I suppressed my surprise at this contact after months of silence. We chatted on about last night's soccer match between Juventus Milan and Liverpool before, in that switch-on switch-off manner of his, he came to the point: he had work for me and was I in the market?

'You must be desperate. You know I've quit the game.'

'Some professions are not for quitting. Your retirement was never convincing. It is time to give up the pretence. So … I ask again, are you available for work?'

'Maybe.' The word passed my lips with no help from me. It left me mildly stunned. After all, for over a year now I had been dealing him a strictly negative answer to that question.

'You mean it?' The surprise in his voice was a manifestation

8

of the surprise I felt. 'You really are ready to go back to work?'

'Maybe,' I said again, only now it sounded more like 'probably'. My damp skin was chilling. I towelled parts of it one-handedly.

'But this is marvellous news!'

'Yeah, well, don't throw your toupee into the air just yet, Giorgy. I'll need convincing.'

'You want more money? This can be arranged.'

It was gratifying to know that my services were so valuable. And after a fourteen month furlough the desire to find a new purpose in life was becoming a necessity.

'The subject, is he a bad 'un?'

'The worst,' Giorgy confirmed.

Thus far in my work I had only ever accepted contracts on bad guys. I had managed to convince myself that by eliminating bad guys I was saving some good guys and gals from their clutches. Sanctimonious? Maybe. Naive? I hope not, but the inner me needed some sort of vindication. I couldn't have killed an innocent. Not coldly, deliberately, for wages. Yet, of course, I had once done just that, if not for a fee, certainly in pursuance of profit.

I trusted Giorgy enough to accept his unqualified assurance. He had never steered me wrong in the past.

'Where?' was the all-important, ultimate question. There were countries where I now feared to tread, or at least to ply my trade, and Giorgy was aware of it.

'Do not worry. This one is in Morocco.'

'Well, at least the sun shines there.'

'You don't need sun, my friend. For your kind of sickness, you need work, purpose, something to occupy you and keep your mind off dead Italian girls.'

'Ouch. You know how to punch low, Giorgy.' I sighed hard into the handset and a chuckle came back at me. 'But you're not wrong. Email me the when and where, and I'll see you then and there.'

After he rang off I postponed completion of my shower. Instead I raided the bedside bottle for my morning pick-me-up, which I carried out onto the balcony. Even this early the sun struck like a death ray, and the tiles were warm underfoot. The house was on a split level, built into the hillside, and the outlook across the valley and the village of La Massana should have been a tonic for my glazed eyeballs. It wasn't though. These days my outlook was all monochrome.

A minibus was rattling down the road towards the village, raising a dust cloud. Nearer at hand the ice-blue prow of my two week-old Aston Martin jutted out below the edge of the terrace. Normally I garaged it but last night Simone – giggling, wriggling, strewing scraps of clothing about the place – had also needed garaging and the car wasn't even in the contest. Beyond the Aston the water of the kidney-shaped swimming pool twinkled like tinsel in the hard sunlight. Luxury villa, luxury car, luxury pool, not to mention a forty-foot yacht berthed at Sitges, in Spain, these were only the more obvious signs of affluence. All purchased, it has to be confessed, with blood money.

My nearest neighbours, Lucien and Madeleine Bos, a retired French couple, were breakfasting on their patio. They waved. I returned the gesture.

I drained my glass and sat in the all-weather armchair that stood in a corner of the balcony, there to dwell upon Giorgy's latest proposition. The next step was a meet, at which the minutiae would be revealed. My ruminations didn't revolve around the job itself but around my change of heart, the prospect of an end to my retirement. Had I reached the fork in the road I had seen coming? To go back to my former trade would be not so much a road to the sunlit uplands as a descent to the dark depths from whence I had crawled. The only thing in its favour was the incentive to get me out of bed in the morning that it would provide. Giorgy's assessment of what ailed me was right as far as that went.

The downsides to going back to my old wicked ways were many and prodigious. I had been lucky in my profession. My forty-one contracts had left me with the equivalent of close on ten million US dollars in a variety of secret bank accounts, and still relatively free to come and go in all but a handful of countries. Why go back to killing, with its attendant moral dilemmas and risk of incarceration for life or even, in many parts of the world, execution? Crazy. Yet what were the alternatives? Carrying on as now, filling the empty days and hours and minutes with screwing and drinking, and popping pills? Purpose and direction were what I lacked, and a contract would at least provide those. Even in this second decade of the new millennium, demand for my unusual skills had not diminished. People still wanted people killed, and the motives were the same as ever: jealousy, spite, revenge, rivalry, hatred, family feuds ... And of course profit, the biggest killer of all.

Just this once then. One more contract, then I really would retire.

The hollow laughter was inside my head, but no less loud for that.

*

Giorgy was waiting, as arranged, at the American Bar, which looks out on Marseille's Vieux Port. There he lounged, partly screened from the sun under a faded Coca-Cola parasol. Cool and chic in a cream lightweight suit and burgundy silk shirt, dark glasses shielding the greater part of his handsome, lantern-jawed face, deep in an Italian newspaper – *Le Giornale*, what else?

'Will you take something, André?' he asked in his fluent

French, when the preliminaries were behind us, indicating his own empty beer glass.

'Vodka with ice, thanks,' I responded in the same language. I was at least his equal in French, thanks to my Québécoise mother (dead, these past six years), who was also to blame for my given name. My very English father had preferred Andrew, his own middle name, but my mother pooh-poohed this as vanity, and the compromise outcome was André. Anyhow, Dad had registered his protest by always calling me Andrew.

I sat down beside Giorgy, not opposite him. Conversing discreetly is easier side by side.

'Stick to English,' I cautioned as he took a breath to speak. The subject we were about to discuss was not for other ears and French therefore best avoided. An example of the ultra-caution I applied to all my professional doings. It had kept me out of prison and/or an early grave. So far.

Giorgy nodded assent. A bulging reinforced envelope passed from him to me.

'One hundred thousand euros in five hundred notes, one hundred thousand US dollars in thousand bills,' he said and couldn't resist his customary smirk, as if he'd just that minute run them off on his own printing press.

This was the down payment, fifty per cent of the full fee, less his commission. The balance was payable immediately before execution of contract, and no balance meant no execution. Those were my terms, take 'em or leave 'em. They had not always been so favourable to me, but certainly in the last few years before my 'retirement' I had been writing my own contracts.

'Confident, aren't you, I'm going to do it?' I said, but stuffed the package inside my check sports jacket, which would be an answer in itself as far as Giorgy was concerned. Sure enough, his smirk broadened.

My vodka and another beer for Giorgy were placed before us on the table. The waiter shoved a tab under the edge of the metal ashtray. I took a big swallow of vodka, the ice tapping against my teeth. People swirled past, intent on their own affairs, only occasionally sparing an incurious glance for the people seated at the tables.

'And the subject?' I prompted.

'Ah.' Giorgy transferred another envelope from his pocket to my waiting palm. It was brown and weighed very little.

'Seems light,' I remarked. 'Short of information?'

A breeze wafting in off the sea ruffled his straight, scalpel-parted hair. He smoothed it down before replying. Not a hair out of place, that was Giorgy.

'The information is adequate, do not fear.' He eyed a Junoesque brunette in a floral skirt as she strode past our table. His sigh was seriously heartfelt.

'The girls in this city are extra-special, do you not agree?'

'I do agree.' I did too. I knew several Marseilloises intimately, in the literal sense.

We had passed the time of day. The rules of *politesse* had been observed. I debated whether to whistle up a refill but decided against. I didn't want to use up my quota too early in the day. So I stood up, transferring a pair of sunspecs from shirt pocket to nose. Giorgy was smiling quizzically up at me, eyes invisible behind his own dark glasses: oval Ray-Bans, very in. Or maybe not so in nowadays. I had lost interest in keeping track of fashions some years back.

'You know, you interest me, André. As a human being, that is.'

'Oh yes? You mean the way a rare bug under the microscope interests a scientist?'

He snorted faintly. 'In a way, I suppose. You obviously have an educated background, which alone is rare among contract killers. You also have compassion for your fellow man, otherwise why refuse contracts on moral grounds, as you occasionally do. You know, you have never told me how you came to enter this profession ...'

Nor was I likely to. My life history was not for public consumption. Why should I explain to Giorgy how the only difference between killing for Queen and Country, as I had once done, and killing for profit, was the size of the pay cheque? Or how my gorgeous loving wife would not have died twelve years ago but for the 'Department' and its contempt for the individual and devotion to the State, right or wrong. Morally speaking, I was now on at least as high a plane as in the days when I took my orders from a senior civil servant to whom the life of others was of less value than a dog turd.

So all I said was, 'If I *were* to tell you, you'd know more than was good for your health.'

The smile slipped.

'That almost sounds like a threat. You are sure you want this job?'

'No, I'm not. But I need it.' I was still clutching the slim envelope. I saluted him with it. 'You'll be hearing from me.'

'Don't leave it too long.' He made a noise in this throat. 'There are rumours ... gossip, if you prefer, about you. It is said you are drinking heavily.' He was clearly embarrassed. He signalled an apology with his hands. 'Not that it is any of my concern. Unless it affects the quality of your work, unless you make a mistake. You understand? The Syndicate is not tolerant of mistakes.'

Giorgy was little more than a high class liaison man for *Il Sindacato* – the Syndicate – a likely *cognoscenti* euphemism for the Unione Sicilione, who for reasons undisclosed occasionally employed sub-contract enforcers in preference to their own kith and kin. In the past I had never asked why and wasn't about to ask now. I didn't care. So long as the days were busy and my life had meaning, I was content to remain ignorant.

'Mistakes, Giorgy?' I said, and my tone was light. I reached down and with calculated condescension patted his cheek. 'I won't make any. Just be sure you don't either.'

His resentment was naked but he rode it like the gentleman he professed to be, forcing a smile back into place. He even offered to shake hands.

'I am your friend, André,' he said reproachfully, as we clasped. 'A true friend. Perhaps even your only true friend.'

Perhaps he was right. The professional killer treads a lonely path.

Two

A fortnight later I was in Tangier, a city, like Marseilles, infested with crime. Unlike Marseilles it is ramshackle, dusty, and smelly; stimulating, lively, vivid, and a den of intrigue. A city of kebabs and couscous, hookah and hashish, and of musicians playing Berber melodies from a long dead past. And since 9/11 gently simmering with anti-Western sentiment. As yet the jihadists were in the background. Waiting, no doubt, for a sign from Allah to commit one of their atrocities.

The modern-traditional Atlas Rif Hotel was to be my centre of operations. Although less Europeanised than the Intercontinental and the newer Moevenpick along the bay (held to be the best in town), I preferred it for the combination of proximity to town centre and beach, its private balconies, and its superbly-equipped gym. On the seaward side all rooms enjoyed a magnificent panorama clear across the Strait of Gibraltar.

The hotel staff were a predictably mongrel bunch. The door of my taxi was opened by a very black African decked out in braid and brass, and keen to maximize his tip. My bags were snatched from the taxi-driver's grasp by a youngster in traditional Moroccan dress, equally motivated by monetary advantage. The girl at the reception desk was blonde, probably Nordic in origin: cool, brisk, wearing severe glasses and speaking flawless French, and wouldn't have touched a tip with a sterilized fishing rod.

'*Monsieur* Melville,' she said, in a voice that made you feel she cared, all warm and cosseting. 'Welcome to the Rif Hotel. May I have your passport, please?'

André Warner as an individual was in cold storage. For the next few weeks I was Alan Melville, complete with credentials to that effect. The central and most vital component of this collection of IDs and credit cards was a passport created by a different process from that approved by Her Majesty's Passport Office. In my case you took the genuine thirty-two page article in its virgin state (2000 euros apiece from a corrupt clerk at a British Embassy, the location of which shall be nameless to protect the guilty), added a genuine unflattering photo from one of those automatic booths, and mixed well with the talents of an Irishman known to me only as 'Freddie'. Freddie was a failed currency forger, with seven years in Dublin's Kilmainham jail to prove it didn't pay, who had now discovered his true vocation. At the end of forty-eight hours of his ministrations, in exchange for five thousand US greenbacks, you had a passport that was good for crossing any frontier, anyplace in the world. It even passed the electronic scanning process.

I obtained all my bogus passports in this fashion.

All my details having been entered into the computer, plus some tedious form filling 'for the authorities', I was led to the lift by the bellboy in Arab attire, for a creaky ride to the top floor and Suite 604.

'Anything else, sir?' the bellboy enquired in French that was anything but flawless, as I paid him off with a twenty-dirham coin.

'Yes, bring me a bottle of vodka and a bucket of ice, will you?'

He certainly would. It meant a second tip.

It was around four in the afternoon, the outside temperature in the middle thirties Celsius, and the immediate priority was a cold shower. Subsequent to this, naked but for a towel, I explored my quarters, comprising bathroom, bedroom and sitting room, all plush and spacious by modern hotel standards. The furniture, which included a fancy chaise-longue, was solid-looking, the woodwork Moorish filigree, and the bed big enough for two to romp on, should opportunity knock. Sliding doors led from both rooms onto an enclosed balcony. I opened the one in the sitting room. Sea breeze, heavily perfumed with ozone, stirred the full-length net curtains and an indistinct skirl of Moroccan music dribbled in.

I took my Swarovski binoculars out onto the balcony, there to sweep the Bay of Tangier with its shifting shades of blue and its frieze of surf that sparkled like a diamond necklace. The shoreline to the east was wreathed in haze, land and sea blending with no delineation between. To the west, rising grandly above the general concrete sprawl, was the medina, the old town, with its fortified *kasbah*, overlooking the port, where a crane was lowering a wooden crate into the hold of a rusty freighter.

The binoculars were powerful: 10 X 40, with a zoom facility. I zoomed in on the packed beach, passed over the ranks of sun worshipping European bottoms, a ripe invitation to the beheading brigade. From the beach I traversed eastward past the suburb of Plage and on to where the buildings petered out. But the grandiose villa at the very tip of a promontory that I was seeking lay beyond Cap Malabata, the other horn of the bay, and was lost in the haze.

From behind me came a diffident cough.

'*M'sieu* ...'

My vodka and ice were served. To the bellboy went the honour of loading the ice into the glass, stripping the seal off the bottle and pouring. More dirhams changed hands and he left me to my dubious pleasures. The liquor slid down my gullet, so cold it burned. The second was better still, injecting frozen fire into my bloodstream. Showing restraint, the third I merely sipped, topping up the ice and returning to the balcony, blinking at the transition from shady interior to white glare.

Unaided by the binoculars I contemplated the street directly below – the Avenue d'Espagne, teaming with vehicles and humanity. The traffic was inclined to be Gallic in character, plenty of hooting and squealing tyres and exchanges of insults. A movement on the next balcony to the left caught my eye, and I glanced casually over the waist-high wall that separated all the suites. Stretched out on a sun-bed, her nose in an electronic book reader, was a woman in bikini top and shorts: European or North America at a guess. Slim figure, dark brown hair, lightly-waved and cut fairly short. Speaking as a well-rounded roué, the overall package wasn't bad at all.

Even as I scrutinised her, she raised her head from her gadget and shaded her eyes to return the scrutiny.

'Good morning,' I said, 'or should it be *bonjour.*'

'Good morning is fine.' American with a dash of Antipodes. Unusual combination. No warmth in it though.

'Just arrived,' I informed her, hoisting a chummy grin. It wasn't returned. No matter, perseverance was my middle name. 'Terrific view. That's Spain over there, I guess.' I gestured northwards with my glass, ice clinking. 'Pity the Rock's out of sight though.'

'Which rock would that be?'

Was she pulling my leg? Her expression said not.

'Well … Gibraltar, of course.'

'Oh. Sorry, geography's not my strong point.'

'You've never been there then? To Gib, I mean.'

From her discouraging frown you'd have thought I was about to suggest an immediate elopement to the place.

A flat 'No.'

So far, it was uphill work. But at least we were communicating. As I was about to extol the attractions of that disputed piece of real estate she stood up abruptly and went indoors. My half-open mouth shut with a click of teeth and my shoulders mentally shrugged. Plenty more grapes on the vine.

My glass was somehow empty. I re-entered the sitting room to replenish it and crashed down on the chaise-longue, which sighed but otherwise held firm. Supine, I think more clearly, and I wanted to knock my plans into a semblance of shape. Tomorrow was to be a working day. I would rent a car, drive the twenty or so kilometres along the coast to the rich man's settlement of Petite Europa for a casual look-see. Then I would decide if the hit was to take place there, at his villa, and if not, begin the surveillance process, the recording of his comings and goings, locating his soft spot, and so on, a process that had been known to take up to a month. Giorgy had assured me that our man was in residence, and Giorgy's assurances were almost always good as gold.

'According to his private secretary he will be at the villa from 18 June to the end of the month at least,' was precisely how he put it. Today was 20 June.

After a while, under alcohol's deadening influence, plotting became a strain and I dozed off.

My sister Julie (christened Juliette), who had recently moved with husband and two daughters from Toronto, Canada, to London, England, expected a postcard whenever I travelled abroad. Her elder daughter, my niece Cathy, collected them and mounted them on the walls of her bedroom. In some places the wallpaper was no longer apparent.

I chose a card depicting part of the *kasbah*, scrawled some trite message on the back, and signed off with a security-conscious 'A', as was my wont. For the sake of exercise I strolled into town to pop it into the box at the main post office in Rue el Msallah. Duty done. I had no other obligations, no commitments, no ties. I used to prefer it like that. Nowadays though, travelling alone was becoming last year's fashion. Same as living alone.

From the post office I taxied to the three-rosette Damascus Restaurant in the quieter, southern precinct of the city. It was renowned for its *haute cuisine marocaine*, but I discovered that gastronomically speaking it wasn't what it had been on my only previous visit. Either that or else my palate had grown fussier.

After lunch, a leisurely return stroll to the Rif, there to catch up on some homework. It was cooler today and overcast, though still warm enough for sitting on the balcony, accompanied by a bottle, a glass, and a bucketful of ice. And a slim brown envelope.

I drank to absent neighbours before spilling the envelope's contents into my lap: eight items, of which the topmost was a colour studio portrait of the subject on A4 paper. Two other printed photos were of the Petite Europa settlement and the subject's villa respectively, taken from the air. These were supplemented by architects' blueprints of the villa grounds and the interior of the building, plus a large-scale map of the coastline eastwards from Tangier to the town of Ksar es Seghir. The remaining two sheets contained the subject's vital statistics, printed out in good old Times New Roman font.

I ran through it for maybe the hundredth time. The man's name was Akram Al'hauri. He was Egyptian, aged fifty-one, and he ran drugs by the container load. In other words, a regular scumbag. A laconic post-script, "Believed to be engaged in other criminal activities", probably concealed more than it revealed. On reaching the end of the personal profile I refilled my glass and contemplated a sea no longer blue but sludge-grey, coloured only by the small craft and sailboards that darted like dragonflies. A gull coasted lazily past my window on a downdraught and squawked at nothing in particular.

Phase one of the operation was an inspection of Petit Europa, and, conditions permitting, of the villa. Before proceeding though, I needed confirmation that Al'hauri really had stuck to his plan to be here from the 18th. So I looked up his telephone number on his CV and called him using my cell phone.

As unscientific as that.

While it rang I propped the studio portrait on the bedside table, to match the face to the voice. The receiver at the other end was lifted and a bored incantation oozed from it.

'Maison Al'hauri.'

'*Bonjour, monsieur,*' I boomed, full of the spurious bonhomie of a professional insurance tout. '*Etes-vous Monsieur Al'hauri?*'

He wasn't, he was the major-domo, and he wasn't about to fetch his master to the phone to answer a telesales call neither.

'*Je regrette, mais il est occupé.*'

Occupé, i.e. otherwise engaged. Confirmation enough that he was in residence. But just to be sure …

'*Est-ce qu'il sera là ce soir?*'

'*Non.*' A shade more terse, a "mind your own damn business" kind of tone. '*Il va sortir.*'

So he was going out. Short of making a nuisance of myself, I felt I had pushed it as far as I could. The line went dead, taking the decision out of my hands. The cell phone battery icon was flashing a warning so I connected the charger and plugged in. The electrical sockets here are the same as in France, which made it easy.

Object accomplished, I could now press on with phase two, the gathering of data: Al'hauri's daily routine, a list of other residents at the villa, the security arrangements by day and by night, to mention but some of the blanks in my knowledge. Already I was impatient to move the process along. The thrill of the kill wasn't in me yet, but it would be soon enough.

I siesta'd the rest of the afternoon away. My sleep was dreamless for once. On awakening to the long shadows of evening, I changed into shorts, T-shirt, and track shoes, and went down to the gym. A punishing 90-minute work-out later, showered and dressed casual-smart in a cream linen suit, I set off to buy me some hardware. And I don't mean hammer and nails.

Three

An open bottle of Sidi Bughari wine stood on the dining table in the drab little room with its unpainted walls and tacky, Ikea-inspired furniture. The two brothers, Ahmad, the elder, and Yacoub, sat side by side facing me. Since Islam outlaws intoxicating liquor North African Muslims stick to mint tea as a rule, failing this, a concoction known as orange-flower water. This pair were somewhat less than devout. They downed two glassfuls of wine apiece while I was still checking mine against the light for foreign bodies.

Yacoub made a drinking motion with his hand. 'S'good. Drink!' he urged me.

'Here's to the hair of the dog,' I proposed, with a silent apology to my constitution. I had a hunch Sidi Bughari and vodka would not co-exist in harmony.

Ahmad, turbaned, gap-toothed, inclined to plumpness, cried, 'Allah to that!' Yacoub, slimmer and better looking, nodded enthusiastically and drank with haste, as if it were an illicit treat that might be snatched away. The third member of the family, Yacoub's wife, watched this performance from the other side of the room in wordless disapproval, eyebrows contracting. In her dark *burka* and veil she was not dressed for levity. I wondered idly if she were naked underneath.

Three toasts later Yacoub jumped up and left the room. When he returned he was armed with another bottle and what appeared to be a rolled-up grey blanket, which he deposited reverently on the table to the clink of metal against metal. Grinning, he then proffered the bottle. Reminding myself I was here on business, I primly covered my glass.

'Later,' I said softly. 'Afterwards.'

Glances were exchanged between brothers, and Ahmad rattled off a fusillade of Arabic at which Yacoub looked sour and rammed the stopper back in the bottle.

'Forgive my brother,' Ahmad said, to an ingratiating display of gapped teeth and large tracts of gum. His French was rough-cast with an Arabic timbre. 'He is still young and inexperienced in matters of trade.'

Yacoub merely glowered.

I waved a permissive hand and turned my attention to the bundle that Ahmad was now unrolling. The plasticky tang of gun oil rose from it.

'It was said you wish for a pistol,' he murmured. 'However, it does no harm to give a choice, hein?'

So, maybe to flaunt the extent of his stock, he had brought both: two rifles, three pistols, all pristine and lightly filmed with oil. He sorted and arranged them on the grey blanket as if setting out a market stall.

The rifles were superfluous. I planned to hit Al'hauri close up. Ahmad, like any streetwise salesman, was quick to suss where my interest lay. He thrust a pistol at me.

'This my top seller.'

I made no comment as I examined his offering, a 9mm Beretta 92F automatic, a type I had used on many occasions. Magazine capacity a healthy fifteen rounds, in a double column. Ensuring the gun wasn't loaded, I operated the slide. As always, it felt natural in my fist, as if we were made for each other. A marriage made in hell.

'It was said you prefer a revolver,' Ahmad purred, 'but I can assure you the Beretta is of the highest reliability.'

'So I've heard.' I squinted along the barrel, tried to get a feel for the balance. A full magazine would increase the weight by a significant amount, making it butt heavy, a point in its favour.

Yacoub tugged at my sleeve. '*Ceci plus bon*,' he said, mangling his French in the manner of a British tourist.

'*Ceci*' was a second Beretta, and for all my close links with the gun trade it was a first encounter with the awesome 93R.

The basic format and profile of this pistol correspond to the 92 but mechanically they are chalk and cheese. The 93 is, in fact, a variation on the machine pistol theme, incorporating a 3-round burst facility and an extended magazine holding twenty rounds. My views on handgun design being conservative, I was critical of most attempts to create a fully-automatic pistol. It's never been done with outright success – even the famed German Schmeisser was really a military machine carbine whose folding stock gave it a pistol-like appearance. On the other hand, it was claimed that the Beretta, thanks to a combination of the low cyclic rate of fire of under 120 rounds per minute, a prominent muzzle brake in the elongated barrel, and most of all the folding front grip, made for a steady shooting platform.

Ahmad reached across me, emitting Sidi Bughari fumes. 'Here is the selector ... you can choose single shots or automatic.'

I nodded and thumbed the selector catch from SAFE through FIRE to BURST, the last-mentioned distinguished by three red spots in a triangular grouping.

'What would this little gadget cost me?'

Ahmad clucked and sucked his teeth, a sure auspice of impending extortion. Not that, privately, I minded paying over the odds. When you buy an illegal firearm through an established trafficker you are assured of top grade merchandise and, no less important, top-grade ammunition. Most of all you also buy secrecy. No comebacks was the unwritten warranty among armourers. In the past I had had my own network of suppliers on whom I could call. For this, my renaissance job, I was relying on Giorgy's.

A shadow darkened the Beretta as I turned it in my hands. I slewed round in my chair. Yacoub's wife was beside me, so close her hip grazed my shoulder. Her huge, burnt-sienna eyes, which were the only visible part of her, fastened on me and remained on me as she reached over to touch the Beretta. Her breathing quickened as she stroked the barrel slide, making tracks in the oil with her fingertips.

I looked at Yacoub. He was unmoved, regarding her imperturbably. Ahmad seemed faintly amused.

I held the gun out at Yacoub's wife. 'Here, take it. Don't be afraid of it.'

From behind the veil came a hiss of breath, and she recoiled as from a venomous spider. Ahmad laughed, a nervous honk.

'She is a jihadist, *monsieur*,' he sniggered. 'She and others would have a revolution here in Morocco and make us into slaves of Isis if they could. For that, many guns will be required.'

Pinpoints of orange flickered in the burnt sienna eyes. That was the only display of emotion that escaped the veil. Then she retreated to her chair, back to her submissive world, back to being the wife of a Muslim.

'To resume, then.' Ahmad pushed a stray black strand from his forehead. 'You will see I have also brought a revolver, just in case ...'

But I had fallen in love – if that's not to make an obscenity of the word – with the second Beretta. I clutched it still, the walnut butt plates warm yet somehow cool to the touch.

'You will take the Beretta.' Ahmad sounded confident.

'The price. You haven't said.'

He smirked, shrugged. 'Does it matter? To a man like you the price is of no consequence, is that not so?'

'None at all,' I agreed. 'If you try to cheat me I'll simply break your arm and we'll say no more about it.'

Yacoub gave off a cackle and dug an elbow in Ahmad's side. Ahmad swiped back at him but he jerked away, out of reach.

'Very well, *monsieur*. The price is twenty thousand dirhams, including ...' he tacked on hastily as my expression hardened, '... one hundred rounds of ammunition. American ammunition,' he stressed. 'Remington.'

Twenty thousand dirhams was about two thousand dollars, which has an expensive ring, though it wasn't much above the going rate for an illegally-imported 93R.

'Fifteen thousand,' I offered. Bargaining, really, for the sake of it. Meek acceptance of a quoted price is counted a weakness among Arabs.

'Eighteen,' Ahmad promptly parried.

'Seventeen.'

We closed predictably at seventeen-five. A bundle of banknotes passed across the table and a seal was stamped on the transaction with more of the fiery Sidi Bughari.

Later that night, my guts awash with the stuff, and a wholly-illegal firearm concealed under the spare wheel in the Fiat's boot, I had luck and to spare getting back to Tangier and my bed without falling foul of a Sûreté Nationale patrol.

Around dawn, when all but the birds were aslumber, I carried out my survey of Petit Europa. I left my rented Fiat in a dirt road off the highway, approached the settlement on foot, skirting the other villas, to finish up in a tree overlooking the high walls of Al'hauri's palace of a holiday home. Even in this moneyed enclave of Westernisation it stood out as the cream of the cream. Had Al'hauri not been about to depart this life I might have envied him.

None saw me come, none saw me go, and I was back at the hotel in time for breakfast.

The rest of the day was set aside for relaxation, specifically a wander in the markets in the hope of coming across a trinket or ornament that wasn't simply tourist junk. Some hope. It was a plan that was not destined to achieve maturity. It was altered radically and irrevocably around mid-morning, as I left the hotel boutique, glancing over the headlines of the day old *Sunday Telegraph* (a new spate of Isis beheadings in Kurdistan). My attention was caught by a group of three people in the archway between the foyer and the coffee bar: a tall woman in shorts and singlet stood in conversation with a man of slightly above middle-height and rugged build, whose unusually wide shoulders gave him a boxy outline. He was wearing a dark blue shirt and white trousers, both immaculately pressed. His back was to me but his gestures implied agitation. The third member of the group was another female, who was sideways on to me, her features screened by sunglasses and shoulder-length blonde-ish hair. She was also dressed in shorts and singlet that emphasized a slightly boyish figure.

Had I not recognized the tall woman as my neighbour from the balcony I might well have walked on by. As it was, curiosity titillated, I pulled up six feet or so short of the trio, opened out my newspaper, and made a pretence of absorption in it while peeping over the top. The man was doing most of the talking, but *sotto voce* so that his words were absorbed by the general bustle of the reception area. Her responses, such as they were, were mostly monosyllabic. What made the tableau so intriguing was the unmistakeable tension between them. At one point he reached out to grab the woman's

29

forearm. She prised his fingers off with a show of irritation.

Unconcerned humanity flowed around them, oblivious of the drama. I had more or less come to the conclusion that it was no more than a husband and wife squabble, when the woman cried out, 'Will you *please* stop pestering us?'

Why she didn't simply walk away was a puzzle. I decided to lend a discreet hand. Three strides took me to the desk. An enquiring Arab male clerk approached, and, keeping my voice low, I leaned across and, speaking French to ensure there was no misunderstanding, said, 'The lady over there under the archway seems to be having man trouble. As she's a guest here, I suggest you do something about it.'

As the clerk frowned in the direction indicated, the man obligingly made another grab for the woman. Predictably she pulled free, whereupon the clerk, startled, scuttled off through a door behind the desk. Bemused, I was about to take off after him when he reappeared in the company of a massive, moustachioed character enhanced by several tiers of paunch. With the agitated clerk in tow, the moustachioed one bustled over to the little group.

I didn't hang around to watch the outcome of my Good Samaritanship but took my newspaper up one level, to the terraced garden, where I ordered coffee espresso and installed myself among the shrubs and the creepers. Apart from an old man in Bermuda shorts tucking into a pyramid of ice cream, I was alone. The air was windless, the surface of the swimming pool tranquil, a dazzling splash of sunlight.

The waiter deposited my espresso before me. I was tearing the top off a sachet of sugar when the tall woman emerged from the hotel interior and crossed the terrace. She had good carriage – shoulders well back, pelvis thrust forward, projecting a feline self-assurance that complemented her height.

Passing close to my table she glanced sideways, and I raised my coffee cup in homage.

'Problem sorted?'

Her jaw dropped slightly as she slowed.

'I ... beg your pardon?'

'I'm sorry, I didn't mean to interfere. You looked to be in difficulty.'

'Oh, *that*.' Her frown lasted only a moment or two before clearing. 'Aah, I see. It was you who sent that hotel bouncer to my rescue, wasn't it? I guess I should thank you.'

Only guessed? It sounded grudging.

'Not unless I did the right thing.' I smiled apologetically, hoping to put her at ease. 'If I acted out of line, I'm sorry.'

'No ... it's not that ...' She came closer, a diffident sidle. 'May I sit down?'

'Be my guest.' I got to my feet, pulled out a chair. 'Shall I order some coffee?'

'Oh, er ... yes, why not? And could you get a Pepsi or something for my daughter? She'll be along in a sec.' She sat cautiously, as if she expected the chair to be booby trapped. 'I'll pay, of course.'

'My name's Alan Melville,' I said, as I resumed my seat. The pseudonym slid glibly enough off my tongue. So often did I travel under false identities that at times André Warner seemed to be another person altogether.

We shook hands across the table. Hers was cool in both senses. Her fingernails were painted silver, I noticed.

'Clair Power,' she said. The waiter cruised over, took our order without a break in his stride, and carried on to the far side of the terrace to serve some new arrivals.

'Pretty efficient here, aren't they?' I said, making small talk the way you do with a stranger, marking time to see how the land lay.

'Mmm,' she said with a little nod. 'I've been pleasantly surprised. Not that we spend much time in the hotel, we're mostly out sightseeing. We may not get another chance for a long time.'

She fluffed up her short brown hair and leaned back, taking stock of our surroundings, while I took stock of her. She was worth the effort. Her age I put at mid-thirties. In her sexual prime and not bad in the looks department, with her deep-set, blue-green eyes, small soft mouth, and sophisticated veneer. There were some fine lines in the usual places, but these only served to augment her appeal. The impression was of a woman who experienced the pluses and minuses of life.

In a corner of the terrace was a grotto with a waterfall at which tiny birds came to bathe. She was looking that way now, and the dance and sparkle of the water lit up her solemn gaze.

'Is there just you and your daughter, Mrs Power?' I asked.

It was another way of asking if a husband was in the vicinity, and is the sort of question that sets alarm bells jangling inside most unattached women. In this regard Clair Power was true to her sex. Her appraisal, before replying, was shrewd, penetrating, yet far from hostile. A weighing of motives perhaps.

'If you mean is my husband with us,' she said at last, 'the answer is no. Actually, he's ... well, I'm a widow.'

I made commiserating noises.

'It's okay. It happened two years ago. I guess I'm over it.'

'No other children?' I asked, more to get onto another topic than out of curiosity about the extent of her brood.

'No. Only Elizabeth.'

Coffee and a tall Pepsi with two bendy straws were set down on our table. I gave the waiter my room number and slipped him a twenty-dirham note that almost fell apart as he took it. Most of the local currency was in an advanced state of decay.

'You're a long way from home, Mrs Power.' Keeping the conversation in motion was becoming a struggle.

'Clair,' she corrected distantly as she stirred her unsweetened coffee, worrying at her lower lip. As the silence lengthened and I was mentally seeking a suitable platitude with which to break it, she blurted, 'Look, I'm sorry if I seem uncommunicative. I just wasn't sure if I should say anything. Anyhow ... here goes. That man you saw us with upstairs has been bothering me ever since we got here.'

'Really?' I didn't ask her to elaborate, just left an opening in case she wanted to.

'Yes. He ... oh, you know ... keeps asking me out. He even got my cell number from somewhere, and keeps calling me. He even suggested we move out of the hotel and be his house guests.' She snorted nervously. 'You can imagine what for, I suppose.'

A red-blooded male behaving like a red-blooded male, was my silent opinion. The opinion I diplomatically expressed was, 'A visit sounds harmless enough. Especially if he's invited both of you. He can hardly, er ... misbehave while your daughter's around.'

She sawed some more at her bottom lip. 'But why won't he take no for an answer? Why so persistent? Every day, without fail, he pounces on me from ... from nowhere. It's like being ambushed.' She shuddered. 'I've nothing against him as a person. I barely know him, only that his name's Henrik de Bruin, though he calls himself Rik. Oh, and he lives in Holland, and he's not short of money. I'm not off men altogether. It's just *him*. I have a bad feeling about him.' She shot me a hard look, as if wondering why she was exposing her soul to a stranger.

'Don't tell me if you'd rather not,' I said mildly. 'I didn't mean to pry.'

'Oh, but I want to.' Her hand brushed my forearm. Her touch was cool and dry. I imagined it stroking my fevered brow. 'We Anglo-Saxons must stick together, don't you think?'

'The special relationship, eh?' I meant it facetiously but she took it at face value.

'Sure, we have so much in common.' She proceeded to sermonise on the purity of the WASP brigade. I sipped my coffee and pretended to agree, though it's an ideology that bores me. Not to mention the implied insult to lesser species, including me, with my mixed parentage and religious persuasion.

'Something's puzzling me,' I said. Your accent's American but it has traces of something else.'

This seemed to amuse her. 'Australian. My husband was General Manager for the Australian subsidiary of Astra Minerals & Chemicals, and we lived there for most of our marriage. I still carry a US passport though.'

I grunted neutrally and switched topics.

'How's your holiday going, apart from your too-friendly neighbourhood Dutchman? Have you been out into the desert yet?'

She tasted her coffee before answering. 'It's on our agenda but we may not bother. It's just sand, after all, isn't it? More than enough of that in Oz.' She glanced down at her watch. 'Where *is* that girl? She's always wandering off. When she was little her father used to call her Wanderliz.' She rummaged in her bag and produced a smart phone. 'I'd better track ... ah, here she is.'

And here, indeed, she was: almost as tall as her mother, mane of tawny hair, stonewashed denim shorts, clinging dark-blue singlet. Partly because of her height it was hard to be precise about her age. I put her in the upper teens region. Shoulders broad for a girl, build otherwise slender with well-defined plump breasts. Limbs uniformly bronzed by the sun. More than merely pretty. A whole lot more.

She came to us, smiling, her walk a faithful imitation of her mother's. She was a delight to behold and mindful of it.

Not only that. She was the living double of my forever companion, a dead Italian girl, who still stalked my daydreams and my night dreams as vividly as if it were only yesterday when I murdered her.

Four

Clair Power made introductions as her daughter unplugged the iPod cord and spirited it away in her shoulder bag.

'G'day,' she said matter-of-factly, pure Australian.

I unfroze my features and manufactured a stiff smile.

'Hello ... Elizabeth.'

'Call me Lizzy. Everybody calls me Lizzy, except Mummy when she's pi ... cross with me.' Then, spotting the Pepsi: 'Is that for me?' She crashed down into a chair very unladylike. 'Couldn't I have a Foster's?'

'Not while I'm around.' Clair gestured towards me. 'This gentleman sent the hotel people to get rid of that Rik person.'

Lizzy broke off vacuuming Pepsi into her mouth.

'No kidding?' she said, speaking around the straws. She didn't seem particularly impressed.

'And, anyhow, where did you disappear to just now? I was chattering away to you, or so I thought, then I turned round and you'd gone. I felt such a fool.'

Lizzy withdrew the straws from the glass, sucked them dry.

'Talking to Yusuf.'

The irritation on her mother's features was replaced by displeasure.

'Gee, honey, I wish you wouldn't.' Aside, to me, 'Yusuf is the ... what do you call them ... bell-hop? Bell-boy?'

'I know him.'

'He's so good-looking,' Lizzy sighed.

'He's a … he's not European,' Clair countered uncertainly in a lowered voice. 'In any case, we're only here for another week.'

'All the more reason not to keep him dangling on a string. And don't be racist.'

'Now listen to me, young lady …'

While this trial of personalities was in progress I was moved to study the girl and to marvel anew that nature could have created two people as physically alike as she and Pavan's daughter, from such diverse origins. Yet although she was a facsimile of the Italian girl this did not diminish her beauty in its own right. Her cheeks and the deep bridge of her nose were darkly pocked with freckles, and though her face still retained some of the roundness of youth it was already firm of jaw and mouth; she would be a wilful one. But what really struck me was her eyes. Smoky-grey, languid eyelids – eyes that were a lot older than her years. It was in her eyes and her smile above all that she evoked Pavan's daughter, brought her back to life, to sit with me at this table in the play of the sunlight, to the splash and gurgle of the waterfall and the coo of the doves in the cool green trees.

Clair's voice punctured the painful balloon of nostalgia. 'Alan … Alan …'

'Sorry … miles away.'

'You don't mind my calling you Alan, I hope?'

'I insist … Clair. You were saying?'

'I was asking whether you would let a daughter of yours go to a disco alone in a town like Tangier.'

Not in any town if I had a daughter as fetching as Lizzy, was my private sentiment.

'It might not be wise,' I said primly.

'Thank you. I was sure you'd agree.'

'Stop discussing me as if I weren't here!' Lizzy seethed. 'I'm too old to be kept on a leash, Mummy, and it's time you adjusted to that fact.'

'On the other hand,' I said, deftly modifying my stance, 'Yusuf seems a respectable enough lad.'

Lizzy's upright jerk told me I was correct in assuming Yusuf was part of the plan.

'There's the Ranch Discotheque, around the corner and up the hill, a matter of a few hundred yards. It's made up like a Wild West saloon. You could organize a taxi there and back.' Lizzy was bouncing in her seat in an attitude of mock prayer. 'To stop you pacing the floor while she's gone, you could join me for dinner.'

My closing proposition, almost an afterthought, hauled Clair back from vetoing her daughter's night out.

Lizzy was not slow to pounce. 'You'll have a great evening with Mr Melville and I'll be back by ten – promise. *Pleeeease*, Mummy.'

Clair made a resigned puffing sound through her nostrils. Lizzy, scenting capitulation, flung her arms around her neck.

'Oh, Mummy, you're beaut!'

Over Clair's shoulder, Lizzy and I swapped conspiratorial winks.

'Must fly.' Lizzy rose so fast the plastic seat stuck to her thighs and rose with her. 'I've got another windsurfing lesson at eleven.' She waggled her fingers at me in farewell. '*Ciao*, Mr Melville. See you again.'

Off she loped, neat little derriere and legs without end, swerving to avoid the man in the Bermuda shorts, who was also leaving.

'Er … how old is your daughter?' I asked, casually, conversationally.

'It's taking some getting used to,' Clair said, and her voice was gruff with affection, 'but she'll be sixteen next month.'

Sixteen. Only three years younger than Simone. Old enough to smoke, old enough to work, old enough for ... other things.

*

Instead of calling a taxi I conveyed Lizzy and Yusuf to the disco in the Fiat, and arranged to pick them up at 10.30. Lizzy full of bounce, her sort-of-blonde hair tied back with a bright green ribbon that matched her full-skirted dress and her strappy platform shoes. Her make-up was on the overdone side, but so what? I guessed her mother kept her well-reined in, a hallmark of the over-protective single parent, so lipstick and eye-liner were harmless enough forms of free expression.

Yusuf was ill-at-ease in his western style sports jacket and chinos, with hair fashionably spiked. Even Clair was impressed by the transformation, admitting as much as she and I strolled up the alley to Le Detroit Restaurant, the flush of the evening sun dyeing the line of rocks beyond the port blood-red and transmuting the sea to molten metal.

'She'll have forgotten him five minutes after your plane leaves the runway,' I assured her, then stopped and caught her arm to point out a collection of small fishing boats heading harbour-wards, low in the water under the weight of their catches. The sunset's glow tinted them sepia, like a scene from a silent movie.

Clair took a deep breath, held it momentarily in her lungs, then released it in a measured exhalation as if it were some rare and finite commodity.

'Africa,' she said with a trace of reverence. 'It really is kind of special, isn't it?'

'Sure.' We had reached the unimposing entrance to the restaurant, so I guided her through and up a cranked flight of stairs. At the top we were welcomed in French by a robed factotum. The place was about half full, with Europeans in the majority. No sign here of tourists being frightened off by the sons of Allah.

'You don't sound very enthusiastic about Africa,' Clair remarked, once we were settled at our reserved table by the window that ran full length of the wall. The head waiter put a match to an overweight candle, distributed menus, took an order for aperitifs, and withdrew. In the window our reflections floated in a fading canvas of sky and water, and the candle was a beacon far out across the strait.

'For my money this isn't the real Africa,' I said. 'That starts below the equator. Up here is just an extension of the Middle East with a French sub-stratum. It's too Westernised. Or used to be before the jihadists declared war on the non-Muslim world.'

She rested an elbow on the table. 'I take it you have first-hand knowledge of the real Africa, as you call it. Tell me about it.'

Like daughter, like mother, she was at her vivacious best this evening. A simple, low-cut blue dress that hinted at cleavage, set off by a feather boa stole. The webs of fine lines had been smoothed away by creams and cosmetics and her looks were almost girlish. Her hair was neat, curling at the nape of the neck, copper-coloured in the dim lighting. Hair that came alive when she laughed, or nodded, or simply toyed with it, instead of being held fast in a chemical helmet. My designs on Mrs Clair Power were beginning to take shape.

Over the aperitifs, the cross-talk of the thirty or so other diners no more than a background murmur, I told her about the real Africa, specifically about the fever swamps of Angola, where some years ago I had hunted down a Portuguese slave trader. For her ears though, I edited the reasons for that mission and its fatal outcome.

'Did you kill any dangerous game?' she asked.

They didn't come any more dangerous than Carvalho, I reflected. To Clair, I said, 'Only a hippo. When I say "only", I mean that was the only occasion. I don't subscribe to slaughter for its own sake.'

From the à la carte menu we both plumped for *fruits de mer*, combining starter and fish dishes. For the main course Clair chose *poulet au citron* to my *brochette* of lamb. Simple fare. For this evening, I confined my penchant for the finer things in life to the comprehensive wine list: a peerless Chablis Premier Cru 'Vaillons' 1983 to go with the *fruits de mer*, and a 1975 Margaux Grand Cru Classé, that king among wines, to follow. Not that I had pretensions as a connoisseur, I just knew what I liked, and what I liked tended to be expensive.

'The bill will be horrific,' Clair said with a giggle.

'We can always offer to wash the dishes.'

'There speaks a man who never washed a dish in his life.'

Which wasn't true, but I let it pass.

'What's your profession, Alan? No – let me guess. Money no object, so ... lawyer? No, too good-looking ...'

'Thanks. Now you're embarrassing me. If I might say so, you're not so bad yourself.'

The approach of the wine waiter armed with our Chablis, stilled the conversation. I checked the temperature of the bottle and watched him pull the cork with the ease that came from constant practice. I tasted the wine, nodded approval.

'Marvellous stuff,' Clair commented moments later as she tasted hers. 'Silky smooth. I could drink it by the gallon.'

'Don't get carried away,' I said with a grin. Then again, it could work to my advantage if she did.

Our starters came. We ate for a while, then it was her turn to talk about her life in Australia: her husband's employers had sent him there just after their marriage, to help set up a local office. The relocation was expected to be short term, but it didn't work out that way. Lizzy was born about a year later. When Robert died in a road accident involving a drunk, Clair had intended to stay on. They were well provided for: a house of their own, life insurance, a company pension. But all their friends were couples, and as an attractive widow Clair was soon estranged from them. Loneliness and disillusion compounded to make her cast ever-longing eyes homeward, to America.

'Presumably you still have family in the US?'

'Unfortunately, we don't,' she said, prodding aimlessly with her fork at an olive. 'My parents have been dead for some years. My father was an only child. My mother had a sister, but she disappeared back in the seventies to join some cockeyed religious order in South America, never to be heard of again. So I've no brothers or sisters, nor aunts nor uncles.' Her smile was melancholy. 'There's just us – Elizabeth and me.'

As a lone wolf myself I could empathize with her.

'Don't you keep in touch with Robert's parents?'

'They're dead too. Tragic – whoops!' The much-stabbed olive shot off her plate and across the table. I apprehended it, popped it into my mouth. 'Thanks. I'm partial to olives.'

'And that was my last!' She deftly hooked a prawn the size of a sausage from the scattered remains of my meal.

'There – an eye for an eye, a prawn for an olive.'

She chewed with relish, while I watched, conscious of a growing attraction towards this mercurial woman, one minute so solemn, the next so full of fun.

'What was I saying?'

'About your husband's parents.'

The solemnity returned.

'He was terminally ill and went to Switzerland to be euthanized, or whatever it's called. After that Robert's mother just seemed to waste away. She died only a few months later.' Her voice dropped to a whisper. 'Poor darlings.'

'And Robert – was he an only child?'

'No, there's a younger brother called Alistair. He lives in Barcelona. I don't know much about him. He was best man at our wedding, but we've have nothing to do with him since.' She sniffed, hunted in her purse for a handkerchief. 'Gee, this is depressing. Let's not talk about my troubles any more. Tell me yours. What do you really do for a living, for instance?'

This was the signal for me to trot out my well-oiled fabrication about killings on the stock market leading to semi-retirement.

'Not a care in the world,' she said with a dreamy air, when I had finished. 'I envy you.'

We were on our main course by then. Outside, darkness had fallen, relieved only by the lights in the harbour and the reflected interior of the restaurant. In this reflection our eyes met and held for several seconds. It was I who turned away, from the image to the flesh.

'You know you're really are quite a looker,' I said.

She placed her knife and fork precisely on the edge of her plate, and rested her chin on interlocked fingers. Her gaze was steady.

'I'm thirty-eight,' she said softly.

'I'm thirty-nine, but I'm not counting. You're still quite a looker.'

'While the compliments are whizzing back and forth, your eyes are amazing. I've never seen eyes so blue; they're like ... like blue ice.' She shivered. 'See what you've done to me? I've gone all goose-pimply.'

She had too: the fine hairs on her forearms were standing erect, like grass at the bottom of the sea.

'I'd rather heat you up than cool you down.'

Had I gone too far? Her mouth formed an O but her follow-up look was tinged with invitation. Then she spoiled it by enquiring about my parents.

'They're still going strong,' I replied. 'They live in the wilds of Newfoundland. You know, Canada. My dad's English – very. My ma's Québécoise. We meet up now and again.'

More again than now.

'You don't sound very English. The way you talk, I mean.'

'Ah, that's on account of living in Canada until I was nineteen. I grew up North American and never lost the accent.'

'Promise me something, will you?' she said later, over the *corbeille de fruits*.

'Promise? That's a big word for new acquaintances.' I raised my glass, indicating she should do likewise. We clinked, drank the last of the Margaux in an unspoken covenant. 'But if I can, I will.'

'Promise you won't expect too much too soon.' She frowned deeply. 'I'm sorry ... that sounds presumptuous. Who's to say you expect or even want anything from me?'

Before I could answer that, the fancy carved clock on the filigree panel that screened the staircase gave off a tinny chime. It was half after ten.

'Elizabeth ... !'

'Lizzy ... !'

We spoke in chorus, then laughed in chorus.

'We'll have our nightcaps at the hotel,' I proposed, summoning the head waiter.

Which, after a mad rush across town to where a lightly-fuming, arms-folded Lizzy and her anxious beau awaited us, is how we rounded off the evening.

*

Elizabeth Power, who looked like a dead Italian girl called Pavan.

I sat drinking into the small hours, memories of the Pavan girl triggered anew by the entry of her lookalike into my life.

As so often before, I saw the gun barrel coming up in slow motion, saw the scarlet-orange spear of flame spew from the muzzle, even saw the bullet in flight, rotating lazily, deviating by not so much as a millimetre from the straight and true. I saw it strike – that terrible, bone-splintering impact – saw, finally, the spray of bright blood, the bouquet of her quietus.

A sob caught in my throat. I jumped to my feet and hurled the glass at the wall. It shattered as the girl's head had shattered, into a thousand fragments, one of which glanced off my cheek.

'Fuck!' I said, not in an outburst, but deliberately and with depth of feeling. Bad enough to have to endure nightly replays on the ceiling. Now I had to contend with my victim in the flesh, teasing, tormenting, and driving me mad.

Five

After dining on *bastela*, a stuffed pigeon in layers of flaky pastry with saffron, almonds and sugar, in the larger of the hotel's two restaurants, I wandered through to the bar. The bar and restaurant at the Rif are separated by an open-work screen and the division patrolled by a swarthy maitre d', impassive of visage as any Buckingham Palace sentry. The hotel's main bar is convivial, relaxing, and orderly, with the air of a London club, and abounds in much-buttoned leather. The staff are appropriately attentive.

I had an after-dinner date with Clair and out of olde worlde courtesy had made a point of being early. The barman, befezzed and perspiring in his enclave of multi-coloured lighting, greeted me with an easy civility.

'Double vodka and ice,' I ordered. Clair was not of that breed of women who tolerate drunks, so I had renounced the hard stuff all day. Now I felt I could open the sluice just a crack.

'*Volontiers, monsieur.*'

I cocked a leg over a stool and swivelled through a hundred and eighty degrees to survey the floor. The place was not busy: just a few couples and a blond-haired man alone in a corner seat, briefcase open beside him, pecking away at a tablet with two fingers.

'*Monsieur.*' My vodka and an ice barrel were placed on the counter. I added a rock of ice, swished it around.

'*Santé,*' the barman said, lingering to watch me dispose of a good third before another customer called him away. I nursed my glass and savoured the warm glow in my gut, soaking up the soft music that filtered through some hidden speaker. Music to dance to, make romance to. Poetry by Warner. I harboured idle thoughts of another kind of poetry, that of Clair naked and in my bed. Forming a detailed picture was beyond me but the general package, I was sure, would be to my liking. Her body definitely went in and out where it was supposed to.

'Is quiet tonight.'

The voice came from my left and I assumed the speaker was addressing the barman. But the barman, when I looked up, was fitting a spout to a new vodka bottle and had his back to the counter.

So I angled leftwards to face a wide-shouldered man sitting a few stools down from me and looked into the staring eyes of Mr Rik de Bruin, Dutchman, aspirant to play house with Clair. It was an interesting face. European without doubt, yet of obscure ethnic heritage: dark crinkly hair, threaded with grey. Not handsome, not with those pock-marked cheeks and swollen lips, but definitely not forgettable. Vaguely menacing, even. I could understand why Clair was not keen to make his closer acquaintance.

'I say is quiet tonight,' he repeated.

I gave a double nod and hoped he would settle for that. With Clair due to show any moment I didn't want to get drawn into chitchat.

'Friday is usually busy,' he persevered. He was wearing a loud-chequered jacket that emphasized the width of his shoulders. A chunky spirits glass was lost in his grapefruit-sized fist.

'You on vacation here?' I asked, submitting to the inevitable.

'I am renting a villa on the coast, the Mediterranean side.'

He stool-hopped until he was alongside me and extracted a card from his top pocket.

'Henrik de Bruin,' I read aloud. To piss him off I deliberately mispronounced his last name 'Brew-in'.

'De Brown,' he corrected, with just a whisker of irritation. 'Like the English name.'

I trotted out my alias, adding, 'Which *is* an English name.'

I studied his card afresh. Below his name it read *DeB Publications, Egmond aan Zee*. No street address, telephone, cell phone, fax, email or website. This guy was ultra low-profile. Suddenly I was curious about him.

'Egmond aan Zee,' I read off the card. 'Where's that? It sounds Dutch.'

'It's in the north, near Amsterdam, but by the sea. You know my country, Mr Melville?'

'Tolerably well.' I placed the card by my glass. 'What line are you in, Mr de Bruin?'

His forehead grew folds.

'Line?'

'Business.'

'Ah, of course.' He cleared his throat, gulped at his drink before replying. 'I am in publishing. Also movies.'

Well, well.

'And you?' he said, raising his glass again and quizzing me as he drank. His eyes were slightly bloodshot.

I gave him the stock answer.

'You are fortunate to be able to retire so young.' He rubbed his rather prognathous jaw left-handedly. The top half of the little finger had been amputated and the stump jutted out stiffly as if it were stuck on. 'I would also like to retire, but ...' he made a disparaging gesture, accompanied by a travesty of a grin, the fleshy lips writhing like a pair of slugs in an embrace. 'I like even more to make money.'

'Who doesn't? Another of those?' I indicated his drained glass.

'An excellent suggestion. Gin, please.' Then, when the refills came: '*Prosit.*'

'Cheers,' I said. His glass stayed upended longer than mine. 'Is the Rif your local?'

'Local? Ah, yes, I remember. Is what you English call your pub, is it not? The place where you always drink.'

I nodded. 'You've gotten the general idea.'

His pleasure at having recognized the idiom unaided moved him to slake his thirst again. He could certainly soak it up. Were it not for my new-found moderation and looming date with Clair I might have paced him. First to fall down picks up the tab.

'Actually, I am here to meet a lady,' he confided, backhanding a dribble of gin from the corner of his mouth.

'A lady, eh?'

He rocked towards me. 'Business, strictly business. She is staying here in the hotel. If you are a guest, perhaps you have seen her. She has a daughter, a beautiful girl ...'

What the *fuck*? So he was still hankering after Clair. I was half-amused, half-resentful.

'She plays, I think you say, hard to get.' He winked, man to man. 'Tonight, though, I believe she will change her mind.'

I crushed my irritation to ask, man to man, 'How so?'

'I recently buyed a cruiser and today it was delivered to me. Is magnificent. Forty meters long ...' He spread his arms like an angler telling the tale of The One That Got Away. 'Five staterooms, all with satellite television and DVD, sauna, Jacuzzi, gymnasium ... magnificent. She will not be able to resist it. I will take her on a cruise to the Canaries.'

Refusing to believe Clair had double-booked me with this self-styled movie mogul, I merely said, 'Let's drink to your success then,' not bothering to hide my irony. 'I have a feeling

...' I was at that moment distracted by the passage, majestic as an ocean liner, of a lissom black-haired beauty in a glued-on evening dress. She tossed the most casual of glances in my direction, and I twitched the extremities of my mouth as encouragement. For all the interest this come-on generated I might have been the invisible man. She swept regally on into the arms of a hunky Latin-type of about thirty. I detested him on sight. Resented, I mean.

De Bruin had followed my gaze. 'You can dream. She is Elsa Macchioni, a neighbour by me. A *very* hot lady.'

The couple mooched off towards the restaurant where the three-piece band was warming up for its evening stint. Coinciding with their departure, a group of about ten people entered the bar, mostly middle-aged, and if their loud English chatter had not revealed their origins, their dress most certainly would have. De Bruin slid off his stool.

'Excuse me,' he said, and then I saw why: bringing up the rear of the group and in discussion with an elderly man, whose rigid carriage and grey bar of a moustache hinted at a military pedigree, was Clair. De Bruin swooped on her, and I hadn't a hope of dissuading him even if my reactions had been fast enough. Clair glanced up as he homed in and an icy wind of hostility emanated from her.

The strength of de Bruin's obsession with her was extraordinary. Fair enough, Clair was an attractive piece, but in a beauty contest with the likes of the Macaroni baggage she wouldn't even figure. And where, I wondered, was Mrs de Bruin while her man was out on the prowl? At home knitting?

What followed next was an action replay of yesterday morning. Having detached Clair from her moustachioed companion, to the latter's undisguised dismay, de Bruin launched into a harangue, arms flying everywhere, like a bookie at a race meeting.

'Won't you take no for an answer?' Clair's voice was shrill, slashing through de Bruin's, but failing to silence him. Chatter in the immediate area dwindled. A waiter, skipping past with a tray load of empty glasses and goggling at the spectacle, almost ploughed into the English group. Enough was enough. In the absence of other intervention, that peace-loving saviour of damsels in distress, alias Alan Melville, would gallop again to the rescue. It was getting to be a habit.

For openers, I tried diplomacy.

'Hey, Henrik,' I called cheerily, coming up behind de Bruin and slapping him midway between those weightlifter shoulders. 'Aren't you going to introduce me to your lovely lady?'

He gave a start, releasing Clair's arm. The relief on her face was transparent, and she took a fast step back, out of his reach.

I said to him, 'I can see now why you're so keen. Not going to keep her all to yourself, are you, you old rogue?'

My initiative had deprived him of speech. He stood open-mouthed as Clair, entering into the spirit of the stratagem, introduced herself to me.

'I'm Clair Power.' She smiled, extending a languid hand. 'So nice to meet a friend of Rik's.'

The military type also joined in the game, elbowing de Bruin aside.

'My name is Hordern,' he said, smoothing the precision-clipped moustache with a bent forefinger. 'Brigadier Hordern. Retired, of course.'

I reciprocated the introduction.

'Pleasure to meet you, Melville. Friend of Mrs Power, are you?'

I said I was now.

'D'you know this blighter?' he asked, in reference to the outmanoeuvred de Bruin, who was hovering on the perimeter of our little circle, looking thunderous.

At this juncture the "blighter" himself recovered sufficiently to speak on his own behalf.

'Why don't you all mind your own businesses?' he hissed, and suddenly I was on red alert. This was not a man to be treated lightly, still less mocked. 'I am talking to my friend, Mrs ...'

'Friend!' Clair's tone was cutting. 'We hardly know each other, and only that because you keep forcing yourself on me.'

De Bruin's eyes slitted. 'All I have done is ask you to come sailing. Is this a crime?'

Clair glared poisoned darts at him. 'And I've given you my answer.' She turned to me. 'Sorry you've gotten involved in this, Alan, and you, Brigadier.'

A deprecating murmur from Hordern. In the restaurant the band launched into "Temptation," and the hum of conversation resumed as the crisis showed signs of receding.

Then de Bruin's hands, big as gauntlets, shot out to grab fistfuls of my lapel. Caught wrong-footed, I was dragged up close to him. We bumped like fairground dodgems. A spluttered 'I say!' from Hordern overlapped a gasp from Clair.

'So you pretend not to know each other, hey?' De Bruin's nose and mine were inches apart. At this range the pock marks on his cheeks were the size of lunar craters. 'You think to make me look foolish.'

It's against my nature to court trouble, principally because it attracts the attention of the police. De Bruin, although a couple of inches shorter than me, had the solid, indestructible look of a bank vault door. So I didn't react according to reflex or male vanity. I simply said equably, 'Don't do that, de Bruin. You'll spoil my suit. Let's shake hands and part friends.'

He shook all right – not my hand but all of me, and so violently my teeth chattered.

'*Qu'est-ce qui se passe?*' The enquiry came from behind me. I tried to look over my shoulder but it wasn't easy, jammed up tight against de Bruin as I was. '*Monsieur, je vous prie,*' the newcomer said, addressing de Bruin in a placatory voice. '*Il faudra vous expulser à moins que vous ne arretiez pas de faire la bagarre.*' We'll have to throw you out if you don't stop making trouble.

The closing bars of "Temptation" were thumping forth from the restaurant but I doubt that anyone was listening. De Bruin and I were stars of the show.

'*Monsieur!*' The plea was stronger now, overlaid with rising impatience.

De Bruin was still clutching my labels. I was bracing myself to dispense a knee to the groin when all at once the madness went out of him, like a volcano cut off in mid-eruption. He blinked three or four times in succession and released me. I staggered free, serendipitously into Clair's arms.

'Alan?' she said, half supporting me. 'Gee, I'm so sorry ...'

'Blasted foreigners!' Hordern barked, presumably forgetting he was in a minority among multiple nationalities.

The newcomer, I now saw, was the duty manager, who had introduced himself on my first day at the Rif. Young, slightly built, smooth. Until now I wouldn't have thought he had it in him to break up a couple of squabbling toddlers let alone two hefty guys.

'Thanks,' I said to him, slightly out of breath.

'*De rien du tout, monsieur,*' he said with a small bow. He was holding de Bruin by the shoulder, and now attempted to coax him away. De Bruin snarled at him, like a tiger about to pounce on its next meal.

'Keep your hands off me.' Saliva sprayed from the blubbery lips. 'You will hear more of this.'

The duty manager was not overtly impressed by this bluster. He stood aside to give de Bruin a clear exit. The Dutchman's parting shot was reserved for me.

'You, also,' he said, finger stabbing, voice crackling with the static of his humiliation. 'You also I am not finished with.'

The English party took Clair and me under its collective wing, plied us with liquor and sympathy, and insisted we join it in a corner of the bar it had evidently made its own. The men were all retired army officers, it transpired, on a privately-organized tour of North Africa. If the group could be said to have a CO, Brigadier Hordern was it. Clair had met them earlier in the evening.

'We were dining in the other restaurant,' she explained. 'Somebody had mixed up the reservations and Lizzy and I were put on the Brigadier's table.'

'Deuced glad to have you, m'dear,' the Brigadier boomed, confiding aside to me, 'Lost m'wife last year, don't you know. I'm the only bachelor in the party.'

'Some might say lucky you,' I remarked, taking a liking to him, in spite of his blimpishness and his transparent designs on Clair.

'And what about that daughter of hers. A cracker, what? Give her another year and she'll be fighting 'em off.' He knuckled furiously at his moustache. 'My God, she will!'

'Are you here on holiday, Mr Melville?' one of the wives asked – a thin, scraggy-necked old girl with a habit of arching her eyebrows as she spoke.

'In the main. I had some business to transact, but that's all settled now.'

There was much more in this vein as the evening advanced. Clair and I scarcely managed two words to each other.

'Ever do any hunting?' Hordern asked me around midnight.

'Some. I usually spend a week in the Dordogne in the fall and do a bit of pot-shotting with an old friend.'

He nodded at that. 'Tell you what – how'd you like to do some boar hunting tomorrow?'

'Boar hunting?' I stared at him. 'You mean here?'

'Not exactly here. South a bit, not far.'

'That'd be great. But the hunting season doesn't start until the fall, does it?'

Hordern cackled as he dismissed a hovering waiter. 'Only in the game reserves, dear fellow. This will be on a private estate. Belongs to a friend of mine, a Government minister.' He swayed towards me, closed a surreptitious blue eye. 'No names, no pack drill, eh? Just, well, let's call it mutual back-scratching.'

'What's that about back-scratching?' a member of the group on Hordern's right butted in: ruddy complexion, bald head cooked pink by too much sun. Most of the introductions had passed me by, but him I recalled as a former Major of Artillery.

'I was telling our friend here about tomorrow's do.'

The bald head bobbed knowingly.

'Ah. Coming, old boy?' This to me.

'Well, the Brigadier has suggested it.' I smiled at Hordern. 'May I bring, er … a companion?'

Hordern frowned. 'Companion?'

'Somebody you know.' Apologizing, I broke into Clair's tête-a-tête with two of the wives. 'The Brigadier has invited me on a boar hunt tomorrow. Could you bear to come?'

In twisting round towards me, Clair's gaze locked with mine and an ageless message leapt across the divide. It was gone as quickly as it came, like a light flicked on and off, but it required no decoding, nor words to complement it.

'I'd love to,' she said.

Hordern could sign-read as well as I. His frown deepened.

'Like that, is it?' he muttered. 'Only to be expected, I suppose. Young man like yourself.'

'Sorry, Brigadier,' I said softly, for his ears only. 'Fortunes of love and war.'

And I really did feel sorry for the old boy, though not sorry enough to sound the retreat and leave the field clear to him. Consequently, when we went boar hunting the next day, Clair and I went as a couple – a threesome actually, since no way was Lizzy letting us (and here I quote verbatim) 'hog all the fun'.

Six

The track we rode into the forest was rock-hard and bore the faint imprints of the earlier passage of hooves. It clung to the bank of a brown and turgid river for a distance of several miles, before bearing away in an abrupt curve to plunge deeper into the forest. The trees were suddenly taller and more numerous, pressing in, almost intimidating.

It was late morning and the mist that came with the dawn had hung around. It clung to the trees in festoons, like lichen. It was a warm humid mist and it created a cathedral hush in which our voices and the clop of the horses' hooves was muffled. Our guide, who had introduced himself as Moulay, led on his big bay, we guests strung out behind, paired like a column of cavalry. Clair rode alongside the Brigadier and directly behind Moulay, while Lizzy and I were next in line. Clair sat well in the saddle: ramrod-backed, head erect, taut denimed bottom in an easy rise-and-fall. A more than competent horsewoman, and Lizzy at least her peer, handling her horse with a natural panache that I, on my skittish mare, could not even emulate.

'She's been riding regularly since she was four,' Clair had confided to me, with that special fondness that shaded every mention of her daughter. 'I've lost count of all the trophies and rosettes she's collected since then.'

Another eight riders came after Lizzy and me. A couple of women, six men, including a certain Mynheer Henrik – better known as Rik – de Bruin, publisher and movie producer, who was turning up in all sorts of unlikely places. A festering abscess in need of lancing. Not a serious rival, just a serious nuisance.

We had travelled from the hotel by coach as a group, the old soldiers, their spouses, the Powers and me. Plus a handful of other privileged souls of uncertain nationality and status. The trip took an hour, our destination proving to be an isolated hacienda-like residence by the River Hachef, on the very edge of the forest where the hunt was to take place. We were met, not by the anonymous Minister, but by Moulay, immaculate in grey jodhpurs and riding boots, and a khaki drill shirt complete with cartridge pockets, all filled. Deadly business lay ahead.

The mist swirled about us as we descended from the coach.

'It comes from the sea,' Moulay explained. 'It will clear presently.'

The Gunner Major patted him on the shoulder. 'Don't worry, old boy, it's just like home.'

Our coach party was not alone in enjoying the Minister's hospitality; a number of private cars were lined up in chevron along the drive, and a score or more Europeans in hunting togs milled about the lawn. No Arabs were present apart from Moulay and some household retainers.

After refreshments in the form of mint tea and mineral water, it was off to the "Gun Room", an annex to the main building and a treasure house of weaponry. The inventory included a rack of crossbows – sinister black contraptions, combining the stopping power of a gun with the stealth of a blowpipe.

With the exception of a blonde middle-aged German, all the women opted out from actually carrying arms. Clair professed to be averse to the wanton taking of life.

'I'm only here because of you', she said with a touch of shyness. I acknowledged the compliment. Lizzy, though an animal lover, would have given it a go just for the thrill of it, but her lack of experience with guns ruled her out.

'And you, *monsieur*?' Moulay breathed down my neck as I picked up an over-and-under Ruger 12-gauge shotgun from a bench table. 'What is your choice to be?'

'These are all shotguns,' I observed, holding the Ruger to my shoulder. 'Don't you also use rifle for boar?'

'It is not allowed in Morocco,' Moulay replied, his sallow face expressionless. 'If you are accustomed to hunting with a rifle, may I suggest the Supervix Sanglier cartridge. For accuracy the Brenneke round is without equal. You will find a full selection of ammunition by the door.' He nodded gravely and moved on.

I thumbed the top lever of the Ruger to break open the breech. This particular gun has some sophisticated design features, including an inertia-locked trigger fire mechanism, which can be set to discharge either barrel first. Holding it, still broken, in the crook of my arm, I sorted out some of Moulay's Supervix Sanglier cartridges, recognizable by the drawing of a boar on the white plastic casing. I stuffed five in each of the flap-pockets of my drill shirt.

As we congregated in the garden Moulay addressed us in English.

'For those who have never hunted wild boar, I must warn you that he is a most dangerous and tenacious creature, especially when cornered. He may look like nothing more than a hairy pig, but he is a killer. Do not under . . .' he struggled with the translation, '... under-estimate him, I beg you.' His gaze roved over the assemblage. 'The other matter concerns your weapons: I am assuming those of you who are taking guns are familiar with their operation, and I will not insult you by talking about the rules of safety. It is usual on a hunt to carry weapons unloaded, we all know this. However, as I have told you, the boar is a savage animal, therefore guns should be kept loaded in the interests of self-protection. Because of this, it is imperative that the safety buttons are always in place. Are there any questions, please?'

No questions. The next step was to separate those who wished to hunt on foot from those who preferred horseback, and the party thus divided into two unequal halves, the riders being in the minority. All the older women opted to remain at the house. A picnic on the river bank had been laid on for them, to be followed by a visit to the nearby mosque of Aakba Amra. Women in general were not encouraged to join the actual hunt, Hordern told me in an aside.

'The old concubine mentality is difficult to shift, what?,' and his tone implied approval not censure.

At a signal from Moulay horses were led out from the stables. As a very occasional horseman I was allocated a young chestnut mare, frisky but good natured. Clair, who rode weekly, was given a stallion; Lizzy, a good-looking bay mare that she stamped her authority on at once. The mounted party was initially eleven strong, excluding our guide, of which four were women. That is, until a Rolls-Royce Wraith showed up, white coachwork stained ochre from the dust. It braked late and ostentatiously in the last few yards before the house, turning every head.

Moulay welcomed the driver with respectful pleasure.

'I'm beginning to get that haunted feeling,' Clair muttered as we sat astride our grazing horses, waiting for the off.

Watching Rik de Bruin in green hunting kit, hurry off to the Gun Room with the fawning Moulay, I began to get feelings of my own that were nothing to do with spooks.

'What is it about Lizzy and me that attracts the wrong kind of man?' Clair mused, breaking into my sour machinations.

'You make it sound like a regular occurrence. Don't judge all males by his behaviour.'

She chuckled ruefully and gave me what I interpreted as a fond look.

'You're excepted. It's just that this business with de Bruin is a replay of a brush we had with an oil sheikh while we were in Dubai. Did I tell you we stopped off there for a week on the way here?'

I shook my head.

'Well, we did, and quite by accident we met this Arab prince from Abu Dhabi. He wanted me to *sell* Lizzy to him.'

'Obviously a man who appreciated the finer things of life,' I joked, then immediately killed my grin when I saw she was not amused. I reached for her hand. 'Sorry, Clair. That was in bad taste.'

'It was pretty unsettling at the time, I don't mind telling you. He made quite a pest of himself.'

'I can imagine. Do you forgive me?'

Mollified, she squeezed my hand.

'It's behind us now. I just don't need history to repeat itself with our Dutch friend.'

'At least here you're not on your own. Not anymore.'

We moved at a canter into the bosom of that hushed, mist-scrolled forest, strung up and alert as army scouts on patrol behind enemy lines. Only Lizzy was impervious to the general tension. Agog with excitement, she chattered on, an undamable stream.

'Are we really and truly going to hunt wild boar?' she said, glancing yet again at my shotgun in its saddle scabbard. 'I mean, it won't be just some old porker they've let loose to give us a bit of sport?'

'Cynicism doesn't become you,' I said, grinning.

'How do *you* know what becomes me?'

An intended comeback was nipped off as my nag momentarily quickened her pace, her hindquarters levitating painfully out of synchronization with my descending seat. Lizzy hooted with friendly derision.

'You're sitting all wrong,' she crowed. 'You're all stiff, and you're holding your reins too short. Let them out a bit.'

She demonstrated, and I liberated a few inches of rein. The mare, given her head, settled into a noticeably more even stride.

'You see,' Lizzy said smugly, then soberly, 'Do you think we'll see a boar soon?'

'It won't be like that. They don't pop out from behind a tree and say "Yah, can't catch me," you know.'

Lizzy doubled over her mare's arched neck in a spasm of mirth.

'Obviously,' she said, on recovering. 'Everybody knows boars can't talk. They do this ...' Letting go of the reins – and it says much for her horsemanship that she retained absolute control – she stuck her thumbs in her ears and waggled her hands.

Now I was laughing and compelled, quite spontaneously, to view Lizzy from a different slant. She was at that pinnacle of innocent beauty, that transient season of her life which is like a shooting star, rising to a glorious zenith before the protracted earthward slide to decline, decay, and oblivion. Surely, at rising sixteen, she was not so innocent as to be unaware of the impact of beauty such as hers on the male of the species. Not to mention the responsibility that goes with it.

'You don't insist I call you Mr Melville, do you?' was next in the continuing catechism, after only a brief lapse.

'No. Just Melville will do.'

More amusement.

'That makes you sound like the family butler. Melville!' For a kid raised Down Under, she managed the hoity-toity modulation beautifully. 'Dissect me a raspberry, my good man.'

'I'll blow you a raspberry, if you don't watch out.'

She ducked under a low branch without any moderation of pace. 'I *can't* call you Melville. Mummy would go ape. Can't I call you Alan?'

'Sure, but not Al,' I said. Though I would even live with that if she insisted. She had that effect. 'If you're not careful, I'll call you Freckles.'

'Don't imagine you'd be the first,' she said with an ear-to-ear grin.

At this point in the badinage, Moulay called a halt. As we reined back, the sun parted the mist and the rags of grey gathered themselves and fled. The temperature immediately climbed several degrees.

Moulay, facing back down the column, announced, 'We are coming to the place where the boars sleep during the day ...'

As if to prove him wrong about the 'sleeping' part, a snuffling was heard in the undergrowth beside the track. A moment later a boar, not much bigger than a terrier and covered with bristly mud-coloured hair, sallied forth and shot through the space between Moulay and the Brigadier, like a runaway go-kart. Clair's mount reared up, forelegs paddling, but her reactions were swift and composed: she reined in, calming him with a monologue of equestrian balm. The distraction enabled the boar to make good its escape, zigzagging from cover to cover, its progress punctuated by a succession of squeaks and snorts. Though I had yanked my gun from its scabbard, the opportunity was lost.

Even Moulay, faster still on the draw, failed to get off a single shot. The squeaking and crashing faded, and Moulay shrugged resignedly.

'As I was saying, we are at the place where boars are to be found.' This triggered a swell of laughter. 'Anyhow, that one was not much more than a baby. We are looking for much bigger game.'

In front of me, Hordern flexed his shoulders and muttered, 'I should damn well hope so.'

Talk of bigger game reminded me of the unwelcome presence to the rear. I looked back, affectedly casual, exchanged a nod with the Gunner Major, his sun-scorched pate now protected by a Panama hat. De Bruin was at the very tail of the column, partnering the German woman. Our eyes met. No warmth in his gaze.

Clair backed up her horse and eyed me worriedly.

'Alan, you mustn't get involved in this,' she said, her voice lowered. 'I'll fight my own battles.'

Far away across the forest a sputter of gunfire blighted the stillness. As it died away to a concert of echoes, I said clearly and precisely, 'Not while I'm around to fight them.'

She smiled her gratitude and tiny creases radiated from the corners of eyes and mouth. The bloom of youth, so patent in Lizzy, was gone from Clair for good, but the impression of health and vitality and *joie de vivre*, compensated for most of those thirty-eight years. As a woman and as a person she had much to offer. If only I represented half as good a bargain.

'I sure appreciate it,' she said, reaching out and letting her fingertips make momentary contact with my arm.

Moulay, who had been casting around for signs of more game, came trotting back.

'Let us continue, ladies and gentlemen,' he called out.

Claire offered a moue of regret and returned to Hordern's side. Lizzy, who surely never missed a trick in her life, said to me, 'Do you like my mother?'

'What do you think?' I said evasively.

She gave a little snort. 'I think you like her a *lot*, sport.'

With the dispersal of the mist the heat was building to its usual noon crescendo, so I stripped off my windbreaker and knotted the sleeves around my waist. Taking my lead, Lizzy pulled her sweatshirt over her head. Underneath she had on a tank top that stuck to her torso like polyfilm, accentuating the rack of her ribs and the impressive swell of her chest. It was the kind of garment that isn't designed to be worn with a bra, and her nipples prodded saucily at the tissue-thin cloth. And, by God, wasn't she aware of the effect on me? She arched her back in deliberate emphasis of her womanly wares, flicked me a loaded glance with those smoky eyes that were mature ahead of their years, and with a knowing smirk kneed her mount forward. I hoped she never gave that kind of look to the wrong kind of guy.

Whereas previously we had cantered, now we proceeded at a walk. Every so often Moulay would signal a halt and spend a minute or so peering at the ground and listening with a cupped ear. The heat grew oppressive during these periods of inaction, and the shade afforded by the greenery overhead diminished as the ground rose and the ilex oaks thinned and became intermingled with the thinner foliage of the junipers, cedars, and Aleppo pines.

Moulay wasn't about to repeat his earlier mistake; his gun was out and at the ready. The crack of a dead branch, loud as a pistol shot, brought him to a standstill, the rest of us closing up to form a compact mass behind him.

On cue, like an actor making his entry on stage, a boar obligingly appeared. No panic-stricken dash like the other, but trotting out from a patch of shadow to stand in the centre of the track. He could almost have been defying us to encroach further on his domain. And any resemblance between this boar and the little fellow was pure genetics. This boar was not only much heavier and greater of girth, but it carried weapons in the shape of a pair of tusks curving upwards around its blunt snout. The all-over black bristle hide looked tough as armour plate.

The boar's stunted legs trembled as it tensed for the attack. Moulay was cutting it fine, drawing every last ounce of drama from the situation. I was reaching for my own gun when he fired, two rapid shots, like cracks of thunder, that ripped the beast apart in a gush of blood and tissue. Death must have been instantaneous and a tribute to the efficacy of the Brenneke cartridge, for the boar didn't even squeal as it collapsed, a mound of shattered meat. It was almost anticlimactic. This wasn't hunting the way I understood it.

While the shots still reverberated through the trees, a great commotion arose. The crackle of scrub and salvoes of breaking branches were superimposed on screeches and grunts and the drumming of many trotters on hard earth.

'Look out – here they come!' Moulay's shouted warning was redundant for they were already in our midst: great and small, adult and young, tusked and tuskless, a whole community of boars on the rampage. Confusion among us was total. Horses wheeled and bucked, adding their whinnies to the general clamour. A woman screamed, a man bellowed, guns blared. Then the boars scattered, fanning out into the forest. The real hunt was on.

Moulay, Hordern, and the Gunner Major galloped their mounts after the biggest group, which contained at least a couple of prize specimens. Clair, whether of her own volition or her horse's, took off after them. Others of our party were in motion in all directions. The forest resounded to cries of the chase.

Lizzy and I were the last to get going.

'Come on!' she shouted. Standing agitatedly in her stirrups, circling her horse and pointing after a trio of stampeding boars that had split off from the rest of the herd.

Away she bounded in pursuit, crouched over her horse's neck like a jockey. A slap of heels against my mare's flanks, and I accelerated after her, my contribution to speed and direction nil. Luckily the trees hereabouts were widely-spaced and the ground was ever firm, making a fast pace possible. Only the infrequent islands of scrub that clustered together in hidden hollows, as if to draw comfort from proximity, dictated caution. Lizzy by-passed two such obstacles but jumped a third, and my mare, not to be outdone, followed suit, almost unseating me. This kind of riding was far outside my ability. I clung on, all pretence at technique long gone.

But we were overhauling the boars and would soon draw level with them. I judged the time ripe for a snap shot and urged my mare to greater feats of speed so as to bring me up alongside Lizzy, who was riding a parallel course ahead and to my right. Another patch of shrubbery loomed in her path. Predictably she aimed her mount at it, choosing to go over rather than round. So accomplished had been her performance until now I had no qualms as the game beast put on a spurt and gathered its haunches for the take-off, muscles bunching under the velvet coat. Only then, when rider and mount were committed beyond recall, did I see from my oblique viewpoint what Lizzy could not: this particular clump was not only much more extensive than even a trained steeplechaser could reasonably be expected to clear in a single bound, but the terrain dipped away sharply beneath it, forming a bowl. Lizzy would, in effect, be jumping downhill, without being aware of it until too late. A shouted warning would only spoil her concentration. Her only salvation lay in making a controlled crash-landing in the middle of the shrubbery, using it to cushion the shock.

Up she went in a flawless lift-off, horse and rider rising in harmony, fused entities like a centaur. And to give Lizzy her due, no wail of panic escaped her when the lie of the land became apparent, which it would have done the minute she left the ground.

I was already swerving towards the bushes when, with the delicate touch of a pilot setting down a battle-shattered warplane, Lizzy belly-flopped her horse into the densest part of the vegetation. Finally her nerve cracked, wrenching a yell from her lungs. Then horse and rider were gone, swallowed by the bushes, the smashing and splintering of twig and branch coinciding with a sickeningly abrupt termination of that yell.

Seven

The foliage closed over Lizzy in a heaving green sea, and the crashing went on and on. Now her horse was whickering, a high-pitched ululation. I tried not to picture four iron-shod, flailing hooves.

I had reached the bottom of the dip and even as my mare slowed, was dismounting – falling off, rather. Lizzy was there ahead of me, of course. Far from being the broken, shattered figure I dreaded and expected to see, she was actually moving, albeit on all fours like a wounded animal, dragging herself to where the mare lay kicking and struggling to rise.

'Are you all right?' I called out as I rushed to her side, fearing some internal injury.

'Yes ... yes.' A triangle of brown skin peeked through a new tear in the back of her tank top and a deep scratch ran diagonally across, oozing pustules of blood. Incredibly, apart from this, she had no visible injuries. Powdered with dust, hair matted, one tennis shoe missing, these were her only other scars.

Her horse had quietened. She was on her side in the flattened shrubbery, flanks heaving, flashing the whites of her eyes and blowing wetly through dilated nostrils. Lizzy knelt beside her and spoke to her in a non-stop undertone while she explored her legs for fractures. Her touch was gentle yet expert. Her calm presence of mind and her concern for her mount over herself impressed me.

'She's good,' she pronounced at length, and her relief was palpable. 'Just winded, I think. C'mon, girl ... hup!' I stood back as, stage by stage, she cajoled and bullied the mare to an upright stance.

'She's fine.' She patted the mare's glossy neck, and received a nuzzle in return. Instant empathy.

'We'd better get back to the others,' I said.

'No boar's head to put in the pot,' she said with a wry grin. She was a fast recoverer. While she made some adjustment to her stirrups I went to retrieve my own horse, patiently waiting under a cedar tree. Lizzy started foraging around in the undergrowth, presumably for her missing shoe. It was in this state of unpreparedness that our forgotten prey found us.

I had been witness to the speed at which boars were capable of moving, so no surprises there. A soft tattoo, an asthmatic snuffling, these were the only danger signals; these and Lizzy's squeal that spun me round like a whipped top. Her mare had bolted, reins flying free, leaving her helpless before the oncoming monstrosity, a nightmare of a boar, bigger and uglier than any I had encountered in my years of hunting in the Dordogne. Its hideous head was held low, positioned for the upward slash, its tiny eyes glowed like live embers, and it was out to kill.

My mare, thank God, had not imitated Lizzy's. I caught her reins and dragged the Ruger from its scabbard, clasping the walnut stock, jabbing at the safety catch. Both barrels were charged, and Moulay's injunction was never more justified than at this moment, for the boar, its snuffles becoming snorts in anticipation of the kill, was almost upon Lizzy as I fired.

In my urgency my aim was a shade low. The cartridge being solid, there was no spread of shot. It chewed a lump out of the earth under the boar's sagging belly, causing it to stop dead. Its braking was as efficient as its acceleration.

'Run!' I yelled at Lizzy, though it was too late for that. An aimed shot was therefore an unaffordable luxury for the second barrel. I just fired and hoped.

Maybe the fact that Lizzy's life hung on my accuracy, maybe it was the sweat blurring my vision; whatever the cause, I, André Warner, supposed marksman with handgun and rifle, fluffed that easiest of shots. The massive cylinder of lead, capable of inflicting enormous damage, carved a bloody groove across the boar's back, setting off a screech of pain and outrage. And that was all.

But at least the boar lost interest in Lizzy, or perhaps decided she was best left for dessert. It wheeled round to confront me and I was reminded of the hippo I had slain in Angola, in self defence. The difference then was that I'd faced that hippo with a *loaded* rifle.

The boar came hurtling at me, fast as a greyhound. Only half-aware of Lizzy's squealed 'Alan!' I stepped out of its path an instant before contact, like a matador dodging a bull, and brought the double barrels of the Ruger down on the torn and bleeding back as it passed to the side of me. This had no effect on the boar's motivation or its mobility. All I gained, as it turned within its own length, was a heartbeat of a respite. Just long enough to allow me to reverse my hold on the gun and to bring the stock down on the flat part of that ugly skull, between the ears, my arms powered by that superhuman strength all of us tap perhaps once or twice in a lifetime. I hit Brother Boar so hard the stock snapped off behind the trigger guard. But it was the heavy monobloc breech that did the damage, splitting the beast's frontal bone cleanly from side to side. Goo fountained nauseatingly from the fissure. The boar crashed to earth, almost taking me with it.

Lizzy stopped screaming, not at once, but gradually, the scream tapering off to a whimper, letting the silence filter back into the sunlit forest. A prolonged wheeze of air escaped from the great black brute. It seemed to deflate, like a punctured ball, and the tiny glowing amber eyes dimmed, becoming opaque and blind. Saliva dribbled from the gaping jaw. A fly zipped past and homed in on the carcass. Scavengers are never slow to move in.

Lizzy ran to me. It was only natural that she should come into my arms, cling to me, and push her face into my chest. Wanting comfort, perhaps as a daughter from the father she had lost.

'Oh, Alan,' she cried, muffled by my shirt front. 'I thought you were going to be killed.'

No concern for her own near-miss.

'Who, me? I wrestle with a boar a day just to keep in shape.'

She burrowed into me, trembling a little. I stroked her hair and murmured consolation. I don't know how long we stood there like that, as close as lovers, the hiss of the trees overhead and the ever more frantic whirr of flies arriving for the banquet, the only sounds. A spell of sorts had been woven around us and I was somehow immobilized by it.

When, still embracing her, I did at last look up, hoping for a glimpse of one or both of our horses, I was startled to discover we were no longer alone. At the top of the incline, near the spot where Lizzy had commenced her leap, was a man on horseback, still as a sphinx. The orb of the sun was directly behind him, and he, blotting it out, was no more than a silhouette. Releasing Lizzy, I waved to him.

'Give us a hand, will you? We've lost our horses.'

The stranger made no reply. Nor did he show any inclination to help.

'Who is it?' Lizzy whispered.

Slightly spooked, I shook my head and took a pace forward. The mysterious rider made no corresponding advance to meet me.

'Wait there,' I ordered Lizzy, and went up the slope at a jog. Still the rider didn't move; his head, dead centre of the sun, appeared featureless. I recognized the shoulders and the clothes before the man: olive-green shirt and pants, patch-worked with external button-down pockets like mine.

'Is close enough.' The clipped speech was loud in the windless air. He shifted his position, bringing into view the muzzle of his shotgun. After my workout with the boar I was in no shape to tackle Rik de Bruin, even without a shotgun.

'Look, de Bruin ...' I made a supplicatory handspread. 'We've just been attacked by a boar ... our horses bolted.' I spoke slowly, distinctly, so there should be no misunderstanding.

'There is a matter you and I must speak about,' he said.

'You think this is the right time and the place?'

'Is *exactly* the time and the place.' The muzzle watched me, a dead eye-socket. 'You keep away from them, that is all I wish to say.'

'Keep away from who?' Then it clicked. 'You mean Clair Power?'

He didn't answer.

'What she does, who she sees, is her decision, not mine.'

'I say no more.'

'Now just a minute, de Bruin.' I took a pace towards him.

'Stop!' The gun was centred on my chest. 'Believe me, Melville, I could very easily pull this trigger.'

The guy was barking mad, no question of it.

'Alan!' Lizzy yelled from down in the gully. 'What's happening?'

'Keep away from them,' de Bruin repeated, and his words were controlled, measured. No froth at the mouth, no hysterics. 'That is my final warning.'

On that note he dragged his horse around, dug in his heels, and was away in a flurry of hooves.

Perplexed and frustrated, I lingered at the top of the rise until the hoof beats faded, then called Lizzy to join me.

'Who was that?' she asked, as she came up, slightly out of breath. 'Has he gone to fetch help?'

'No,' I said shortly, and she didn't pursue it.

We stayed put, taking it in turns to yell. Twenty minutes later, leading our runaway mounts, Moulay, Hordern and a distraught Clair found us.

Eight

The sand, white and fine as salt, was hot to the touch. I scooped
out a handful and let it trickle through my fingers. An analogy
for the passing years, the sense of time dribbling away, of life
passing me by. Thirty-nine years old and all I had to show was
a dead wife, a string of corpses, and a heap of dollars. No
achievements to look back on with pride. No good deeds done.
A big part of me still wanted to reform, to opt out from the
killing. But I had already tried that and it hadn't worked. Until
I found something to replace it I was jammed in the groove.

Unless ...

'Penny for them?' the woman sitting beside me said.

'Not worth it.' I rolled onto my side and smiled up at Clair.

Her return smile was warm, sincere. She reached out and
twined a lock of my hair around her finger.

'Has your hair always been this colour?'

'Course it has. D'you think it comes out of a bottle?'

'It's almost yellow. Unusual.'

'Let's change the subject. Me bores me. Tell me about you.
Everything.'

A mischievous light flared in the blue-grey eyes.

'Everything? My vital statistics included?'

If that wasn't an invitation to get personal the Warner nose
for matters of the flesh wasn't what it used to be. I hesitated
though. Clair was class, not some strumpet I had picked up
at a boozy bash.

It was Monday and July was upon us. It was also the fifth day running spent, to a lesser or greater extent, in Clair's company. Five days idly fraternizing when I should have been earning my living.

'Don't rush this job,' Giorgy had cautioned. Sound advice. As far as the job was concerned, I was doing like he said. If I was involved in any rush at all it was to consolidate the bond between Clair and me before she resumed her journey to the States. For her, if I was any judge, such consolidation would arise out of the giving of her body. She was conventional in that respect. For me, the physical element carried little weight. The real commitment would have to come from inside. Rik de Bruin's threat was not a factor in the decision-making. When Clair and Lizzy left for America, whether or not their exit from my life was permanent, he was unlikely to follow them. Meanwhile, I had no doubts about my ability to keep him at bay. I would almost welcome a showdown, whatever the risks.

'Up until now,' I said, belatedly to Clair's unprecedented tease, 'you've only shown me the parts that stick out of your swimsuit.' Today's costume was a black one-piece with broad white edging and cut ultra-high in the leg, a style that did marvels for her long legs and slender thighs.

'Up until now?' she echoed, lightly mocking. 'That's a rather provocative remark, Mr Melville.'

Provocative? Hell, I hadn't even kissed her properly yet. My restraint was the stuff world records are made of.

She sat up, unscrewing the cap from a bottle of sun oil.

'Be a darling and do my back.'

I positioned myself cross-legged behind her and squirted amber liquid into my cupped palm.

'We'll be leaving soon, Lizzy and I,' she said, looking out to sea – a sea of humanity as much as water, bathing vacationers packed tighter than spectators at Wimbledon on the last day. Lizzy was someplace in amongst them, swimming the way she rode, like a champion.

'I know.' I wanted to express regret but my tongue was gummed to the roof of my mouth. I went on stolidly working oil into Clair's copper-hued skin. 'Not on my account, I hope.'

'Don't be silly.'

As I reached the base of her spine, a tremor passed through her.

'Stay on then,' I said tentatively.

'I sure would like to, but there are a million arguments against it.'

'For example?'

'Money. This was supposed to be the vacation to end all vacations. We won't be able to afford another like it for a long time.'

'Let me ...' I stopped. I had been about to offer to foot the bill, but gut feeling cautioned me against it. Some women take offence at that sort of thing.

As it happened she guessed the part I left unsaid.

'That's kind of you, but I couldn't.' She rotated on her bottom to face me. 'It's not pride, don't think that, or moral scruples. We just have so much to do. There's Lizzy's schooling, for instance, I want her to enrol for university. Not only that, we need to find someplace to live ...' She laughed, but without joy. 'We haven't even decided which state we prefer. Probably Massachusetts, where I lived before my marriage.'

The opportunity to propose an alternative would never be riper. To take a giant step into the future with this woman – and her daughter. A ready-made family. If nothing else it would serve to drag me off my bloodstained treadmill.

I came close to crossing the divide. Closer than at any time since my abortive venture into a marriage that, thanks to Her Majesty's Secret Fucking Service, had lasted a bare eighteen months. Set against the canvas of purest blue, Clair was at her loveliest. Even with only minimal make-up her principal features – eyes, lips, prominent cheekbones – were as bold as Van Gogh's brush strokes. Her chestnut brown hair, tousled, dried by wind and sun after our earlier swim, made a scalloped setting for them. Looks, a sense of humour, intelligence, she was well endowed. Why seek further?

Yet, like a timid poker player, I let the opportunity slip. I let my future die at birth, my red rose turn to brown, the petals wilting and falling to earth one by one, there to curl and rot and become dust.

'I do want to see you again,' I said feebly. 'After you go to America, that is.'

She smiled at my faint heart's jargon, though it was a smile tinged with sorrow.

'Dear Alan.' She stroked my cheek with long, cool fingers, holding my eyes with hers. 'I could so easily love you.'

Moved, I drew her to me. Our mouths came together in a coalescence of flesh and breath, a clash of gouging teeth and probing, teasing tongues; our bodies enmeshed, thigh to groin, chest to breasts.

Among the other beach users were doubtless those who did not approve of this immodest display of amour from a mature couple. Nevertheless, we let no inhibitions rule us. In full public view, encircled by the cries and chatter of vacationers, we made love in all senses but the physical.

'Mother! Everyone's looking at you!'

The shocked protest dumped an icy douche on our ardour. I left off gnawing Clair's neck. Her fevered panting ended abruptly on a rising note, and she heaved me aside, flushed, wild-eyed, as obviously aroused as any woman ever seduced.

Lizzy, dripping salt water, frog-flippers in one hand, snorkel mask in the other, seemed to soar over us like an avenging angel. Her hair was plastered to her scalp, taking the edge off her prettiness and giving her a pinched, shrewish look that was wholly out of character.

'Sit down, Lizzy,' I growled, conscious of the stares we were attracting from a young family nearby. 'No need to make a scene.'

'*I'm* making a scene?' she stormed, but sat down just the same.

Clair took both Lizzy's hands in hers. 'Darling ...'

That was as far as she got. The required words would not come. Lizzy sat cross legged, with folded arms and glowering expression, immune to blandishment.

'Let me, Clair,' I said gently. 'Look, Lizzy, I can understand it's difficult for you to accept any man other than your father kissing your mother. But you know how much I like her and believe this or not, that was our first kiss, so you can't say we've been rushing things.'

Lizzy unfolded her arms but only to towel her hair savagely. No softening yet. Clair was looking worried.

'It wasn't planned,' I slogged on, picking my words with the care of a teenage Romeo composing a St Valentine's poem for his sweetheart. 'There we were talking about the weather, when suddenly we had this urge to kiss. Some kind of magnetic impulse, I suppose. I guess you could say I'm Power-mad.'

No reaction from Lizzy but a heartfelt groan from Clair.

'Pur-*lease*, Andy, spare me the puns on my name. I've heard every one in the book and then some.'

'Sorry. I'm just Power-less in your presence.'

Clair rolled her eyes heavenwards. From under the towel came a giggle. Lizzy emerged, cheeks furnace-bright.

'Powerless in your presence,' she echoed. 'That's very funny. It may even be original.' She leaned across and kissed Clair's cheek. 'I keep forgetting Mummy is still young enough to want to go out with guys. It still doesn't seem long since Pops ... you know ...'

'Of course, darling,' Clair said, reaching for her spontaneously. 'It's the same for me, it really is.'

They hugged, a small reconciliation. I was touched. Fleetingly, I felt like a voyeur.

'Let's celebrate that kiss with an ice cream,' I said, pointing out the ice-cream vendor in fez and tattered shorts plodding at the water's edge. His invocation to buy – 'Ice ... ice ...' – competing with the crash of breakers and the general cacophony of squeals and yells that goes with any crowded beach. I grinned at Clair. 'After all, it was one *hell* of a kiss!'

She reddened becomingly and delved into her beach bag for some money.

'Race you there,' Lizzy challenged me, tucking a banknote in her bikini top.

She won.

As we walked back, ice cream cones already wilting, she looped her arm through mine. Her shoulder brushed my bicep and the heat of it made me catch my breath.

'Is anything wrong?' she queried at once.

'No, no. A touch of indigestion.'

'Oh.'

Clair waved to us. I returned her wave with a raised cone, like the Statue of Liberty.

'Actually I'm really glad you like my mother, Alan,' Lizzy said, looking down at her feet, not at me, and kicking up puffs of sand as we walked. 'She deserves a break. But what about me?

'Yeah, what about you?'

'No, I mean do you like me too?'

'You bet I do.' I wasn't just humouring her either.

'As much as you like Mummy?'

'Sure.' It came out as a croak. 'Every bit as much.'

She gave a satisfied little nod.

'Good,' she said. 'I'd be bloody jealous if you didn't.'

No messages awaited me at the front desk but, as I turned away, today's person in charge, an elegant Spanish woman I might have cultivated had Clair not been around, called my name.

'Telephone call for you,' she said, her lush red lips curving in a smile. 'Will you take it in a cabin?'

I was directed to cabin number 1, nearest of a rank of three.

'A moment, please,' the Spanish woman said as I put the receiver to my ear. Then a male voice replaced hers and it was a lousy swap as it turned out.

'Mr Melville? This is Rik de Bruin.'

I almost dropped the receiver. Recovering, I responded noncommittally but with civility. I still wasn't looking for a fight with this guy.

'This will be a surprise to you,' he said, and he wasn't wrong. 'I am telephoning to apologize for what I say to you, in the forest. You remember? I was angry.'

It was an unconvincing about-turn.

'Think no more of it,' I said blandly.

'To make amends I wish to invite you to come here, to my villa. We can talk, get to know each other, eh? Possibly do a little business ... you are a businessman, is that not so?'

'Was. Now I'm an ex-businessman.'

His laughter had a hollow pitch. Like his sincerity. I wasn't so naïve. This was sure to be a come-into-my-parlour ruse. Yet I might be able to make capital out of it. Maybe I could kill him in self-defence.

'I'm willing to meet you,' I said. 'But on neutral ground.'

'Neutral? Aah ... *neutraal*.' The Dutch pronunciation was a world away. 'It is agreed.' He suggested a café-bar out at the Cap, the "Chico".

I cut short his attempt at directions. 'I'll find it. Shall we say tomorrow, at ten?'

'Twelve is better. We will have some lunch after, no?'

Which would rule out lunch with Clair, a small enough sacrifice in the interests of peace, yet I grudged it. I sighed and agreed, and that was that.

Nodding my thanks to Spanish Rose, I made a leisurely ascent to the bar where I was to meet Clair for aperitifs. I chose the most secluded of the remaining available tables, ordered a vodka – the first of the day – and the harassed waiter was darting away when Lizzy wandered in, munching a large green apple and wearing a red layered mini-dress that showed a lot of brown leg. I waved and she strutted over.

'Hi, Alan.' She took the seat opposite, crunched into the apple, and grinned through bulging cheeks.

'Hi, yourself. Where's your mother?'

'Coming, coming,' she said airily. 'Eight o'clock, she said you said.' She consulted her large octagonal wristwatch. 'It is now exactly eleven minutes to. So ...' She paused and her voice dropped to a conspiratorial whisper. 'I've got you all to myself for eleven minutes.'

My mouth opened mechanically but nothing came out.

'You look like a fish!' she exclaimed, and aped me.

'Do you always talk with your mouth full,' I said, falling back, in my disarray, on a parental-style rebuke.

Unfazed, she bounced to her feet. 'Do you like my froufrou dress?' Lifting the hem like a can-can girl, she did a double twirl, exposing more than was good for my good intentions. Nor was I the only male noticing.

'Sit down,' I muttered, my cheeks hot.

She subsided back into the chair. Her laugh was low and throaty. I could have sworn the minx was giving me the come-on. Because she was Clair's daughter I naturally tended to view her more as a child than a young adult. Big mistake.

'You planning to see Yusuf again?' I said, a despairing attempt to distract her.

She elevated her nose. 'Yusuf! He's a fucking downey.' Her lapses into expletives and Aussie slang were more frequent when Clair wasn't around. 'Didn't even kiss me the other evening let alone get his fingers sticky. He's a big boy, mind you. If you know what I mean.'

Over the apple those smoky eyes inspected me. I could only blink back at them. My conditioned responses were not geared to such forthright language from a schoolgirl.

'You've gone all puce,' she observed. 'It doesn't match your shirt at all.'

I withdrew behind a generous swallow of vodka. Ought I simply to disregard her provocative talk on the premise that it would then wither away? Or put a deliberate stop to it and thereby tacitly acknowledge that she was getting through to me, sexually speaking.

Thankfully, the onus was removed by Clair's entry into the bar, her height and that panther stride setting her apart from the other women there. Ravishing in an ankle-length, dark-shading-to-light-blue crepe dress and a wide choker necklace that was a blazing rainbow of colours, setting off her long neck and well-shaped head with its dark bouncy coiffure. I rose to greet her with a light kiss on the lips; hers were moist, slightly open, newly intimate. By her thermometer our courtship had advanced several degrees. By mine, we were already in tropical climes. I glanced down at Lizzy and was taken aback by the malevolence that was written there.

It looked as if I had more bridges to build in that direction than I had bargained for.

'So lunch is out tomorrow, I'm afraid,' I said to Clair, encouraging the last dregs from a bottle of Valpierre rouge into her glass.

It was after eleven and the hotel restaurant was almost deserted though the band played on obligingly for lingerers such as us. Lizzy, as punishment for an unbroken, evening-long sulk, had been banished from our presence.

'There's always dinner,' Clair said, adding, 'If you can stand another dose of me and my wilful daughter.'

'Doses of you I could stand for a lifetime.' I could be gallant when the occasion demanded. 'Your daughter I would prefer in more rationed quantities.'

Though I knew Clair's attitude was love me, love my daughter, she was not offended.

'She does have her moody side, I must say. Fortunately, tonight's behaviour was exceptional. She just has to get used to you, to us as an item.'

'Okay, I'm convinced.'

As she laughed gaily, the maitre d' materialized at my shoulder.

'*Un digestif pour madame et monsieur?*' he proposed.

From a list as long as Magna Carta I plumped for Martell "Cordon Bleu" cognac; Clair, less extravagantly, for a Cointreau liqueur.

'No sense in acquiring expensive tastes,' she said.

I handed the list back. 'And coffee, please. Espresso.'

'Only three days left,' Clair said, when we were alone again.

'Time's running out,' I agreed. I looked hard at her, trying to probe her emotions. She returned my scrutiny, unflinchingly, laying herself bare through her eyes. Her hand scuttled across the table to imprison mine.

'Alan ...'

'Don't go back to the States, Clair.' The words jumped from my tongue like a jack-in-the-box. Only I couldn't stuff this jack back inside and shut the lid, whether it was a serious proposition or merely the consequence of drink and soft candlelight.

The entreaty was incomplete. So I nerved myself to follow through, saying, 'Come to Andorra; come home with me.'

Nine

When I drove out of the Rif parking lot the next morning, bound for my appointment with Rik de Bruin, Clair's serenely smiling 'Let me think about it,' was still swirling around my mind. So was a certain astonishment. Astonishment, because I wasn't in love with her. Honest-to-goodness love had been a rare event in my life since Marion's death. Maybe by accident, maybe by design, I had fended off emotional attachments and stuck to physical ones, with or without money changing hands. A couple of short-lived affairs, the second ending tragically, were the only oases in the desert that was my love life and even they had proved to be mirages. Clair was the first woman I had seriously cared for in a while. She represented a catharsis, an end, possibly, to mourning. It was long overdue.

At a suitable spot, once the suburbs were behind me, I pulled off the road, and despite faultless positioning and a winking indicator, was honked for my temerity by a battered taxi. I suppressed the temptation to retort in kind and waited for the cumulus of dust to disperse before emerging to retrieve the Beretta, the spare magazine, and the box of shells from under the wheel in the trunk. Back inside the car I loaded up: twenty cartridges per magazine, every cartridge individually examined for defects, for any blemish that might induce a jam. A jammed gun is the assassin's bogey. Also the reason for my preference for revolvers over automatics. I rejected three rounds and lobbed them out through the window far from the roadside.

Fitting each magazine in turn into the grip, I worked the slide, jacking every last round into the breech and out through the ejector port into my lap. No jams, no snagging. As satisfied as I was ever likely to be, I reloaded and stowed the gun and the spare magazine under my seat. The box containing the surplus shells went back in the trunk.

Secreting a handgun the size and bulk of the Beretta about the person is always a challenge. You can strap it to your ankle or stuff it down your pants' waistband, in the small of the back, and that's about the extent of your options. In the ankle position the gun has to be secured with adhesive tape, making a fast draw impossible. So my preferred option would be the second one, meaning that, heat or no heat, I would have to wear a jacket. To any streetwise villain this would normally be a giveaway. I was banking on de Bruin not being street-wise. About his villainy I was reserving judgement.

Soon after regaining the road I passed a flaking sign bearing the multi-lingual message that the Chico Bar was next on the left, some 500 meters ahead. Which proved to be a bit of a con, because once you were thoroughly committed to the turn-off, a typical Moroccan *piste*, and wondering if perhaps you had made a mistake, a far less-imposing notice informed you that the Chico was "only" 3km more.

The red top of the Cap Malabata lighthouse hove into sight on my left. Otherwise the landscape was uninteresting, just barren earth, scrubby grass, the very occasional stunted conifer. The road began to descend in a succession of hairpin bends. An ancient station wagon had come to an untidy halt on the second of these bends. Edging past I noticed a spare wheel with a bald tyre lying on the ground. Two North African guys in scruffy shorts and singlets were jacking up the front of the vehicle, on the other side. The sea, rich aquamarine and sun-speckled, made its appearance here and so did the Chico Bar. It was a wooden building tucked into the rock face, and fronted by a paved terrace dotted with tables and parasols, and fenced by tattered palms. Wooden steps that looked unsafe led from the terrace down to a cove and a beach with an oily tide mark. A billboard proclaimed WELCOME in five languages, plus a final line of Arabic squiggle. The place had a down-at-heel ambience.

Three unremarkable cars were parked in a gravelled area, shaded by a rock overhang. I tacked mine on to the end beside a Spanish-registered Alfa convertible, reversing in, anticipating a possible hasty exodus. A routine precaution. Down the waistband went the Beretta. It was a tight fit against my spine and bloody uncomfortable. While still inside the car I shrugged into my jacket, light blue, tropical-weight but still a garment too many for the mid-day sizzle.

De Bruin was already installed at a table, his head obscured by a red and white Pepsi parasol. He emerged from under it to shake hands. For form's sake only, no warmth in his clasp.

'Please,' he said, indicating a chair. He was smoking a gargantuan cigar, and spoke with his teeth clamped on it. 'Sit down.'

He wasn't alone. Very much not alone. The girl on his left was maybe a couple of years older than Lizzy, very blonde, very busty, and with a pretty snub nose. Her minuscule halter and short red shorts were cut to emphasize her assets.

'Hello,' she said, with a light Nordic lilt married to an engaging smile.

I returned her greeting and that of de Bruin's other playmate, a younger girl, fifteen at the most. Unattractive brown hair, but with looks that more than compensated for it.

I cast around, as if making a random appraisal. The only

other customers were a young, blond guy, built like an athlete, and a brown-skinned type, dazzling in white slacks and shirt.

'Nice here, huh? You like a drink?'

'Why not? Vodka with ice.'

He spoke to the younger girl, addressing her as 'Bea'. The rest was Dutch, which to me is mostly double-Dutch. Bea scuttled off to the bar.

'You certainly picked an out-of-the-way spot to meet,' I commented for something to say, resuming my survey. A warm westerly breeze was blowing, rattling the parasol and making the palm fronds clack. Gulls and other seabirds wheeled about like Spitfires and Messerschmitts in a dogfight.

Bea returned with a tray of drinks. A gin for de Bruin by the look of it, to which he added a splash of tonic water. The girls were on smoothies.

'Prosit.' De Bruin drank like a man with no tonsils – a single swallow and the glass was half empty. For once, I only wetted my lips. I wanted all my faculties about me.

'You are not too hot?' he said, in clear reference to my jacket. Oozing innocence, maybe real, maybe fake.

'Not at all,' I replied, disregarding the prickle of sweat on my temples. And the Beretta giving my spine hell.

The buxom blonde girl started stroking de Bruin's neck. Bea was more interested in her smoothie. Even when de Bruin reached behind her and jerked up her halter top, exposing pale, barely formed breasts, her only reaction was to dip a finger in her glass and give the contents a stir.

'What do you think of those, hey, Melville?' he cackled. The girl carried on unconcernedly stirring her smoothie. Her vacant, young-old eyes fastened on me, inquisitorially, as if expecting a gush of admiration.

Faintly embarrassed, I looked beyond her. Maybe girls do

graduate to womanhood at an ever-earlier age these days, but reading the statistics in the tabloid press is a lunar journey away from having it shoved under your nose for inspection. Perv I was not.

'You see, Bea,' de Bruin scoffed, 'he thinks you are too young for him. Perhaps Margot is more his type.' He repeated his trick with the halter on Margot. Her breasts were in a different category altogether, with pronounced red-brown nipples, which she rubbed and tweaked as she came round the table to me, teeth bared. She was well rehearsed. She stopped with her breasts inches from my nose, close enough for me to make out the blue latticework of veins under the taut skin. The effect on my prick was devastating. After all, I was only flesh and blood. I glanced uncomfortably at the two men sitting across from us. They were staring at the girl, but without expression, as if the flesh carnival was an everyday feature at the Chico.

She shook her breasts at me, impatiently, demanding a reaction. Her nipples had distended to the size of hazel nuts. Had it not been for the sneering presence opposite, I might have been tempted.

Disturbed by my own weakness, I said gruffly, 'What's the strip show to do with the matter of you and me and Clair Power?'

The sneer vanished. He left off fondling Margot's backside, and leaned across the table.

'How would you like to make some money? A lot of money.'

The question was so unexpected I laughed in his face.

'Doing what?'

He snapped his fingers, and Bea and Margot fled from the table, adjusting their halters as they ran. Their Master's voice, and he hadn't uttered a syllable. I always believed that kind of thing only happened in Arab harems.

'Amongst other things I have a publishing business,' he said, idly tapping his empty glass with his left hand, the stump of his amputated pinky jutting out. 'Well, that is what I call it. We produce movies for DVD and Internet. The material is specialist ... sorry, specialized, and the demand for it grows more every year.'

I was ahead of him. Or thought I was. 'You mean porn?'

'Porn, yes, yes, of course.' Impatiently. 'But there are many kinds of porn. Soft porn, hard porn. Fetish, BDSM, torture porn. Even snuff porn. In any case the profits are better than you can imagine. Fortunes are being made, by me and others.'

He picked something up off the floor, tossed it on the table in front of me. It was a bulky envelope. It was not sealed so I peeked inside. It was stuffed with mauve €500 banknotes. I placed it on the table between us.

'Very generous. Is this to cover the cost of my gas for coming here?'

'It is less than one day's receipts from subscriptions to my websites in the UK.'

If he meant to impress me, he succeeded. It looked like a lot of money. I noticed Bea and Margot watching from the doorway.

'What's the proposition, de Bruin? Are you offering to pay me to star in a dirty movie with the girls?'

'That as well, if you like.' The cigar was back in his mouth, waggling. 'But, no, let us be serious. The proposition is a piece of the action.' The outdated Americanism was in keeping with the rest of his posturing. Phoney as a plastic suit of armour. 'There is a vacancy for director of my UK business. Not just a job, as a partner.'

'I'm not interested in that kind of action.'

The cigar described an airy curve.

'You don't have to be. You sign checks, you sign receipts,

you hire and fire beautiful girls. You fuck them too if you feel like it. It is a legitimate business.' He tapped the envelope and added, 'You get paid in cash.'

'How much is in there?'

'Fifty thousand.' His bulging eyes glinted. 'This is the retainer. You will make this much every two weeks, for two days work a week.' A snigger. 'If you can call it work.'

I mulled it over. Not the offer itself, but the over-the-topness of it and the motivation. The breeze played on my face, flicked my hair on and off my brow. Down in the cove the sea burst against a spit of rock, throwing up an arc of spray, while further out, in the strait, shipping crept across the horizon, like models on a war games board. Routine sensations, routine sights. Yet my conviction that I had been lured into a trap was growing. In the half-hour I had been sitting here, with the Beretta reshaping my backbone, no new customers had shown up. Neutral territory? I didn't think so. De Bruin either owned the Chico Bar, or the owner was in his pocket.

'So?' De Bruin's voice quavered with impatience. 'What do you say to my offer?'

No matter how busy my brain, I would keep my responses natural and my suspicions to myself.

'You must want something more from me than my services,' I hedged, resolved to act out this farce to its foregone conclusion. But to de Bruin it was no farce, as his reply made clear.

'Nothing at all.' More puffing at the cigar. Ash tumbled to the table, was wiped away by the breeze. 'All I am requiring is that you cease to meet or contact Mrs Power and her daughter. Easy, hey? You do nothing, you get fifty thousand euros now, and a guaranteed income for life. Like they say in England, money for old rope.'

The cards were now face up on the table at last. Except for

the joker, still buried in the pack. The joker that was the key to it all, the joker that would reveal *why* de Bruin sought to separate me from Clair.

'Are you in love with her or something?' I asked him bluntly.

His face closed up.

'My interest in her has nothing to do with you. I am making you a commercial proposition to stay away from her. It is a business deal. It also happens I am thinking you are a man I can do business with.' He forced the irritation off his face, replaced it with an ingratiating smirk. 'Now ... do you accept? A simple yes, or a simple no. Simple, eh?'

Crunch time. I leaned forward, partly to ease the discomfort of the lump of ironmongery in my waistband, partly to make it more accessible.

'No, de Bruin, I don't accept.' I tensed involuntarily as I spoke. 'If you really want to know, I think you're off-the-wall crazy. I think you're one sick puppy.'

He reddened, then shot a glance at the beefcake boy and his Arab companion. The pair were sure to be in cahoots with him. Odds three-to-one, then. The girls didn't count. I hoped. A certain girl karate expert had once shown me the error of underestimating the alleged weaker sex.

But de Bruin hadn't yet expended all the arrows in his quiver. A second, fatter, envelope made the trip from floor to table top.

'Perhaps you value your contribution more highly. There is another hundred thousand.'

I didn't react, so he tapped the envelope with a thick forefinger. 'A hundred and fifty thousand euros. It's yours, here and now, you need do nothing. Just agree to leave the Powers alone.'

That was when, heedless of consequence, my cool deserted me.

'Fuck you!' I snarled and leapt to my feet. My fist smashed into de Bruin's ear. It was like hitting a concrete slab, but he went over in a somersault, chair and all.

After that events moved in a fast, confused farrago. De Bruin was temporarily out of it. Happy to relate, the girls did not rush out to give a demonstration of karate, kung fu, or kamikaze. They retired behind a slammed door, which left only the beefcake boy, who flexed biceps and looked danger-ous, and his Arab chum, who just looked out of his depth.

While I was still blowing on my bruised knuckles, around the corner of the building came another duo, both Arabs in *burnous* and turbans. Both brandishing daggers, straight out of Ali Baba and the Forty Thieves, not to mention every tourist bazaar in Tangier. I almost laughed at the amateurish-ness of it. De Bruin might be a king in the world of smut, but he was out of his depth in my world.

Then the sound of running feet to the rear alerted me to a new threat. Heading this way at a canter were two men in shorts and singlets, late of a certain disabled station wagon. With de Bruin also surfacing from the wreckage of the table and parasol, the odds were looking sicker by the second. Amateurs or not, they were numerous enough to do me harm.

Time to level the odds. I yanked the Beretta free. It came easily, removing no more than a couple of layers of my skin.

'Hold it!' I shouted, and nobody was running anymore. Nobody was shouting orders or flashing daggers. Even the gulls seemed to go quiet, leaving only the crash of surf and the bumpety-bump of my heart.

I hooked down the forward grip and flipped the selector onto its three-burst setting. The two with the daggers were closest, so I covered them first. Then, when I was sure we had an understanding, I swung the pistol through a semi-circle to where two statues from the station wagon stood, comically arrested in mid-stride, then finally back to the mastermind himself.

De Bruin was holding a handkerchief to his flattened ear and hadn't moved from the table. Beefcake slowly turned his head towards him, seeking guidance.

'All right, all right,' de Bruin shouted, flapping the handkerchief like a flag of surrender. 'We let you go, Melville.'

Big of him. Being let go wasn't enough though. I took a backward peek at the station wagon pair. They were behaving themselves, even to the extent of clasping their hands behind their necks, unasked. Arabs have a lot of respect for guns.

I beckoned de Bruin. 'Come here. The rest of you, on your bellies.' I repeated the instruction in French.

De Bruin stayed put. The rest, taking their cue from him, stayed vertical.

I lifted the gun and ripped off a three round mini-burst, a hacking cough of gunfire. Birds erupted by the hundred from every ledge and crevice, dimming the sun and blotting out all sound with their cries. The blizzard of thrashing wings took a while to disperse. When quiet was restored I lowered the long barrel to fire a second burst, a fraction above head height. To a man, and in concert, the minions hit terra firma, and de Bruin started walking towards me, albeit on dragging heels. Amazing what a little lead slinging will do.

De Bruin stopped, leaving a meter of so of space between us. He licked his slug-like lips.

'Two hundred thousand euros,' he said. 'I will give two hundred thousand. A hundred and fifty now, the rest later today.'

'You never give up, do you?'

I went up to him, and we stood there, a foot apart, breathing hard, glaring at each other. Then I lashed him across the bridge of his nose with the gun barrel, so abruptly he had no hope of avoiding the blow, and so violently that the jolt travelled all the way to my shoulder. A shout of pain, a gush of blood, and he fell to his knees in the gravel.

I stepped away from him, panting a little.

'Let that be the end of it, de Bruin.'

Giorgy called me on my cell phone. He was brief. 'The Al'hauri job is off,' he said flatly.

When I thought about my lack of progress over the past week I was more relieved than disappointed.

'It's your lost deposit,' I returned, and let it go at that. You don't discuss a cancelled contract on an hotel terrace. Anyway, with $200,000-plus already banked, I could afford to be philosophical.

Over a second beer I pondered the reason for the cancellation, a phenomenon without precedent. Was my professionalism in doubt? Was it on account of my dawdling? No, scratch that for a reason. Giorgy himself had urged me to take it slowly. If he was growing impatient an ultimatum would have been issued. Nobody, not even the Syndicate (*especially* not the Syndicate), writes off two hundred Gs without having examined and discarded all alternatives.

Professionally, I concluded, I had no cause for self-reproach. At a personal level, I was pleased. It would leave the field clear for me to focus on winning Clair.

As far as that went, the only impending squall on an otherwise placid sea was Rik de Bruin. Our mutual enmity was now out in the open. After the pistol-whipping at the Chico Bar I would have to watch my back. His nose was bloody, but I had to assume he would still carry on plotting. I didn't under-estimate the man. He had demonstrated a willingness to pay mega-bucks to take Clair from me. Fantastic? Yes, but it was happening. It was a fact. Be it lust, love, or midsummer madness, he was bent on having her. What was more, the initiatives were all on his side. To stay ahead of him I would have to perform the impossible feat of staying alert twenty-four hours a day.

The beer and several vodkas gradually took the edge off my chagrin and I gave up brooding. A waiter, red-fezzed, matching bumfreezer jacket, responded with alacrity to my raised finger.

'*Encore un vodka, s'il vous plait.*'

Strictly for medicinal purposes, let me say.

It was after midnight. In my room I picked up the phone and called Clair's number. It rang for so long I thought she must be asleep and was about to hang up when the receiver was lifted.

'Yes?' Very wary.

'It's me. I didn't wake you, did I?'

'No, no. I was in the bathroom, removing the gunge. Anything wrong?'

'What are you wearing?'

A tiny inhalation of breath, a pause.

'Not much.' A longer pause. 'Well, nothing actually.'

'Good. Describe yourself.'

An incredibly salacious giggle was followed by the burr of a dead line.

Ten

We dined *à trois* at the Marhaba Palace, a typical Moroccan eating establishment with a mini-orchestra and a boy who does the celebrated Rif tray dance. All very fine if you go for the Muslim concept of music and dancing boys. Clair lapped it up anyhow, which was good enough for me. Afterwards we went for a wander in the Medina amid the jostle of late night shoppers and gawkers, Clair and I hand in hand, Lizzy scouting ahead, detouring into this bazaar and that boutique.

'Hey, look at this!' she effused, trying a gold lamé caftan up against her. 'How much is three thousand dirhams in dollars?'

'You'd never wear it,' Clair said, hauling her away under the resentful scowl of the hovering saleswoman. 'Let's find something more suitable.'

'*Suitable*? Fucking drab, you mean!'

'Lizzy!' Clair said in outrage. 'Don't use that kind of language with me.'

Lizzy glowered incandescently then shrugged and muttered an apology of sorts. We drifted into a jewellery store and, my ears shut to Clair's protests, I treated her daughter to a heavy bangle in antique Berber silver that looked like a manacle on her bony wrist.

'Alan, you're super!' a mollified Lizzy carolled, and as I counted out endless notes into a creased brown talon she planted a smacking kiss on my cheek.

I made light of the expenditure. 'It's only money.'

Clair slid her arm through mine and nuzzled up against me.

'That was extravagant and definitely undeserved,' she reproved, 'and I ought to make her give it back. But I'm an indulgent mother, so I won't.' Her lips settled fleetingly on my chin or thereabouts. 'Thank you.'

'It was my pleasure, really. Now let's find something for you.'

She tittered girlishly. 'You've spent enough on us this evening.'

'What else should I spend it on? I don't exactly scrape by on welfare, you know.'

Thankfully, she didn't take my boast as a cue to probe further into how I did scrape by. So far she had shown no tendency to pry.

We coasted along with the human tide, down the narrow, airless street, importuned with tiresome regularity by youths, persistent and prevalent as flies at a picnic.

'No, we don't want a guide,' I would snap as they fell into step beside me. 'And I don't want any bloody kif. *Maintenant, foutez le camp!*'

They seemed to get the message.

At a crossroads, under the walls of the Royal Summer Palace, we came upon a store specializing in jewellery made from coral. Clair went into raptures over this stuff and, since she couldn't decide which piece she preferred, I forked out for a co-ordinated set, comprising necklace, bracelet, tiara, and ring. André Warner, big spending fool. In truth, I was enjoying having someone to spend on.

'You mustn't, you mustn't.' Clair was at once agitated and thrilled.

'Chill out, sweetheart. It only sounds a lot in the Mickey Mouse money they use here.'

With these purchases, though it was not my agenda, I

seemed to have bought a large chunk of goodwill. Clair's kiss was bold lips-to-lips and conveyed much more than gratitude. Lizzy affected not to notice, but for a tightening of her lips. Learning to live with the idea of her mother having a boy friend was never going to be easy for her.

In the Petit Socco plaza we pounced gratefully on the only spare table outside the Café Central, and for a while watched the world go by – and "world" was not a misnomer, for the nationalities represented were too multifarious to name or count: from the obvious, well-fed American, groaning under cameras and optional extras, through olive-skinned Latin, to moon-faced Chinese and blacker-than-ebony East African.

Claire and I had ordered mint tea, with a light beer for Lizzy. She downed it in a gulp before, with a flash of teeth, deserting us for a boutique next door, to browse over racks of dresses and other feminine frippery. Whenever she took off like that it made us nervous, but Clair was adamant about not being over-protective.

'I can't watch her every minute of every day,' she explained.

I admired her enlightened approach.

'Brave of you.'

'So long as it doesn't turn out to be foolhardiness.' Her eyes sparkled as they focused on me. 'That aside, she's giving us a few minutes alone together.'

'Great, so let's not squander the gift.' I enclosed her hand in mine. 'Have you thought any more about my offer?' Even as I resurrected the subject, I was unsure which I feared most – acceptance or rejection.

'I've done little else.'

'Tomorrow's your last full day here,' I pointed out. 'Even if you don't make a decision, we ought to do something special to celebrate the end of our vacation. With or without you, I'll be leaving on Friday at the latest.'

'Yes ... I see.' She bit her lip. 'But tomorrow, I ... I shan't be seeing you, Alan.'

I made no effort to keep my disappointment private.

'Please don't be upset,' she said, laying a consoling hand my arm. I was not consoled. 'It's not that I don't want to ... I do. Very much.'

'Well, what then?'

'I need a breathing space, or I should say a thinking space. To clear my head and make my decision free from your distracting presence.'

'Fair enough. If you must, you must. How will you pass the time?'

'It's all planned,' she said, around a bright smile. 'We've booked a rental car and we're going to drive to Asilah. Do you know it? It's a little fishing port on the Atlantic side, very old and very lovely. So the blurb says.'

I grunted. Stuff the blurb. Blurbs were full of bullshit anyway.

'We'll be back by early evening,' she said.

'Be careful. Some nasty people lurking in the bushes these days. A couple of ravishing Westerners would be a gift from Allah.'

'It's a guided tour, don't worry. We'll be a group of twenty or more, so I don't think we'll be in any danger. When we get back we could meet for drinks, if you like.'

'If I *like*?' I growled. 'I'll break down your bloody door if you don't show up.'

We said our good nights in the corridor outside her room. Lizzy, a continuing model of discretion, had gone up ahead of Clair.

'Are you going to invite me in,' I said, as we separated from a kiss that set me afire with primeval urge.

'I can't, really. Lizzy's next door. She ...' Her hands fluttered like a humming bird's wings. 'Oh, Alan, please be patient just a little longer.'

I pulled her to me, roughly. She gasped as our lower bodies came together and my desire was communicated to her.

'Don't play games with me, Clair.' I released her, and her back bumped against the door.

'Games?' Her voice was shaky. 'If only you knew how much I've wanted ...' She bit the sentence off short, kissed my cheek with her fingertips. 'Good night ... darling.'

She turned and was gone, the door closing behind her softly but with a certain finality. Now it was just me in the dimly-lit corridor, her 'darling' still resonating in my ears, and the vaguest residue of her perfume titillating my nasal passages. I sniffed it in, slow and deep, like a *bon viveur* savouring the bouquet of a vintage wine. It was all I was going to get this night.

I was not so moonstruck as to completely forget the menace of Rik de Bruin. He would come looking for me, sooner or later, I was sure of it. So, instead of Clair, I took the Beretta to bed with me. It was a lousy substitute.

'Encore, monsieur?' the waiter at the Café de Paris enquired, with a meaning bob at my empty glass.

Encore? That would make four vodkas slopping around inside me and it wasn't yet noon. I oscillated a negative finger, paid the tab, and ambled off down the slope of the Rue de la Liberté. It was market day and the square at the foot of the hill heaved with colour, an iridescent sea. I swam into it. Shoulders shoved, elbows dug, and small boys darted between legs, steering old baby carriage tyres at the end of a bent piece of wire, Tangier's ubiquitous home-made toy. On the far side of the square I staggered free of the throng, squeezed like a pip from a lemon.

One o'clock. I sat down under the veranda of the Africa Bar, on what used to be called Rue de la Plage but is now something unpronounceably Arabic. Here the sea breeze tugs at the white table linen and brings the tang of the ocean to garnish your meal. I managed not to order a fifth vodka. Such strength of will.

The waiter brought me a French newspaper. The words made no impression. It might as well have been a blank sheet. Two o'clock. Yawn. Mooching around waiting around for Clair's return, waiting to learn my fate, was not my idea of a fun way to pass the day. Notwithstanding that the answer could transform my life.

I ate listlessly. Tasteless sandwiches with refrigerated beer to flush them down. I was sorely tempted to call her on her cell phone. Resisted the temptation with difficulty. She wouldn't thank me. Give her space, my sterner side chided.

Three o'clock. Time seemed to be slowing down.

I decided to take a drive. Anyplace would do. Any activity, even sitting behind the wheel of a car, was better than this. Until I discovered once again that the inside of a car that has been standing in the afternoon sun, in July, in Africa, is no fit place to be. The air conditioning did its best but even working flat out it was fifteen minutes before it started to chill the sweat on my skin. By then I was sitting in a puddle of my own making.

My route chose itself. Out towards the airport, a straight nondescript stretch of highway. Dodging the potholes kept me on the alert. Other vehicles were sparse and mostly commercial. I didn't speed. The local law is very free with its on-the-spot fines.

After a while the novelty of just driving wore off and I turned in at a roadside bar. Mindful of Clair's opinion and its increasing relevance to me, I shunned the hard stuff. Pure lemon juice with a dash of soda. I knocked it back in one, paid up, and drove back the way I had come. At least I had killed some time. It was now after five, the sun already in free-fall westward, the blue turning to pink above the horizon. The highway was busier than on the outward journey, when the heat had kept it free of all but mad dogs and this particular Englishman. An open Porsche zapped past, male driver, female passenger, her features lost in the golden swirl of her hair. German license plate. My Fiat was no competition. Moreover, it was developing a knock in the engine compartment. I didn't dare push it too hard.

Once past the airport the road became straighter and wider. I was relaxed. My penance was almost over and I was eager to see Clair at the hotel. I may have hummed a tune, played scales on the steering wheel rim, laid tentative schemes for the future. I don't recall, the memories were eradicated by events about to unfold.

At the roadside a white P in a blue square gave notice of a parking zone 1000 meters ahead. It registered only in my subconscious. When the site itself came up I gave it a sidelong glance, as a motorist will glance at any break in the monotony of the open road. It was set back behind a straggle of petticoat palms. Parked here were a small, cream sedan and a grey BMW. Between the two cars a small group of people, of which two were female. The men were dark-skinned, in Western dress; one of the women, a tall brunette, had on white shorts and a yellow shirt. Clair had a yellow shirt, I mused ...

Christ!

My reverie was blown to fragments. The parking area was already behind me but I saw in detailed replay the interaction: a man's grip on Clair's arm, her attempts to pull free, the other men closing in to restrain her; saw Lizzy trying to intervene.

Even saw the terror on her face.

All this flashed before me, a frozen frame. The implications defied instant explanation but those Arabs weren't just touting *bric-à-brac*. I braked, standing on the pedal so hard my backside left the seat. The wheels locked, inducing a howl of rubber on asphalt and a skid that fell just short of uncontrollable. After an interminable few seconds of drama, I managed to bring the Fiat to a juddering standstill, half-on, half-off the verge.

A horn blared behind me, remonstrating with good cause, and a car whipped past. I crunched gears, seeking reverse. Come on, you bitch, come *on*! Crunch, whirr, crunch ... there! Foot flooring the accelerator, the car taking off backwards like a greyhound from a trap, and to hell with the traffic coming at me on a collision course. Let them get out of my way.

More horns trumpeted, a regular fanfare, followed by a squeal of brakes. A car clipped me as it careered past; a glimpse of the driver's face, mouth agape in disbelief, then he was gone.

The distance I had to cover was less than a quarter of a mile, but it was the longest quarter mile I have ever driven. Another car rushed at me, yawed past, control hanging by a thread. Next came an old bus that flung a solid wall of wind and dust at me, missing by the thickness of a coat of paint.

I swung into the slip road, slewing the car round on the handbrake. I was nearly too late. The party had broken up, the BMW was in motion, U-turning away from me. Inside, a jumble of heads, two of which presumably belonged to Clair and Lizzy for they were nowhere else to be seen. If I let them get clear of the parking area I would lose them, no doubt about it. The BMW was the 7- series, capable of 150-plus mph. My Fiat would do well to achieve half that. Even now the

Beemer was accelerating away, opening up a gap between us. I pounded my fist on the steering wheel, screaming obscenities after it. Much harm it did them.

The Beemer slowed slightly, to wait for a break in the stream of traffic. At that moment the nearside rear door flew open. A slight figure tumbled out, rolling over and over on the asphalt to disappear in the uncut grass that bordered it. Female, a pennant of blondish hair ... Lizzy! The Beemer came to a lurching halt, and an Arab in patterned shirt and jeans emerged, landing in a cat-like crouch, glancing in his uncertainty from where Lizzy had come to rest, to the Fiat, then back again to Lizzy.

As I accelerated at him, his arm came up and the metallic extension to it was not an artificial limb. A tiny pop, like the pulling of a cork, and the windscreen frosted over. The bullet made a flitting sound as it missed my head by an inch or so to exit through the rear window. I spun the wheel, hoping to upset his aim. Another pop and a side window shattered, hurling glass over my shoulder. I braked hard, churning up a dust-storm. While the Fiat was still rolling I dived through the door, cracking my elbow on the pillar and hitting the ground in a clumsy slither, badly grazing my unprotected forearms and thighs.

In deference to Moroccan sensibilities I had again consigned the Beretta to the spare wheel well. No use at all in an emergency. A bullet spanged off the trunk lid and away into the great beyond. Without much hope I looked towards the highway where lay possible succour. Couldn't the people in those passing cars see what was happening here? And if they could see, would they rush to intervene? I didn't think so. This wasn't England, and I wasn't among friends.

A yell from Lizzy made me forget about flying bullets long enough to peer around the wing. The Beemer was still in place, smoke dribbling from its twin tailpipes. Inside, heads bobbed frantically. Clair wasn't making it easy for the bastards. Good for her. The gun-toting Arab was stooping over Lizzy whose bare legs were kicking at him, holding him at bay. There might never be a better opportunity. I stood up and wrenched open the trunk. As I dragged the spare wheel aside there came the familiar popping cork sound, coinciding with the appearance of a star-shaped tear in the raised trunk lid. Though I wasn't to know it then, I owed his poor aim to a well-directed kick in the crotch from Lizzy. Next time he won't miss, I told myself, hauling the spare out of its recess.

I scooped up the Beretta and dropped flat the very instant the Arab fired again. Another miraculous miss slammed into the Fiat. By then I was in a 'go' situation. Pistol shooting from a prone position was not my forté, but the Beretta's firepower was such that I could afford to be prodigal with my ammunition. I never got the chance: the Arab's last bullet had done more than just perforate the Fiat's bodywork. I smelled the gas fumes a second or so before the car went up in a plume of flame, throwing out a concussion that would have blown me away like a feather in a hurricane had I been upright. As it was I suffered only a light grilling to the back of my neck and legs from the initial fireball that enveloped me. A frantic scramble took me away from the heat and the flames and the choking black smoke. Somewhat the worse for wear, but ready to go to work.

The Arab was unprepared for my emergence alive from the inferno. He was staring at the blazing Fiat, perhaps admiring his handiwork. I shot him as his gaze shifted from the car to me. I had actually drawn a bead on his chest, that most substantial part of the human frame that makes it the sniper's favourite target, but failed to compensate for the muzzle jump when on automatic fire. As a result, my three rounds ripped through his neck to exit in a geyser of blood. His collapse was instant, soundless, and total. And satisfying.

Above the roar and the crepitation of the flames I heard the surge of the Beemer's engine as it moved off, the open door slamming shut. With Clair still inside! Rising to one knee, I pumped bullet after bullet at the rear wheels – to aim higher was to risk hitting Clair or the fuel tank. Sooner a hostage than her death to bludgeon my conscience. The Beemer shrugged off my bullets, gathered speed, and whatever mischief my bullets had done hadn't depleted the horses under the hood. It crossed the highway against the traffic flow, almost causing a pile-up, and was out of sight in no time.

Passing cars were at last, too late, slowing. Not stopping, simply moderating their pace. All the better to view the pyrotechnics.

Even in my rage and distress I was still mindful of my own precarious circumstances, armed as I was with an abbreviated machine pistol and saddled with a corpse. My old instincts urged me to run. If the police got involved, as they must, I could expect to be held for questioning or worse. To help Clair I had to have freedom of action. Lizzy was another factor. Now on her knees in the grass, staring after the Beemer, calling 'Mummy ... Mummy ...' over and over in a strangled, incredulous voice. Deserting her was not on the cards, I had to stay and brazen it out. It was the gun that would condemn me and make a criminal of me. If I could account for the gun, the rest of my story need not be far from the truth.

A possible deception vaguely forming, I hurried across to where the dead Arab lay, his head in a bloody halo, lips drawn back over yellow teeth, the snarl of his epitaph. I dragged a long-in-the-tooth Walther PP fitted with a sound suppressor from his slack grip. With my shirt tail I wiped the Beretta clean of my fingerprints, smeared his all over it, then re-printed it with mine before throwing the weapon from me. It slid across the hard surface in a spray of sparks. Again I used my long-suffering shirt to wipe the Walther clean of the Arab's prints and loped into the scrub beyond the parking zone. As I passed Lizzy, who was still on her knees, distraught, crying, I touched her lightly on the shoulder. Letting her know she wasn't alone. She sobbed my name but much as I wanted to comfort her I had other priorities and they couldn't wait.

Burying the gun without tools would have taken too long, so, about a hundred yards into the scrub I hurled it high into the air and watched it tumble to the earth maybe a further fifty yards distant. If the police did an intensive search of the area it was bound to turn up, but it was the best I could do in the circumstances.

As I rejoined Lizzy, a car finally peeled off the highway to investigate the blaze. A second car followed close behind, overtaking it on the access road.

The second car had white paintwork and a flickering red light on its roof, and the lettering along the doors proclaimed SURETÉ NATIONALE – Moroccan French for "Police".

Eleven

Morning. The monkey chatter of children at play, the unmistakable creak of a swing and of a ball bouncing on a gravel surface.

This was not the usual backcloth to my daily awakening. I was not in my soft bed, in my five-star hotel room, serenaded by piped radio music and pleasurably anticipating delivery of a pot of fresh-ground coffee and warm croissants. In fact, I was in a cell. The bed I lay on was hard and narrow, and the mattress was about as comfortable as a sack of coal. Harsh electric light bounced off the bare concrete walls and ceiling and the only natural light entered via a grill set high in the wall. Fresh-ground coffee existed only in the imagination.

In the next cell a man groaned, then sneezed, not once but a whole spluttering paroxysm. I grimaced. A junkie, by the sound of it. Tangier had its share – more than its share. I had seen them draped around the port area or mooching in the *kasbah*. Emaciated, unkempt, begging. Or so spaced-out from a recent shot as to be oblivious of the world outside.

I sat up, and now it was my turn to groan, at the twinges that arose out of this routine act. Too many soft beds in too many soft hotels ill-prepared you for prison conditions. Not that I was under arrest, as the happy-go-lucky sergeant, dapper in grey with black accessories, had assured me. No, I was merely a detainee. A material witness, held for questioning. See, I could even keep my watch and the belt of my shorts.

They hung on to my wallet and manufactured credit cards though, and unless I had grown naive in my middle years, they would have been round to the hotel for a nose through my belongings. I had no worries there. The only incriminating piece of luggage had been the Al'hauri dossier, and this I had destroyed when the contract was cancelled. Before incarcerating me for the night, they took my fingerprints.

A footfall sounded in the corridor. Breakfast, I hoped. I hadn't eaten since being brought here.

The feet stopped at my door. The observation panel flipped back and a square of brown face regarded me unwinkingly.

'Bonjour,' I said, forcing cheerful unconcern into my voice, as if he were from room service. Grunt from the panel. Bolts crashed, keys clunked, and the door swung outwards, exposing a policeman. He made a loose beckoning motion, and I rose and walked stiffly towards him.

To judge from the lack of tabs and stripes about his tunic he was of lowly rank. He was also alone and unarmed, a favourable sign for my status as witness rather than suspect.

'Par ici.' He directed me down the corridor. Another door swung open on another policeman. Black gun belt and holster prominent. My optimism dimmed.

They took me up three levels to a large and untidy office with a window that filled most of one wall and overlooked a dreary apartment house development. I was shown to a chair before a desk in the centre of the office and left to my own devices.

Overhead, directly above the desk, was an old-fashioned ceiling fan. It was rotating lazily, creaking a little like an old galleon in high seas. It was barely necessary, as the day was still young and the breeze coming through the open window, agitating the venetian blinds, agreeably cool. Right in front of me was a row of three identical black telephones, the old-fashioned type with coiled cables, all knotted. From there my gaze drifted over the severe furnishings: dark heavy wood throughout, apart from a row of steel file cabinets. Papers and books were strewn any old how over every flat surface. My stomach gurgled in objection to the unaccustomed fast. I yawned – tension, not tiredness.

'Ah, good morning.' The cheery greeting came from the doorway behind me. I twisted in my seat to receive a matey slap on the shoulder from a well-built guy with a square beard. My hand was pumped like a long-lost brother's.

'Sorry to keep you waiting,' he said in impeccable English. 'My name is Ramouz. Commissaire de Police Ramouz.'

'How do you do?'

'Very well, thank you.' He marched around the desk and settled in the swivel chair. He was about fifty, grey invading the black silky hair but not the beard. 'I am the head of the Sureté Nationale here in Tangier.'

An important personage then. Flattering, you could say. A carnation adorned the lapel of his fawn, lightweight suit. He bent his nose to sniff at it, his eyes cowled, probing me. A little humility in the presence of the exalted never does any harm.

So I said, 'I'm honoured. I appreciate your seeing me personally, *Commissaire*.' The way I said it made it sound as if this were a business appointment not an enquiry into a homicide.

'Would you care for coffee or tea?'

'Coffee. Thanks.'

He rustled up coffee by phone, then steepled his fingers and rocked back in his chair to fix me with a hard cop stare.

'I haven't had any breakfast,' I pointed out, taking the initiative. 'In fact, I've had nothing to eat since I was brought here, and only water to drink. And I'd like a shave.'

He chuckled. 'My apologies, Mr Melville. The service here

is not quite up to the standard of the Rif. These, er ... oversights will be rectified presently. In the meantime we must decide what is to be done with you.'

'Done with me? What do you usually do with people who try to prevent a kidnapping?'

'Is that what it was?' His eyebrows had edged upwards, but the tone remained smooth as butter.

'Didn't the girl tell you? Miss Power.' I frowned at him. Until this moment I had assumed Lizzy was in safe hands. 'Where is she? Is she okay?'

'Oh, oh, so many questions.' He made soothing motions. 'Do not worry about the young lady. She is being cared for by my wife.' He smiled then, and that at least was genuine. 'I also have daughters.'

'If she ... if Miss Power is all right, then she must have explained to you that she and her mother were abducted by three Arabs.'

Ramouz nodded. 'Oh indeed she did.'

'She also presumably explained that she escaped from the car but her mother didn't, and that one of the men came after her to drag her back into the car.'

The nods continued. We were making progress.

'And that I disarmed the man and shot him with his own gun.'

Now the bear-like head was still.

'It is there we enter what I believe is known as a grey area.'

I had not expected my story to be accepted at face value. Some embellishment was called for.

'Then let me colour it black and white for you, Commissioner. This is what happened: the man who went after Miss Power was armed. He shot at me and set my car on fire. Presumably believing me to be incinerated inside it, he turned his attentions to the girl. Are you getting the picture? She's a gutsy kid, she didn't make it easy for him.' In all essentials this was close to factual. Ramouz's moderately-pigmented countenance showed neither belief nor disbelief. I continued, 'While he had his hands full I tackled him from behind; I once trained in unarmed combat.' It was true, courtesy of the British Secret Service. 'He was one very surprised kidnapper when I took his gun away.'

'You ... took it away?'

'Want me to demonstrate?'

Ramouz made a pretence of alarm. 'No, no. That will not be necessary.' He drummed softly on his desk blotter. 'So far I am inclined to accept your story, Mr Melville. What I am not clear about is why, having disarmed the man, you then shot him.'

This was the tricky part. I had my improvised explanation ready. It was riddled with flaws, yet not implausible.

'It was a sort of accident ...'

The door opened on an underling bringing refreshments, consisting of a pot of coffee, its aroma preceding it, with two diminutive cups and a dish of pastries, all on a copper tray. I suspended my narrative.

'An accident, you were saying.' Ramouz decanted coffee for both of us. 'Please elaborate.'

'Fortunately I know a bit about guns,' I said as I selected a pastry. 'I was an officer in the British army. The gun I took off the kidnapper was more like a machine pistol but, well, not at all complicated. And the safety catch was off. Anyhow, as I was saying ...' I frowned disingenuously. 'Or was I saying? Never mind. The thing is, at the point when I knocked him down his friends decided to help. They got out of the car. They were both armed, they fired at me and missed, I fired back, a short burst. At the same time the first guy threw himself at me, and ... and ... well, he just got in the way of a bullet.'

To my culpable ears it sounded weak. Perhaps therein lay its strength, though. A cleverly crafted lie can excite more suspicion in a cop than a bumbling account such as mine.

'Who was he?' I asked, between munches of pastry. 'The ... you know, the dead man.' I put the pastry down as if the talk of death had killed my appetite. I just hope I wasn't overdoing the ham.

'The man you killed? At any rate, do not be concerned that he was a worthy citizen. He was a known pimp and drug peddler called Lalla Yousef. We believed he had left the country. It seems we were wrong.' The interrogatory stare, lately relaxed, was reinstated. 'Tell me, how did you come to be there, at that spot, at that particular time?'

'Pure chance.' Another truth. I licked pastry flakes from my fingers. 'I'd driven to Asilah for the day. Mrs Power and her daughter were also there, but independently, as they had their own transport. I was on my way back to Tangier when I witnessed the abduction. I recognized the Powers from the road.'

'Oh? While you were driving past at, what, sixty, seventy kph?' His tone was incredulous.

'Not facially, but by the clothes they were wearing.'

'It's fortunate that you did. Otherwise we would be investigating a *double* kidnapping.'

Ramouz extracted an unopened pack of American Chesterfield cigarettes from a drawer, peeled off the cellophane, thrust the pack at me.

'Thanks, I don't.' My stomach grumbled in protest at the interruption to my breakfast. I tried to avert my eyes from the uneaten pastry. 'What are you doing about tracing Mrs Power?'

'Everything that can be done.' He drew on his cigarette, holding it between the roots of index and middle fingers, and sucking through the funnel of his clenched fist.

'Have you tried calling her cell phone?'

'No, because it was not with her when she was taken. She left it in her hotel room, charging the battery.'

'How do you rate your chances of finding her?' When he made no reply, I said, a shade more forcefully, 'Do you expect to find her alive?'

Again he declined to reply, asking me instead, 'Have you any opinions on the motive behind the abduction? I understand you and Mrs Power had been seeing each other regularly.'

'We have, yes,' I said, amending the tense. 'As for the motive ...' I was reluctant to pass my theories on to Ramouz. The Warner rulebook stated that information must never be volunteered to the police beyond the minimum necessary to save your own hide. I sighed inwardly. Forget the rules. This was about Clair's hide, not mine. If help was available, I had no right to obstruct it.

'Yes?' Ramouz prompted.

'A Dutch guy has been hanging around her, called Henrik de Bruin. He kept pestering her, wouldn't give up. He tried to buy me off. You might want to write this down,' I added, when he made no move to record my revelations.

'Do not worry. The recording machine has been running since you came in.'

Smooth bastard. Around a crooked grin, I went on, 'Naturally. Anyhow, as I was saying, this de Bruin character was obviously besotted with her.'

'Bee-sotted? You mean he wanted to fuck her?'

'Very subtly put, Commissioner. But, yes, that was my conclusion.'

'Enough to abduct her? That does not seem very likely, Mr Melville.' Ramouz toyed with a pen. 'Even so, we will follow it up. Tell me all you know about him, including a physical description.'

I complied, but only in part. The existence of de Bruin's residence in Tangier I kept to myself. Checking it out was going to be my first move, and I didn't want the police trampling through it ahead of me.

'Is her family rich?'

'Most of her family is dead. Including her husband. No, there's no financial incentive I can think of.'

Ramouz blew a perfectly symmetrical smoke ring before mashing his cigarette in an ash tray. He had consumed about a third of it.

'Were you ... *are* you going to marry her?'

My instinctive reaction was to laugh off the idea. Certainly marriage had not formed part of the immediate plan. Then, on a hunch it might reinforce my innocence if I were thought of as Clair's husband-to-be, I admitted it was under review.

'I have asked her. She's thinking it over.'

Ramouz heaved a sigh that might have been disappointment. I guessed he was coming round to accepting my version of the incident as true in its essentials. He got up to switch on the air-conditioning and boost the speed of the ceiling fan, for the room had warmed up in the last half-hour. Sunlight, striped by the blinds, lay across the desk and the patterned rug that covered much of the floor. Before resuming his seat he altered the slats to deflect the light upwards.

'Would you mind telling me what business you are in?'

I dished up the usual yarn, now so familiar I could have recited it backwards. If you tell a lie often enough, I find, it becomes indistinguishable from the truth. I was at pains to stress my comparative wealth, making sure he understood I had no need to break any laws to provide life's luxuries.

'Stocks and shares are to me as the mysteries of outer space,' he confessed.

'All you need is good advice, and a certain amount of luck.' That much I *did* know.

Another cigarette travelled from pocket to mouth.

'Luck, eh?' He lit up, inhaled with the transparent relish of a nicotine addict. 'Police work also requires luck. I suppose you have some proof of your financial situation.'

I scratched my bristles. 'I don't carry bank statements around with me, but if you insist I can produce the necessary references so you can do your own checking. I've about seven or eight thousand dollars' worth of travellers checks in my suitcase at the hotel.'

He smiled thinly. 'We know. You also have a large amount of cash.' The hard cop stare was back in place. 'More than is legally permitted.'

'So fine me.' My anger was not contrived. He was scratching around for justification for holding me. If a minor infringement of the currency restrictions was the best he could do, I was on safe ground.

One of the black telephones shrilled. Untangling the cord to bring the receiver to his ear cost Ramouz several curse-laden seconds.

'*Si?*' he barked, listened frowningly then acknowledged in Spanish, the dominant language in this part of Morocco. Signing off with a grunt, he replaced the receiver. The cord immediately re-entangled itself.

'A representative from the British Consulate is here,' he informed me.

'To see me? How did they know where to find me?'

'We notified them, naturally.' He blew another of his smoke rings, studied it critically as you might study an antique of uncertain provenance. 'An American with Australian citizenship is kidnapped, leaving a child, who also has Australian citizenship, without parent or guardian. A British subject kills a Moroccan citizen. These are not everyday occurrences, even here in Tangier, Mr Melville. The tourist business is an important source of revenue for my country. We have enough problems with the Jihadist threat. Where our foreign visitors are concerned, we try to be especially scrupulous.' He glanced up as the door opened. 'Ah ...'

Our Man in Tangier was tall and spare, with a cap of jet black hair contrasting with his death's head pallor and matching tropical suit. Ramouz greeted him with total correctitude if a noticeable lack of warmth.

'May I present Mr Melville?' he said, and I rose for the customary rites. 'Mr Formby.'

'Vice-Consul,' Formby amplified frigidly. The turbulence from the fan ruffled his hair, and he glared up at the ceiling in unconcealed irritation. He gave the impression of being a man who would irritate all too easily. 'Is Mr Melville ready?'

'Are we going someplace?' I said in surprise.

We were, I learned, going to the Consulate.

'I have finished with you for the time being, Mr Melville.' Ramouz said, supplementing his words with the little sigh all cops give when parting with what they consider to be police property. 'But you may not leave Tangier without my permission, and under no circumstances must you attempt to leave the country.' A pause, a drumming of fingers on desk top. 'We have, of course, confiscated your passport.'

The grin that accompanied the last piece of news was sardonic, as if he were aware that the lack of a passport would not keep me in Morocco if I chose to abscond. It's not as if it were the genuine product.

For the sake of form though, I assumed an affronted air.

'I resent the slur on my character, *Commissaire*,' I said, playing the honourable English gentlemen to the last. 'Mr Formby, I'm all yours.'

Formby sniffed. His disapproval was unspoken but implied that people who have their passports confiscated are not nice to know. Ramouz, with more of that notorious police reluctance, passed my wallet and credit cards across the desk. I checked that none were missing, signed a receipt and minutes later Formby and I were out in the street. A white Ford Mondeo with CD plates awaited us, illegally parked in the block of shade cast by the police building.

Well, I was out of the can, though it was a reprieve, not an acquittal. Ramouz wasn't to be taken lightly, affable though he was. I wouldn't put it past him to keep digging for dirt until he found some that would stick.

I prevailed upon a grudging Formby to detour via the Rif and allow me ten minutes for ablutions and a change of outfit. Even such an insensitive soul as his could perceive that shorts, especially shorts bearing the scars of kidnapping, fires, and shooting, not to mention doing service as prison pyjamas, were not suitable attire in which to go calling on Her Britannic Majesty's Consul.

Years ago, when the British Diplomatic Service set much store by appearances, the Consulate General was an opulent mansion, fittingly set in the Rue d'Angleterre. This is the main artery through Consulate country to the south west of the old town: a district of tree-lined streets, parks and gardens, peace and tranquillity. When Thatcher came to the throne, as ever for reasons of economic exigency, the establishment was moved to a couple of floors in a seedy office block near the equally seedy Place du 9 Avril 1947. One of these days I would make it my business to find out what happened on that date.

On arriving at the Consulate, Formby, who had spoken only in monosyllables during the drive, hustled me through the double frosted-glass doors, distinguished from similar neighbouring frosted-glass doors only by the royal coat of arms above them. From there we proceeded to the innermost sanctum, the Consul's eyrie.

In direct physical contrast to Formby, the Consul was short and rotund, and completely hairless. Half-moon spectacles sat on his button of a nose. He had a homely, lived-in presence, like a room in a house full of children. Formby did the introductions and bowed out.

'Take no notice of Formby,' the Consul said, mind-reading to perfection. 'He's a robot. Efficient, unflappable, and indispensable. How'd you get on with friend Ramouz?'

Disconcerted by the sudden switch of topic, I looked blankly at him.

'Sorry, old boy. Always swapping and changing, my wife tells me. You'll get used to it.'

The guy was so genial, you couldn't but warm to him. In carefully chosen phraseology, I explained that Ramouz and I had come to a *détente*.

He nodded at that. 'The shooting – an accident, I imagine.'

'Correct. As I told the *commissaire*, I'm a bit out of practice when it comes to guns.'

He tugged at the blob that did duty for a nose. 'You must have found the jolly old boar hunt a bit of a trial then.'

My flesh seemed to contract. How much was implied by that throwaway remark?

The twinkling eyes had ceased to twinkle, had become opaque like a darkened mirror. The innocuous exterior was no more. We were getting down to nitty-gritty.

'Look, old boy, you could be the fastest draw in the West for all I care. I'm not prying, believe me, I'm not. I only heard about the boar hunt in casual conversation with Brigadier Hordern, whom I believe is an acquaintance of yours. My problem is not what to do about *you*, but what to do about that young lady in there.' He jabbed a thumb at a door in the far corner of his office.

'Lizzy? Is she here then?'

'Where else? Ramouz and his wife looked after her last night, but clearly the responsibility rests with the Consulate. With me.'

'But she's American, or Australian – take your pick. What's the British Consulate got to do with it?'

'Simply this: the nearest American consular office is in Casablanca. The nearest Australian consular office is in Paris. We occasionally help out.' He fixed me with a stern gaze. 'And let's not forget that *you* are British.'

'Anglo-Canadian actually.'

'Your passport is British.'

My phoney passport was British, at any rate.

For no reason I could put my finger on, I had a premonition he was leading up to something. Conditioning me, in his jovial way, for disagreeable news. I made no comment. It wasn't my place to smooth his path.

'So, as I was saying, your familiarity with guns is not an issue. You might have trained as a sniper in the British Army, for all I know or care.' He was making excuses for me, justifying my reticence for his own ends. 'Your attempt to save Mrs Power places you fair and square on the side of the angels and as far as I'm concerned makes you "respectable", if you'll forgive the anachronism. Respectability is an absolute prerequisite, old boy.'

Now bewilderment merged with my misgivings.

'Presumably,' I said, in some exasperation, 'you intend sooner or later to decode this gibberish into plain English, like wot she is spoke.'

He tittered behind his hand. 'Quite right, old boy.' He peeled off his spectacles, levered his round body out of the chair, and began to pace back and forth behind his desk in a peculiar hop-skip gait.

'I understand you were close to Mrs Power.'

'I *am* close to Mrs Power, yes,' I said, rejecting his use of the past tense. Ramouz had also slipped into the historic when speaking of Clair. The portents were obvious and ominous.

'Quite so. I do apologize.' He left off pacing to fix me with an earnest gaze. 'However, we must face up to the possibility that Mrs Power may not ...'– cough – '... be restored to us.'

'Yes.' I had faced it the previous day, even as the BMW had blasted off down the highway.

The Consul was no longer pacing but standing at ease, regarding me, directly below the forty-year-old portrait of the monarch that hung on the pastel green wall. Neither of us spoke. I was lost in my thoughts, anxiety for Clair being uppermost. Someplace in the room a clock ticked. Even with the air-conditioning churning, it was hot. The Consul took out a large white handkerchief and passed it across his forehead.

'Have you any idea why Mrs Power was taken?' he said.

I said I hadn't but told him as much as I knew of her background and circumstances, pretty much the same fiction I had fed Ramouz.

'So you were going to marry her?'

I wasn't about to quibble over distinctions.

'That's about the size of it.'

'Good.' The nod was unqualified satisfaction. My apprehension came rushing back. 'That being the case, I take it you will be willing to accept responsibility for Elizabeth in the event that . . .' Another cough, a clearing of the throat. 'In the worst eventuality?'

It was out in the open at last and less of a shock to the system than it deserved to be.

'It needn't be official, old boy,' the Consul said hastily, interpreting my silence as rejection, 'and it most certainly wouldn't be permanent. After all, the girl has an uncle in Spain, I believe. We shall be contacting him at the earliest opportunity. In the meantime, someone has to step up to the plate and accept responsibility. A family friend like yourself, for instance. It's important for Elizabeth's peace of mind and stability. A strictly temporary measure, I assure you.'

If it was an appeal, it was unnecessary. The idea of abandoning Lizzy had never crossed my mind.

I said, 'Just so long as you understand that my relationship with Mrs Power is of very recent vintage. Elizabeth might not want me as a stand-in custodian. She knows nothing about me.'

The Consul rubbed his hands together, clearly pleased by my tractability. 'Let's find out, shall we? Let's ask her.'

He hop-skipped to the door in the corner, flung it open.

'Would you care to join us, my dear?' he cooed into the room beyond.

As he stepped back, Lizzy came out – a pale, woebegone travesty of the Lizzy I knew, with red-edged eyes and slumping shoulders. Until her gaze alighted on me, a friend in a wilderness of strangers.

'Oh, Alan!' she cried, and came to me at a run.

I held her as I had done once before, not so very long ago, both the giver and receiver of comfort, making vicarious contact with Clair.

The Consul, standing on the sidelines, beamed approval. He had his answer.

Twelve

On leaving the Consulate Lizzy burst into tears, starting a trend that was to continue on and off through afternoon and evening. What with the bitter pill and worry of Clair's disappearance, the further niggle of my suspended passport, and now the burden of responsibility for a teenage girl, I wasn't feeling too chirpy myself. Lizzy and I were confederates in doom and gloom.

We had returned directly to the hotel. The staff at the front desk had learned of the drama, and much sympathetic clucking and head-shaking came with the key cards. This provoked renewed snivelling from Lizzy, and I hustled her up to her room where she agreed to lie down for an hour, on condition I didn't leave her alone. So, while she curled up on her bed and felt miserable, I sat out on the balcony and felt miserable. With the sun past its meridian, it was moving into shade. A pair of Clair's sandals lay under the other chair, toes pointing inwards like a little girl's. Somehow, seeing them there, waiting to be reclaimed, heightened the unreality of the situation. It also deepened my desolation, which drove me to telephone room service for a bottle of vodka. Stupid, weak, pathetic bastard, I silently berated myself as I hung up.

With the vodka came Yusuf. By then Lizzy had dropped off into a restive slumber, so thankfully I could drink without an audience to pass judgment on me. As I drank, I pondered the view and the various courses of action open to me. I steadily became ever-so-slightly smashed. A familiar pattern.

I also prayed for the telephone to ring. It didn't, of course.

In the early evening Lizzy woke up and shuffled barefoot out onto the balcony. Listless, hair a mess, a sodden handkerchief balled in her fist. A lost, lonely waif.

'Sit down,' I said, trying for an avuncular smile.

She sank into the chair. 'What are you drinking?'

I rotated the bottle so the label was on her side.

'Vodka,' she said, wiping her nose on the back of her hand. 'You can keep it.'

'That's a relief.'

My feeble humour drew an equally feeble tremor from her lips.

'Pour me one anyway, will you?'

I sent her to fetch a tooth glass.

'I don't expect there's been any news about ... about Mummy,' she said watching the colourless liquor splash into the glass.

'No, honey. No news.'

She looked at me, misery drawing lines that were obscenities in so young and lovely a face.

'Who ... ?' she began to ask. 'No, I mean *why*? Why did they do it? Mummy isn't rich. Or important. Only to me.'

'And to me,' I said, a gentle nudge that she wasn't on her own in this.

She sipped her vodka. No change in expression.

'I'd forgotten how tasteless it was.' She smacked her lips. 'Give me beer any day.'

'There's some in the ice box.'

She twisted the handkerchief round and round.

'Do you think she's all right, Alan? I mean *really* all right.'

Desperate not to hurt her, I resorted to white lies.

'Bound to be.' The words reeked of platitude. 'Kidnappers

always treat their victims well.' Not true. 'If they didn't, the ransom wouldn't be paid.' Not true. 'To them it's a business, you see. A way of getting rich quick.' That was true, at any rate, only Clair didn't have any money or any rich relatives as far as I knew. 'Your mother is just a piece of merchandise to be sold back to the people who care about her.'

'But who's going to pay?' Lizzy stared at me. She had unerringly put her finger on the weakness in my postulations. 'Will you pay, Alan?'

Would I? Yes, the private me replied, quite firmly and at once. I would pay to get her back.

'Yes, Lizzy, I will. If they ask me.'

'How much? How much will you pay?'

No deception was required. I would pay the price of Clair's freedom even if it took all I owned. Although I didn't love her as I had loved Marion, or even Gina, who had died accidently at my own hand less than a year ago, I had been ready to build my future around her. If, God forbid, she was never seen again, it wouldn't wipe out what we'd had together, short-lived though it was. It's called obligation.

It was thus with an untroubled conscience that I was able to say, 'Whatever it costs, I'll pay.' I reached for her hand, gave it a squeeze. 'We'll get your mother back.'

It was a meaningless pledge. Unless I was a whole three hundred and sixty degrees off-track, no payment would ever be demanded, for Clair was not a conventional kidnap victim. And if I was correct in that surmise, I could also say with certainty who had masterminded the operation.

Rik de Bruin.

'Any news, Commissaire?'

'No, Mr Melville. We have heard nothing. And we have found nothing.' Meaning no corpse had turned up yet.

'Oh, well done.'

Sarcasm is cheap but I couldn't help it. It was Sunday morning, nine o'clock-ish. The abduction had taken place on Friday, a whole forty hours ago. Forty hours of no bloody progress.

'We will keep you closely informed, Mr Melville. Be assured.'

I smashed the phone down. Be assured. Standard cop humbug and about as reassuring as my own placatory drivel about kidnappers and ransom money.

Lizzy was sleeping in her own room. After my chat with Ramouz I went to rouse her and ran into a deputation outside my door: Brigadier Hordern and a handful of picked cronies.

'Morning,' I said, a trifle curtly.

'We heard about Mrs Powers.' This from the old Miss Scraggy Neck. Her face was that map of tragedy that some people can turn on and off at will. 'How absolutely dreadful.'

'Power,' I corrected. 'No "s". Yes, it's a bloody mess.'

They meant well, these throwbacks to the sunset of the British Empire but they were no use to me.

'Actually,' the Brigadier said, knuckling his moustache, 'we came to see if you need any help. With Mrs Power's daughter, don't you know? Must be a bit difficult for you ... a single man, what?'

Idiotically perhaps, I resented the suggestion that I wasn't cut out to be a caretaker guardian. It wasn't that I disagreed, but I'd have taken the orphan population of Tangier under my wing sooner than admit it to this crowd. Or maybe he was hinting at something else; impropriety, for instance. Man of a certain age with an under-the-age-of-consent nymph.

'Thanks, but I'll manage.'

I pushed past them into the corridor and walked the few yards to Lizzy's door with the do-gooders at my heels.

'If you're quite sure ...' Mrs Scraggy Neck's tone implied that, sure or not, the task was beyond me.

I rapped on Lizzy's door.

'Quite sure.' Hearing Lizzy's invitation to enter, I slipped into her room and gently, smilingly, shut out the circle of wrinkled faces.

Lizzy was on the balcony, dressed in black leggings and a red T-shirt many sizes too large, with a Virgin motif across the front – Richard Branson's company logo, not a statement of her chastity. Her eyes were still a bit pink and swollen, but she had brushed her hair and was outwardly in control of her grief.

'All right?' I enquired.

'Oh, more or less. I was just thinking ... you know, Mummy is out there somewhere; probably not very far away.'

'In the next building even.'

Her hand jumped to her mouth.

'Not that close. She couldn't be.' She leaned out over the balcony, peering along the promenade as if she expected to see her mother waving to her from a window. The Virgin motif was on the back of her T-shirt too.

I dragged her away. 'Let's go and have breakfast.'

'No ... no, I couldn't eat.'

'Try, at least,' I said, doing my guardian stuff. 'Then there are some things I must do.'

The Consul had offered a baby-sitter facility, 'in case of emergency'. An acknowledgement that I might wish to go into round holes where a fifteen/sixteen-year old girl would be the squarest of pegs. Was he thinking of a brothel?

Whether or not, in making the offer, he had brothels in mind, he reacted with mild surprise when I took him up on it.

'So soon, Mr Melville?'

'Only for a few hours. An urgent business meeting.'

Lizzy, being Lizzy and clinging to me like grapes to the vine, was even unhappier about the separation.

'It's very important, honey,' I soothed. 'There's an outside chance I'll dig up a lead on your mother.'

It wasn't smart of me to raise her hopes, but this was one jaunt I had to do all on my own.

Next, I organized transport, renting a newish Renault Megane from the same company as before (they were most understanding about the incineration of the Fiat, maybe because it had been clapped out). A spate of form-filling later I was heading east out of town at somewhat more than the speed limit.

De Bruin was staying in a rented villa, coincidentally not so far from that of the reprieved Abdul Al'hauri. No secrecy need shroud this visit to the Petit Europa. Up the private road and round the first bend in a squeal of rubber. The road forked. The left fork bore the name Rue du Bord de la Mer. A couple of hundred meters on I came to a street with no exit: Impasse de Florentin. This was the address given to me by Lizzy from the card de Bruin had given Clair in the hope that she would accept his invitation to a cosy evening in front of the telly. Number 5 was my destination. I drove into the street and up to the last house. It bore a discreet 5 beside a bell-push on the right pillar of a massive timber gate that would not have disgraced a mediaeval castle.

The gates were not guarded, nor were they locked. I walked right in, making no attempt at stealth. Weaponless; the thread of my credibility with Commissaire Ramouz was too slender to bear the strain of another gunfight. In putting my own safety at risk I was gambling that de Bruin would flinch from a second assault. I hoped that one literal bloody nose was enough for him.

The grounds of the villa were not quite up to the opulence

of Al'hauri's pad but your average multi-millionaire would find little to carp about. The lawns were watered to an emerald green, their borders crammed with flora from everyday marigold to exotic bougainvillea. Trees had been planted so as to provide large tracts of shade, mostly palms, pine, and oak, their foliage browned by ozone, while in a corner, where two walls met, was a great rampart of bamboo. Water dribbled from a waterfall of rocks into a crescent-shaped pond crossed by an ornamental bridge. Some landscape architect someplace had been given a spade and a blank cheque, and told to get on with it.

My appraisal of all things horticultural was ended when a young blond-haired man in baggy swimming trunks stepped out from behind a fat palm, barring my path. I recognized him as de Bruin's watchdog, the beefcake boy. From the trapezium-shaped foresight I also recognized the stubby revolver in his fist as a Ruger GP-100 Magnum. Nice gun. If nothing else it showed I had been upgraded from the status of harmless sucker to dangerous sucker.

'You are trespassing,' he said in English with Germanic undertones.

'So I am. Where's de Bruin?'

'Mynheer de Bruin is not here.'

I weighed the prospects of taking the gun away from him without getting holed. And then of matching his two-hundred-plus pounds of lightly-oiled muscle and sinew against mine. Not to mention a probable fifteen year age discrepancy in his favour.

'When will he be back?' I asked reasonably.

'Next year.'

I didn't take this seriously. 'I'll wait.'

Beefcake waggled the gun. 'He is not coming back, I tell you. He has returned to home.'

'To Holland.'

'Sure.' A sneer. 'If you want to see him, you got a long walk, mister.'

From an unseen part of the lot a girl's voice called, 'Christiaan!' and then what sounded like 'Flook!'

Beefcake alias Christiaan cocked his handsome head sideways to bellow '*Houd je mond*!' which, if I recalled my phrasebook Dutch correctly, was an impolite way of saying 'be quiet'.

I took advantage of this distraction to push past him, reckless in my resolve. Ignoring his shout, I broke into a trot and rounded the corner of the building a couple of lengths ahead of him. And went no further.

Two girls adorned the poolside: Bea and Margot, de Bruin's little pieces of fluff from the Chico Bar. Both were naked but for a sheen of sun oil and a red choker around Margot's throat. If that were all, I might have taken it in my stride. What pulled me up was not their nudity but the naughty things they were doing to each other. Right under the drooling lens of a movie camera, complete with crew: cameraman, boom operator, clapper girl, and the rest. I was still held in thrall of this epic-in-the-making when Christiaan came up behind me, announcing his presence with a gun barrel in my kidneys. I let out a grunt of pain. A battery of eyes swung towards me. A tall, skeletal man with an upsweep of grey hair as high again as his forehead stepped clear of the group, yelled 'Cut' to the cameraman, and fired off a terse challenge at Christiaan.

Christiaan's answer was lengthy and complicated, only the words *Engelsman* and *Engelse,* Dutch for Englishman and Englishwoman, conveying anything at all to me.

The skeletal one contemplated me warily, as if I were a chained beast and the length of my chain indeterminable.

'I am called Martens,' he said, switching to fluent English.

'Mr de Bruin has gone away. Now will you please do the same.'

'Not until I find out what he's done with Clair Power.'

'We know nothing of this lady. Can't you see we are making here a movie?'

I could see. I could also see what kind of movie they were making.

'Now please go,' Martens insisted, his voice petulant.

While this conference was going on, the girls had come out of their clinch. Bea, the younger one, was now flat on her back, dragging her hand in the water, remote from the controversy around her. Margot had assumed a crouch, legs spread unnecessarily wide, mine to drool over. Out-and-out exhibitionism.

Christiaan made a grab for me, but I elbowed him away. I was too committed now to back off meekly, confident anyway that nobody was going to put a bullet in me just for gatecrashing.

'Wait!' Martens moved forward, raising a mediatory hand. 'No violence, please.' He said unintelligible things to Christiaan, who promptly lowered the gun and looked sulky.

'You,' Martens then said to me, coming within throat-grabbing distance, which was brave of him considering my present mood. 'Explain, please, what you want, and I will try to help. We want no troubles here.'

I bet they didn't. Ramouz would have loved to bust up this party.

It was just conceivable this Martens had no knowledge of de Bruin's interest in Clair, so I damped down my aggression for his benefit.

'To speak to Rik de Bruin is what I want. Has he really gone back to Holland?'

'Last week. Do you want to search the house?'

Christiaan growled an objection. If Martens heard, it didn't faze him.

'If you like, you can look.'

The camera crew, all Europeans as far as I could see, were hanging onto our exchange, as hushed as mourners at a burial.

I decided I had nothing to lose by taking Martens up on his offer. 'Okay, I'll look.'

This didn't go down well with Christiaan. He covered me with the Ruger and rumbled menacingly in Dutch.

Martens shrugged. 'He says he must go with you. It is because he is the *bewaker*, the keeper of the house. It is his responsibility.'

'Fair enough.' Then to Christiaan, 'Come on, body beautiful. You can be guide.'

By giving me the run of the house Martens was as good as proving neither de Bruin nor Clair were there, though that didn't mean to say they were in Holland. I went through the motions anyway, checking the place out from basement to loft. Having kicked up a big stink, I could hardly do less.

Twenty minutes or so later, my mind's eye still reeling from visions of the master bedroom with its vast four-poster, gold lamé drapes, and yellow tinted mirrors covering every flat surface including the floor, I re-emerged onto the terrace, Christiaan dogging me closer than my shadow.

'You are satisfied now?' Martens shouted across; he was arranging the girls' extremities, presumably for optimum artistic effect.

I signalled an affirmative and let Christiaan escort me to the gate. After a period of repose the gun was again muzzle foremost.

'Do not come back,' he said as he slammed the gate shut.

'Don't count on it, gorgeous,' I returned, and left him scowling through the bars.

Thirteen

From de Bruin's house I drove to Ibn Battouta airport, on the opposite side of the city. A polite enquiry about 'my associate, Mr Rik de Bruin', at the Royal Air Maroc desk, accompanied by a high denomination euro note, was met by frenzied checking of passenger lists but an ultimate blank. I fared better at KLM, the next obvious choice. More currency passed across the counter. Mynheer de Bruin had taken the Saturday flight to Amsterdam. Alone? A dusky finger punched more computer keys and there on the screen flashed a Mynheer Hock, de Bruin's travelling companion. Whoever he might be.

No way could Clair be passed off as Mynheer Anybody, with or without her co-operation. Ergo, she hadn't accompanied him. The next obvious step was to check all female passengers, though she would hardly be booked under her real name. The contents of my wallet were further depleted and the good-natured KLM clerk did a second scan of the passenger list for me. It proved nothing, as several lone women had travelled that day. Somehow, I couldn't see him taking the risk of letting her travel with him openly.

This left just a single line of enquiry and the lengthiest of long shots. Ahmad and Yacoub, gun merchants, from the Tangier suburb of Charf. No obvious connection between them and de Bruin existed. We had done our business before I even met Clair, before the confrontation at the Chico Bar. But people who move in the criminal domain have their ears and noses to the ground. When rumours circulate, they are usually part of the circuit. Snippets are harvested, and retained as possible future bargaining tools.

With this in mind, I rolled up at the seedy little villa with its down-at-heel date palm and scraps of wiry grass trying to eke subsistence from a patch of land that was mostly sand. The front door was open, behind an insect screen.

'Anybody home?' I called through the screen. A cat mewed from within. '*Il y a quelqu'un?*'

My summons was answered by younger brother Yacoub. He was wearing the same outfit as on my previous visit, only grubbier and wrinklier. It looked like a nightgown, so maybe he slept in it too.

'Ah, Mr Englissman,' he said. His greeting was natural enough. If he had anything to hide it wasn't apparent in his demeanour.

He invited me in, a further indicator of innocence.

Is Ahmad around?' I said, as I trailed after him, into the living room. Standing by a stove in the kitchen nook was Yacoub's wife. She was preparing a concoction of food. The burnt sienna eyes swept over me, disconcertingly hostile.

Nawal, you remember Mr Warner,' Yacoub said to her in French.

Oui.' This was her first ever utterance in my presence. She continued to stare at me as I accepted Yacoub's invitation to sit.

Ahmad not home,' he said. 'He no live here.'

No matter,' I said in French, which would be his second language after Moroccan Arabic. 'You can probably help me.'

'*Bien. Voulez-vous encore une arme? Je suis à votre disposition.*'

In other words, if I was in the market for another gun, he was my man.

'It's not about guns, Yacoub.' Puzzlement wrinkled his smooth brown forehead. 'It's about information concerning the kidnapping of a friend of mine.'

His quick glance at Nawal could have been guilt, incomprehension, or just a loving look. If he was ignorant of the incident, this would be a wasted visit. If he was privy to it, I needed a sign. Then I could go to work. Until that point, I was still his friend and client.

'I do not know this woman,' he said, under a barrage of silent signals from his wife.

'Kidnapping is not my business.'

The giveaway had come easier and faster than I expected.

'What woman?'

'The woman who was ...' Yacoub broke off, blinking like a semaphore lamp.

In Arabic, Nawal fired off a string of vituperation at him. He was in trouble. I almost felt sorry for him. He would be sleeping in the spare room tonight.

'*Allez-vous en!*' she snarled at me. A not-exactly polite request to leave.

'Not just yet, sweetheart. First, tell me what you know about the woman who was kidnapped? If you like, you can begin by explaining *how* you knew my friend was a woman.'

Yacoub's lips trembled. 'I didn't know, *monsieur*. I ... I was guessing ...'

'So you're a good guesser. That's very helpful. Now you can guess where they took her, okay?'

His frightened glance at Nawal told me he was at least as terrified of her as of me. Suddenly he bolted towards the door to the room where the guns had been stored. I was off my chair and smashed into him as he pulled the handle. We went down in a bundle. He didn't fight me but he worked bloody hard to get free. As he eventually subsided in defeat and I got up on my knees, a hard object slammed into the back of my head. It was badly aimed, more of a glancing blow, but it was enough to disorientate me. I subsided on Yacoub, who was not enthralled at taking my weight. A second blow, square on my back, hurt without incapacitating. It also made me mad.

With Yacoub serving as a rug, I got to my feet, deflecting Nawal's third strike with her iron *cous-cous* pan. It connected with her husband's shin instead of my skull. He howled. I yanked the pan from her fist and flung it across the room. Shattering noises ensued.

Disarmed, Nawal switched to her inbuilt weapons, notably claws as long as a leopard's. After suffering a scratch across the jaw and narrowly avoiding a poke in the eye, I discarded the rules of gentlemanly conduct. A punch in her niqab-ed mouth with all my weight behind it was enough to subdue her. Her eyes slid under her eyelids and she crumbled without a murmur. Instead of rushing to her side, Yacoub headed for the entrance door on all fours. He didn't quite make it before I caught up with him.

'*Sois sage*,' I advised him. Be good.

'Leave me alone!' he squeaked, rolling onto his back and kicking at me.

I slapped his cheeks, one after the other. Not too hard, just enough to calm him. He curled up like a hedgehog in protective mode, his head tucked in his arms.

'Listen to me, Yacoub,' I said, keeping my voice low and level. 'All I want to know is who kidnapped the woman and where they took her.'

'Why are you asking me?' he gibbered. 'It was a gang from Casablanca, not Tangier men.'

I sighed. Whether he was lying or truthing, I couldn't tell. That's the trouble with duress. Victims will lie either to save themselves from punishment or to buy time. Ordinarily, I would have been inclined to beat it out of him and risk its veracity. But I didn't dare jump off the precarious fence of legality I was now straddling here in Morocco. If word reached Ramouz, I would be back as his guest, minus the pastries.

'Don't give me that,' I snarled at him and bunched my fist for launching. 'I want names and locations quick, or you're going to need plastic surgery.' I may have gotten the French for "plastic surgery" wrong, but he reacted by moaning and shielding his face, so I reckoned the gist of it got through.

'I only know what I heard in the Medina,' he blubbered behind his hands. 'It was only gossip, *monsieur*, I swear.'

'So where do I find the Dutch guy, Rik de Bruin?'

'Who?'

'*L'hollandais.*' I grabbed the front of his *burnous* and shook him. His head thudded on the tiled floor. 'Rik de Bruin. Don't pretend you don't know him, you little shit.'

'No, it is not *un hollandais,* I tell you, it is some men from Casablanca.'

Behind me I heard movement, accompanied by a feminine groaning. Yacoub's wife was returning to the land of the conscious. In truth I was more worried about her than him. The so-called weaker sex fight dirty. That aside, mixing it with women wasn't really my style.

Time to move on. I salvaged my pride by leaving a threat hanging in the air.

'Okay, slimeball, I'm going to check it out with my contacts in town. If I find out you've been lying, I'll be back and you and your brother will be two sorry assholes.'

It might have carried more weight if I had some "contacts in town" to check it out with.

Back in my room at the hotel, with Lizzy still out of my

hair, I treated the scratch on my jaw with antiseptic cream, and sat down in front of the phone. In the whole world I could call to mind only five people who might – and it was a huge might in every case – be able to shed light on de Bruin. Giorgy was one; my old friend and former SIS compatriot Tony Dimeloe was another. Longer shots were Freddie, my Dublin-based passport maker; Tagd Corry, my armourer in the UK, and Paul Masson, a Marseilles-resident rackets boss who owed me a favour.

Giorgy first. My call to his business line was answered by a woman, who spoke only Italian, but managed to convey to me that he was out of the country. I tried his cell phone, but it was switched off. With Tony I had better luck. Unusually for a Saturday he was at his desk.

'Well, hel-*lo*!' He sounded sincerely pleased to hear from me. 'Where've you been hiding?'

'Where people like me usually hide,' I quipped non-committally.

'It must be ... what? Six months at least. I got married last week, by the way.'

'Really? Congratulations, old son.' He was the wrong side of forty, so it wasn't too soon. 'Tell me more.'

'No, let's save the catch-up for our next meeting. Are you over here?'

'No, I'm in Tangier. And I've gotten a problem.'

He chuckled. 'So long as you don't need money. What's up?'

I gave him an abbreviated version of events to date, skipping my involvement with the police. As a British government employee Tony would instinctively shy away from anything that might cause friction with foreign powers, especially Arab ones. I also omitted to mention Lizzy.

When I finished, he made sympathetic murmurings and

said, 'So how can I help? You're not expecting me to send a gunboat, are you? I doubt the navy has any left.'

'Thanks for the offer. But joking apart, Tony, I just want anything on file about a guy called Henrik de Bruin, Dutch, about thirty-five, may or may not have a company called DeB -' I spelled it out, '- Publications, which may or may not be located in a town called Egmond aan Zee, in the Netherlands.'

De Bruin's name meant nothing to Tony. I hadn't expected it to. What he did have to offer was access to computer files on every known and suspected criminal world-wide, so if de Bruin had any sort of record it would soon surface. Whether the databank would lead me to Clair was questionable. It was better than nibbling my nails.

'This woman's important to you, eh?' he said sympathetically.

'It's even more complicated than that,' I said, thinking of Lizzy.

'It would be, knowing you.' I heard the opening chime of his desktop coming alive. 'Give me forty-eight hours.'

'Could you make it twenty-four?'

A grunt. 'Oh, hell, why not? What else have I got to do but run errands for you and give up my days off? Give me your cell phone number and I'll text you.'

Text me. Security always to the fore with Tony.

'Thanks, chum. I owe you one.'

'More than one, boyo.'

'Yeah. Say hello to the wife. I look forward to meeting her.'

'Fuck off. I wouldn't let her within a mile of you, you bloody Casanova.'

On that bantering note I hung up and moved to the next on my list.

For security reasons Freddie was loath to pass on any client details, even for payment. I didn't blame him. The forged passport business relies on client discretion. In the end, after much hand-wringing, he checked his files and confirmed that he had never supplied a Henrik de Bruin. It was probably true. And it didn't help.

Tagd Corry, another Irishmen, kept me in firearms. De Bruin, being on the white collar side of crime, was unlikely to have much call for guns on a regular basis. Still, I was leaving no trails unsniffed.

'Ah, to be sure I've never heard of him,' he piped in his Ulster brogue. 'But you know, Mr A, if he's the top man, it's not likely he'd come a-buyin' in person. Most likely he'd be sendin' one of his lads.'

Most likely he was right. We chatted for a minute or so longer, and I left him to his lethal trade.

Finally, I called Paul Masson. He was out. I left a message with his answering service. To minimize the inconvenience to him (he was a man easily pissed off), I asked him only to call if he knew of de Bruin.

End of enquiry leads for now. I hadn't expected much, and so far I hadn't gotten much.

The shadows were lengthening. If I knew Lizzy – and I thought I did by now – she would be fretting to be rescued from the clutches of a certain Mrs Haslam, a secretary to the Consulate. My private agenda listed a final source of information: electronic, not human. In the hotel lobby was a Wi-Fi Internet facility. It was here, with a glass of vodka within reach, where I set out to trace de Bruin with the help of Google.

The name de Bruin threw up de Bruin Aeromaintenance, de Bruin Group, de Bruin's Greenhouses, and a whole host of individuals who might or might not have been related to friend Rik. Too many to pursue. DeB Publications gave me the Department of Environmental Biology (DEB), which published material on Integrative Organismal Systems, whatever they might be. Still, under the DeB search engine I did make a modest find: DeB Publications of Amsterdam had a website 'under construction'. It featured a stylized naked woman with a bullwhip looped around her body, suggesting I was on the right track. The site was due to be up and running by October 1st. Not a lot of use to me in July.

Depressed and suffering from a rising sense of impotence, I gave up the hunt for now. A couple of vodkas numbed the dolour. Afterwards I drove to collect Lizzy from the home of Mrs Haslam. The Haslams, who had a sixteen-year-old daughter, occupied a first floor apartment just off the Place du Maroc, on the southern edge of town. I parked in a residents-only bay, and was barely out of the car when Lizzy exploded from the building and came at me across a wizened lawn, amid incoherent cries of relief.

'You've been so long,' she whimpered, her arms like a steel band around my waist. 'I thought you weren't coming back.'

Over her shoulder I nodded meaninglessly at Mrs Haslam, who had followed Lizzy out and was watching worriedly from her porch. A Diplomatic Service wife who might have been fifty, such demonstrative behaviour was not for her. Upper lips should always be kept stiff.

'Did you find out anything?' Lizzy demanded, clutching at me.

'Not much, I'm afraid. It was a dead end.'

Mrs Haslam came up and made as if to comfort Lizzy. 'You can stay here tonight if you wish, my dear.'

'No thanks,' Lizzy said ungraciously, not looking at her.

Half of me was tempted to overrule her. The other half suffered twinges of guilt at my eagerness to unload her on someone else.

'Kind of you to offer,' I said in an effort to make up for Lizzy's lack of courtesy. Motoring back into town, I gave her a mild ticking off. 'You've blown it there, Freckles. Mrs Haslam won't want you again.'

She snorted. 'Who cares? She's a vulture. If you put anything down, she swoops on it and whisks it away. "Tidiness is next to Godliness",' she mimicked.

'I thought it was cleanliness.'

'Oh, she said that too, don't worry.'

'But what about her daughter? Didn't you have much in common?'

'Apart from both being girls – no!'

I grinned, accelerated past a dithering motor-scooter, and turned into the Rif parking lot.

No messages for us at the desk. Lizzy rode the disappointment well, better perhaps than me. She was learning to overcome the fear and the uncertainty, if not yet facing up to the probable outcome.

Fourteen

By Monday morning, the fourth day since Clair's abduction and still no news from Ramouz, I was ready to savage the carpet. To keep me sane and Lizzy from brooding I took us windsurfing. It proved to be good therapy. Like many young Australians Lizzy was no stranger to the sport and though my technique was on the rusty side we were evenly matched. Helped by a light west wind and temperate seas we finished the session with honours even at four wipe-outs apiece.

Afterwards we sat on the screened terrace at La Pergola Bar, which abuts onto the beach, chuckling now and again at the mishaps of other windsurfers, especially the obvious novices. Until today Lizzy hadn't laughed since Clair went missing. It was too much to expect that she was turning some kind of corner; to raise her spirits at all was a breakthrough.

Lounging here in the heat, adding an extra dimension to my tan and slurping iced vodka, I felt not a little ashamed at my uselessness, at my inactivity. By all that was logical I had no reason for self-rebuke. The police were far better equipped than I to trace Clair, and unless Tony came up with something I was bankrupt of leads anyway. Plus, I had Lizzy to mother. All that said, I still reckoned I ought to be doing more than warming a chair with my backside and rotting my gut with booze.

Then Paul Masson called back on my cell phone. He was not forthcoming. His background was gambling and protection, he reminded me. The porn business was alien territory, and white slaving too repugnant even for his taste.

'My second wife used to complain that I treated her like a slave,' he joked. 'But that's as close as I ever got to owning one, let alone trading in them.'

'Stay tuned, will you, Paul?' I asked him. 'If you hear anything at all, bell me.'

He promised to do just that. In truth, it was another dead end.

'If only we knew she was all right.' Lizzy said, her voice wistful, as I tapped the cell phone disconnect bar. 'I could bear the rest.'

My sentiments to a T.

'The police will be doing all they can,' I muttered, hoping the words carried conviction. 'They'll find your mother. It's only a matter of time.'

I sounded like a parrot.

The bouts of weeping were now behind her, and she was as pretty as ever in her white bikini, if somewhat finely drawn. A month from now, she had informed me, she would be sixteen. At what age did a girl metamorphose into a woman? Through my sunglasses I studied her surreptitiously, again considering her as a woman. Better placed than most to reap the ripest fruits of life, with her bright personality, her intelligence, her high spirits, and the external packaging of those perfect features. Especially the sleepy smoky eyes and the mouth that was made for ...

Christ, what was I thinking of? Clair was prisoner of a gang of Arab thugs and here was I fantasizing over her teenage daughter. I felt a deep sense of shame.

'Couldn't we hire a private detective?' Lizzy suggested, tugging a comb through a refractory pony tail. 'People do, don't they?'

It was an idea. I didn't immediately discount it.

'Well?' she said when, after a few seconds, I hadn't responded.

'Sorry, honey.' I patted her hand. 'I was weighing the pros and cons. Let's give the police a bit longer. They don't take kindly to private enterprisers getting under their feet.'

She sighed. 'If you say so.'

Next to report in was Tony Dimeloe. The text message announced its arrival a few minutes after the twenty-four hour timescale. I was just about to go under the shower; I stood there and read it bare-assed naked.

> hi Alan
> you may be onto something with yr mr de b.
> he is known to Interpol. seems he was arrested
> in bratislava slovakia 8 yrs ago in connection
> with a snuff film. You are familiar with snuff films
> arent you? your man held for several weeks
> while police investigated alleged death of young
> girl supposedly in making of film. body never
> washed up & de b was released eventually
> without charges. the report mentions local
> speculation that he bribed police chief. since
> then neither sight nor sound of him at any rate
> not in Interpol records. film never surfaced far
> as we can tell. sounds like a nice chap. sorry
> not to be more help. if I can do anything else
> just yell.
> samantha (new mrs dimeloe) says hello.
> up yours. Tony.

Informative but not helpful. De Bruin might even have been innocent of the charge. The snuff movie and the missing girl might never have existed. Officially, de Bruin was clean so far as the world at large was concerned. What with

Ramouz's lack of progress, it was beginning to look as if I was Clair's only hope of salvation. Bereft of leads as I was, it was a pretty forlorn hope.

No contact at all from Giorgy, my "only true friend".

That evening we dined at Le Detroit where, a million evenings gone by, I had also dined with Clair. Though the food was assuredly exquisite, it might as well have been sweepings from the gutter for all the impression it made on my palate. Lizzy only played with hers, shoving kebabs around her plate, prodding moodily at her eggplants. Talk was desultory and trite.

Earlier, Ramouz had contacted me, forestalling my call to him. Delivering his no-progress report, he had sounded weary, defeated even, as if he had lost faith in achieving a result.

'Call yourself a bloody policeman,' I seethed, when he had finished.

'Careful, Mr Melville.' Some of the familiar bite returned. 'I'm still not entirely satisfied about *you*.'

Touché. I glared at the receiver, caution dulling my rage.

'Have you considered,' I went on, in more respectful tones, 'that she might have been taken out of the country?'

Sigh. 'Naturally. And naturally we cannot be sure.'

When I had relayed the gist of this conversation to Lizzy, she became withdrawn and taciturn, and stayed that way throughout the evening. The restaurant staff did their best to inspire her. Flapping and fussing over her as if she were royalty, tempting her with this and that succulent dish – baby squid, lobster, snails, and later strawberries and figs. Their efforts were not well-rewarded. She was beyond consolation.

A little after ten we left, to walk the kilometre or so back to the Rif. The breeze had died away as it often did at dusk, and the moon was up in a clear, star-crowded sky. It was a night for lovers and loving. If Clair had been here we might by now have attained that status. As we came to the concourse of the Avenue d'Espagne, that hang-out of junkies and ne'er-do-wells, Lizzy noticed my abstraction and gave my sleeve a tug.

'Want to see something really hilarious?'

I grunted. 'Sure.'

'Take a look at this then.' She plucked a compact from her shoulder bag, opened it and thrust it under my nose.

I stared at my own lugubrious reflection in the little round mirror. 'Well, what?'

'The ugly mug, of course. Don't you think it's a scream?'

In spite of my gloom, I couldn't help grinning.

'Oh-oh,' she said, in mock reproof. 'You shouldn't have done that. You've gone and cracked your make-up, I can see all the wrinkles underneath.'

'That's what comes of having plastic surgery on the cheap,' I sighed, and we chuckled together convivially. I was still chuckling when a solid object slammed into the side of my skull and spread me all over the sidewalk.

I was hurt. Badly enough to be content to lie there and want to be left in peace and get well soon. Except that all around was yelling and cursing and no consideration at all for the afflicted. So I rolled over onto my back, the better to see what the fuss was about, and in so doing felt the wind of a descending iron bar, double-handedly wielded by a large, hooded Arab. The bar struck the sidewalk with a clang, a near enough miss to sting my cheek with sparks and chips of stone. The closeness of my escape wiped away the wooziness like mist before a hurricane. I grabbed the business end of the bar as it left the ground for a second go at my head and gave it a vicious twist, ripping it from the hands of my attacker.

Back on my feet, still as wobbly as a sailor after a month at sea, I kicked the hooded one in some hopefully vulnerable spot. He hit the sidewalk, making a lot of noise. This left me free now to tackle two other Arabs, similarly hooded, who were getting the worst of an encounter with the clawing, spitting wildcat that was Lizzy. I wasn't even sure she needed my help. One of the Arabs was hopping around, clutching his privates, the other was doing no more than hold her off. I ignored the hopping Arab and whacked the other across the shoulder blades with my new toy. Bones snapped audibly, and the accompanying screech must have carried across the Strait. Hey, this was *fun*!

The late owner of the iron bar now rejoined the fray, plucking a long tourist-bazaar knife from the folds of his *burnous*. I twirled the bar at him like a medieval knight with a broadsword and he gave ground, stumbling, his features in shadow within the hood.

'You all right?' I shot at Lizzy, who was standing apart in a defiant Karate-style pose.

'Yes, yes, don't worry about me. I'm a tae-kwon-do green belt.'

Just another of her multiple talents.

My next vicious swipe with the bar would have ripped the big Arab's nose off had my reach been just a wee bit longer. It convinced him he was on the losing side. From the depths of the hood issued a rasping command. As abruptly as they had pounced our attackers were gone, the injured pair hobbling off in mutual support down an unlit side street, the Arab with the knife forming a rearguard.

The pedestrian traffic, which had inexplicably melted away during the fracas, came back to life. A fat guy walking his dog rushed up to enquire in breathless French, were we hurt, and weren't these muggers *tout à fait affreux* and should he call the police.

I answered no, yes, and no especially to calling the police. Even as a victim of an assault I wanted no more of Ramouz's hospitality.

'No harm done,' I assured the fat man. Except to the side of the Warner cranium, which, on examination, was found to be leaking red stuff. At the sight of my stained fingers Lizzy gave a cry of distress.

'You're bleeding, Alan!'

'M'sieu!' Fatso squeaked in alarm. 'Vous devriez voir un médecin.'

Reluctantly, I was inclined to agree that I should seek medical help. 'We'll get the hotel to send for a doctor.' More belated Samaritans were approaching, so I said hurriedly to Fatso, 'Thanks for your concern,' and hauled Lizzy off across the street.

'Are you really good?' she asked worriedly.

'Yeah, I'm good,' I said, making light of it. 'How about you?'

She rummaged in her bag. 'Here, let me try and stop it bleeding. It's running down your neck.'

We stopped. She produced a ridiculous tiny handkerchief with embroidered edges. While I stood and chafed under a street lamp, she dabbed uncertainly at the wound.

'Sorry,' she said whenever I flinched.

At the time I had been too dazed to notice the pain; now it was throbbing, a rising tempo of hammer blows between brain and bone. Which reminded me I was still in possession of the iron bar. I wasn't inclined to ditch it just yet.

With the completion of Lizzy's repair work we moved on. The bar came in handy as a walking stick, though a Zimmer frame would have served better, I was that shaky.

'Were they really muggers?' Lizzy asked. 'I've never been mugged before.'

Nor had I.

'Muggers? Probably.'

No, not probably; not even possibly. It was an amateurish, ham-fisted attempt at removing me from the scene, to leave the field clear for Lizzy to join her mother.

'Which little bird told you we'd been mugged?' I asked Ramouz as I settled in the interviewee's chair before his desk.

He seemed surprised by my ignorance.

'The doctor, of course. In Morocco all injuries caused by a third party must be reported to the authorities.'

I fingered the dressing above my left ear. Seven stitches had been inserted in the wound and the ensemble was smarting furiously, unresponsive to a heavy dose of painkillers.

'So all right, we were mugged. It's not unknown here in paradise, is it?'

Ramouz was impervious to irony this morning.

'Not at all unknown, to my regret,' He fashioned one of his famous smoke rings and studied the tip of his cigarette with an obviously affected negligence.

'We sent your fingerprints to Scotland Yard,' he said conversationally.

Oh-oh. My prints were definitely on record in the UK. Not as a criminal, and not at the Yard, but as an SIS operative, under my real name, of course. If Ramouz discovered I was in his country with a false passport he was sure to make me suffer. Fortunately, I was confident that MI6 wouldn't have released my real name.

'Since I'm clean, they presumably had nothing to offer.'

'Precisely,' he said, still absorbed in his cigarette. 'They had nothing to offer.'

His voice carried a trace of resentment, suggesting that the response from MI6 had not been a straightforward "Not known to us". The reaction to Ramouz's enquiry over there would have been a closing of ranks. Spies, even when retired, enjoy the protection of their former employers.

'I want you and the young lady to leave Morocco at once.' Ramouz's attention finally transferred from the cigarette to me. 'And that is not a request.'

I didn't try to hide my bewilderment.

'For your own safety,' Ramouz added, and so matter-of-factly that I had to take him seriously.

We matched stares. His had the force of law and order behind it.

'It wasn't a straightforward mugging, is that what you're telling me?' Although I knew as much already, that knowledge was meant for my brain only.

A series of slow nods. Through the spiralling smoke his gaze was unwinking.

'The same gang as kidnapped Mrs Power?'

More slow nodding.

'That,' he said, 'is what our sources tell us.'

'Fair enough.' No reason now to continue the facade of ignorance. 'Let's say I agree there's a link between the kidnapping and the mugging ... the attack. I'm still not running away. I can't leave without Clair, or at least without knowing what's happened to her.'

Ramouz was hesitant. 'You must accept the probability that she is ... no longer alive. Five days have passed. We have received no demand for money from the kidnappers, no messages of any description. Whatever the motive, it cannot have been financial.'

'There's still time.' My voice was uneven.

'You think so?' The uplifted eyebrows said it all. 'If money was the motive, how do you explain last night's attack on you and the girl?'

In the street a bicycle bell tinkled. More distantly the

rumble of a bulldozer from some building site. Out there were people who wanted me dead and Lizzy in bondage with her mother. It didn't scare me for my sake, only for hers.

'So you don't think their objective was to put me out of action temporarily, you think they're out to waste me ... to kill me.' It sounded like an accusation, and I suppose it was: I was accusing him of keeping it from me.

He hooded his eyes and said, 'I can only speculate. However ...' He ground his cigarette into the brimming ashtray, 'they know you are a threat. If they can remove you for good, cheaply, why let you live? A hundred dollars would do it.'

I considered last night's attack afresh, as an attempt at murder rather than disablement. It was the method employed that made me dubious – an iron bar? Killing tools don't come any cruder than that. Yet had that second blow connected with me instead of the sidewalk, it would have done the job efficiently, if messily, enough. The knife too. Tourist junk, sure, but lethal tourist junk. On reflection, Ramouz's hypothesis was credible.

I wrestled with my thoughts, trying to put them in order.

'Commissaire... about Lizzy ... Mrs Power's daughter...'

'Yes?' Ramouz, grinding his cigarette into the brimming ashtray, had assumed a politely enquiring look.

'I can't just take her away. What I mean is, I'm not her legal guardian. Where am I supposed to take her?'

'There is an uncle, is there not?' He stirred his papers until he found what he wanted. 'In Spain?' Reading from a typescript, 'Alistair Power. Last known address: Baya el Figuera no. 221A, Barcelona. He would appear to be – how is it in English?– next-of-kin?'

It was true that I could deliver Lizzy to Uncle Alistair in transit to Andorra, and that the inconvenience would therefore be minimal. But it wasn't the mechanics of that operation that troubled me. It was the tacit desertion of Clair, the scuttling off home. The foisting of Lizzy on some unsuspecting relative, who might or might not be prepared to honour his obligations.

And where did it leave Lizzy (and me) if he wasn't?

'It can't be done, *Commissaire*. Whatever the risks in staying here, I can't leave yet.'

Ramouz bared teeth that were stained yellow with tobacco. 'I understand, my friend . .' (we were *friends*?) '. . and I respect your reasons. Yet you can and must leave. If you force me, I will have you physically expelled. You must understand it is the safety of Miss Power that concerns me, more than your own.' His raised hand forestalled my question. 'She is at risk through her association with you. The men who abducted Mrs Power and who attacked you are being orchestrated by a single agency, that is clear. These gangs have little compunction about meting out injury and death to whoever stands in their way. And a girl as pretty as Miss Power may have worse to fear than death alone.'

Coming from a policeman for whom I was developing a lukewarm respect, I had to take this caveat at face value.

I got up. 'If I'm to leave the country, I'll need my passport.'

Giving me a long look he opened a drawer in his desk and restored to me that intrinsically worthless yet indispensable document.

'The dossier on you remains open. It may never be closed. Am I speaking clearly enough for you?'

His features were so composed, so bland, it was impossible to tell whether I had just received a serious warning-off or no more than an exhortation to "watch my step".

He rose slowly and with a kind of majesty, like a modern-day Nero. 'You and Miss Power are booked to fly out by Air Maroc tomorrow morning. To Barcelona via Madrid. This gives you the rest of today to see the Consul about the arrangements regarding Miss Power's uncle.'

'Nice of you to organize everything,' I said, with a cynical smile.

His face altered in some subtle way, became as bleak as a Siberian landscape.

'Just don't come back, Mr Whoever-you-are,' he said. 'Ever.'

Fifteen

From Police Headquarters I drove directly to the Consul's private residence in the sleepy suburb of Boubana where, it being Saturday and the Consulate closed, I had deposited Lizzy.

The Consul's wife, a homely woman with the abstracted air of someone whose physical person and spirit were in two different places, conducted me through the surprisingly modest bungalow to a yard at the rear, abutting onto the Christian cemetery. The Consul was there, in a faded deck-chair encircled by paperwork. There too was Lizzy, in skinny jeans and a crop top, horizontal in a swing seat. A tablet was propped on a cushion inches from her face, her iPod plugged into her ear. In passing by I pecked her cheek, was rewarded by a pale smile.

The Consul left off poring over diplomatic bumph, glad, I suspected, of the excuse.

'Can I offer you something, old chap? Orange juice, grape-fruit juice?' He indicated twin carafes on a rustic table under the dome of a cedar tree, the only mature timber the yard contained.

'Nothing stronger?' He didn't rise to the hint. 'Orange then, please.'

Tumblers in hand, ice cubes chinking, he and I strolled down the crazy-paved path that wound through a labyrinth of flowering shrubs.

The Consul opened by saying, 'We cabled Mrs Power's brother-in-law, Alistair, several days ago. We've also informed the Consulate in Barcelona. Mr Power has not, so far, replied.'

'And the Consulate?'

'They acknowledged. I telephoned them this morning, in the absence of a reply from Power, and asked them to verify the address.' He halted and sipped at his drink. 'I gather you have to leave tomorrow.'

'"Have to" is right. They're deporting me.'

'Yes.'

He spoke as if it were to be expected. I glanced sharply at him. 'Did you protest on my behalf?'

As we came to an area screened by shrubbery he halted again. 'Let's get this straight, Melville, I'm having no diplomatic incidents here. If Ramouz wants you out, you're out. Look at it from his perspective: since you came, he's had a kidnapping, a killing, and a serious assault. Tourists like you he can do without.' He consulted his orange juice as if it were his oracle. 'Don't make waves, there's a good fellow. You have to think of the girl's safety.'

'Yeah,' I said heavily. 'That's what he said too. But suppose I left without her, that would make her safe, wouldn't it?'

The Consul looked dubious. 'In that case, who would take care of her?'

'Take care of her? She'll be sixteen soon. She doesn't need a nanny.'

'Your compassion does you credit.'

'Fuck you,' I said under my breath. He was good at making me feel bad.

'Commissaire Ramouz feels you ought both to leave Tangier,' he went on, taking my protest as null and void. He made a clicking noise with his tongue against his teeth as he pondered. 'I imagine he believes Elizabeth is also in danger.'

'But only,' I persisted, 'because of her association with me.'

I took a swig at my orange juice while he worked out further objections. The yard was full of the scent of flowers, and bees were everywhere busily harvesting pollen, hopping from bloom to bloom. The Diplomatic Service, I noticed, was not short of funds for horticultural projects; the yard was not only exquisitely maintained but well-watered. And the price of Moroccan metered water is said to be on a par with the price of wine.

The late afternoon sun switched off abruptly as it sank behind an adjacent, two-storey house. The insect noise abated, as if the sun's decline were a signal to down tools and go home. We strolled on, the Consul massaging his dimpled chin.

'Let me put it another way ... Ramouz tells me the chances are almost nil of Mrs Power being found ... alive.' His voice fell to a whisper for, as we emerged from the shrubbery, we came in sight of Lizzy. She was watching us covertly, no doubt aware she was the topic under discussion. That her well-being was to some extent being picked over.

Poor kid. To have her fate batted back and forth between this affable but weak diplomat, governed above all by the soft option, and me, dealer in death, whose only loyalties were to the great gods Dollar and Bacchus, and who simply wanted out. I was again shamed by my readiness to abdicate responsibility. Yet even had I been willing to take Lizzy under my wing on a short-term basis, my qualifications for the post were meagre.

'Let me put a proposition to you.' The Consul steered me onto another path that looped away from the house, keeping us out of Lizzy's earshot. 'At some point, at the very least until she is eighteen, we will have to place Elizabeth in care. At the moment this uncle in Barcelona is our best bet. Indeed our only bet to date. If we pay your travel and accommodation expenses, will you ...' He became flustered, rolled the tumbler back and forth across his forehead to cool it. 'Will you take Elizabeth to Barcelona and deliver her to him?'

Deliver her. To the Consul, Lizzy was a package. True, the package was human, and therefore lip-service must be paid to its sensibilities. But, these formalities apart, the only criterion was safe conduct away from A (the Consul's domain) to B (Barcelona or anyplace else where a sanctuary of sorts might be found for it).

My liking for the man had turned to dross as he unveiled his buck-passing solution. No matter that I was neck and neck with him in the scramble for an easy exit.

'That's not a proposition,' I remarked, keeping my animus tightly screwed down. 'It's a bloody, king-size favour. But don't worry, Ramouz has already asked on your behalf.' I laughed without humour. 'Only *he* didn't ask.'

'Ah.' The Consul's gaze was set in a straight line ahead.

'Could it possibly be Ramouz was doing your bidding? Making it official, just in case I refused?'

Twinkle, twinkle went the little eyes.

'You'll do it then?' No denial, no attempt even to justify his subterfuge. 'Royal Air Maroc flight RM017, from Ibn Battouta Airport at 11.30 tomorrow morning. The tickets will be waiting for you at the hotel.' A smirk. 'First class, naturally.'

'Such generosity,' I sneered. 'When it comes to sidestepping its obligations, HM Government's purse strings are ever loose, eh?' He made no comment, a dumb admission of the truth of my slur. 'You say you haven't made contact with this Alistair guy. How do you know he's still there, or still in Spain, even?'

'We don't, not for certain. Elizabeth tells me he emailed her mother in April and he was still living in Barcelona then.

160

Elizabeth tried to email him this morning, but the message was rejected as undeliverable. He must have changed his email address, which doesn't necessarily mean he's changed his physical address. If it turns out that he's moved on, you'll have to contact the Consulate in Barcelona – a Mr Alan Rees, for preference. They'll organize accommodation while they decide how to play it. You may be required to stay on there until Power is traced.'

'Detained at Her Majesty's pleasure,' I murmured. 'Presumably Elizabeth has her passport. Her mother might have been carrying it when she was abducted.' A desperate, last-ditch tactic, bound to fail.

'No problem in that direction, old chap. I checked with her.'

As we sauntered on, I contemplated my sneaker-clad feet, comparing them with his, diminutive in supple white moccasins that shouted money. Like many senior diplomats abroad he most likely had private means and a generous expense account. The hardships, major and minor, that touch the lives of ordinary mortals, would not disturb his lot.

'Just supposing Lizzy's uncle isn't there,' I said, 'be his absence temporary or permanent, what's to stop me doing a runner and leaving your Barcelona crowd holding the baby?'

As we came around a curve in the path and in view of the terrace, Lizzy was coming to meet us with purpose in her stride. She was done with sitting passively on the sidelines.

'What's to stop you … er, doing a runner,' the Consul hedged, in the tone of a holy man confronted with blasphemy. 'Well, a couple of things, I would have thought. The police might yet trace Mrs Power. How would it look to her if you had ditched her daughter?'

The sneaky bastard had it all figured out.

'And the second thing?'

Now he smiled with real warmth, the cherub in him glowing through.

'Your conscience, old chap, your conscience.'

The airline tickets were indeed at the hotel front desk. I didn't even have to ask for them. In expediency the Diplomatic Service moves with the speed of an antelope.

Lizzy said curiously, 'Aren't those airline tickets?'

I nodded. 'Let's go where we can talk.' I took her elbow and propelled her upstairs to the bar, to a secluded corner table, where I ordered the usual poison for me and a beer for her.

No sooner had the waiter gone when she said, 'You're leaving me, aren't you?' Her eyes were big and round and dewed with unshed tears.

'No,' I said roughly. I threw the tickets on the table between us. 'Two tickets, please note. One for you and one for me.'

'Oh,' she said, blinking. 'I thought ...'

'Don't think,' I snapped, snatching the vodka from the waiter's tray. 'Just ... trust me.' Which was asking a lot since I didn't even trust myself in this matter.

'But we *can't* go, Alan,' she said, and my heart turned over at the anguish in her voice. 'We've got to stay here until Mummy ... until she comes back.'

'Look, Freckles ...' I took both her hands in mine; hers were trembling. 'The police believe it's dangerous for us to stay on here any longer. Now, for myself I don't give a damn, but I can't take chances with you.'

'I don't mind taking chances. This will be like running away.'

It was. But it wasn't my choice. I tried to explain as much. I explained that Ramouz was expelling me from Morocco, and that the Consul required me to convey Lizzy to her uncle.

'Will you come back here afterwards to wait for Mummy?'

'I can't come back. The Police won't let me on account of that man I killed.'

'But he deserved it!' She sniffed. 'I haven't got a hanky.'

I passed mine across and she blew her nose lustily into it. She laughed shakily.

'Now I've made it all snotty.'

'Be my guest,' I said. 'Look, there's Yusuf'

The bell-boy was hovering by the entrance, trying to catch Lizzy's attention.

'Go and talk to him,' I urged. 'Tonight's your last chance for a date.'

'Stuff that. I don't want a date.'

'It'll help take your mind off things.'

She gave me a beseeching look. 'If you're not going to come back for Mummy, what will you do? After you've handed me over to Uncle Alistair, I mean.'

'Stick around in Barcelona, what else?' I hadn't really thought about it but it wouldn't inconvenience me to stay on for a week, say, to see her properly settled. And hope still remained, fast diminishing, that Clair might turn up unharmed.

'I'll find an hotel near your uncle's place and we'll phone the police here every day for news about your mother. Okay?'

'Yes, I suppose so.' Sulkily.

'Good girl.' I touched her cheek lightly with the palm of my hand and she sandwiched it with hers. It was an extraordinary, intimate gesture and it startled me. The flesh of my palm seemed to burn.

'Go and put Yusuf out of his misery,' I said sharply, to cover up my confusion, and that, hiding her heartache behind a brittle gaiety, is what she did.

A pair of cops drove us to the airport. Ramouz's private escort service making sure we didn't miss our flight. When they deport you from Morocco they do the job properly. We even had flashing lights to make us feel important.

Like most third-rate airports Tangier-ibn Battouta is a modern but uninspiring supermarket-like structure with a lot of glass and metal, and an apology for a control tower, set down in a suitably flat slab of otherwise non-productive land. The single runway looks the same as runways the world over.

After passing through the police barrier, travellers trek across the apron, which is overlooked by the usual viewing area for goodbye wavers and plane spotters. Some compulsion made me glance up there as our passenger crocodile shuffled across towards a Royal Air Maroc Boeing 737. It was a glance that brought me to a shocked standstill, causing the passenger behind to blunder into me.

'So sorry,' he murmured in best Queen's English, though the fault was all mine. I wasn't paying attention, anyway. I was transfixed by two broad silhouettes at the viewing platform rail, and the interest was strictly mutual. The bigger of the two was Christiaan, the beefcake boy, in a black sleeveless T-shirt that accentuated his bulging biceps, the sun's rays striking his golden locks and creating a halo effect that was surely not merited. His companion, his equal in width but a few inches shorter, was less casually attired in short-sleeved beige shirt and matching slacks, and was reported to be in distant Amsterdam.

'De Bruin.' My lips formed the name of their own volition.

A tug on my sleeve and Lizzy's 'Tired already?' dragged my eyes away. The tail of the crocodile was passing by.

'What's the matter, Alan?' She was quick to sense all wasn't well.

'I think I've forgotten my wallet ...' Indecision anchored me to the asphalt, locked the muscles in my legs.

'No, you haven't. You had it when you bought me that magazine.'

The last straggler detoured around us and I looked up once more at the platform. A number of observers still leaned against the rail, some waving to emplaning relatives or friends, but the Dutchmen were gone, a conspicuous gap marking the spot they had occupied.

Unthinkingly, seeing only a red mist of hate, I started back to the terminal.

'Alan!' Lizzy's yell followed me and reason returned as swiftly as it had departed. As a *persona non grata* deportee, I would never be allowed back through the police barrier. Actually, I would never get as far as the barrier: our escorts were standing by the departure lounge door, conscientiously making sure the plane didn't leave without us.

'Alan, they're waiting for us.' Lizzy's plaintive cry, accompanied by her wrench on my arm, turned me back towards the airliner.

'What the fuck did you do that for?' she demanded, holding on to me tightly, as if a puff of wind would blow me away.

'I saw somebody,' I said, done with pretext. 'I thought I recognized him ...'

She was not slow to get my drift. Her hand went to her mouth, her step faltering.

'To do with the kidnapping?' she said breathlessly, too damn sharp for her own good.

'Yes ... I mean, no. I was mistaken.'

She looked over her shoulder. Now *I* was doing the hustling.

'Come on, Freckles. I told you it was a mistake.'

By then we were at the foot of the boarding stairs, and being welcomed by a hostess in a fetching Arab rig of Air Maroc red and green. We were the last to board. Within minutes, as we coupled up our seat belts, the engines were winding up. For speed and simplicity the procedures at these smaller airports leave the Heathrows and JFKs standing.

'Are you sure it was a mistake?' Lizzy said, peering out through the oval window.

'I told you.'

She seemed to accept this. As we taxied to the runway she flipped through her magazine, not reading, just turning pages. When the takeoff proper began she dumped the magazine instantly, sitting up rigid in her seat – from exhilaration, as it turned out, not fright.

'I'm nuts about flying,' she declared, face flushed.

The grey strip of concrete dropped away and we headed westward in a steep climb, crossing the massive parapet of dunes, nature's breakwater, holding back the Atlantic.

'It looks so clean,' Lizzy remarked of the sea, and these were her last words during the entire fifty-five minute flight. Which suited me, since it left me free to try and fit this new piece into the unfinished jigsaw puzzle surrounding Rik de Bruin. Had he come to the airport to make sure I really was leaving? How did he know which day and which flight? Mulling over this latest development started up a pulse in the healing wound on the side of my head. I touched the spot cautiously, smoothing my hair over the strip of band-aid that the doctor had earlier substituted for the original dressing. The pain was gone; all that remained was a mild discomfort from the pull of the stitches and a bald patch the size of a 2-euro coin.

I gave up on de Bruin and fell into a doze from which I was awakened by Lizzy shaking my arm and piping, 'Seat belt, Alan,' in my ear. Minutes later we touched down at Madrid where we were to make our connection via the Spanish domestic carrier, Spanair, to Barcelona.

As we drank tasteless machine-made coffee in the transit

lounge, Lizzy sank into gloom, her short vividly-patterned dress seeming suddenly frivolous, even disrespectful, like a loud suit at a funeral.

'We shouldn't be here, you know,' she moaned. 'We shouldn't have left my mother.'

It rang like an accusation and it cut deep. Privately I raged against Ramouz, against the Consul, and, of course, against de Bruin. For Lizzy's benefit I maintained a neutral front and recycled some empty reassurances about the cops knowing best. It might have helped if I believed it.

'It's all right,' she said in the next breath. 'I know you really feel the same, and that you've no bloody choice.' She exhaled with feeling through her nose. 'I won't bring it up again.'

'Bring it up as often as you like. Better that than simmer in silence. That way you end up blaming everybody.'

'I wouldn't do that. I never have secrets from my friends.' She shot me an anxious look. 'We are friends, aren't we?'

'The best of,' I assured her. 'I hope we'll always be.'

'So do I. Then there must be no secrets between us. Agreed?'

It was a compact I was to be reminded of often in the weeks to come. At the time though it didn't seem such a big undertaking to give.

'Agreed.'

II

Lizzy

Sixteen

Alan Rees from the British Consulate had booked rooms for us at the Diplomatic, a luxurious modern box just off the Avenida Diagonal, the multi-lane speed track that bisects Barcelona from east to west. Our rooms were eight floors up and air-conditioned, naturally, with Sky TV and free Internet Wi-Fi connection. The outlook from my window was of endless rooftops, stretching into the fume-blurred distance. The sea was on the other side. It would be. The British Government was footing the bill.

I phoned Rees for an update on Uncle Alistair, but he was out and nobody else was in the picture.

'Let's just go round there,' Lizzy suggested. 'I've got his address.'

'To your uncle's? Best to phone beforehand.'

She shrugged. 'I don't know his number, so we can't.'

No number appeared in the local white pages either, and we drew a further blank with the Telefonica information service.

We were still mulling it over when my room phone chirped. Señor Alan Rees from the Consulate, no less, was waiting downstairs. That settled the what-to-do-next debate.

He bounced out of an armchair the moment we walked through the automatic doors into the lobby. A dapper stick of a man, around my age, with crinkly black hair and a pronounced Adam's apple. Spanish blood ran in his veins, for all the Anglo-Welshness of his name and his pure Oxford accent.

'You must be Mr Melville,' was his opening shot. 'Too much of a coincidence, based on the descriptions we were given. Alan Rees, Vice-Consul.'

Hellos were said and at Rees' suggestion we retired to a pair of long settees placed at right angles in a corner of the lobby.

'Rooms all right?' Rees enquired as we made ourselves comfortable, Lizzy next to me, Rees on the other couch.

'No complaints. But we're having trouble with a phone number for Elizabeth's uncle. Nothing in the book.'

Rees nodded worriedly. 'Yes, odd that. We've already made enquiries at the address Tangier emailed us. Sent one of the clerks round to flush him out, so to speak. Nobody home, I'm afraid, so not sure he's still in residence.'

'So you know this Baya da Figuera?'

A worried nod.

'Off the Ramblas. Not the most salubrious part of town.' He coughed into his fist. 'To be truthful, it's a bit of a slum.'

A man the size and shape of Miley Cyrus's infamous wrecking ball wobbled through the hotel lobby towed by a dog small enough to fit in your pocket. People moved out of the man's trajectory like the Red Sea parting for Moses. It was either that or be bowled over.

Rees was saying something about tracking Alistair Power down.

'I wish you luck,' I said.

'Of course, he may have flown the coop altogether, so to speak.'

'Will it take long?' Lizzy asked worriedly.

'I'm afraid I can't say, my dear. If he has moved on it won't be an easy task without, so to speak, spending money. And the Treasury doesn't like parting with its shekels these days.'

'So to speak,' I said bitchily.

A passing glare, then, addressing Lizzy, he said, 'But we'll do our best, be assured of that.'

Nothing was left to say. He departed, in a state of mild pique, without shaking hands.

'You pissed him off,' Lizzy observed. I took it as a reprimand until I spotted the sparkle of mischief in her eyes as she added, 'Pompous little prick.'

'Remind me to talk to you sometime about how refined young ladies are supposed to speak,' I said, only half-joking.

She snorted. 'Who said I was refined?'

I couldn't help laughing. 'Come on, let's go for a swim.'

'Okay, boss man.'

We had the hotel pool to ourselves, but after a few frenetic lengths Lizzy got bored and went off to the bar. I joined her there presently and in the faint hope of shedding some light on her gloom put in a call to the Tangier Police HQ. Ramouz wasn't around but a sergeant gave me an update: no progress, no news.

No hope, was what he didn't say, but that's what he meant.

For our first full day in Barcelona, as an alternative to trying to resolve Lizzy's future, I planned to drive down to Sitges, an historic seaside town about forty km south of the city. It tends to be a bit touristy, with its "pubs" and fish-and-chip shops, but chunks of its original character and architecture remain essentially intact. More than you can say for many Spanish resorts. The local populace includes a notable gay contingent. So long as you keep away from their haunts, they don't impose on you.

Sitges was also the current home berth of my boat, *Seaspray*, a partially customized forty-four foot sloop. I hadn't mentioned the boat to Lizzy, intending to surprise her. As far as she was concerned this was an ordinary day trip. It wasn't until we were descending the stone steps down to the pretty if overcrowded marina that she cottoned on.

'We aren't going on a boat trip, are we?'

'It's an idea.'

'Oh, beauty! I love boats.'

It did me a ton of good to see her face light up, dissipating the cares of the last few days.

We came to the harbour wall. *Seaspray* was moored near the mouth, anonymous in a forest of masts. I picked out the gnome-like figure of Alfredo, huddled over the companion hatch. Always fiddling, always tinkering, that was Alfredo. Sixty years old at least, and dried by the sun and the hot winds that blew straight across from Africa to the consistency of a *croûton*.

As we drew alongside *Seaspray* I came to a stop. Lizzy carried on a couple of paces further, then, realizing she was on her own, about-wheeled and gave me a puzzled look.

'This is as far as we go,' I said.

The puzzlement cleared from her expression.

'This one? Aaah, I get it. She's *yours*, isn't she?'

'Yep. Come aboard but take your shoes off. High heels and wooden decks don't mix.'

'Oh, Alan, a yacht! It's so cool, really grouse ...'

Grouse? I took it as a favourable commentary, and led her, still enthusing, across the gangplank. As *Seaspray's* stern dipped fractionally under our weight Alfredo glanced up, his monkey face cracking into a grin of welcome.

'Good morning, Señor André,' he piped, removing a cheroot that was a near-fixture from the corner of his lipless mouth. He was wearing his usual bent and battered fedora hat, a threadbare singlet, and patched knee-length shorts. Fortunately, since my Spanish was only a grade above phrase-book basic, he had a functional command of English. I employed him as maintenance man, watchdog, and occasional crew, for a retainer in untaxable black money.

To save complicated explanations, I introduced Lizzy as my niece. She didn't seem to mind. Nor did she seem to have noticed Alfredo's use of my real name.

'Hello, Alfredo,' she said and switched on that sunny smile, so seldom seen of late, that brought forth the full flower of her prettiness. From that moment on Alfredo was a captivated man. The cheroot was discarded. Clutching hat to scrawny chest, his baldness revealed for all to appreciate, he bowed and swore allegiance and everlasting devotion.

'I'm not really dressed for boats,' Lizzy pointed out, plucking at her dress, as Alfredo scurried off below decks to organize refreshments. 'I thought we were just going walkabout.'

'Don't fret. You won't be expected to climb the mast, you're strictly a passenger. Just sit down and enjoy the experience.'

'Good day for sail,' Alfredo chortled as he rejoined us, precariously laden with three cans of Mahou and three tumblers on a tray. Beer was the only kind of alcohol I kept on board.

It was, as Alfredo observed, a good day for sailing. The type of day yachtsmen go into raptures over: wind light and steady, veering between south and sou'-west. Strands of cirrus lazing above the high plain to the north posed no threat down here at sea level.

The beers disposed of, we all donned life jackets and got under way. With the aid of 90hp of Perkins diesel engine we nosed out from our cramped berth, and through the tight harbour mouth, encountering a see-sawing swell as soon as we left its protection.

'Fetch my sunglasses, will you, honey?' I said to Lizzy, who was standing beside me at the helm. 'You'll find them in a cabinet above the chart table – first right after the kitchen.'

'Okay.'

Up forward a halyard was flapping. I hailed Alfredo, drawing his attention to it and he left off untying the mainsail gaskets and went forward on all fours like a baboon.

As Lizzy came back out on deck a wave flicked us beam on, forcing her to grab at the coaming.

'Oh! It's rough.'

She was wearing a pair of blue-framed sunglasses, property of an old flame, burned out three months since. She handed me a second, less exotic pair.

'I borrowed the sunnies.' She tapped the blue frames. 'You don't mind, do you?'

I assured her I didn't.

'Who do they belong to?' she asked, after a short silence.

'A friend,' I said.

More silence, longer than before.

'Have you ever been married, Alan?'

'Uh-huh. Once upon a time.'

Alfredo signalled we were clear of the shoal and I turned back onto our original course. As we came round with the wind abaft I cut the throttle. This was Alfredo's cue to crank the mainsail halyard. We lost momentum, the engine now idling, the sail beginning its ascent to the masthead in little jerks, the canvas crackling like far-off thunder as the wind caught it.

'Can I help?' Lizzy offered.

'Not this trip. If you like, I'll give you some basic tuition when we're back in harbour. For now, just soak up the sensation of silent motion. It either grabs you or leaves you cold. There's no in-between.'

The mainsail was up, and as I killed the engine *Seaspray* leapt forward as if catapulted. Her bows parted the sea, hurling a fantail of spray so high in the air that the sun caught it and turned it into a rainbow.

Alfredo came crabbing back over the cabin roof, unperturbed by the pitching motion. A near-half century fishing the Med in clapped-out, leaky hulks had endowed him with the sense of balance of a tightrope artist.

'Going good, eh, *señorita*?' he babbled at Lizzy, showing off his English. His wide grin exposed crumbling brown molars between two of which a fresh cheroot had been wedged.

'It's ... it's beaut!' The animation in Lizzy's face was not fake; she really was hooked. She came to stand by me at the wheel, steadied herself with a hand on my shoulder.

We were now running with the wind on our starboard quarter, bearing away slightly to port to follow the coastline. *Seaspray* was plunging like a dolphin, revelling in it.

'More sail?' Alfredo proposed, sucking on the cheroot. For him we could never crowd on enough canvas. Reefing wasn't in his vocabulary.

'Why not? Let's see what she can do when she's really trying.'

As I turned to windward, *Seaspray* heeled sharply, and Lizzy's hip bumped mine. 'I think I'm in love,' she said, her mouth close to my ear.

My head snapped round. '*What*?'

'In love. With *Seaspray*, with sailing.' A slow smile reshaped her lips. 'What did you think I meant?'

As if she didn't know.

Seventeen

An envelope was waiting at the Diplomatic when we returned that evening. I drew from it a single flimsy sheet topped with Her Majesty's coat of arms and *Dieu et mon Droit* slogan. The hand-written message read:

Mr Melville— have traced Alistair P. Address now 18 Espoz y Mina, Barcelona 4, off Avenida del Parallel. Apartment 3D, 3rd floor. Let me know if you need any help. Regards A.R.

'We'll go tomorrow,' I said, showing it to Lizzy.

'Okay.' The lack of eagerness was marked. Maybe she wasn't expecting overmuch from Uncle Alistair's new habitat.

Dawn, overcast and unseasonably cool, did little to boost morale. Rain spotted the pavements as we breakfasted. Lizzy was moody and withdrawn.

'Once more unto the breach,' I quoted with spurious cheer as we piled into a Mercedes taxi, the latest sleekest model, and with a non-speaking driver who carried us to our destination at the pace of an ambulance answering an emergency call.

We left the Avenida del Parallel in due course and first impressions of the district were not unfavourable. Tenements, yes – most of central Barcelona consists of multi-storied apartment blocks – but trees lined the street and the pavements were wide, and the parked cars looked cared for. Then we made a left turn and my hopes plummeted as the environment changed for the worse, then another left turn which put us in squalorsville: festoons of washing, grubby kids, grubby adults, overflowing garbage cans; an ambience of futility.

'Oh, no.' Lizzy's cry was muffled by her hand. The driver glanced at her in the mirror and said something in Spanish that was outside my comprehension.

'Wait,' I told him as we got out opposite no. 18. *'Espere aqui.'*

His head jiggled an acknowledgement, and we almost ran past a trio of loiterers into the entrance hall. Ignoring the array of nameplates we went straight for the elevator. Its scarred and dented doors were hung with a lop-sided piece of card that read *NO FUCIONA*, the second word a misspelling. Wrongly spelled or not, it meant the elevator wasn't working. So to the stairs, bare concrete, littered with all shapes and sizes of flotsam. On the flight between the first and second floors a lout of about eighteen was lounging against the wall. He lifted the hem of Lizzy's dress as she passed. She turned, kicked his wrist hard enough, with luck, to dislocate it. He reeled away, howling and clutching the injured limb.

'Come on.' Impressed, I dragged Lizzy after me up the last few steps, inwardly cursing. Unless all the indicators were wildly out, Alistair Power was going to be no use to her.

No. 3D had a bell-push. I thumbed it and for good measure hammered on the door. A toddler wearing a torn dress and clutching a naked headless doll, eyed us solemnly from a doorway at the end of the passage.

Lizzy stood listlessly beside me, mute in her misery, her powder-blue dress incongruous in these fetid surroundings.

3D opened. Rock music thudded forth through the gap. A beanpole apparition with long, unkempt blond hair and beard was framed before us. Its only garment was a pair of sawn-off denim shorts frayed at the bottoms.

'*Si?*' the beanpole grunted.

'Alistair Power?'

'You a pig?' he demanded truculently in American-accented English.

'No. Are you?'

He stuck out his beard, drew hard on a loosely-packed cigarette that had the stink of a joint.

'A joker, huh?'

'Does Alistair Power live here?' I said, with controlled politeness.

The apparition did a practiced lip curl. 'It's Alis you want, is it? Stay here, I'll fetch him – if he can stand up.' He retreated into the poorly lit interior of the apartment.

'I want to see inside this hole,' I said to Lizzy, and set off after the beanpole who had gone through a door at the end of a short hallway.

Setting aside the usual niceties, I barged through the door with Lizzy tagging along behind, and into a kitchen-living room. I barely got beyond the threshold. My shock tolerance is high, but in the context of a prospective home for Clair's daughter I was momentarily paralyzed by the goings-on that confronted me. The room itself was in semi-darkness, the only window being screened by a roller shade. It contained about ten people, of whom three or four were girls, not much older than Lizzy at a guess. All present were in varying stages of undress. One of the girls hadn't a stitch on, and another, in bra, stockings and garter belt, backside thrust ceilingwards, was giving oral sex to some creature, presumably male, on the floor.

The gasp from Lizzy summed it up. I was still adjusting to the concept of a sex party at 10.30 in the morning, when a gaunt individual, bearded, thin but with a flabby gut, rose from the room's only armchair.

'You looking for me, sunshine?' he said, with a casual insolence that made me itch to sock him.

'If you're Alistair Power, I am.'

'Alan!' Lizzy clutched at me, her fingers digging into my forearm.

Power, who was supposedly in his late twenties but could have passed for forty, thrust his beard at me. 'What do you want, man?'

I brought Lizzy around to my side.

'This is your niece.' If I'd said 'This is your life' and shoved a mike at his ugly mug he couldn't have been more taken aback.

'Hey, Alistair's an uncle!' someone hooted, setting off a gale of laughter.

'Hi,' Power said, eyes hooded, to Lizzy. To me, 'What's she doing here?'

'Her mother's disappeared. You're the only surviving relative.'

Lizzy tried to pull away. 'Alan, I can't …'

Power gaped, taking a step back. 'You mean … you've brought her to stay? Here? With me?'

That made three of us appalled by the prospect. I looked around the room – a room thick with smoke, reeking of pot, incense, and cheap wine. The girl in bra and stockings had rolled onto her back and was sprawled, legs apart, as if posing for a sleazy magazine.

'Hey, Alis, don't be anti-social.' This from the beanpole. 'We're kinda short of cunt and this one's a real looker. C'mere, niecey.' He reached out and yanked Lizzy from my grasp, his hand cupping a breast. 'Tits kinda small but I guess they'll grow. We can give 'em . . .' At that point I filled his loud mouth with my knuckles. I felt and heard his front incisors snap. Down he went, landing on top of a naked girl, who objected vocally to being used as a safety net.

Lizzy, released, staggered against me. Power bunched his fists and looked pugnacious, while the other male members of the commune, the beanpole excepted, slowly came up off the floor. Five in all, with Power.

'Which asshole is next?' I said with a confidence that wasn't justified by the odds.

Power paused, glancing down at his felled associate, whose jaw was smeared with blood and hung lop-sidedly. Broken. Well, bloody good!

The other weirdoes were bunched up behind Power; they would take their lead from him. Eliminate Power then. It was easy. A crunching left to his ear, the twin of that I had used to flatten Rik de Bruin, then a right to the breadbasket. It was like punching marshmallow and it arrested him in mid-descent. Finally, as he collapsed, retching, a kick to the crotch to neatly round off the demolition job. The crash when he went down to join the beanpole released the roller shade, which wound up in a rush. Daylight surged in, bright as an arc lamp. From the cries and shrieks you'd have thought I'd disturbed a nest of vampires.

'Who's next?' I repeated, over Uncle Alistair's twitching form.

Lizzy was clutching my arm, but not from fear. She had proved in Tangier that she wasn't short of spunk. With her tae-kwon-do skills she was probably capable of doing more damage than I.

Nobody offered to be next. There remained four of Alistair's pals still able-bodied, and though they could easily have bested us had they acted in concert, they backed off, drugged eyes fearful, mumbling unintelligibly.

'Wait at the door,' I ordered Lizzy.

'Who *me*? No chance, mate. This is all for one and one for all.'

'Hey, man, chill out,' one of the girls whined.

Unable to come up with a witty rejoinder, I turned and, hustling Lizzy ahead of me, quit that stinking hole in search of clean air. I slammed the door after me so hard the handle came off, moving Lizzy to a half-hearted giggle. Grinning foolishly, I jettisoned the handle, and we walked back down the corridor into a gathering of tenants, presumably drawn by the disturbances in 3D.

'*Narcotics*,' I grunted by way of explanation as we forced a passage. 'Drugs.'

This was met by an awed 'aah,' and they went into a huddle, leaving us to make good our descent. With luck some public-spirited soul among them would tip off the police. Alistair Power and his pals would be looking at the world through vertical bars for many a long year if ever they were busted for drugs this side of the Pyrenees.

Our taxi was still outside, double-parked, the driver picking his teeth with a match.

'Home, James,' I said, thrusting Lizzy in ahead of me.

'Home?' she said, slumping dejectedly in the corner of the seat. 'Where's that?' She cupped her face in her hands. No tears but she was crying inside. As for me, I had no answer to her question, and no comfort to give worth a damn.

'Lizzy!'

'Lizzy!' mocked the echo. 'Lizzy-Lizzy-izzie-izzie-zie-e-e-e ...' It travelled down the valley, startling a flock of magpies out of the sun-crisped grass.

'Lizzy! Where are you?'

'Areyou-areyou-you-you ...'

'Oh, shit!' I stumbled forward, swerving between the knobbly little rocks that dot the slopes here on the French side of the Pyrenees. Heading nowhere in particular. Just searching, with increasing desperation. Standing in one spot and hoping didn't seem the thing to do.

We had driven non-stop from Barcelona in a Hertz Audi, to cross into France at the town of Bourg-Madame. This area is celebrated as the sunniest in France and today's weather had fortified this statistic. A picnic lunch had been the natural choice.

We shopped for materials and accessories at a mini-super-market, and drove on out of Bourg-Madame as far as the first suitable site. We dined by a gurgling stream, on a rough and ready salad, liberally enhanced with a bottled garlic dressing and accompanied by pâtés, cheeses, and the obligatory baguette. To wash it all down, a modest red wine from the Pays de l'Hérault.

After lunch Lizzy, in an uncharacteristic burst of domestic-ity, had washed our plastic tableware in the stream and afterwards wandered off in search of 'the ladies'. Hereabouts, such facilities were to be found only in a ditch or behind a rock.

I stretched out shirtless to siesta in the debilitating heat. Sleep didn't come easily, beset as I was with anxiety over my escalating obligations. Eventually though I must have dozed off, for when I next gazed upon the sun it was dropping behind the 8,000-foot summit of the Font Negre, and my skin was cool, bordering on chilly.

And Lizzy was nowhere around.

At first I searched without alarm. Then, as the cast of my net grew wider and the sun dipped below the mountain's crest, transforming the valley into a realm of shadows, real worry set in. Before long I had ranged a mile or more from the car, searching fanwise, calling her at intervals. Now and again I looked back on the off-chance she had returned to our picnic spot. Cars, miniaturized by distance, wound past it, engines buzzing in low gear. Otherwise no movement, no flash of the bright yellow shirt she was wearing. Dusk fell all too fast. I raced for higher ground, for a vantage point from which to scan the whole valley.

At the top of a slope of scree I sat down. A moonless night closed in and the stars sprinkled their dust across the vastness of space. The outline of the mountains blurred and fused with the darkness into a black backdrop. And I kept on calling, until my throat was sore with it and my shouts so hoarse they no longer produced an echo.

As far as I was aware no four-footed creature more savage than a fox inhabited these lower levels of the Pyrenees. What harm could have come to her, I asked myself, to the extent that she was incapable even of responding to my calls? The obvious explanation still didn't occur to me.

Down on the road vehicles still droned uphill, a necklace of lights. Maybe she was back at the car, waiting for me. Though it was an empty hope, it was a step up from no hope at all. A last hoarse 'Lizzy!' that provoked a flutter of wings in the darkness, and I set off.

Without a flashlight, it was a nightmare of a descent. I tripped over rocks, plunged into ditches and hollows. I tore my chinos in several places, cracked my crazy bone, and bruised every toe more than once. The wound above my ear throbbed too, in sympathy.

Finally, I was brought down by an unidentifiable obstruction that went 'Oh!' and then as I sprawled across what was undoubtedly a living being, 'Ow!'

'Lizzy? Is that you?' Though the voice was hers I couldn't believe it. That after all these hours of searching I had actually found her by accident.

A moan, a subdued 'Yeah.'

'What happened?' My own hurts retreated into oblivion. My groping fingers contacted flesh. 'Are you injured?'

'I wasn't injured till you trampled on me.' She moved, sat upright, wincing. Now the pale smear of her face was discernible, half hidden by tousled hair.

'What the hell happened to you?' Anger was displacing relief.

'Nothing happened to me.'

Mystified and not a little put out, I squatted on my haunches. 'But I've been calling you. You must have heard me.' I shook her roughly. 'You bloody well ran away, didn't you?'

'Piss off,' she retorted, her tone flat. Then a sigh. 'Oh, all right ... yes.'

'But why? I'm taking you home to Andorra with me. Isn't that enough?'

'You don't really want me,' she said sulkily. 'You're just being kind. *That's* why I ran away – to relieve you of the burden of being so bloody kind to me.'

'Oh, my God.' I sank back on my haunches, shaking my head. This just wasn't my scene at all. Not only that, the wound in my skull was pounding anew, making any rational thought a trial.

The headlights of a U-turning vehicle flicked across the mountainside, momentarily lighting up the strained features opposite me.

'Now listen to me,' I said, trying to keep the frustration out of my voice, 'the reason I'm looking after you is first and foremost I owe it to Clair ... to your mother. Secondly, I actually do care about you and what becomes of you. I'm not going to fob you off on some hippy uncle, or couldn't-care-less diplomat, just to get you out of my hair. No one's making me take you with me. My arm hasn't been twisted, bribes haven't been offered. It's all my own idea, and we both hope that it's only a temporary situation, don't we?'

'*You* do, anyway.'

'Because …,' I said, declining to rise to that barb. 'Be-*cause* we both hope your mother will be set free or found or whatever. And if she is, then maybe my home will be yours anyway. You did know I asked your mother to come and spend some time here?'

A snuffle.

'Sort of.'

'So look at it another way: you're the bait that will entice your mother into my lair.'

The snuffle became a giggle.

'Am I going to be like Rapunzel in the tower, waiting to be rescued by a handsome prince?'

'You'll be free as a bird,' I promised her. 'For as long as you want to stay.'

A murmur of wind funnelled down through the valley, and I sensed rather than saw Lizzy shiver.

'That might be a bloody long time, Sir Galahad.' Her hand came into contact with mine, clutched it. 'I don't think Mummy is …' She caught herself and shivered again, transmitting the convulsion to me through our handclasp. She was still unable to voice the possibility that Clair was gone forever. Maybe she never would, short of confrontation with her dead body.

'Keep hoping, like me. Pray a little.'

'I do. A lot. Every night.'

Pins and needles had attacked my legs. I straightened up,

hauling Lizzy with me. The sweet-talking was over. It was decision time.

'I'm going home,' I said firmly, and would have looked her in the eyes if I could have seen them. 'You coming?'

'Just one thing,' she said as she brushed herself down.

'Go on.'

'Why did Alfredo call you André?'

'It's Spanish for Alan,' I improvised.

Funny, I know, but more than anything this one simple question warned of the tiger traps lying in wait on the road ahead.

Eighteen

In the pre-dawn of the morning after Lizzy's birthday – a lacklustre affair, long on gifts, but short on guests, games, and party spirit – I came awake while the rest of Andorra still slumbered.

Came awake and stayed awake. Before I killed the Pavan girl I had gone about my high-risk business these twelve years and loss of sleep was an uncommon event. Currently I had even less cause than usual to gnaw my nails: no professional demands to satisfy, no contracts pending, none needed (in the financial sense). The omnipresent fear that I had slipped up over some detail and that at any moment might come the legendary small-hours knock on my door so beloved of novelists, had faded to the insignificance of a microdot.

'No worries, mate,' as my guest might have put it in Down Under parlance.

No, at the core of my insomnia was that very guest. Sixteen years old yesterday. Fatherless, almost certainly motherless. Effectively relative-less. Stuck with me as I was with her, pending the advent of a someone with a legitimate claim on her, or a move by me to evict her. The second option was a non-starter. Ruthless I could be, callous I was not.

Two weeks had passed since our homecoming. Every morning of every day of those weeks, I had religiously telephoned the Tangier police department. Every morning the reply was the same. Progress zero. For them and for me

Clair was already long dead. Possibly for Lizzy too, though the ultimate acceptance was still withheld. Less painful, perhaps, that she should come to a creeping acceptance of the fact.

Most days I left her much to her own devices, and she would spend hours in what was now "her" room, which was the larger of the two guest rooms, complete with ensuite. Once a day, at no particular hour, she would emerge to swim a few lengths of the pool or make a pretence of eating, while in reality doing little more than rearrange the food on her plate. Now and again she had accompanied me into Andorra-la-Vella, but for all the impact the principality's lively little capital made on her she might as well have stayed at home and moped.

From the farm above the Bos's house came a triumphal cock crow. Dawn was imminent. The oblong of the balcony doors behind the heavy drapes was paling, the furnishings materializing all around me. As yet they lacked form, as if viewed through a soft filter: the wall-length mirrored vanity, the two bureaux, all in yellow pine; the doors leading to the dressing room and the en-suite bathroom where I had recently had installed a Jacuzzi whirlpool bathtub. It was a bright, sunny room, even when the real sun wasn't out, if on the Spartan side. The only embellishment I had allowed it was a painting of a sunlit glade in a forest in the Dordogne, hung above one of the bureaux. Somehow, having a female about the place on a regular basis, was making me notice the austerity of my environment.

My thoughts shifted from the retrospective to the prospective. To consider, for instance, what was to be done about Lizzy's future. If I was to be her temporary unofficial refuge, a plan was required. Maybe attendance at a finishing school for a year. An establishment of repute, with residential facilities. Far from Andorra. No involvement by me other than paying the bills, a cheap premium for seeing Lizzy settled and out of my hair. The overall priority was to ensure that she lacked none of life's fruits, and then I wanted out. O– U– T out.

And yet ... and yet ...

By coincidence, as if privy to my indecision, Lizzy came back to the land of the living that same morning, a butterfly emerging from its cocoon. Off-blonde hair brushed to gleaming, a smear of eye make-up, the little blue dress that was of such simplicity that it drew attention to her freckled, porcelain beauty, as well as displaying lots of long golden leg. She had her mother's build. Tall and lean, with the shoulders of an athlete.

'Can we go shopping today?' she asked, shredding a croissant. That was progress too. Usually she picked at them.

We were breakfasting on the terrace, served by Señora Sist, my new housekeeper (her predecessor had flounced out of my employ after a row about cleaning up certain of Simone's unwholesome discards). Señora Sist was an Andorran-born, gentle soul of fifty-odd, who had taken Lizzy's installation in her stride and accepted her status as the daughter of a close friend who had "just disappeared", as if such happenings were commonplace. She spoke French rather than Spanish, which was a major factor in her selection.

'I don't see why not,' I said to Lizzy. I viewed her revival with circumspection. It might be no more than a blip on the graph. On the other hand I could always give it some encouragement. So I asked her how she was fixed for money.

'Er ... that might be a problem. All I've got are some Australian dollars and about three hundred dirhams.'

I spread butter on a roll. 'Like me to change it to euros for you?'

'You're a real sport, sport. I'll go and fetch it.'

'No rush,' I said, increasingly impressed by this new-found energy. 'Finish your breakfast.'

Just then Señora Sist appeared with the coffee. Lizzy flashed her such a brilliant smile that she reared back in surprise.

'The *mademoiselle* is feeling much better this morning,' she observed to me, in French.

'Yes, I am.' Lizzy had made some modest progress in the language in the last week or two, mostly via the medium of the TV I had contributed to her growing inventory of personal effects. '*Je suis mieux.*'

Señora Sist was delighted. '*Je me sens mieux*,' she corrected. '*Mais bravo!*'

'*Vous êtes gentille*,' Lizzy ventured, and garnered more gushing plaudits.

'Your French is really coming along,' I said, as Señora Sist retired to the kitchen.

Lizzy peered at me round the stalk of the parasol. 'Did you think I spent all those hours in my room staring at the ceiling?'

'Certainly not,' I said glibly. 'I assumed you spent it watching the box.'

'Ho, ho. I detect disapproval.' She spooned a dollop of chocolate spread from the jar. 'I do like this Nutella. We used to have it back home but Mummy rationed it.'

'Good thing too. The way you're scoffing it, you'd be the size of an elephant. Do you know how many calories there are in that jar?'

She stuck out a chocolate-striped tongue. 'Who's counting?'

Señora Sist placed my mail by my plate, and replenished my coffee cup while I flicked through the half-dozen envelopes, a mixture of circulars and bills. Plus my coveted *Sunday Times*, which was airmailed to me direct from the UK. It was two days old when it was delivered. I tore off the wrapper and sorted through the various sections. In the house were a plethora of unopened packages containing earlier issues of the paper, delivered during my absences. Every six months, Senora Sist arranged for them to be collected for recycling.

'Alan …'

'Mmm?' Scanning the business pages, I was only half paying attention.

'I know you only telephone the police every evening because you promised you would.'

I stopped reading, peered at her over the top of the newspaper. The lightheartedness was gone. Her eyes were bright but free of tears. A tic at the edge of her mouth was the only symptom of agitation.

'Well … you don't need to go on doing it. Not every day, anyway.' She shrugged unhappily. 'That's all.' The tic became a wavering smile, then she got up and walked with bent head into the house, leaving me staring sightlessly at my own reflection in the glass of the patio doors.

Shopping was not my favourite pastime. I only accompanied Lizzy because she needed a guide and interpreter, and in case she ran out of money. We spent the best part of the afternoon in an Andorra-la-Vella boutique called Els Fills d'America, a cramped, sweltering establishment whose only saving grace was the proprietress, a sultry Frenchwoman of about my own age. Out of habit I chatted her up while Lizzy did what her sex excels at, trying on this dress, those jeans, that swimsuit, and failing to make a single decision. She worked through fifty per cent of the stock, from a full-length gown for formal occasions to a swimsuit that made even my jaded eyes bug. It was in white lycra, technically one-piece but with more cut-outs than material.

In my role as surrogate parent a prudish side to my

character that I hadn't known existed was exerting itself. I gave the swimsuit the thumbs-down on moral grounds, only to discover afterwards that she had bought it anyway. The girl had more than a trace of exhibitionism about her.

'Nobody notices anymore,' she said when I gave her a ticking off.

Nobody except the voyeur, the rape artist, the sexual psychopath.

And me.

The unusual and experimental nature of my relationship with Lizzy required that hurdles of one form of another be cleared daily. The shopping expedition took place on Wednesday. On Thursday we coped with our first social callers.

My neighbours Docteur Lucien Bos and his wife, Madeleine were in the habit of dropping in for an aperitif about once a month. I enjoyed their company and was mildly flattered that this wealthy, articulate French ex-government minister and his well-preserved wife should have come to regard me as a friend, so soon after I had set up home in Andorra. Their visit was inevitable. The need to explain Lizzy's presence as co-host was also inevitable. I was as prepared for it as I could be, my script rehearsed and as close to the truth as made no difference. From the propriety angle, I had nothing to be ashamed of.

That Thursday was muggy, the sun softened by skeins of high cloud, and storms were forecast. When Lucien and Madeleine arrived on foot, I was clearing a blocked sprinkler on the lower of the two lawns while Lizzy was up on the terrace, at work with paintbrush and oils.

'Bonjour, bonjour, cher ami!' came the cry, and I abandoned the sprinkler at once, glad of the excuse, but in a state of funk about how to convince them it was all perfectly innocent.

This morning Madeleine was walking in her own private

patch of shade, cast by a Stetson with a brim as big as a bicycle wheel. We brushed kisses to the cheek.

'*Comment va?*' Lucien said, as we clasped hands warmly.

Madeleine was shading her eyes towards the terrace.

'Come up and meet Lizzy,' I said, since concealing her was not an option. At least she was wearing the relatively modest swimsuit from her original wardrobe and not the brazen scraps I had been duped into buying.

'Lizzy?' Madeleine echoed, though she must have seen her about the place. Probably through binoculars. '*Qui ça?*'

She may well ask. As we mounted the steps I explained all, sticking close to the literal truth. They'll never believe it, I thought, as Lizzy slid off the sun bed to meet us, a sultry goddess to the last bronzed inch, with a poise that made nonsense of her age. They'll take it for granted we're playing house together.

'*Enchanté, mademoiselle,*' Lucien enthused, beaming through his gold-framed specs. Madeleine, by disposition more reserved, was equally unaffected.

We sat down around the patio table, and Señora Sist bustled out with aperitifs.

'André 'as told us about your mother,' Madeleine said to Lizzy in English, her voice husky with sympathy. 'You poor child. I am very sorry for you. I 'ope she will come back soon.'

Lizzy stared down into her apple juice. 'Thank you.'

'If we can do anything to 'elp, André,' Lucien said, 'do not 'esitate to ask. Anything at all.' If the emphasis contained a hidden message it was too abstruse to fathom.

'I appreciate that, Lucien.'

There, for the present, the subject rested. The chat became inconsequential, and my neighbours took their leave a half-hour later, having invited us to a dinner party the following week.

'Nice people,' was Lizzy's summing up as she went back

to her easel. She dabbed a blob of green on the hillside. 'Is André French for Alan as well, the way it is in Spanish?'

My call to Ramouz was the first in a week. I was fortunate to catch the great man as he was tidying his desk before heading home.

'Even policemen have homes to go to,' he said, a good-natured grumble, then gave me a rundown on developments, the long and the short of which was that he had called off the hunt.

'It's been nearly a month and we are no closer to an arrest than we were in the beginning. There are other cases requiring my attention.'

My expostulations were as arrows on armour plate.

'It is no use to shout, Mr Melville. You have to accept that Mrs Power is almost certainly dead.'

Dead. So that was it. To have it acknowledged by official-dom was an icy shower on the last feeble flicker of my hopes. I imagined him unconcernedly puffing a smoke ring at the ceiling fan.

'Are you still there?' he shouted down the line.

'I'm here. Look, Ramouz, I'm coming back. I'm going to do your fucking job for you.'

It was a hollow threat.

'Mr Melville, should you be so unwise as to return to Morocco you will be arrested and, if the pistol we discovered nearby where Mrs Power was abducted means what I think it means, you may look forward to a long stay inside one of our excellent prisons.'

Almost from the moment I disposed of it I had thought no more of the Arab's pistol. In Ramouz's cop brain, attuned, as are all cop's brains, to suspect, such a find would automatically be interpreted as evidence of wrongdoing on my part.

I said no more, but left him listening to the dialling tone. The discovery of the gun was an irrelevance. Clair was my only concern. Clair, who was now written off, officially deceased. Clair, who was doomed to be no more than a fading vacation romance. Boy meets girl, the chemistry clicks, avowals are made, a shared future hinted at. Then, when the vacation is over and the protagonists return to their respective folds, it proves to have no substance. To be like footprints in the sand, washed away by the next incoming tide. Usually the only leftovers are a superficial regret and a sprinkling of memories to reminisce over in the ensuing weeks; nothing lasting. In my case, the regrets were deepened by tragedy and the leftovers unlikely to fade so readily. You can't consign a real live, sixteen-year old semi-dependant to the scrapbook of the mind.

While I was pacing away my frustration, Lizzy came into the room.

'It's about my mother, isn't it?' She had on a flour-dusted apron and hands that were white to the wrists. She looked as if she were wearing gloves.

'Don't worry,' I hastened to reassure her. 'They haven't found her ... her body or anything. But, well, they're going to call off the investigation.'

She sank into the low, curved couch, more bewildered than distressed.

'I don't think I understand. Have they found the men who did it then?'

Such naivety.

'Not exactly. What I mean is, no, they haven't.' I sat beside her. I felt tired. Tired of cover-ups, tired of diplomacy and making light of disaster. 'But they've stopped actively follow-ing it up. From now on they'll wait until a positive clue or lead turns up before they take any action.'

In my efforts to paint a picture less bleak than the reality, I was over-explaining.

She took it calmly.

'I see. Or I think I see.' She tucked her legs under her and fixed me with that steadfast gaze that was so disconcerting. 'I heard what you said on the phone. That stuff about going back to Morocco and doing their job for them.'

'Hot air. I can't go back.'

'Because of leaving me?'

'Partly. And other things.'

A door slammed, and Señora Sist, her daily stint done, called out, *'Bonne soirée, Monsieur* André, *bonne soirée*, Leezee. *A demain!'*

A second slam and the house was quiet once more.

'Tonight,' Lizzy said, 'I'm cooking dinner.' She splayed her flour-gloved hands for my inspection as proof.

Cook dinner is what she did. A Waldorf salad starter, a little heavy on the apple, and a brace of steaks cremated Aussie-style to follow. I'd dined better, but as her first culinary foray since taking up residence it was the right side of edible.

Having complimented the chef, I asked, 'Why the candles?'

She had unearthed, from God knows where, a long-forgotten candelabra and a pack of emergency candles and we faced each other through bobbing flames.

'It's more romantic.'

I assumed this was an attempt at whimsy.

'You may not feel much like it,' I said, 'but a heart-to-heart discussion between us is long overdue.'

'Is that so?' Beyond the flames her face was shadowy. She had taken her hair back, leaving long ringlets dangling over her cheekbones, and had on elaborate earrings that clinked at the slightest movement. Since I last noticed she had acquired a nose ring. My views on facial furniture tended to be conservative, but I knew better than to air them. She was wearing the ankle-length dress I had bought her in Andorra-la-Vella. It was more daringly cut in front than I recalled, and she had just enough curve in that quarter to justify it. It was hard not to be conscious of the shadow between her breasts, despite my pathetic efforts to look elsewhere.

'You're looking very lovely tonight,' I said impulsively.

The change that came over her was disturbing: her mouth parted, her eyelids drooped, transforming girl into woman. It was like a glimpse into the future. I was confused by it, and even more by its impact on me.

'Are you trying to chat me up?' she said, her voice dropping an octave. Her body language told me it wasn't meant jokily.

'Let's get back to this heart-to-heart,' I said shakily. 'We have to decide where you're going to live, in the longer term, that is.'

She received this calmly enough. 'You have to decide, you mean. I'm in your hands.'

I studied her, wondering if she spoke out of petulance or the reality of her situation.

'You can't stay with me indefinitely …' I began, and that was as far as I got. A shutter came down over her face. It became still, mask-like, hostility radiating from her.

'We have to sort out the legal position,' I wallowed on. 'I'm not your legal guardian. Others probably have a much stronger claim on you.'

'Uncle Fucking Alistair, for instance.' So much scorn in so short a sentence.

I had to grin. 'I think we can eliminate dear Uncle Alistair.'

A moth came blundering into the candlelight, rushing at the flames. The heat forced it back but round it came in a wide sweep for a second attempt at immolation.

'Silly creature,' Lizzy murmured, and gently swatted it out

of the danger zone. To her, even a moth was precious. Then, looking me in the eye, 'There is nobody. No blood relative that can be traced. There was some nutty aunt who went native in South America a million years ago. She could be anywhere now. And she'll be absolutely ancient, I should think.'

'Your mother mentioned her. But what about close friends?'

'In Australia?' She drained the dregs of the solitary glass of wine I had allowed her. 'No such animal. We had two types of acquaintances, those we socialized with and those we didn't. After Daddy died and all the sympathy had been dished out, most of them faded away. Some of the guys came pestering Mummy for you-know-what, but she was ripper at seeing them off.'

The occasional Aussie idioms still sounded like transplants in her speech. Out of place somehow, on this side of the world.

'All right, Freckles. No relatives, no close friends. My qualifications for the job still look lousy.'

The carriage clock on the room divider chimed the hour. The atmosphere was easy, intimate. Two months ago, on an evening such as this, I had probably been sitting at this table opposite Simone, eating a meal cooked (badly) by Simone, and afterwards carrying Simone up the curved staircase to bed. And Simone was only three years older than Lizzy.

Frowning, thoughtful, Lizzy tapped a cocktail stick on the rim of her glass, beating time with the clock chimes.

'Mummy was going to come here and stay with you, wasn't she? Where she goes, I go. As far as I'm concerned you can't have better qualifications than that.'

'But you can't be certain she was going to say yes. She was still thinking it over.'

'I'm certain.' The stick snapped in her fingers. 'She talks everything over with me. Involves me in all her decisions.

That's one of the things that make her such a super mother.'
A gruffness crept in. 'She treats me like an equal.' The smoky,
sultry eyes focused on me. 'So you see, Alan, you have every
right in the world. What's more, I choose you. Out of all the
applicants clamouring to be my guardian, I choose *you*.'

That was pretty unequivocal. I was in deep without a
lifebelt. Nobody was going to haul me out except me.

I glanced at my watch. 'It's late,' I said, though it was only
a few minutes past eleven.

'Okay,' she said, readily enough. 'I'll clear the dishes away.'

'They can wait. Señora Sist will see to them in the morning.
You get off to bed.'

'Yes, master. Do I get a goodnight kiss?'

'Go to bed,' I said, and the harshness of my voice made her
recoil.

'Yes, master, right away, master, fuck you kindly, master.'
Her resentment put on record, she whirled from the room. I
listened to her rapid ascent of the stairs, the rat-tat-tat of her
heels on the bare pine boards overhead, the violent closing
of doors.

I slumped into the nearest chair and buried my face in my
hands. Lizzy had succeeded in expelling the demons of my
guilt over the Pavan girl, only to replace them with new
demons, no less active, but living rather than dead. No longer
did I grieve a young life snuffed out. Now I was merely torn
apart by conflicting passions and obligations. Never was a
surrogate parent less suited to the job.

Nineteen

The pact of no secrets between us had been easier entered into than honoured, and it came back to plague me regularly through that hot July as it slipped into hotter August. Shit, I had more secrets than a spy ring. For instance, an all-night rendezvous with Simone at the Hotel Coma, in Ordino, when the protracted lack of sex became irresistible. This absence I passed off to Lizzy as an 'unavoidable business meeting'. For Simone other fabrications were required to justify the hotel venue. Members of my family were vacationing here, was the excuse. The lie to Simone was of no consequence; the lie to Lizzy conscience-rending.

Secrets aside, the major event of the month was a visit to the International School of Paris, high-class place of learning for high-class expat kids. Insofar as Lizzy romped through the entrance test, the expedition was a success. She, however, was less than enthralled about the prospect of going there.

'Bloody school,' she grumbled on the return flight, staring gloomily out of the window. Below, the landscape was of the mountains of the Massif Central, sun and shadow alternating on their flanks.

'So you don't like the idea.'

'It sucks.'

'So why did you agree to come?'

'To see Paris.' A long pause, then, almost shyly, 'And to please you.'

The ability to come awake fast was among my most useful attributes. The yell of 'Alan, Alan, quick!' that shattered my dead of night slumber, firstly launched me from my bed, and secondly sent me scrabbling under the edge of the mattress for the Colt Python, my lethal bedmate. Within seconds of waking I was in full defensive mode.

'*Quick!*'

I hurtled out of my bedroom and into Lizzy's with all the finesse of a rampaging rhino. Her light was off. Moonlight streamed through a foot gap in the drapes, projecting a white zone across the bed, now empty. Lizzy herself was by the window, her back to me, staring out across the terrace. Not a panic situation after all.

'What is it?' I demanded, uncertain, hovering in the doorway.

Her stare swivelled to me. She let out a squeal and dived for the bed, pulling the sheets over her head.

Bemused but relieved that she was obviously okay, I crossed to the window and stood where she had been standing, wrenching the half-drawn drapes aside to do a sweep of the moonlit terrace. Nothing was stirring, not even the tips of the huddle of elephant grass, planted by Maurice a year ago and already taller than a man.

'What was all *that* about?' I said, perplexed at being rudely awakened for a non-event. I moved towards the bed and contemplated the human form under the sheets. 'Was it a nightmare?'

'No ... no ... I don't know.' Her words were muffled. 'I heard voices outside.'

Convinced it was no more than a bad dream, I sighed and returned to the window. The landscape was bled of colour by the August moon, and lifeless apart from a pair of yellow pinpoints of headlights descending the road into La Massana.

At this hour even the crickets slept. A feather of breeze twitched the drapes and chilled my skin. I strained to hear – a footfall, a suspicious rustle of bushes, any hint at all of a presence. The stillness was absolute.

'Nothing,' I announced. I closed the shutters and switched on the ceiling light. I considered doing a tour of the house and yards. If Lizzy insisted on it, I would. But when I turned from the window to ask her, she was still under the sheet.

'It's safe.' I told her, jumping to the wrong conclusion. 'You can come out now.'

'Not bloody likely!' came the retort. 'You've got nothing on.'

'Oh, Christ!' I cast about for a modesty preserver. A bath towel, draped over the dressing table stool, served. It was damp and smelled faintly of bath oil.

'Sorry, honey. *Now* you can come out.'

She peeked fearfully over the top of the sheet, cautious as a snail emerging from its shell.

'You've got a gun,' she observed.

'Only a small one.' Best to pass it off lightly. I perched on the edge of the bed, laid the gun beside me, finger-combed the disorder from my hair.

'Is it real?' she asked.

'It shoots bullets, yes. Lots of people around here keep them for self-defence. Does it frighten you?'

'It gave me the Jimmy Britts when I first saw it. Now I'm glad. It makes me feel safer.' She moved her legs restlessly under the sheet. 'Who do you think it was?'

'A bad dream?'

She made a dismissive gesture. 'No, how could it be? I was awake, I got out of bed. I heard at least two blokes down there, talking. They shone a light on my window.'

'Did you actually see them?'

She shook her head crossly. 'They must've run off when I yelled for you.'

'Maybe you were hearing things in your sleep.'

'Don't be fucking stupid.' Indignant now, she got out of bed and stomped off to the bathroom. She was wearing a pale blue T-shirt thing, covered with garish, abstract patterns in red and dark blue.

Water gurgled in the bathroom. She returned with a tooth glass full and stood before me while she consumed half the contents. A hiccup, then an accusing 'You don't believe me.'

A visit by prowlers wasn't out of the question. Burglaries were not unknown, even in low-crime Andorra. Reserve judgement, then.

'Go back to bed,' I said. 'See how it looks in the morning. Daylight puts things in a different perspective.'

'If you say so.' She deposited the glass by the bed, crawled back under the sheets, stretching like a drowsy cat. 'But it wasn't a dream. They weren't speaking English. Or French.'

'We'll talk about it tomorrow. I'll leave your door open.'

'Don't forget *that*,' she said, pointing at the Python.

I picked it up, feeling a bit ridiculous, as if I had over-reacted.

'Good night, Freckles.'

'Night, Alan.'

As I re-entered my room the towel fell off.

At breakfast next morning Lizzy, unexpectedly, was willing to concede that it might have been a dream after all.

'Even you and that gun don't seem real anymore.' She tittered behind her toast. 'Were you really in the nuddy?'

I squirmed. 'Discussion of my nudity is hereby declared a no-go area.'

Breakfast was concluded in more or less orderly fashion. Afterwards, while Lizzy cleared away the dishes (it was

Señora Sist's day off), I went outside in the already thickening heat and around to the east face of the house where lay Lizzy's bedroom. No matter what platitudes I had fed her, my built-in self-preservation meter would only stop ticking if I eliminated the alternative explanation, namely that the prowlers had been real.

No traces of interlopers on Lizzy's bedroom's side, not so much as a trampled cigarette butt. The ground was baked hard and the grass was struggling to survive, so brittle it crunched underfoot like frozen snow. Only the flower beds were kept moist, including the strip of soil between the gravel path that ran parallel to the house wall on three sides of the building. This section was planted by Maurice, my part-time gardener, with rosemary, alyssum, nasturtium, and every bloody flower known to man, all irrigated by an automatic sprinkler system.

I continued my survey, round to the north wall. My attention was caught by what looked like a single shoeprint in the flower bed. I crouched for a closer inspection. The shoeprint was of a heavily ribbed sole, as of a tennis shoe, and was pointing away from the wall, suggesting someone had been standing there. Next to it a clump of lavender had been flattened. By one or more other feet, presumably. Anyone standing there would have been invisible from Lizzy's window.

Had Maurice come across such desecration he would surely have erased the print and tended the blooms. It was therefore very recent.

What price Lizzy's bad dream now? I proceeded to do a sweep of the immediate area for other signs of trespass. When Lizzy hailed me from the terrace I was still at it.

'Looking for treasure?'

'No, a four-leaf clover,' I quipped, already thinking about the precautions I needed to take for her safety.

'It might be wise,' I let drop casually, over morning coffee, 'if you slept with your shutters fastened in future.'

Lizzy was instantly on the alert. 'Because of a dream?'

Sometimes she was too sharp for her own good.

'Because of peace of mind. Mine as well as yours.'

'You really think I saw someone, don't you?' she threw at me. 'Is that what you were searching for? Clues?'

I sidestepped the question. 'The reason I want you to keep your shutters closed is to put a curb on that busy imagination of yours. Satisfied?'

She acceded with an ill-grace, and showed her annoyance (or disbelief) by whirling off to 'bash the bones'. Lizzy-speak for playing the piano, at which she was more than merely competent.

The second precaution would be harder to justify, and would stretch my ingenuity and her credulity to the limit. The house was palpitating to the plinkety-plonk of the Bechstein when I locked myself in my den, the only room in the house barred to Lizzy. Not that it contained much that was of a secret or sensitive nature: a couple of handguns, a rack of hunting rifles, ammo for all of these. Also my private papers, including bank statements and shares certificates. On the desk a rather grainy photo of my parents, taken before I was born, and another of Julie, Willie and their girls, taken last year.

Otherwise just books, mostly comprising scruffy paperbacks unsuitable for public display, some unlovely ornaments, and an HP laptop computer I used for booking hotels, flights and suchlike. But it was for a hand gun that I came to my retreat. Not just any hand gun, a rather special revolver, made by Reck of West Germany. In profile similar to the Colt Python. Firing, not bullets, but what is best described as a mini-shotgun shell, a 9mm round that has the appearance of a blank cartridge case but contains, in addition to the explosive charge, some forty to fifty pieces of bird shot, each roughly 1.5mm in diameter. The ideal deterrent. Capable of inflicting pain, or *in extremis* disablement by blinding, yet not lethal. Into the cylinder of this nasty piece of work I loaded four cartridges, leaving the chamber under the hammer empty to prevent accidental discharge; the next chamber in line anti-clockwise, I loaded with a blank. This to allow both giver and receiver a last chance for reflection, before the second squeeze of the trigger and its consequences.

I introduced it to Lizzy during an afternoon stroll up the hill, following the goat trail towards the hamlet of Erts. We stopped walking while she examined the weapon. In her slender brown hands it was an obscenity.

'Don't touch the trigger,' I cautioned. 'It's loaded.'

'You said the bullets aren't real.'

'I said they can't kill, which isn't the same. But they can cause injury. Look.' I demonstrated how to swing out the cylinder, indicated the empty chamber, extracted the blank round from the chamber next to it. Let her handle it while I explained how it differed from an ordinary bullet.

By then we were sitting side by side on a great grey slab of rock alongside the trail. I exchanged the blank for a *cartouche à grenaille*, as the shot-filled slugs are styled. She held it as if it were a loathsome insect.

'I couldn't deliberately blind someone,' she said with a shudder. 'Even a really bad person.'

'Blinding is a last resort,' I said patiently. 'Shoot low. Aim for the legs, or the arms. It's like being stung fifty times all at once. That's all. Enough to hurt, not to maim.'

'Ugh. How can you talk about it so bloody clinically? You make it sound like a scientific experiment.'

Emptying the shells onto the rock, I got her to hold the

pistol and practice pulling the trigger. She needed both hands, which was no bad thing, making for a steadier firing platform. Then I taught her how to cock the hammer for slower, more premeditated shooting.

It was hot up there on that bare, scorched hillside. I was in shorts and loose-fitting shirt, Lizzy in shorts and a white cotton shift with a bold NOW! emblazoned across the front, and still we sweated.

'What shall I aim at?' she asked, clasping the gun, her forefinger laid along the bottom of the chamber, well clear of the trigger. The way I was teaching her. 'How about that Coke can?' She pointed the gun barrel.

'Sure,' I said, mopping moisture from my eyes. 'It's only a blank anyway, remember.'

The first shot, being blank, served to condition her to the gun's kickback and the noise. These cartridges go off with a bigger bang than the real thing. Birds erupted in clusters all along the slopes, setting up a bedlam of twitters and squawks.

'My ears are ringing!' Lizzy complained as the echoes of the gunshot ping-ponged across the valley.

'Sorry, I should have brought ear protectors. It'll go away in a few seconds.' I re-arranged her hold on the pistol, settling the butt more snugly in her hand, hooking her left forefinger around the front of the trigger guard for greater stability. 'Now, listen up. The next round isn't a blank, so try and hit the can. Cock the hammer for the first shot, then just keep firing, slow and easy. And don't yank the trigger back. Sque-e-eze. At this range you shouldn't miss.'

And, by God, she didn't. The range was about five yards, optimum for this gun. Four shots and with each of them the can skipped a foot or so.

'Hey, this is fun,' she exclaimed, while the air was still twittering with the resonance of her last shot.

We went to examine the can. It was in tatters. Many shots had passed clean through, others rattled around inside. I kicked it away, into a gully.

'You shoot well,' I said, genuinely impressed.

She made a pretence of blowing smoke from the muzzle, stuck the gun down the front of her shorts, and swaggered about, thumbs hooked in belt loops.

I said, 'Don't ever do that with a loaded gun.'

I took it from her and showed her how to eject the empty shell cases, catching them in my cupped palm.

'We must do that again,' she said as we moved on up the track, innocent ramblers once more. 'Tell me, though, why do I need to learn to shoot? Can a gun make dreams go away?'

'All right, no need to keep hammering it home. So it probably wasn't a dream. Burglars, most likely.'

'Hoo-bloody-ray, you've finally admitted it.'

Whatever the ambitions of last night's visitors – simple theft, voyeurism, rape even? – having thwarted them once didn't rule out a replay. Since I couldn't keep Lizzy company twenty-four hours out of twenty-four, a measure of self-protection was required. The means and the know-how I had now provided. The will to use them was up to her.

'New house rules. In future you keep your shutters locked when you're in bed. Agreed?'

'You told me already.' Wearily.

I put my arm around her bony shoulders and it seemed natural that hers should encircle my waist. Like father and daughter. Sort of.

'Anyhow,' I said, 'you'll be off to school in a couple of weeks.'

'Will I? I haven't decided yet.' She sighed and pushed back a strand of damp hair from her forehead. 'I love being here, being with you. If I went away I'd be miserable.'

I let that go by me. I'd be miserable too. More than I dared to acknowledge publicly.

'Let's stay focused on the matter of your self-defence,' I said, then we came to an abrupt halt as a large mottled brown bird did a vertical take-off from behind a clump of grass beside the path. So tightly drawn were my nerves that I made a reflexive grab for the gun in my pocket.

The bird, a fat partridge, wheeled away sunwards on fright-driven wings, uttering a liquid, whistling call.

'Go on,' Lizzy prompted. 'About my self-defence?'

'Yeah, right. All I ask is that you keep this gun in your bedside drawer. Remember, shot number one is harmless ... just a big bang. It's the rest that count ...'

That night passed, free of incident. I lay awake for most of it, as taut as a violin string, waiting for a yell that never came. As the empty hours dragged by, my worries about Lizzy's safety receded, were ousted by other worries. Notably my ever more ambivalent attitude towards her.

On the one hand she inspired in me the urge to cherish and protect. It was a non-sexual urge. Parental and entirely honourable. Rising above the temptations she daily dangled before me, by her scantily-dressed presence and teasing behaviour. See-sawing between the demure and the outrageously seductive. Far from innocent, she nevertheless evoked a sort of hands-off purity.

I was conscious of the trust implicit in my guardianship. It was a trust I didn't take lightly. It was my honour that shackled me and made her inviolate, as much as her extreme youth. Thus out of my night of unrest came a resolve to behave impeccably and irreproachably. As Clair would expect. If carnal satisfaction was all I needed, other outlets were available, and after all Lizzy would soon be flying off to Paris. With her would fly temptation, if not longing.

'I'll really miss you,' she had confessed again before going to bed.

Me too you, Freckles. My God, I will!

Lack of sleep made me irascible next morning.

'Talk about getting out of bed the wrong side,' Lizzy chirped, herself back to sunny side up. 'You must have got *in* the wrong side as well.'

'Grrr.'

Señora Sist breezed out onto the terrace, likewise infuriatingly cheerful, la-la-ing snippets of music from Carmen.

'*Quel beau matin!*' she cried, as she replenished my cup.

Later, Lizzy set up her easel on the terrace. She was working on a watercolour of the view towards the Bos residence.

'Got a date with your girlfriend tonight?' she enquired, all sweet know-nothing, without break in the rhythm of her brush strokes.

I left my chair to stand to inspect the fruits of her toils. As a modest connoisseur, sadly with no artistic talent of my own, I derived a vicarious pleasure from seeing the picture take shape.

I swung her round by her shoulder to face me. 'Just for the record, girlfriend or no girlfriend, I like having you around.'

She swallowed, her eyes narrowed and probed mine, as if seeking a hidden meaning behind the sentiment.

'In that case I might decide to stay.'

Never short of a comeback, that was Lizzy.

Twenty

Aside from Lucien and Madeleine, our only regular visitors were Maurice the gardener, and the mailman. Consequently, the day the vacationing couple invaded our little haven it was a major event.

Until then it had been a typical morning. Me on a sun bed on the terrace, skipping through a turgid biography of Lenin, Lizzy performing at the easel. Most days, after an hour or so of brush-wielding she would feel like a break and seek me out in search of amusement. Today was no different.

'Come on, lazy!' She pulled at my wrist and the sun bed slid several feet with me still aboard. 'Ten lengths of the pool and the winner pays for a champagne supper tonight.'

My laugh was derisive. 'Suppose you win?'

'Easy. You lend me the money.' She laughed back at me, gaily, even happily, then accelerated across the terrace, her tanned frame in fast, fluid motion, her hair a tawny backwash.

By the time I left the lounger she was in the water and had covered nearly half the length of the pool. She could swim like a porpoise and I had to work hard to get past her, which I did as we turned for our eighth length. She didn't look at me as I passed. Her face was set with concentration; she expected to be beaten – that she could tolerate. The objective was to avoid humiliation.

I won by a few feet. The grin she flashed at me as I hauled her from the pool denoted her satisfaction with the result. It was then I noticed that her navel had grown a piece of jewellery. First nose, now navel. Which part of her anatomy next?

'You're improving,' I said.

'Yeah. In a week or two I'll beat you, just wait.' She picked up her discarded towel. 'I wish Mummy was here to see ...'

Her face altered, the happiness draining away like water off sealskin. I drew her to me, giving comfort. This was a function I had performed often during our weeks together. She needed a lot of hugging. Commentary was secondary, a garnishing.

'Oh, Alan,' she whimpered into my chest, 'I miss her so. I still miss my dad, too, even after all this time.'

'Sure you do.' She made me feel like crying for her. I stroked her hair and murmured sweet anythings that came into my head.

Her arms were clamped around my waist, her nose around my left armpit. Shivering.

'You're so nice to me.' She looked up, and her eyes, damp, sparkling probed mine. 'Much too nice for a spoiled brat like me.'

'Don't be a nong.'

She smiled at the Aussie vernacular, wiped her nose with a forearm. 'I don't deserve you, really I don't.' She blinked shyly, touched my cheek with timorous fingertips. 'I ...' She broke off, looking past me and frowning. 'Hey, we've got visitors.'

I turned. A green car of uncertain provenance was nosing into the drive. It crawled towards the semi-circular parking space, propelled by a stammering diesel engine. Andorra plates, male driver, female passenger. Strangers. Mentally I went onto Yellow Alert. Not because they looked suspicious or dangerous, just part of Warner's survival kit. They parked tidily beside Señora Sist's moped. The clattering ceased and the doors swung outwards simultaneously, like flippers.

'Hello there,' the man called up to us. 'I hope we do not disturb you.' He was of middle-height, thinning blond hair, with a vacuous sort of face.

I nodded neutrally. Looked from him to the woman: she had mid-brown hair carelessly done up in a bun, and was on the stocky side, with thick, muscular legs. Both she and the man wore shorts; hers were easily a size too small.

'Do you mind if we come up?' the man said, with a hint of apology. His English was accented, maybe Germanic.

'Be my guest.' I indicated the steps that wound up to the terrace in an elongated S. The pair ascended hand-in-hand. Honeymooners? Neither of them would see thirty again, but maybe it was second time around.

'Sorry to disturb you,' the man said again as they mounted the terrace, addressing Lizzy. And Lizzy, exuding goodwill to all God's creatures, smiled broadly, a splash of white in a bronzed setting.

'G'day,' she said. 'Are you lost?'

The woman answered. 'No, no, nothing like that.'

The man laughed, a shade too heartily. 'No, no,' he echoed, as if the idea were ludicrous.

'What can I do for you, Mr ... er ... ?' I enquired civilly.

'Grahvermarker is my name.' He stuck out a small, slender hand; the palm was sweaty. 'It is spelled g-r-a-v-e-m-a-k-e-r.' A giggle, embarrassed. 'In English, it means gravedigger.'

'Hello,' I said neutrally.

'This is my wife.' He indicated the woman, his hand extended, palm upward.

'Mrs Gravemaker.' I raked up a stiff smile.

'Are you on holiday?' Lizzy asked.

Gravemaker regarded her in open appreciation, as any

heterosexual male might be expected to do. 'Yes. We are staying in Encamp. We come every year.'

'Yes,' his wife trilled. 'It is such a beautiful place.'

'Do you live here, Mr, er ... ?' Gravemaker went on, his turn to play the name game. I confined my reply to a curt affirmative. My identities, real and bogus, were jealously guarded.

'How can I help you?' I said then, an edge to my voice.

'Well, you see ...' Gravemaker dragged a peeling forearm across a peeling brow. He looked hot. Perspiration darkened the armpits of his shirt. 'We are looking for a property to buy. We were on our way to meet an *immobilier* in Andorra-la-Vella, when we saw this house. It's so ...'

'Magnificent,' Mrs G supplied.

Gravemaker's mouth twisted, as if he found his wife an irritant. Then he shrugged. '*Ja*, magnificent. We wondered if perhaps you wish to sell.'

'No,' I said shortly.

'Ah.' He didn't seem unduly deflated.

'Are you from Holland?' Lizzy asked Mrs G.

She confirmed it with a duck of the head.

'From a village near Groningen, in the very north of Holland.'

'I went to Holland once.' Lizzy's face screwed up with the effort of recall. 'I was only little and I don't remember much about it except the windmills and the canals. We went on a boat with a glass roof and rows of seats like a bus.'

'Amsterdam,' Mrs G said.

Gravemaker studied Lizzy again, with a trace of slyness I didn't care for. It was as if he were sizing her up, perhaps pondering her relationship with me. The natural assumption would be father and daughter. Unless he had reason to think otherwise.

He was scratching under a damp armpit, his gaze now transferred to the house. It stood well on its elevated site: the L-shaped layout, the timbered gables and second floor balcony compensated for its modern styling. It had been built by a Spaniard from Granada, but the only Andalucian influence was in the archways enclosing the dining room. The blend of natural colours – beige stucco walls, dark woodwork, chocolate coloured roof tiles – complemented the backdrop of green hillsides and steel-grey peaks.

'It really isn't for sale,' I said, and flung out an arm to take in the amphitheatre of the valley. 'There are plenty of other properties on the market.'

Gravemaker made a non-committal sound. His wife just simpered. They showed no inclination to move on.

'Would you like a drink?' Lizzy asked them. 'You look so hot.'

I willed them to decline.

'Er … thank you.' Mrs G, bemused, glanced at her husband. 'That's very kind.'

'Yes, very kind.' Gravemaker had no reservations about accepting. 'Thank you, Miss …?'

He was at it again, fishing for names.

'I'm Lizzy. He's Alan.' Introductions made, she ran into the house calling for Señora Sist. A moment later she was back, with the good *señora* in tow.

Drinks implied seats. I erected the big parasol over the table and various soft drinks were ordered from Señora Sist, who doted on surprise callers.

'Are you staying long in Andorra?' Lizzy said. Small talk came naturally to her.

'A few days, a week if necessary.' Whenever she spoke, Mrs G darted a worried glance in my direction. Maybe I was making my displeasure too obvious. I pasted a meaningless smile on my face to put her more at ease.

The drinks arrived on a tray and Lizzy distributed them. An awkward silence descended, broken only by the clink of ice cubes as thirsts were slaked. Gravemaker drank in short, sharp bursts, sluicing the lemonade around in his mouth like a wine taster.

'Is your wife away?' he said to me.

'No.' I didn't expand. What business was it of his?

'Alan's not married,' Lizzy said, and my heart contracted. She was so guileless it was painful. Now conclusions were sure to be drawn about our being shacked up together.

'Oh.' Gravemaker gulped lemonade; his cheeks bulged.

I stuck sunglasses on my nose and pretended I was invisible.

Two girl cyclists in short shorts were wheeling their boneshakers past the drive entrance, chattering non-stop. A dusty old pick-up, careering downhill, honked them appreciatively, earning shouts of derision and an unladylike double salute. The pick-up honked a retort and rattled on, streaming dust.

'We must go,' Gravemaker announced at last, his smile taut.

'Thank you very much,' his wife said, and in rising treated me to an old-fashioned stare.

Lizzy was alone in her insouciance. 'You're welcome to come again, whenever you like.'

I gnashed my teeth behind tight lips.

'Goodbye.'

'Goodbye, and thank you again.'

We waved them back to their car and off the premises. The exhaust vomited billows of blue smoke, hinting at impending mechanical disaster. Lizzy linked her arm through mine. 'They were nice.'

Nice. Everybody was so goddamned nice.

'If you say so.' My head was pounding. A real drink was

the only cure, but having jumped off that particular merry-go-round for Lizzy's sake, I meant to stay off. 'To be candid, I didn't greatly care for them.'

'Misanthropist. They're just a couple of Tulips from Amsterdam.'

'Groningen,' I corrected absently, returning to the sun lounger. High up in the aching blue a hovering bird of prey caught my eye. As I watched it went into a stoop, tumbling earthwards like a stalling aircraft, a plunge that spelled death for some unwary denizen of the hillside.

Lizzy went back to her painting and I went back to my book. All very domestic, all very tranquil.

The tranquillity lasted less than twenty-four hours.

Lizzy cycled into the village for her music lesson in the morning, now a twice-weekly routine. I always offered to drive her, she always declined. The independent streak coursed fiercely through her veins.

In her absence I did a stint in the kitchen, experimenting with a recipe for salmon *pâté*. The sun was shining, the birds were singing, and aside from the ever-present shadow of Clair's disappearance, the world wasn't too bad a place right then.

When Lizzy returned, bringing her own special sunshine to add to the natural kind, I was popping the *pâté* in the fridge, well pleased with the result of my labours.

'Hey, Alan, guess what?' she said breathlessly, as she came over and pecked my cheek.

'I can't. What?'

'I saw that Dutchman in the village just now.'

I started to clear up the debris from my culinary toils. 'The gravedigger guy? So what?'

'No, not *him*!' She was seriously agitated, fists clenched, almost bouncing with impatience. 'The one with the English name. Or if it wasn't him, he's got a twin brother.'

'English name?' I said with only half an ear, as I swept debris into the trash can.

'You know, Brown. That man who was always hovering around Mummy.'

It belatedly permeated my grey cells.

'Brown? You mean de Bruin? From Tangier?' I gripped her arms so tightly she squeaked with pain and surprise. 'You've seen de Bruin? *Here*, in Andorra?'

My apprehension rubbed off on her. Her eyes grew wide, fear dilated her nostrils.

'In the village. He was just driving along the road. He didn't stop or anything.' She wriggled to break free. 'Alan, you're hurting.'

'What?' I released her as if she were white hot. Thumb-shaped bruises bloomed on the soft flesh inside her upper arms.

'Oh God, I'm sorry ... I didn't mean to hurt you, honey.'

'It's all right.' She massaged both places ruefully. 'Cave man. Look, maybe it's a coincidence. No need to get snaky. Don't worry, he didn't offer me sweets to get in his car.'

Only then did I remember that Lizzy was ignorant of de Bruin's complicity in her mother's abduction. She had no cause to see him as a threat.

'You're right.' I turned to the counter, made a show of dumping utensils in the sink.

'I don't suppose you liked him on account of him always hanging around Mummy,' she said.

'That's about the size of it.' I took a grip on myself. My heartbeat wound down. 'Not only that though, he was ...' I needed to justify my over-reaction. 'I found out afterwards he's a criminal of some sort, possibly mixed up in the slave trade. So you'll see why I'm not anxious to have him hanging around *you*. You don't want to end up in a sheik's harem, do you?'

She considered this. 'Funny you should say that. While we were in Dubai ...'

'Clair told me about the Arab prince,' I said curtly. 'You may not know this, but thousands of young people of both sexes go missing every year and are never seen again. God knows where they end up.'

A toss of the head.

'I can look after myself.'

I didn't dispute it, but I couldn't help thinking about the Dutch girls, Bea and Margot, de Bruin's playthings. Forced, induced, bribed, or whatever to appear in a lesbian porno-movie. Bea, if anything, had been even younger than Lizzy.

'Did de Bruin see you?'

'I don't think so.' She opened the fridge and foraged inside. 'Jesus, Alan, if I'd realized you were going to make such a bloody stink I'd have kept quiet about it.'

Thank God she hadn't.

De Bruin in Andorra. Add to that, an impromptu visit by two Hollanders. House-hunting tourists? Or spies carrying out a reconnaissance? And was there a link between Grave-maker and Lizzy's night-time prowlers? It couldn't be ruled out.

Lizzy poured Orangina down her throat, straight from the bottle. Her worried frown told me she suspected I was keeping stuff from her. She could read me too well.

Hit or run were the options. De Bruin didn't scare me. I would welcome a one-to-one confrontation. If he could deliver Clair alive (taking for granted that he instigated her abduction), I might kill him quickly and cleanly afterwards. Then again I might do it slowly and messily.

Only my private pledge to Lizzy made me hesitate. The prowlers' visit had proved she was already in danger, either on her own account or through her association with me. The amount of protection I could provide while simultaneously hunting down the Dutchman was limited. His resources manifestly exceeded mine, and his troop train was already rolling while mine was stuck in the sidings, waiting to get up steam.

I made the decision. To run.

'You've only two weeks left before you start school,' I reminded her. She pouted. School was very much a sore point. 'What do you say to a short cruise on *Seaspray*?'

'I'd say … beaut-ee!' She flung her arms about my neck and we whirled around the kitchen like ballroom dancers, her gaiety as always infecting me, temporarily snuffing out doubts and inhibitions.

It was the soft option. Remove us both from circulation until Lizzy was due to start at her swank school (I hoped), thereafter leaving me unencumbered to deal with de Bruin for once and for all. As a plan, it was sound. My intentions were good.

Meanwhile, I needed information about de Bruin, so that evening I telephoned Giorgy. He had never returned my call from Tangier, but this time I struck lucky. He answered the call in person.

'I have no work for you right now, André,' he said a little tersely, before I had a chance to explain. In the background I could hear voices so perhaps my timing was bad. 'Next month, probably.'

'Forget that. I just want to pick your brains. Have you heard of a Dutchman called Rik de Bruin?'

Several seconds passed before he responded.

'Possibly.' Now the tone was guarded. 'Why do you ask?'

Possibly meant certainly. But it would be all too easy for him to fob me off over the phone. We had to meet.

'What I have to say is not for an open line, Giorgy. Could we meet up at the weekend?'

It turned out, after some grumbling and flicking through the pages of his diary, that he could but didn't see why he should. He was more exasperated than suspicious.

'You must convince me why I should inconvenience myself merely to satisfy your desire for information.'

'If I could tell you more, I would. How about I buy you lunch?'

He surrendered in the end, as I was sure he would. Unhappy, but resigned. Too curious to refuse. The venue agreed on was Cap d'Agde, the French Mediterranean vacation resort, approximately equidistant from Andorra and Giorgy's Antibes base. I only hoped I wasn't digging my own last resting place.

Twenty

Seaspray toppled off the edge of the world. Swooping like a big dipper, down, down, into a trough so deep that the wave crests on either side rose to half the height of her masthead. The shudder of the hull as it nosed into the translucent green travelled up through my feet, and through the wheel to my hands. Then we were climbing again, sluggishly, staggering under the water's weight, up the side of the next thundering wall of green.

Lizzy and Alfredo stood at the front of the cockpit, clinging to the coaming on the cabin roof, each secured, like me, with a brace of safety lines. As we slithered over the escarpment of water, Alfredo turned to make a circle of finger and thumb, denoting approval, delight, and all those other passions that wild seas and a bucking deck inspire in lovers of sailing.

This was no storm. Just water sculpted by high winds into spires of foam and froth that caught the sunlight and scattered it like liquid gold dust. And I loved it for the same reason that the explorers of yesteryear took to their cockleshells of boats and crossed limitless oceans. Because to pit myself and my boat against the might of the sea and to win was to temporarily conquer the last unconquerable element on earth. Its hazards were narcotic and the greater the danger the more mind-blowing the high.

We were some thirty hours out of Sitges and crossing the Golfe du Lion, notorious for its volatility. My troubles were behind me, healed by wind and spray and ozone. We were running close-hauled, the north wind butting at our port bow, Cap d'Agde away to the north-east, was still over the horizon.

'All right?' I bellowed at Lizzy, as we rocketed out of another trough.

She could only bob her head vigorously.

By all the rules of seamanship I should have put in a reef. We were down to just the mainsail but even that was too much canvas for the conditions, and we rocked and rolled more than was comfortable. Yet we were never in any danger. Alfredo and I were immune to high seas but Lizzy surprised me, lapping up *Seaspray's* contortions like an old salt. We completed the final leg of our run across the gulf unreefed, and suffered no worse than a soaking.

In Cap d'Agde harbour we picked up a spare buoy easily enough, and set about making *Seaspray* shipshape, aglow with the thrill and satisfaction of having taken all the sea could throw at us and gone the distance.

'Enjoy it?' I asked Lizzy, as she helped me to stow the staysail.

'*Enjoy* it?' she breathed, unclipping the halyard and snapping it onto the pulpit; she was learning fast. 'I *loved* it.'

'I never had kids of my own to share it with.' I peeled off my lifejacket. 'You're like a being from another planet to me.'

'Green skin and pointed ears?' She wiped damp hair from her salt-glistening cheeks. 'Is that how you see me then – as the daughter you never had?'

If only it were that straightforward.

'Er ... well, no, I can't say I do exactly. I'm not qualified for fatherhood, and I don't feel old enough. I've led too solitary an existence for too long.' I fell back on a tired old cliché. 'We're just good friends really, I suppose.'

'Just good friends?' She fixed me with a searching look.

'We're more than that, aren't we? We must be more than that. I don't see you as a friend or a father.' Her grey eyes were searching. 'You're extra-special. Unique.'

Inside my skull an alarm bell was jangling faintly, as it always did whenever we got onto the tricky subject of her and me and how we fit together.

'Maybe you should pop me in a jar of preservative,' I joked, straining to keep the dialogue light.

Rejecting my levity, she looked directly at me and through the window of her eyes laid her inner self bare. I knew what she was leading up to and it scared me.

'It's no good, sweetheart,' I murmured, forestalling her next utterance. 'You and me ... it's impossible.' The words just slipped out. Words of regret for a love I couldn't contemplate. Daren't contemplate.

She didn't flare up, though she might easily have taken my regret for condescension. Instead she turned away, her back stiff with my rejection as she saw it.

Alfredo saved me from further gaffes by emerging from the saloon armed with steaming metal mugs.

'Señor André, señorita ...' We took the proffered vessels, with relief on my part. Lizzy and I had brushed fenders, but the damage was superficial. For now. Maybe one day, maybe soon, would come the head-on collision.

A change of clothing, and the three of us went ashore for lunch, afterwards to explore the pastel-toned canyons of Cap d'Agde. Named after the promontory on which it sits, it is no more than a purpose built vacation factory growing, like others of its ilk in the littoral between the Camargue and Perpignan, faster than weeds in a wet climate. The buildings are Moorish in theme, each in harmony with its neighbour. Only the tourist hordes spoiled it and without them there would have been no town in the first place.

By evening the wind had dropped. The clouds fled inland and a red and gold drape rang down on the day. Lizzy and I dined on the catch of the day at a restaurant in the harbour. Minus Alfredo, who had gone off in search of a game of *pétanque*.

As we finished eating, a boy of about ten came in and went swiftly from table to table dishing out leaflets. TORO PIS-CINE shouted the blurb at the top.

'I know what *toro* means,' Lizzy said, 'and isn't *piscine* swimming pool?'

'Correct.'

'Bulls swimming in a *pool*? It has to be some kind of circus. Let's go and find out. It's tonight.' She pointed to the date.

So, in the absence of other attractions, we did go and find out. It took place in an oval arena. No bullfighters and swords, just heifers with bossed horns, a dozen or so teenage youths, and, in the centre of the area, a plastic pool, about eighteen inches high.

As we sat entranced by the antics, Lizzy clung to me in her excitement. My awareness of her was heightened in equal ratio to my diminishing awareness of the crowd, who faded to a homogeneous blur. Only the two of us remained: me and Lizzy. Close as lovers, yet far apart as two planets.

The heifer was at full gallop, lunging and feinting at the fleeing figures. The crowd aaah-ed as a youth, striving to reach the pool, stumbled; then cheered when the heifer overshot, allowing the youth to scramble up and belly flop into the pool, which the heifer is supposed to shun. Only this baby hadn't read the rules ...

Rules, convention, morality. The shackles that held me in check. If ever the links were to snap, only the gossamer veneer of self-restraint would stand between Lizzy and the beast that lurked inside me.

My rendezvous with Giorgy was for 2pm on Sunday, outside the Voile d'Or Hotel, which looks out over the marina. It was essential to achievement of my objectives however, to hold our discussions in absolute seclusion. On board *Seaspray*, and at sea, would meet that requirement.

Anticipating Giorgy's refusal to rumple his ever-immaculate drapes by paddling out to *Seaspray's* mooring in a dinghy, I had bribed an official of the Yacht Club d'Agde et du Cap to lease me a temporarily vacant berth in the marina, only a minute's walk from the Voile d'Or. Now access to my boat was by the luxury of a gangplank, complete with handrail. Even Giorgy could not reasonably object.

This party was not for such innocents as Lizzy and Alfredo. I packed them off ashore, impressing upon Alfredo in an aside, that he was not to leave Lizzy alone.

'Not even when I must pee-pee, Señor André?' he demurred, with a lipless, toothless grin.

'Not even when you must shit-shit,' I retorted, and the grit in my voice wiped away the smirk. 'And I don't care if you mess your pants. Just don't ...' I prodded his flat, bony chest, 'let her out of your sight. *Entiendas, amigo?*'

'*Si,* Señor André.'

Lizzy liked her banishment not at all, and was predictably earthy about it.

'One of these days you'll realise I'm not a kid to be sent out to play whenever you want to talk business. Business? Big fucking deal!'

But this was the only wave she made, and when we parted company after lunch she pecked me on the cheek to show no hard feelings.

'You brought your cell phone, didn't you?' I said.

She patted her shoulder purse. 'Never without it.'

'See you back on board at six,' I said, and unthinkingly

patted her bottom. It was not sexually motivated, but she pivoted round and eyeballed me, a reflective smile tweaking her lips.

I walked away fast, thrusting a passage through the vacationing multitudes to arrive before the Voile d'Or at two on the nose. Giorgy, there ahead of me, materialized from behind a rack of picture postcards. In dazzling white from collar to the soles of his shoes apart from a red handkerchief flopping from his top pocket like an open wound, and an anachronistic red cravat with white spots snuggling under his chin. Flicking a probably imaginary speck from a slender lapel. Always immaculate, no matter where or when.

His handshake was less firm than usual. Cooler.

'You are looking well,' he commented unsmilingly.

'You too. Younger than ever.' I couldn't resist the dig. He recognized it for what it was, and a shadow of resentment clouded his countenance.

The press of humanity was forcing us under the awning of the postcard boutique. I fetched up against a beefy, wide-shouldered man. I apologized in French and he replied in drawling English: 'That's okay ... André.'

A frisson of alarm ran through me at this familiarity from a stranger. I gave ground, opening up space between us. Ready for combat.

'Easy, André, easy.' Giorgy murmured in my ear, also in English, in which he was fluent, but used only when he had to. 'This is Baker. A colleague. Baker, say hello to André Warner.'

Baker grinned broadly. 'Hi, André.' He was easily a couple of inches taller than me, six-three or four, and a whole lot wider. Fleshy-faced and with a blond stubble where most of us have hair. He was sweating copiously, not surprising in that unseasonably dark wool suit. But then a lightweight cloth is useless for smoothing the outline of a shoulder holster.

I ignored him and the grin died. To Giorgy I said, 'What's the idea?'

'No idea at all, André. Baker and I have business in Toulouse tomorrow. We are travelling together.' He shrugged, almost convincingly. 'That is all.'

My reflection in Giorgy's sunglasses was strained. Baker was no more a mere travelling companion than I was here for a day out at the seaside.

'Okay, so he's not really a watchdog. But when we talk, we talk alone.'

'No, André,' Giorgy said gently. 'Where I go, he goes, or this meeting is at an end. When a man like you asks to meet a man like me in search of information he must expect certain precautions to be taken. We do not play children's games, you and I, *hein*?'

I swallowed my resentment. For now, I couldn't afford to do otherwise.

'I've taken precautions too,' I said. 'To ensure we can't be overheard. My boat is here, so we can have our little chat on board, out in the bay.'

My tone was flat, as if Giorgy's acceptance were a foregone conclusion. He frowned. Baker looked from him to me. Awaiting a directive.

'It's cooler out there,' I said.

'Oh, very well. How far is it to your boat?'

'No distance at all.'

We quit the protection of the awning, and hacked through the bovine masses, most of whom were going in the opposite direction. *Seaspray's* anodized mast was easy to pick out. It reflected the sunlight, appearing to be sheathed in silver lamé.

'That's her,' I said over my shoulder to Giorgy. His response was a grunt. Not a boat enthusiast, then.

When, on arriving at the quayside, I invited him to step onto the gangplank he almost changed his mind.

'I think perhaps this is not a good idea.'

It was either stand firm or abort. I had nothing to lose.

'Come on, Giorgy. Give a little. I've played ball with you, accepted your sidekick. This is for all our benefits.'

He scowled, then waved Baker on ahead of him.

'Check it out below,' he ordered, and the goon, with a hard glance at me, moved past him and down the gangplank. I made to follow, but Giorgy's outstretched arm barred me.

'We wait, André.'

Several minutes passed before Baker surfaced, red in the face (it would be sweltering down there), to give the all-clear.

Giorgy grinned crookedly. 'You are not offended, André? It is not that I mistrust you, you understand.'

I shrugged and stood aside while he went aboard with nervous mincing steps. Baker was sprawled on a seat in the cockpit, cheeks puffed out, sapped by the punishing heat.

'We'll get under way,' I said to him. 'Once we're clear of the harbour you'll be able to take your jacket off.'

This oblique reference to the hardware under his armpit drew a tight grin from him. No amount of tailoring can completely soften the bulge, even of the flattest automatic. Giorgy, who never went armed, had already removed his jacket and was fussily folding it. He wore red suspenders. Funny how you can know a guy for years and still not be acquainted with his sartorial idiosyncrasies. Down the back of his shirt a stripe of damp.

I alone, in my cotton slacks, short-sleeved shirt, and the Panama hat I fetched from the cabin, was dressed for the conditions. I alone was wholly prepared for the next act. Baker didn't worry me. He was a factor, that was all. In my mind he was already catered for.

We puttered out of the harbour under diesel power, past the ranked yachts and cruisers and the artificial island with its citadel of apartment blocks. Somebody waved from a second floor balcony. I returned the salute, eased the wheel to port to take us through the harbour mouth. As we cleared the longer of the two jaws a pleasure boat, packed with tourists, went fussing by, tooting a warning, her wash smacking against *Seaspray's* hull. We undulated merrily. Giorgy clutched at the jib winch, losing colour, of which he didn't have much in the first place. Baker, on the other hand, lapped it up.

'Swell tub, André. Ain't been sailing since I was a kid.'

'There's beer in the fridge.'

'Gotcha.' Baker lifted his hulking frame from the seat. He was light on his feet considering the bulk he carried. 'Boss?'

Giorgy wanted only mineral water.

'Beer for me,' I said.

The sea was, as I had prophesied, calm. Even beyond the shelter of the Cap, where a refreshing cat's-paw of breeze sprang up to lick at us, the waters remained unruffled.

'Gonna put some sail on her?' Baker asked, as he ripped a beer can from a pack and handed it to me.

'Not this trip. I don't think your boss would appreciate it.'

Giorgy swigged Perrier water straight from the bottle and made no comment. An island fortress, squat, crumbling, slid by to starboard.

'This is far enough,' Giorgy said. Some of his colour had returned, and he was no longer clinging to the fitments.

It wasn't far enough for me, but to press on would have been to precipitate a showdown. So I set the engine to idle, and switched the wheel onto Autohelm before going forward.

'What are you doing?' Giorgy called after me, still suspicious.

I kept on going. 'Dropping anchor.'

I did too, only not as far as the sea bed. According to the chart the depth of the water here was over twelve feet. I paid out an estimated ten feet of cable and clamped it there. Ostensibly we were immobilized. In reality we would drift with the prevailing current. The breeze was from the north-east and would push us farther out to sea. Farther from witnesses.

Baker was attacking his beer when I clambered back into the cockpit. Giorgy, watching me constantly, was occupying the seat over the sail locker, which didn't fit my scheme of things at all.

'Excuse me, Giorgy,' I said. 'Would you mind moving to the other side?'

It was as painless as that. No song, no dance, he swapped from port to starboard. To justify the request I opened the locker lid and rummaged about among the sail bags, careful not to disturb the magnum revolver secreted there.

'Lost something?' Baker had come up behind me, stealthy as a cat burglar, and was breathing down my neck.

'Anchor securing pin,' I improvised. 'Doesn't seem to be here.' I slammed down the lid before he could offer to help.

He grunted.

I yanked off the metal ring off my beer can and guzzled sociably. 'Take a look at that,' I said, pointing towards a large, three-masted schooner crossing the horizon. 'I'll fetch the glasses.'

With the Swarovski binoculars we took turns to watch the schooner's regal progress along the skyline. Even Giorgy was stirred by it.

'You don't see many sights like that nowadays,' I said with real regret, stuffing the binoculars back in their case.

'You're a romantic, André,' Giorgy remarked, loosening

his white silk cravat. 'I never realized it. I wonder that you can sustain it, yet still do what you do. *C'est une paradoxe.*'

'Whatever,' I said, not caring to be analyzed by him.

'But come, we have spent long enough sailing your little boat, and making the small talk. Out here ...' He looked from left to right, 'we are completely isolated, which suits us both. Let us discuss whatever it is you wish to discuss.'

I considered insisting on Baker moving out of hearing range. The big American was on his third can of beer, periodically belching or jacking up a buttock to fart explosively. Giorgy showed distaste, but no inclination to reprimand. Maybe Baker was a bigger cog in the machine than his uncouth country-hick demeanour suggested.

My querying eyebrow cocked in Baker's direction brought a head-shake from Giorgy.

'He stays,' Giorgy said firmly, in French.

So, no more delaying tactics.

'Tell me what you know,' I said, also in French, 'about Rik de Bruin.'

Giorgy had the poker player's faculty for inscrutability. Baker, while possibly uncomprehending of the French, stiffened at the mention of de Bruin. He didn't leave off guzzling though. Beer from the uptilted can trickled down his chin, forming an amber dewdrop on the underhang.

'Before I do, *if* I do, you must tell me why you ask,' Giorgy said heavily. 'Be warned, André. De Bruin is a man with friends in high places.'

'A friend of the Family, perhaps?' I bantered.

This punning reference to the Mafia likewise made no impression on Giorgy's deadpan.

'Rik de Bruin is an associate of the Syndicate and that is all.'

I made a show of studying my beer can. 'It's not enough. And your coming here today proves something.'

I hoped he didn't ask me what it proved, because I had no idea.

Baker had grown increasingly restive since the switch to French. Now he said roughly, 'Stick to English, huh?'

'Very well,' Giorgy said, adding an apologetic shrug for my benefit. 'Tell me,' he said to me, 'why you are interested. I will listen. But you place me in the position of a lawyer representing two opposing litigants.'

'In case you ain't gotten the message, Warner,' Baker sneered, 'de Bruin is a blue-eyed boy.' He let loose a bark of laughter. 'Hey, how do you like that? Blue-eyed de Bruin!' Another bark. He slopped beer into the ever-open cavity in his face, choked, and regurgitated most of it over his own shoes. 'Fuck!' The can clattered onto the well deck and rolled towards me.

Giorgy's repugnance became more pronounced. He slid along the seat away from Baker.

'Do not mind Baker,' he said in French. 'He is not used to mixing with civilized people.'

'I told you to speak English,' Baker growled, popping the seal on another beer. 'You wanted me along on this caper, after all, Giorgy.'

'Just do your job, that is all I ask.'

Giorgy removed his cravat altogether and mopped his neck with it. He was beginning to look decidedly rumpled.

'What is it between you and de Bruin, André?'

An open speedboat, twin outboards howling, cut across our stern, ploughing a foaming furrow through the placid waters. Bronzed, bare-bosomed forms were draped along its hull like hunting trophies.

'Well?' Giorgy demanded.

I told him.

I told him about Clair and about Lizzy. About the kidnapping and the killing and the subsequent assault on me. I told him about the threats, and about de Bruin's appearance at the airport the day I left Tangier. Finally I told him that de Bruin was now in Andorra. A coincidence too far.

And throughout the telling I sensed that none of this was news to Giorgy.

Twenty-One

A wave, whipped up by a freak gust, smacked against the hull, and *Seaspray* rolled a degree or two with it. Giorgy clutched unnecessarily at the binnacle, and looked shoreward with longing.

I grinned at him without humour. 'Nothing to say, Giorgy?'

'Only that your annoyance is understandable. How do *you* explain de Bruin's behaviour?'

'If I could explain it, I wouldn't need you. But since you ask, I'll give you my take on it. At first I thought he was just infatuated with Clair. Obviously it wasn't that straightforward. Nobody in his right senses kidnaps a person out of infatuation. On top of which the bastard is still hounding me, so I finally came to the conclusion it's the daughter he's after. The mother just got scooped up in the trawl.'

'You can't be certain it was de Bruin who kidnapped this woman friend of yours.'

'Maybe it was one o' them sheiks,' Baker sniggered. 'Collecting concubines or whatever they call 'em.'

Giorgy flipped him a bleak glance. To me, he said, 'If de Bruin was attracted to the woman, but had nothing to do with the kidnapping, it is possible ... I say, possible ... he believes she is living with you.'

'I can't accept that. Even if she were, would he really go so far as to abduct her?'

'But her daughter *is* living with you – correct?'

I hadn't mentioned it.

'How do you know?'

He made a dismissive sound in the back of his throat.

'We know. That is enough. Do not worry, my friend ...' He reached over and patted my knee, 'we will not broadcast your ... affair. Your little foibles do not interest us.'

I came up off the seat. 'Now listen, Giorgy . . .'

Then Baker was between us, right hand inside his jacket, left hand pressing me down.

'Cool it, Warner. Nobody's blamin' you for screwin' the kid. She's a juicy little chick, that's for sure. Did you get a load of that sweet little ass, Giorgy?' He gurgled appreciatively. 'And we saw you feelin' it.'

I went from hot to cold and back to hot. He was just baiting me, I told myself. Don't be a sucker, don't rise to it. I wasn't looking for a fight. All I sought was a lead on Rik de Bruin. Taking an innuendo or two on the chin was a small enough price.

'I might make you a present of her when I've finished,' I said, faking a grin. This was the kind of language Baker would understand.

He whistled. 'Gee, that's pretty white of you, André. Hey ...' He inclined towards me conspiratorially, 'she give head?'

I shrugged, as if to imply it was a foregone conclusion.

'She *swallow*?' he persisted, almost panting.

'Cut it out,' I snarled. My tolerance had its limits.

'Enough of this,' Giorgy intervened, his voice icy. 'On the subject of de Bruin I will speak frankly, André. It is true we are aware of what is happening. However, he is, as I have said, under my protection. I cannot intrude. I can only advise you.'

His predatory features relaxed somewhat, liberating some of the compassion I knew was in him, though it was buried deep and only ever exhumed in private.

'Advise me then.'

'Leave him alone. Whatever he does, let him be. When he has what he wants he will leave you in peace.'

'So what exactly does he want? Maybe I can give it to him.'

'I think not. Just do not stand in his way. He is a business-man, not a gangster. He will only act against you if you … obstruct him.'

'Obstruct him? From snatching Lizzy? If you think I'm going to stand back and let him do it, you're living in Won-derland.'

'André …' Giorgy stretched out a hand. 'You should go away. I can give you a new contract, here and now. In Brazil.'

I shook my head. Both of them were regarding me with an intense curiosity, as if I had just stepped off a flying saucer.

'Not only that,' Giorgy went on. 'We will pay more. How does five hundred thousand sound? And not just for this contract but in the future too. It is agreed?' He was patheti-cally eager. 'I have with me a down payment, in good faith.'

I didn't react. I was content to let him make the running, to see how far he and the Syndicate would stick out their financial necks for the mighty Rik de Bruin.

He reached inside his neatly-folded jacket and withdrew a fat envelope.

'One hundred and twenty-five thousand. If you take the contract now, you will receive the balance of the usual fifty per cent tomorrow. Here.' He shook the envelope under my nose, as if inviting me to smell it.

First de Bruin, now Giorgy. Everybody offering me money to be a good boy and not stick my nose in where it wasn't welcome. What was I to deduce from this generosity but that de Bruin was invaluable to Giorgy's principals. Deals were being done, and very big deals at that, to judge from the amount of hush money swilling around. Let him be, was

Giorgy's entreaty, take an inflation-busting pay rise. Likely as not he'd have given even more, had I demanded it.

But this wasn't a matter of money. For once in my professional life, I wasn't to be bought.

No good would come of further debate. I did a swift recce. The fortified island was now well to the rear and the town itself was a fusion of pinks and beiges and pale greens. We were the only craft this far from the shore, other than the big stuff plodding along the sea's periphery. Circumstances were as favourable as they would ever be.

'We're drifting. Anchor must have dragged.' I drew their attention to the island, now a good mile astern.

'Let it drift,' Baker grunted, expansive with beer. Only two cans remained of the original twelve. As I sized him up, assessing his ability to function with so much booze inside him, he shook a cigarette from a flip-top pack of Camels and lit up with a Zippo lighter. His hand was steady enough.

'No!' Giorgy said sharply. 'Please return to the harbour, André.' He was still clutching the envelope. Probably in a sweat about being dunked in the Med with it. 'Please, André. I cannot swim.'

'You won't have to swim.' I vacated the seat and lifted the locker lid trying to keep my movements natural, yet sensing they were wooden and theatrical, telegraphing my intentions.

The butt of the gun, a German Korth .357 magnum revolver, reputedly the world's most expensive mass-produced handgun, protruded from the staysail bag. I grasped it, almost lovingly and tugged the three inches of barrel free. In that same instant my shoulder was grasped and I was spun sideways to smash into the wheel, its rim gouging my spine and forcing a shout of pain from my lips. Baker, who else. Now he was closing in, hands balled into fists, cigarette still drooping incongruously. I had managed to hang on to the

Korth, but he seemed not to notice it. Maybe he was made of bulletproof steel.

So I let him look down the muzzle, let him take note of the long cylinder that spelled magnum and a bullet capable of dismemberment. Yet anger, not fear, flared in the piggy eyes. The massive frame bunched, ready to launch. He was too committed, or maybe too smashed, to back down. He was paid to protect. Behind him Giorgy was rising. In him was fear enough for both of them. I could smell it on him.

'Be sensible, Baker.' I prodded him with the Korth so hard that he gasped and stumbled backwards. Still no fear there. Frustration, yes, and fury, now boiling over into madness, goaded at last to the ultimate folly. His hand dived inside his jacket and he was fast all right. The signals to my brain were a succession of freeze-frame movements, my vision acting as a viewfinder, the shutter opening and closing, click-clack, click-clack, and my own responses seeming sluggish, reluctant. My finger was squeezing the trigger, it felt stiff, resistant to the pressure. Baker's gun was clearing his jacket, a compact square automatic, sure to be double-action, sure to have a round already chambered.

Impressions came fast: of the spurt of orange from the Korth's muzzle, a darting mayfly of flame that bloomed and died within a heartbeat, and of the report, thankfully emasculated by the open space of the sea. Of the slap the 150-grain cartridge made as it penetrated flesh and sinew; of the spurt of blood, a gory mist, momentarily speckling the blue beehive of the sky. Of Baker, hurled towards the gunwale, his head snapping back, the cigarette spinning one way, his gun another, skating across the cabin roof. Of Giorgy ducking instinctively, then trying too late to prevent Baker from going over the side, and almost being dragged with him.

Baker hit the water, raising a crescendo of spray, soaking Giorgy, who was left slumped across the gunwale, half-out of the boat. I moved in on him and he wrenched round to ward me off.

'No ... no!'

He needn't have worried. A dead Giorgy would be no use to me. Floundering noises from under the stern were overlaid with American-twanged cursing. Likewise a dead Baker would have been an embarrassment. I had aimed for his right shoulder and my aim had been true.

'Give him a hand,' I ordered Giorgy, who was so manifestly relieved not to be in the drink too, that he rushed to obey and was soon straining to haul his failed watchdog back on board. Retrieving a man overboard without proper gear is no picnic, especially if that man has a useless arm and a waterlogged suit. But I wasn't about to join in.

While this was going on I checked for indications that the gunshot had not been heard by others. All was as normal. No busybodies racing to investigate.

My hat had come off during the skirmish. I reclaimed it and sat down at the very stern, putting the steering binnacle between me and the struggling pair. Baker had managed to hook a foot over the gunwale. Giorgy had a double fistful of his jacket lapels and was braced against the side of the binnacle, grunting with the effort.

'No hurry,' I said, resting the Korth along my thigh.

Baker's white face rose over the cockpit rim, like the moon coming up. A last Herculean heave from Giorgy and the pair of them crashed into the well together. Pure slapstick.

Baker was tough. Ignoring Giorgy, he got to his feet and stripped off his jacket, exposing the empty pocket of the shoulder holster. The bullet had gone in an inch below his collar bone and hadn't exited. The blood that stained his cream shirt had been diluted by the water to *rosé*. Fresh outflow was already darkening it anew.

He unstuck his shirt from the wound. Didn't so much as wince. An authentic hard case.

'Bastard,' he said, his voice unsteady.

'Next time it'll be your head.'

He looked searchingly at me, perhaps remembering that killing was my daily bread too.

'Do nothing, Baker,' a damp, dishevelled Giorgy, crawling onto the seat, croaked.

And what could he do? But glower – and he did plenty of that.

Although Giorgy's chest was going like a bellows from his recent labours, he found enough lung space to fling an assortment of Italian expletives at me. At least they sounded like expletives.

'You are skating on very thin ice, André,' he said, reverting to English to make sure I received him loud and clear.

'Giorgy,' I said, patiently, as to a recalcitrant child, 'don't threaten me. I never wanted to make an enemy of you, but I have to know what game de Bruin is playing. He's already taken my woman ...'

'You say,' Giorgy interrupted.

'You think I'm doing this for *fun*?' I said, stung to anger.

Giorgy produced the red handkerchief and mopped seawater from his face and hair. 'It will do you no good. I don't know myself why de Bruin is to be left alone. All I can say is that he has influential connections in the Middle East. Oil money.'

'Giorgy!' Baker growled. 'You got a big mouth.'

'What does it matter?' Giorgy retorted. 'He knows what is going on. It is useless to pretend.' He turned back to me. 'I am only acting under instructions. You must believe this,

André. In this matter I am little more than a message-carrier, and the message to you is keep away from de Bruin.'

Oddly, I was inclined to believe him. Tactically though, I wasn't quite finished with him yet.

'You're lying, Giorgy.' I hooked back the hammer of the Korth. Giorgy shrank away from me; Baker, ashen-faced, made a feeble gesture of restraint, then sagged against the cabin wall, clutching his smashed shoulder, his fingers red-dyed.

'André ... I swear.' Giorgy spread his arms, a wordless appeal.

The gun barrel was centred on his left kneecap.

'Do you know what happens to the kneecap when a bullet goes through it?'

He just stared.

'It shatters like glass,' I said. 'Into tiny, tiny fragments. The pain is excruciating. Indescribable. The reconstruction job is complicated and painful. They may have to bond a metal casing to whatever bone is left, or even replace it with an artificial joint, or even amputate your leg. Sometimes they can't ever repair the damage, and even if they can you'll always have a limp. Always walk slowly. Always have pain.'

Sweat trickled from his hairline. His mouth writhed, no speech issued from it. The veneer of prestige and persuasion was finally stripped away.

'Bad enough to lose one knee,' I went on, twisting the knife. 'Imagine losing both.'

'All right, all right! You have made your point.'

The buzz of an outboard cut through our discussion. A dinghy crewed by two men or youths scudded by, off *Seaspray's* port bow, indifferent to our presence. No salvation there for Giorgy. His hopeful look faded.

'I'm waiting,' I said. 'But not for much longer.'

'He is providing a … a service for my principals.' His voice was a tremolo, his eyes averted from mine. Baker kept his counsel; he didn't relish a kneecap job either. 'My principals have taken a major share in de Bruin's business interests. They have much invested in him, so they will not be pleased if you … harm him. That is it. That is all I know.'

'This business of de Bruin's,' I mused aloud. 'Pornography – is that right?'

A dispirited nod.

'Porn barons are ten a cent. What's special about his set-up that makes it so attractive to your crowd?'

This time a shake.

'This I truly cannot tell you. It is for a specialized market.'

Specialized. De Bruin had used the same word.

I questioned him for another ten minutes. Around in circles we went, always to arrive back at our original starting point. Every route led to a wall of ignorance that couldn't be bulldozed down. I was tempted to make a demonstration – shoot off an ear lobe or the tip of a little finger. But it wouldn't have advanced my cause. As things were, he was just the right amount of scared. Physical damage might even have encouraged him to invent something.

As the sun dipped towards the west and its fire dimmed, and Baker grew grey from loss of blood, I had to conclude that the well of Giorgy's knowledge was dry. Such as it was, I had it all.

'If you want to dress his wound,' I said to Giorgy, 'you'll find a first aid kit in the saloon, above the seat.'

Playing Florence Nightingale wasn't his style, but he could hardly sit by and let Baker bleed to death. He stumbled off down the companionway while I went forward, gun in belt, to haul in the anchor.

I made for Rochelongue, a tiny hamlet of rundown vacation homes along the coast, where a natural jetty was formed by a finger of black rocks.

'André, *mon ami*,' Giorgy said, clutching my arm, as we edged up the rocks. 'I understand why you did what you did this afternoon. Because we are friends, I am willing to overlook it. But that is all I can do. I cannot protect you.' He pressed the envelope, now crumpled and splotched with damp, on me. 'Take this. Go to Brazil.'

'Can't be done, Giorgy. Thanks all the same.'

'That makes twice you have said "no", André.' His face twisted with genuine regret. 'You are gambling with loaded dice. Forget de Bruin. If you do not, you are finished.'

'Thanks for the advice.'

I had to man the wheel and throttle so as to keep station with the rocks, leaving Giorgy to make the transfer from deck to dry land all on his own. He managed it without mishap and helped the crudely bandaged Baker, now somewhat revived, thanks to liberal applications of First Aid cognac

'If you really want to make a contribution,' I called to Giorgy, 'keep de Bruin away from me. If I don't see him, I can't hurt him. Pass the word along, huh?'

'Forget him!' he shouted. 'Go to Brazil.'

'Stuff Brazil!' I waved and opened the throttle. *Seaspray* went astern, slipping away from the rocks.

My only true friend, was how Giorgy had described himself when we met in Marseilles. If that were true, I was now friendless.

On 26 August we sailed for home. The weather had cooled over the last few days, and the blue was now often blotted with cumulus. The wind was from the north-east, light, steady, benign.

26 August was also my fortieth birthday. A party was

improvised. Lizzy, working with the most basic of ingredients, baked a cake at sea. It was a sunken disaster, but the three of us scoffed it anyway. Forty years old. I supposed it would hit me sooner or later that I was now in the fast track to my fifth decade on earth. Maybe I ought to acquire some of the trappings, like slippers and a pipe. Lizzy thought the idea hilarious.

Alfredo asked to be put ashore at Barcelona on the second morning, to visit his daughter. Since weather conditions were set fair and Sitges less than three hours sailing from Barcelona, I agreed we could dispense with his services.

'I'm glad he's gone,' Lizzy said as we chugged out of the Estacion Maritima around mid-day, passing a towering container ship with more rust on her plates than paint.

'Alfredo? Don't you like him?'

'No, it's not that. He's a sweetie.' She was on her back on the cabin roof, adding another layer to her already magnificent tan. Wearing a striped bikini that was only just short of indecent. 'It's just that I prefer it when there's just you and me.'

Oh-oh, here we went again.

Sitting up and crossing her legs, she went on, 'I had a hateful dream last night: I dreamed Mummy was with us.'

'On the boat?'

'At the house.'

'What was so hateful? The waking up?'

'You mean like when you still think it's real?' She shook her head, making her pony tail wag.

'I wish it was that simple.' She rested her elbows on her knees and her chin in her hands. Her gaze was as direct as ever, probing my soul. I smiled back at her and the response was instant sunshine.

We were clear of the port and amongst a host of other small craft. I would wait until we had sea room before hoisting sail.

'Going to tell me about it?' I asked. She had fallen quiet and was prostrate again, face to the sun.

'It was hateful.' From where I sat the rise and fall of her breasts was discernible. 'You see, Mummy was at the house and ... and we were all together. It ought to have been marvellous ... perfect. I ought to have been happy.'

'But you weren't, I take it.'

'No.' Pause. She brushed a hand across her eyes. 'I didn't really want her to be there. I kept wishing she would go away. I even wished she was ... well, dead. How could I have wished a thing like that?'

'As you say, it was only a dream. It meant nothing. Forget it.'

Most of the other boats had dropped behind. It was time for some real sailing.

'Let's hoist some canvas,' I said briskly. 'Come on down and drive, will you, honey?'

'Okay.' She jumped up, wriggled her feet into a pair of flip-flops, and scrambled sure-footedly down into the cockpit.

I rotated the wheel until we were heading due north to the wind's nor'-east, and cut the throttle.

'Just hold her on that.'

'Aye-aye, skipper.'

The mainsail was only loosely stowed, and raising it was a simple matter of winching up the halyard and rigging the boom vang. The spread of canvas began to belly long before it was fully extended, stiffening into the shallow curve that makes for optimum performance.

'Hold her on that course!' I shouted to Lizzy as I started back to the cockpit, keeping to windward of the mainsail. Even in relatively mild conditions a sudden change in direction can whip the boom across and any object in its path will most likely be swept over the side.

I relieved Lizzy at the wheel and set about changing tacks, to bring us back on course. South-west, then west-south-west was our heading, running before the wind, the mainsail sheeted right out. Restful, carefree; sailing at its least demanding. I stood at the wheel, relishing the sting of sea spray on my bare chest and the music of the hull's surge through the water.

Lizzy, hugging her knees in the corner of the cockpit, said, 'Alan, we never talk about sex.'

No secrets. Remember? An easy pact to make, not so easy to keep.

'Should we?'

'Are you embarrassed to talk to me about it?'

'Should I be?'

She rolled over and balled up the towel she had been lying on. I easily avoided it.

'I hate you!' she yelled.

'Sure you do.' I grinned at her, and after a brief glare she responded in kind. 'Is there something in particular you want to know?'

'Sort of,' she said, her brow wrinkling. 'Not the technical stuff, fucking and all that, I had that all sussed years ago. No, I just wondered if, you know, you've got a regular girl friend.'

'Only a casual one,' I said, and made a small correction to our compass bearing. A patch of swell lifted us, and water broke over the bows, flinging spray back as far as the cockpit. Then, suddenly, it was calm again. A passing reminder that the sea is never at rest, never completely trustworthy.

'Do you ... you know, fuck with her?'

No double entendres for Lizzy. I couldn't help grinning.

'You're so subtle.'

'All right then, Mr Prissy, do you make love with her?'

'How does mind your own damn business sound? Do I ask about your sex life?'

She contorted her features into an exaggerated moue.

'*What* fucking sex life? Since we left Oz I've been living like a nun. Hadn't you noticed?'

I just nodded warily, wondering where this catechism was taking us.

'Alan ...' Now she was hesitant, almost diffident. I braced myself mentally for some highly intimate probing. 'What would you say if I was to go ...' She was up on her feet. A wriggle of arms, a flexing of shoulders, and a scrap of black and white flew across the cockpit, 'topless!'

And topless she was. Creamy breasts with jutting nipples, in flagrant and exciting contrast to the rest of her bronzed body. Nor was she bashful. She pirouetted for me, a slender, shapely Venus, and lit a fuse of passion inside me.

The uneven pounding of my heart throbbed inside my head. My throat contracted. I couldn't speak.

She interpreted my loss of voice as disapproval.

'Cat got your bloody tongue?' she said crossly, hands on hips, and her pout, like the rest of her, was in the young Bardot class.

'Lizzy ...'

She adopted a suggestive stance, cocking a hip at me, the pout metamorphosing into parted lips and a teasing tongue. She was into all the tricks.

I cleared my throat and with it my vocal chords.

'Cover yourself up,' I said thickly.

She went very still, hand still on thrusting hip. '*What* did you say?'

'I said cover yourself up!' Even as I spoke I was conscious of over-reaction. 'And don't ever do that again.'

She slowly unfroze from her come-hither pose.

'You can go and fuck yourself, you fucking faggot!' she

seethed, and turned and stomped off towards the companion-way, collecting the discarded bikini top en route. That was the last I saw of her until we docked in Sitges harbour.

Twenty-Two

More disconcerted than ever by Lizzy's undermining of my defences, I set out to prove to myself that I wasn't really besotted by a schoolgirl. In the week following our return home I all but abandoned her for an extravaganza of debauchery in the arms of complaisant, undemanding, always-available Simone, who wasn't much older than a schoolgirl herself. Seven nights in a row I descended upon my accommodating Grenobloise. Daytimes too, when she was free. She accepted this new "up" in our up and down affair readily enough, though she wasn't entirely lacking in curiosity.

'Is it true you have a girl living with you?' she asked, after an energetic session that left me feeling all of those forty years.

'Yes. But not the way you mean it.'

Her chuckle was sardonic. She stubbed out her after-sex Gauloise, and discharged a twin plume of smoke at me through her nostrils.

'My dearest André,' she murmured, 'it is *exactly* the way I mean it.'

Trust a French girl to put a sexual slant on any relationship, whether or not it existed.

Unsurprisingly, Lizzy, who had been slow to recover her natural bounce after her humiliation on *Seaspray*, did not take kindly to my frequent and sometimes lengthy absences.

I managed to avoid any dissension though, until the Monday of what was supposed to be her last full week in Andorra before the start of the new school term.

I had spent the afternoon and evening with Simone, demonstrating to both of us how I could get by without Lizzy. After our second stint she began to menstruate and immediately, as was the norm with her, went right off sex. Consequently I had returned home early in the evening, slightly the worse for fornication and much the worse for drink.

Señora Sist was still there, working overtime. She made no bones about her disapproval.

'It is not right that you are away so much,' she remonstrated. 'And everybody knows you are seeing *that* girl.'

Thanks to me, Simone had gained a certain notoriety of late.

'What girl?' I said dully, my intake of vodka insulating me against all censure.

She went off home in a huff.

I fixed another hefty slug of my favourite painkiller, selected a Brahms album on the iPod, and stretched out on the couch. Under the combined influence of music and dissolution I drifted away to a dark and peaceful place.

When I awakened all was quiet. No lilting Brahms, just wind, butting at the corner of the house. The carriage clock told me it was eleven thirty-five. I felt shagged-out. Decrepit.

I became conscious of the smell of perfume. Prodigious though the effort required, I flopped my legs off the edge of the couch and rearranged the other parts of me into a semblance of sitting upright. My left arm felt dead. I massaged it, and looked straight into the troubled eyes of Lizzy. My focus was blurred: her features didn't look right.

'How long have you been here?' I slurred, backhanding a thread of drool from my chin.

'I want to ask you something.'

My vision was steadily clearing. She was kneeling at my feet and had on the garish blue and red night shirt.

'Have you been out screwing again?' she flared.

My brain was too woozy to concoct a story.

'What if I have?'

If I had learned anything at all about Lizzy in the two months or so I had known her, it was that she could not be fobbed off with equivocation. A direct question deserved a direct answer and no messing about. That was her ethos and it was not for compromising.

'I reckon I could fuck better.'

I blinked and my vision unglazed a little. That was when I realized what looked wrong about her: she was wearing make-up. Not just the usual touch here and there but great dollops of it – eyes in black pools, mouth red as fresh-spilled blood, cheeks plastered with foundation, over-emphasizing the bone structure to create an almost skull-like effect. It was a whore's mask.

While I was taking this in, a slow process, given my condition, she got up quickly. In a single flowing movement, practiced as any nightclub stripper, she pulled the nightdress over her head and cast it aside. It was a re-enactment of her performance on the boat. Underneath she had on matching cotton briefs and that was all. Her eyes on my face, she dug her thumbs in the waistband and down went the briefs over her thighs, over her knees, to her ankles, forcing her to crouch awkwardly. Then she straightened and stepped out of them, proud in her nakedness.

'What are you doing?' I said, my voice seeming to come from the bottom of a deep shaft.

'Don't you like my body?'

It was a delightful body. The golden brown of her skin was

made glossy by the artificial lighting, and her legs were long and smooth and svelte. I ached to reach for her and accept what she was offering. After all, I was human, I was male. Only the foreknowledge of the shame that would come after, as surely as winter follows summer, prevented me. I reminded myself, as I had done so often these past weeks, that she was sixteen years old, and only just that. A child, albeit with very much a woman's body. Not only that, she was in my care. In my safe-keeping.

'Don't you like my body?' she repeated, resentful now. 'Isn't it up to the standard of your precious ... *Simone?*' She spat the name as if it were a fly that had got in her mouth.

Simone was one secret I hadn't planned to let her in on.

'Lizzy ... honey, this isn't right. You know it, we both know it. Your mother ... She and
I ...'

'Who's to know except you and me?' The tone was shrill, unnatural, like the fire that blazed in her eyes.

'That's just it. *I'll* know! And it's me who'll have to live with my conscience, not you.'

I was trying. As God – if he exists – was my witness, I was trying. Then Lizzy, done with talking, took the initiative. She seized my hand and clamped it to her breast, to that soft, tender badge of her womanhood. Her nipple was hard as a pebble against my palm. Her breath was a blowtorch on my face, her open mouth on mine, smothering my protests.

'Love me,' she moaned, between clumsy, intense kisses. 'Love me, *fuck* me!'

'No, bugger it!' I thrust her away, more roughly than I intended. She rolled off my knees and hit the floor on her back with a crash and a squeal.

While she was sorting herself out I staggered away from the couch and made for the nearest door. Through the kitchen

I lurched, out into the warm night, heading noplace, anyplace, just away from her and the road to moral doom that she stood for.

Another storm broke that night. A crashing finale to the five month drought. Winds lashed, rain descended in a solid mass, thunder and lightning provided the usual special effects. Wilder, more turbulent than the storm that raged inside me. Incomparably less devastating.

It drove me back inside in the small hours, to warily re-enter the living room. My trepidation proved groundless. Lizzy still occupied the couch, was still naked, only now she was aslumber, her painted mouth slightly open, adding to her air of vulnerability. Scribbles of mascara ran from her lower eyelids over her cheeks.

Sick at heart, I scooped her up into my arms. She was no lightweight. The curtain of her hair swung loose, tinted golden by the yellow lighting, its form as ever-changing as waves in a stormy sea. She spoke my name sleepily and snuggled up to me, almost purring. My fingertips beneath her armpit sank into the edge of her breast; her flesh was cool. The wanting returned, stirring within me like a restless embryo. I stifled it, teeth clenched, eyes fixed straight ahead. She was a child, only a child.

I mounted the stairs, carried her into her room, detouring around strewn garments. When I laid her gently on the bed, she half awoke.

'Alan,' she murmured, eyes still closed, clutching at my arm. 'Don't leave me.'

I drew the duvet over her. I kissed her forehead, bringing a ghost of a smile to her painted lips.

And walked out.

Next morning the rain was pelting down as solidly as ever. Lizzy was booked for a French lesson in La Massana and would normally have cycled there. Since her sighting of de Bruin I was unhappy for her to travel anyplace unescorted. The rain was a convenient excuse for me to take her in the car without appearing over-protective.

In La Massana the deluge had turned roads into rivers, fortunately still fordable. Having dropped Lizzy a hop and a skip from the door of her tutor's apartment house, I sat out my vigil in the bar of the Gran Hotel Font opposite, wiping the condensation from the window every once in a while. Neither de Bruin nor any of his known henchmen passed by. Nor the Gravedigger couple. If it hadn't been for Giorgy advising me to let de Bruin alone, half-confirming that Lizzy was his target, I would have been inclined to write off her encounter with the Dutchman as a case of mistaken identity.

My doubts I kept to myself as I drove Lizzy back up the hill. In fact I didn't have much to say at all that morning and neither did she. We were both uncomfortable over the events of last night. So much so that, after a wolfed lunch, I escaped to Lucien's in search of less emotive company.

Madeleine was out and Lucien was glad of an opportunity to discourse on his favourite subject – politics. We talked about climate change, the current state of the world's economy, ISIS and other Muslim issues, and the rest. Once again I went home with a gutful of alcohol, and spent the evening slumped in front of the box. On my own.

About once a month I would go bargain-hunting in Andorra-la-Vella, to prowl the back street bazaars and rummage through bric-à-brac, hoping to come across some dusty *objet d'art*. My success rate was dismal, but it was an amusing pastime, not to mention a form of education.

This particular expedition, which took place on a Thursday morning, I was bent over a trestle table outside one of my regular haunts, extricating from the junk a pair of tongs that might have done duty in some Inquisition torture chamber, when a passing elbow jostled me.

'*Pardon.*' The accent was guttural, Nordic. I responded with an automatic '*Je vous en prie,*' dismissing the incident. The next moment my hand was grasped and pumped, and I was facing the Dutchman who had dropped in at my house, unasked, with his wife. The Gravedigger couple.

'Ah, it is you,' he said, full of bonhomie. 'So nice to see you again, er ... Alan.'

'You too ... er ...'

'You have forgotten.' A gush of forgiving laughter. 'No matter. Pim Gravemaker.'

With the Dutchman was a short, scrawny man, pasty of complexion, wearing a T-shirt several sizes too large and a pair of patched, faded jeans. I had seen him hanging around the Bar Raco de Valls, gathering place of the town's ne'er-do-wells.

Gravemaker introduced him. 'This is Miguel. He works for the *immobilier* who has been helping us find a house.'

It would have been impolite to call him a liar, so I settled for unspoken incredulity. Even in easy-going Andorra, estate agents' assistants don't look and dress like hobos. Much of Miguel's face was hidden behind octagonal sun-glasses. The mouth, however, split into a friendly enough grin.

Gravemaker made a show of peering around me. 'And where is your young companion today?'

The answer 'at home' was stillborn on my tongue. Irrationally maybe, I still entertained suspicions about this man. The Dutch connection and all that. So instead, I said airily, 'Oh, shopping someplace. And your wife?'

'The same. Look ... we are renting a house, not far from yours; why not visit us?'

'Sure.'

'Tomorrow? You will come tomorrow?'

I stalled. 'Give me a call in a few days.' Only when Lizzy was despatched to Paris would I feel safe to socialize again.

'Give me your number. I will telephone you on Saturday.'

'*Messieurs.*' The store owner had come to hover in search of a sale. '*Vous désirez quelque-chose?*'

I was still in possession of the tongs. I unloaded them on him and said, 'Not today, thanks,' and left him grinning hopefully and ingratiatingly at Gravemaker.

Lucien, presumably with the purest of motives, had sent his nephew round to meet Lizzy. Jean-Phillipe was a dark good-looking youngster and cocky as a rooster. He had arrived the previous evening with his parents, Lucien's sister and her husband.

Lizzy's encounter with Jean-Phillipe was instructive. Hunting for a pair of swimming shorts in the dressing room, I overheard a snatch of conversation between them as they sunbathed by the pool. He was hitting on her and giving a decent account of himself. Most girls would have been impressed. Not Lizzy. Her brush-off was a tart 'Come and see me when you're grown up.'

This cameo brought home to me the reality of Lizzy's extreme youth. With her looks, boys would line up for her favours. Jean-Phillipe was only blazing a trail that many more were destined to tread. All of them young, which was as it should be. What depressed me as I eavesdropped, was my shame in even mildly resenting the boy as a rival, as if Lizzy were my prospective lover. Part of me was increasingly out of control, running downhill, no steering, no brakes. And lying just ahead was a hairpin bend and a vertical plunge to certain oblivion.

Gravemaker didn't ring on Saturday because I hadn't provided him with a number. That was the good news. The bad news was that he and his wife called in person. When, around dusk, the beat-up green Seat bumbled into the driveway, trawling the perennial blue smoke, I was retreating indoors for the night. With the advent of September the evenings up here above the thousand meter line were beginning to chill. Upstairs, rock music was churning.

Yellow headlights swung across the terrace, and I hoisted a welcoming rictus and a nominal salutation. Be the Gravemakers friends or foes, harmless or malevolent, I wasn't ready to antagonize them. Playing the innocent was a game at which I had more practice than most.

The Python was in its usual place in my bedroom. While the Gravemakers parked below the terrace I raced upstairs, startling Lizzy who was proceeding in the opposite direction, still wriggling into the top half of her track suit. Her hair was damp and she smelled of shampoo.

'Hey!' she squealed as I charged past. 'We've got visitors.'

'Go and let them in then,' I snapped, without turning or slackening my pace. 'I'll only be a minute.'

'Why not use the downstairs john?'

There being nowhere to secrete a gun the size of the Python about my person, I had hoped to slip it behind a cushion in the living room, where we would entertain our visitors. The Gravemakers were too quick for me though. As I hit the foot of the stairs Mrs G's coo of rapture reached me through the open door of the living room: 'Oh, what a lovely room! So much wood– and that *cheminée*! I do love French *cheminées*.'

A dresser, a massive oak structure with an oval mirror and many drawers, stood in the hallway. Into a drawer went the Python. If I needed it in a hurry ... Well, I just hoped I wouldn't need it in a hurry.

'Hello there!' I bounced into the room, bursting with phoney goodwill.

'W-we came to invite you to our party,' Gravemaker said, blinking furiously, as if afraid I was about to fall on him in fury. 'I hope it is not inconvenient.'

'Not at all, not at all,' I blathered. 'Do sit down. A drink perhaps. Lizzy get some ice, will you? Mrs Gravemaker, what's your poison?'

She reared back. '*Poison*?'

'Ha, ha!' Gravemaker nudged her teasingly. 'It is an English joke. It means what do you like to drink.'

No hardware on him, I was relieved to note: lightweight slacks free of bulges, close-fitting grey sweatshirt, the only bulge being his tummy. Likewise his wife, as far as I could tell without a strip search. She had on a flared pinkish dress with tight bodice. She wasn't even toting a purse.

Drinks were distributed, and as dusk slid into twilight and lights sparkled down in La Massana, I sank into an armchair nursing a king-size vodka.

We were barely settled when Mrs G leapt up, almost spilling her Cinzano Rosso, and asked if she might use the ... er ... er.

'Out the way you came, turn right, then first left.'

'Oh.' Confusion. 'Perhaps Lizzy ...'

'Lizzy, take Mrs Gravemaker to the er-er, will you?'

Lizzy stifled a giggle. 'Okay.' Her smile was wide and natural. I was to remember it.

'I wonder if I might trouble you for a little more soda,' Gravemaker said as Lizzy conducted his wife from the room.

'No trouble.' I set my glass down, relieved him of his, and transported it to the bar in the far corner for a two-second squirt. It was now ninety-percent soda, but that was his business not mine.

When I turned he was by the patio doors, looking out onto the illuminated terrace. The wind had risen with the fall of night and was soughing through the archway around the side of the house, ruffling the surface of the swimming pool.

Gravemaker blew his nose and thanked me for his debilitated drink.

'Cheers.' He drank in nervous gulps and nodded his approval. 'Much better, thank you.'

I smiled politely and further insulated myself with vodka. Lizzy returned with Mrs G. They seemed to be getting on well together.

'Lizzy was showing me your salon,' Mrs G bubbled, fingers fluttering around the locket that hung from her neck. 'The furniture looks antique.'

'It is.' I was rather proud of the dining room with its Louis XIV decor. 'You should see my insurance premiums.'

'Please?' My humour was incomprehensible to her.

So I explained, which made for some dutiful mirth, then moved on to other equally trite and uninteresting topics.

Whether on account of the drink or the company, I was beginning to feel distinctly light-headed. While I was puzzling over this the door-bell rang. Which was odd because I hadn't noticed any vehicle lights and it was impossible to enter the drive unseen from this room at night. That alone should have alerted me; in fact, it did but only belatedly, after Lizzy had rushed off to answer the door.

'Wait!' I shouted, out of a vague sense that something was out of kilter. But already a voice reached me from the hall: 'Good evening, miss.'

Lizzy's exclamation of surprise was instantly converted into a cry of pain. It galvanized me into movement. The exact nature of the danger was as yet ill-defined, shapeless like figures in a fog. Yet danger there was, and the thrill drove me to toss my drink, glass included, into Gravemaker's face, before rushing from the room. Weaponless and, for all my forebodings and my mental vigilance and my preparations, caught as wrong-footed as could be.

My callers were two in number and male in sex. The one was blond and muscular, only too well remembered as Rik de Bruin's right-hand lackey in Tangier, name of Christiaan. His companion was a new acquaintance: smaller, wirier, and all in denim.

Christiaan had an arm lock on Lizzy. She was squirming feebly. His grip didn't allow for much free-play, and her tae-kwon-do skills were no use unless she could break free. Denim Suit had eyes only for me, and I only for the thing he was pointing at me, at gut level. This particular thing consisted partly of a silencer tube, accounting for a good half of the total length. The curved magazine suggested automatic fire capability.

'Let her go,' I snarled at Christiaan. I was mad but not mad enough to argue with the gun. Christiaan just snickered. Gravemaker joined us, dabbing vodka from his eyes. Denim Suit tossed him a small automatic.

'Tell him to let her go,' I pleaded with Gravemaker, judging him to be the senior member of the group. A backhander across the mouth was all my grovelling earned me. I licked blood from a split lip.

'What's happening, Alan?' Lizzy quavered, wide-eyed.

'Nothing to be frightened about, little lady.' The speaker was a fourth man, stepping over the threshold. Christiaan and Denim Suit moved deferentially aside for him.

Fleshy lips contorted in a jeering grin, staring eyes, crinkling at the corners in his triumph; the persona of menace that sat astride his shoulders like a Horseman of the Apocalypse. It came as no surprise to see here on my doorstep the pitted features of Rik de Bruin.

Twenty-Three

'Whatever it is you want,' I said to de Bruin, 'just don't hurt her.'

Appeals to better nature would be wasted on these people, about that I had no illusions. Still, rather a wasted entreaty than none at all.

'Let us sit down and behave like civilized people,' de Bruin proposed, at which Christiaan and Mrs Gravemaker hauled a swearing, struggling Lizzy off upstairs.

So we sat in the living room while bumps and crashes resounded overhead. Something breakable smashed. The cessation of noise when it did eventually come was abrupt. Ominously.

If only I could think straight. But now that I was seated again the earlier giddiness had returned, was worse if anything.

'No harm will come to your little lady,' de Bruin reassured me. He sat directly beneath the floor lamp so that the light threw a shadow across the upper part of his face. 'Save your concern for yourself.'

The threat that lay behind that piece of advice made no impact on my fogged brain.

'Are you going to explain?' I said thickly. 'Or do I have to guess?'

'You can please yourself. As far as I am concerned ...' he gave a baying laugh, '... you can remain in ignorance.'

'What did you do with Clair Power?' I demanded.

De Bruin's stare was blank.

'Is she alive?' I said.

'Is who alive?'

It was becoming an effort to speak. My tongue felt swollen, a fat sausage filling my mouth.

'What are you doing to the girl?' I mumbled. Voices reached me faintly from upstairs. Whatever had been done to Lizzy, to subdue her, was not sweet-talk. And this was the girl I had sworn to protect ...

'Questions, questions. Soon you will have no need to ask questions ... Warner. That is your real name, is it not? André Warner?'

Answering was not worth the effort it would take.

He eyed me pensively. 'Do you feel a little tired, by any chance?'

Denim Suit cackled and waggled the silenced gun at me.

'Do you know what a barbiturate is, Mr Warner?' Gravemaker said.

'Barbit ... bart ...' I gave up.

'Barbiturates,' Gravemaker repeated softly. 'Nembutal. Goofballs.'

Drugs? They had *drugged* me?

'In your drink,' Gravemaker confirmed. I didn't remember asking him. 'Virtually tasteless.'

If I still had control of my facial muscles I would have laughed. People only put drugs in drinks in Agatha Christie whodunits. But what was happening to me was no fiction.

De Bruin's image was fuzzy, like an image viewed through frosted glass. I squeezed my eyelids tightly together but when I opened them it was no clearer. The light hurt, making me squint.

'You ... shits,' I croaked.

'That's it.' De Bruin again. 'Call us bad names. You will feel better. But hurry ...' Through a haze I saw him check his watch, 'your time will soon be up.'

Denim Suit cackled again, a sound that was chilling in its mindlessness.

Upstairs a gun went off.

Once, twice, three times the shots crashed through the house. Everyone froze. I was the first to thaw. The effort required was gargantuan but, fear for Lizzy temporarily shredding the fog, I leapt out of the chair and ran, or rather reeled, towards the door. Ahead of de Bruin and the rest by seconds only. I didn't expect to reach the door without taking a bullet or two. But for whatever reason de Bruin wanted me not merely alive but unharmed; his 'Don't shoot!' command had a panicky ring.

The stairs loomed ahead, stretching upwards to infinity, swaying as in an earthquake. Or maybe the stairs were static and all the swaying was me. Somehow I forced my legs up the steps and, as I reached the top, Christiaan staggered out of Lizzy's room, clutching at his face. He moaned gibberish. I chopped him on the side of his bull neck and almost broke my wrist. It was enough to topple him though, and in toppling his hands spread to break his fall, exposing a face pitted with dozens of tiny holes, oozing scarlet.

Of course – the shotgun-pistol.

Happily for me, Christiaan's fall had projected him down the stairs to collide with Gravemaker who had been within grabbing range behind me. I didn't linger to watch the show but the sound effects were satisfyingly cataclysmic. Hope rekindled, I lurched into Lizzy's room. Vaguely aware of feet pounding the stairs anew. Lock the door, must ... lock ... the ... door.

Thankfully the key was in the lock. I kicked the door shut, turned the key with stiff, bloated fingers. It was a solid door but it wouldn't stand up to a sub-machine gun. Although I didn't know it then they were as anxious to avoid making bullet holes in the house as they were in me. The guns were mostly dressing.

My fading vision took in the scene inside the room. Lizzy was on her back on the bed, the Gravemaker woman astride her, striving for possession of the gun that Lizzy held in a grip so tight that the tendon on the inside of her wrist stood out like a length of rope. In the passage outside, a foot thudded against the door. Move, Warner, *move*, you lazy bastard!

The signals were getting through to my extremities clearly enough, only the motive power was lacking. It was as if I were wearing weighted boots. Then Lizzy let rip a yell for help that sucked me forward like a sluice pump. I grabbed Mrs G by the shoulder. She wriggled free without much effort and dove into the space between bed and wall. Lizzy, pistol flailing, lunged after her. I caught her ankle and, expending most of what little strength remained to me, dragged her back onto the bed.

'Not now!' I mumbled, my mouth full of tongue. I prized her fingers from the gun, which I then used to crack the skull of the cringing woman on the floor. Effective, if a little ungallant. The gun slipped from my fingers. I lost track of it, which was a shame.

Lizzy clutched at my shirt front. 'What do they want? They ... they've given me an injection. Do you think I'm going to die?'

'Injection?' I couldn't make any sense of it. 'Got ... got get 'way.' As if to instil in me a little urgency, the door creaked under another assault. On the other side voices were raised in dispute. Again the door shuddered.

'Must escape,' somebody said. Me, I think.

Lizzy's face crumpled. 'They've done something to you as well, haven't they?' She looked around. 'The window ... it's not far to the ground. We can jump.'

I nodded and my head felt as if it was about to fall off.

'Jump,' I agreed, without understanding.

Lizzy flung the double window wide open. Cool night air eddied in, reviving me a shade. Enough, with Lizzy shoving and pulling, to home me in on that gateway to salvation.

'You first,' I wheezed.

'No, you.'

Wood was splintering someplace close by. I didn't argue. I couldn't remember the words anyhow.

How we made the transition from window to ground will forever remain a closed cell in my memory. I have a muzzy recollection of clinging to the sill by my fingertips, and of my body jarring and my neck snapping back, and of cool grass tickling my nostrils. The sound, remote now, of the bedroom door giving way coincided with Lizzy landing beside me, light-footed as a cat.

A yell in Dutch told me they were only a jump behind us.

'Come on!' Lizzy dragged me off my stomach, and together we plunged down the slope, skirting the terrace with its bright lights.

Shouts from behind. Still no bullets flew. They weren't needed. Any minute now I was likely to come to a standstill of my own accord. I tripped on a tuft of grass, taking Lizzy down with me. It wasn't a heavy fall. I was just glad to lie down.

Lizzy crawled over to me. 'Rattle your dags, Alan, it's not bedtime yet.'

With only minimal contribution from me, she had me up and moving. It was a mystery where she found the strength.

Then we were standing before the garage. Well, Lizzy was. I slithered to the ground, a useless deadweight.

'We must take the car.' The voice came from miles away. Something stung my cheek. It could have been a slap. I was too tired to care. Another slap. And quite a few more. I growled, some of the cotton wool wiping from my brain.

'Alan, get up! They're coming.' Slap-slap-slap. 'You must get up ... the car.' Slap-slap.

'The car? What about it? I raised an arm to ward off the blows that were loosening my teeth in their sockets. The murk shredded, and Lizzy's sweet face leapt into view, every line, every contour sharp-etched. I blocked a slap on its way in. 'All right, all right, you can quit the rough stuff.'

Partially revived, I pushed her aside and tottered to the garage door. Normally this was opened remotely but the remote control was presently on a shelf in the living room. Fortunately it had a manual back-up in the shape of a combination lock.

'Is the key gadget in the car?' Lizzy asked, clinging to me while I spun the dial.

It wasn't, which meant using the spare clamped to the chassis in a magnetic box. Explaining all that to Lizzy was beyond my present powers of speech, so I settled for an affirmative grunt.

The lock tumblers tumbled sweetly. The up-and-over door clattered up on unoiled rollers and simultaneously the night was bisected by a flashlight beam above. A hushed call followed. Rubber soles padded across the terrace. The beam was criss-crossed by another, like searchlights seeking enemy bombers.

Inside the black cavern of the garage I stumbled and fell against the runabout, a Peugeot 205 I had inherited from the previous owner of the house as part of the deal.

'Switch the lights on,' I said unthinkingly to Lizzy.

'What! They'll know we're here!'

'Oh, yeah ... yeah.' I pushed her towards the Aston, followed unsteadily and went down on my knees beside the driver's door to grope under the bodywork.

'Stop wasting time!' Lizzy, uncomprehending, hissed.

'Key here,' I muttered. My flash of lucidity was on the wane. My fingertips felt numb, incapable of distinguishing metal from plastic.

Running feet, the crunch of gravel. Any moment now they would be on us. I barked knuckles on bolt heads, gouged skin on a flap of metal. Part of the chassis shifted, a ghost of movement – there it was! I dragged the little magnetic box free of the frame to which it was attached. I plucked the key fob from the box, almost dropping it. More vital seconds were lost while I clambered into the driving seat, every action awkward and robotic, my limbs unresponsive. Torchlight found us, flooding the rear window.

A yell, summoning reinforcements. I recognized Gravemaker's voice. Divine forces must have taken charge from then on because I sure as hell had no hand in it. No need to insert the key fob with this car. The engine fired at a touch. The forces even selected reverse for me and switched on the lights.

'Look out!' Lizzy's warning tugged my head round.

Gravemaker was beside my door, pistol thrust forward, mouthing in Dutch. He didn't scare me. I was invincible. I thumbed the internal door lock pad even as he wrenched at the handle. He kicked the door. My insurers wouldn't like that, I thought crossly.

Handbrake off. Thank you, divine forces. Clutch out, accelerator down. Backwards we went on squealing tyres with a thrust that tumbled Lizzy against the dash, which fortunately on the DBS is passenger friendly.

A human figure was briefly illuminated in the back-up lights. It leapt sideways, but not quickly enough. A glancing blow that didn't slow us by a single mile per hour, and all behind was wide open spaces. I braked savagely, spinning the rear wheels so that gravel sprayed against the inside of the wheel arches like buckshot. I shifted from Reverse into Drive. The divine forces fumbled it, going into Park instead. Lizzy was back in her seat now and belting up, none the worse for her mishap. Still no shots. Noise was out. Noise meant neighbours phoning for the police. For now, I guessed they would rather let us escape than shoot. We took off, rear wheels spinning, tail wagging. Down the drive we tore, slipstreaming gravel. Round the tight left-hander, then a straight run to the drive entrance, slowing for the road out of habit. Which way? I couldn't even make that simple choice.

'Go *on*.' Lizzy urged. I was squandering our lead, and she at least grasped that. Behind, yellow headlights stabbed in the night. 'They're coming, they're coming!'

I turned left, up the *pista forestal*, thinking to make for Lucien's house. By pursuing me there, de Bruin would throw away the anonymity he had so far preserved. Then I had second thoughts, which proved I was still capable of thought. I couldn't inflict this gang of thugs on my friends. So when the fork came up I continued on, down the narrow, snaking road into La Massana. Had my cerebral quotient been firing on all cells, I might have made for the local slammer, overcoming my natural aversion to crying on the shoulders of the police. But when the option did finally occur to me, the police station receding in the rear view mirror.

The main street of La Massana runs along the side of the town, more like a by-pass, enabling us to blast through at some grossly illegal speed. At the junction where the N3 bears away to the right I carried straight on, taking the Ents road. No specific destination in view, no ultimate sanctuary. Just keeping the car on the road was challenge enough.

The adrenaline rushing about my bloodstream had so far kept me from complete collapse. Now, as we left La Massana behind, crossing the bridge over the River Valira, all I had to do was hang on to the wheel. Yet torpor was again stealing over me, attaching weights to my eyelids, and turning my limbs to lead and my brain to mush.

Driving conditions couldn't have been better: dry road, clear night, traffic negligible. The Aston stuck to the crumbling asphalt like a leech, the fat tyres never once losing traction. Ahead of us the xenon headlight beams cut a fleeing crescent through the darkness, now lighting up the occasional villa or cottage, now swinging across a snow marker post or crash barrier on some precarious bend. In the mirror, on bend-free stretches, the lights of another car twinkled.

'They're after us,' Lizzy piped, bouncing in her seat. She was as lively as I was enervated.

'Don't ... worry.' Speaking was a real effort. 'Never ... catch ... up.'

Never, that is, if I could only stay awake.

Now lights were coming at us from ahead, closing fast, flashing imperatively. I cursed, dazzled but couldn't find the dip switch stalk. The lights ripped past and left me blinded and fighting a wheel that had acquired a will of its own, tugging at my hands as we mounted the verge. I heaved the wheel over, too far – we swerved across the road, struck the opposite verge, which by happy chance kicked us squarely back into line.

And throughout it all not a peep from Lizzy. She was a spunky kid all right.

Now she reported, 'They're gaining!' She sounded more thrilled than scared.

That near-smash had cost us ground. It wouldn't have mattered if I wasn't drugged out of my mind. The Aston had oomph and to spare. But I was fast sliding into a warm, welcoming emptiness, my decline now gilded by hallucination. The climbing road was no longer firm but slipping and sliding, in perpetual motion, a fast flowing river with frothing rapids and rocks that lay treacherously just below the surface. A river that was pushing us back into the embrace of our pursuers. Go faster, go faster, urged an inner voice. My foot obediently squashed the accelerator to the floor. We took a bend at an impossible speed. Now even Lizzy was unable to suppress a squawk of alarm.

Faster still flowed the current, faster still I drove, the ascent steepening, the rapids becoming a cataract. On and up, in magical defiance of gravity, to the very top, cresting it ... Lights burst upon us. Tyres yelped, a horn blared in alarm. I braked harshly, provoking a rear wheel skid, corrected, over-corrected. We hit the nearside verge at an angle, mounted it on two wheels, flattened a line of fence posts. Out into the blackness beyond, engine racing as the Aston became airborne, revs going off the scale, lights washing the great empty bowl of the night sky.

Lizzy screamed, just once. Then came other noises: a crunching and rending apart of metal and a splintering of glass. Then ... nothing.

Twenty-Four

Awakening.

A darkened room. Bare, impersonal walls. The whirr of an electric motor. Not night: a bird was singing lustily outside an open window. A draught of air licked at me, cool and sweet, prickling every follicle of my scalp, calming my pattering pulse.

Elsewhere, heat and cold overlapped. From the neck down I was afire. Sweaty, yet shivering. Trembling, yet still.

Was this death?

The doctor was French, in his thirties and fast losing his sandy hair. He was also brutally efficient without the zombie professionalism of so many of his brethren. His last name was Henry, his first name never mentioned. Typical of his race in that respect.

'You are feeling better today. I can see it in your face.'

I conceded that much.

'Eating too, at last.' He glanced towards the cleared plates on the breakfast tray. 'I am encouraged.' He studied the graph clipped at the foot of the bed.

Earlier, I too had studied the graph and been none the wiser.

Three days had passed since my return to full sensibility. My faculties, mental and physical, were now on the trail back towards normal. Though still weak I was at least capable of putting two and two together. And even of occasionally making four.

Dr Henry parked his behind on the edge of my bed. His examination of pulse, temperature, blood pressure, visual and aural reflexes was swift yet far from cursory.

'Good, good, good,' he said, examination over.

'That's a relief. You can take the rest of the day off.'

Ironic English-style wit is usually wasted on French-style mentality. Dr Henry was no exception.

'No, no, I couldn't possibly. You are not my only patient, Mr Warner.'

'Now I'm disillusioned.' I threw in a grin to show I wasn't serious. 'Which brings me to a question, or, rather, a number of questions, if you can spare me five minutes of your time.'

'Questions are a form of therapy,' he said pompously.

That, I thought, rather depended on the answers.

'For starters, where am I?'

'Toulouse.' Surprise number one. 'Centre Hospitaliet de Purpan.' He said it with pride, as if it were his own creation.

'What happened to the young lady who was with me when the accident happened?'

He blinked worriedly. 'What young lady? For that matter, what accident?'

As likely as not he had been off-duty when I was admitted.

'My car ran off the road. A girl was with me at the time: her name is Elizabeth Power. Australian-American, sixteen years old. I'm her guardian.'

'I see.' He tapped his teeth with a fingernail. 'Go on.'

I elbowed myself up into a sitting position. 'What do you mean – "go on"?' My voice shot up. 'I crashed my car, and I want to know what happened to my passenger.'

'Be calm, *monsieur*,' he said, making soothing motions. 'I will try and explain. We know of no accident, nor of any car or companion. You were found at your house in Andorra by your, er … neighbour, Doctor Bos.' I stopped breathing. I couldn't believe what I was hearing. 'You were in a coma, unconscious, on your bed.'

'Coma? On my own bed?' I was yammering. 'I don't understand.'

Compassion lightened Henry's austere features.

'You must not let it trouble you. Everything will become clear in due course. You need rest, a lot of rest. An intravenous overdose of cocaine has a traumatic effect on the mind ...'

I grabbed a handful of crisp white lapel. 'Cocaine? What are you raving about? What cocaine?'

The bedside manner stayed unruffled.

'You don't remember. This also is perfectly normal.' He smiled reassurance, patted my shoulder. 'In such circumstances a slight memory loss is nothing to worry about.'

Loss of memory? Was it really that? I pressed my temples to stimulate rational thought. When at length I spoke again I was icy calm.

'I don't know much about cocaine, doctor, but would I be right in thinking it induces a feeling of exhilaration? Gives you energy?' He frowned at me. 'I mean, it doesn't make you feel sleepy, does it?'

'No. But you yourself must be aware of its effects.'

'Never mind that.'

My last memory, before I drove the Aston through a fence, was of drowsiness, of torpor. The opposite effect to that of coke.

'How long have I been here?' I said, changing tack.

Henry got off the bed and consulted the chart. 'Not quite a month.'

'A month!' Shocked, I looked at my wrist, to confirm the date from my watch. It was watchless. 'That's impossible. What's the date?'

When he told me, I still didn't believe him.

'Mr Warner,' he went on, 'you have been in a coma for most of that period. You are very fortunate indeed not to be dead. The dose you took would have killed most men your age, I can assure you.' His mouth tightened primly. 'It is likely that the police will wish to interview you. Not so much about the drug taking itself as about your ...' Here the primness gave way to out-and-out distaste, 'sources of supply.'

The police! Such visitors I could do without.

'Also Doctor Bos arrived in Toulouse last night. I took the liberty of telephoning him when you emerged from your coma. You have him to thank for your life, also for this private ward.'

I had wondered about that.

'I'll pay my own bills. Is Lucien – Doctor Bos – going to visit me?'

'He has expressed a wish to do so. You permit?'

'For sure.'

'Very well, *monsieur*.' His natural respect for a fee-paying patient had been restored. 'I am to contact him at his hotel. Meanwhile, I suggest you try and sleep.'

'You can't be serious. From what you tell me I've been asleep for a whole fucking month.'

The obscenity served only further to lower his opinion of me. Not just a junkie, but a foul-mouthed junkie.

'For that, if I may say so, Mr Warner, you have only yourself to blame.'

On which self-righteous note I was left to the joys of my private ward, to absorb Henry's revelations and to ponder the fate of Lizzy. This mental exercise kept me busy (but left me little wiser) until Lucien's familiar head popped around the door in the early afternoon. My pleasure at seeing him was intense, my handshake reflected it. For once though, he crushed my fingers rather than I his, such was my enfeebled condition.

'Where's Lizzy?' I shot at him while he was fetching a visitor's chair – a moulded plastic job, the kind they run off by the million for hospitals and doctors' waiting rooms. He sat, crossing his legs with exaggerated care.

'I was hoping,' he said, his tone guarded, 'that you were going to tell me.'

I groaned unreservedly at this confirmation of my fears.

'They say you arranged for me to be brought here. How so?'

'Your condition was very grave, my friend. The level of treatment you required was beyond the resources of the hospitals in Andorra. Toulouse is my home town. I believe I may have mentioned this.' He had but it was the sort of forgettable detail that never takes root. 'The Chief Administrator of this hospital is a friend of my brother. So – *voila!*'

'No complaints, Lucien. I'm alive and that's recommendation enough. But I don't understand what happened.' I leaned towards him and caught hold of his wrist. 'Tell me, before I go cuckoo.'

The pale sunlight streaming through the narrow window was not kind to him. It suddenly struck me that Lucien Bos was an old man. Like the poplar trees outside my window, their leaves tumbling more or less continuously with the coming of fall, he was visibly in decline. Crumbling slowly.

'Aren't you well?' I asked him, conscious of how much I owed him.

'It is nothing. A little trouble with the heart ...' He shrugged. 'Age comes like the night. It is inescapable.'

I was saddened. My own troubles faded into insignificance.

'You know how grateful I am for all you've done.'

His smile contradicted the melancholy in his eyes.

'I know.' He found a new position, exchanging legs crossed for legs outstretched. 'You ask what happened, but in truth there is little to tell. It was on the Sunday evening. Knowing Elizabeth was due to leave for Paris on Monday, Madeleine and I came to wish her *bon voyage* . . .'

He told a lengthy, laborious tale which I managed not to interrupt. He and Madeleine had found my house locked but not shuttered. Perhaps, they had debated, Lizzy had left a day early; perhaps I had driven her to the airport here in Toulouse. Odd she hadn't come to wish them goodbye. To assure themselves the house really was empty they had walked round to the kitchen door, which proved to be unlocked. They entered, and I owed my survival to their trespass. Their unease led them upstairs, ultimately into my bedroom. There I reposed, breathing but only just, in close proximity to a quantity of uncut cocaine. Also to hand were a hypodermic of the disposable variety, a length of cord for swelling the veins, and a sterilization kit (I was a *responsible* junkie).

I was rushed to the little hospital in Andorra-la-Vella for emergency resuscitation. When I failed to respond, I was transferred to Toulouse early on Monday morning.

To lie in a coma for a month while Lizzy ... While Lizzy what?

'No sign at all of Lizzy in the house?' I went through the motions of asking.

'No. Some of her clothing appeared to be missing.'

'Lucien,' I said, and fixed him with a gaze he couldn't avoid. 'I want you to know that I have never in my life injected myself with drugs. A few months ago I was dabbling a bit, you know the kind of thing. Grass, a couple of lines of coke now and again, but I quit when I got back from Morocco.' He hadn't looked away, which was a good sign. 'Do you believe me?'

'I must. Because if I do not ...' Here a wry grin pulled his face out of shape, 'it will mean I am a poorer judge of character than I thought I was. And I am much too vain to admit this.'

I sighed explosively and sank back into my pillow. I felt I had just crossed an Arnhem of a bridge.

'Something has been puzzling me though,' he said. 'Your car was found on the road to Ents, badly damaged. How do you explain this?'

That was confirmation that I wasn't completely off the wall.

'It's a long story, if you're sure you want to hear it.' When he nodded, I went on, 'It really starts in Tangier. You remember how Lizzy's mother was abducted there?'

'Certainly.' He produced a pack of cigars, then remembered where he was and put them away with an exaggerated sigh. '*Une affaire très bizarre.*'

'But no less true for that. You may also remember my mentioning a certain sleazeball, name of de Bruin ...'

Four days after Lucien's visit I took my first tottering steps, using a nurse as a willing prop. The extent of my debility shocked me.

Not for long. A daily two-hour stint in the superbly equipped gymnasium, and within a week I was as fit as ever. During this period I had ample opportunity for introspection. For assembling and reassembling the mosaic of events prior to my discovery by Lucien. I had to assume Lizzy had emerged unscathed from the accident. According to Lucien the police had found no traces of blood. The car had landed on all fours and been brought to a halt by a low stone wall. So much for the crash, of which I remembered only a lot of noise.

Entering the realm of pure speculation, de Bruin had arrived on the scene, removed Lizzy and me back to the house where, while still unconscious, I had been injected with a potentially fatal dose of cocaine. It would be surmised, as Lucien had surmised until I enlightened him otherwise, that I had overdosed myself. An occupational hazard with junkies, hardly rates a post mortem. As for Lizzy's disappearance, that would be shrugged off. With me gone, who would organize a search on her behalf? Señora Sist? Lucien and Madeleine? They might be concerned, even worried, but I couldn't see them going beyond making a statement to the police.

As with Clair, so with Lizzy. Carried off by the same Dutch scum, for God knows what slimy purpose.

And I had let him do it. I had much to answer for.

The bad dreams of old returned that night. Just like before, only now Lizzy was there alongside the Pavan girl. Both of them accusing. Contemptuous. Screaming hate.

I woke up in total darkness, slippery with sweat from head to toe, the virus of a new guilt poisoning my system. Only this time I had the means to purge it. And the intent.

My only other visitors during my convalescence were more concerned with my misdeeds than my health. Two French detectives – Lieutenant and Brigadier, the latter rank equivalent to Sergeant in the UK – civil yet persistent, borrowed the Administrator's office to interview me. The immunity afforded by my British passport and Andorran domicile carried little weight. When in France, French laws rule, and Andorra is in any case also subject to French legislation.

Unlike Lucien the cops did not unquestioningly accept my version of what had taken place, even though it was essentially factual. All that concerned them was the source of my drugs. They even proposed an amnesty.

'Tell us where you buy the stuff, *monsieur*, and we will not press charges.'

A classic *quid pro quo*. If only I could. They didn't call me a liar. Just composed their faces into tableaux of bored disbelief. Regarding my inability to reveal my sources as misplaced loyalty, not ignorance.

At a superficial level I was co-operative. The only major detail I withheld was de Bruin's identity, referring to him, as I had to Lucien, as 'a Dutchman called Hendriks'. I also altered his description so as to make him unrecognizable. Not because of any desire to obstruct the processes of law and order, even less because of any high-flown concepts of honour among thieves. In protecting Rik de Bruin I was serving my own interests. He had taken too much from me to be left to the slow-grinding wheels of justice. There had still remained room for doubt over his involvement in the abduction of Clair. In the case of Lizzy, no doubt at all. From now on, where Rik de Bruin was concerned *I* was now the law.

The morning of the day after my visit from the police, I discharged myself from the Centre Hospitaliet de Purpan. To much head-shaking and clucking by Henry.

'You should stay for at least another week,' he said dolefully.

Another week in this place and I would be a candidate for the nut foundry.

The account was presented and payment requested there and then. Foreign patients have a habit of vanishing without trace, I was tartly informed by the accounts clerk. I wrote a cheque for 24,000 Swiss Francs, drawn on the Schweitzerische Kreditanstaltbank, Zurich. Medical care in France comes dear. Funny, too, how readily they accepted my cheque with no more supporting documentation than my Swiss Driving License.

By taxi to Toulouse Matabiau Station, then by train to

Barcelona, a minor red herring for the police to nibble at. I would dismount at the tiny town of L'Hospitaliet-près l'Andorre and from there proceed by taxi to Pas de la Casa, the Andorran frontier town that welcomes more visitors than the Eiffel Tower, due to the principality's tax-free shopping. It was growing dark and drizzling steadily when I paid off the taxi at the edge of town. Wisps of mist straggled down the roadside ravine, and the nine thousand foot summit of the Cirque de Font Negre was cloaked in cloud. Dismal. Like my spirits.

My plan required that I conduct my business incognito. That I enter and exit Andorra before the local law got wind of it. Crossing the Franco-Andorran frontier is simplicity itself when you know the ropes. Anyplace out of sight of the frontier post will do. Total darkness further improves the prospects of making it without being pinched, that is if you don't mind falling down the odd crevice or plunging over a precipice. The lights of Pas de la Casa enable me to avoid the most dangerous pitfalls, but I still spent as much time on my knees as on my feet.

A little before ten I slunk into the Andorran side of town like the Man With No Name in a spaghetti western. Cold, wet, muddy, and exhausted. Forty-five minutes later, now warm, but still wet, muddy, and exhausted, I was climbing from a taxi a mile or so short of my house. The nefarious purpose of my visit necessitated a few precautions, like not giving my address to gabby taxi-drivers.

A cold shower later (the heating was off), revived and dressed in black cords and black leather coat, I was push-starting the Peugeot runabout. Fortunately it was all downhill from the garage door. Equally fortunately the battery, after months of inaction, had enough life left in it to send a spark to the plugs. The engine spun and caught, rattling like a can full of nails.

Andorra-la-Vella was quiet, the summer season long gone, the winter not yet arrived. The main thoroughfare, Avenida Princep Benlloch, slick with rain, no longer a bumper-to-bumper train of vehicles. Business as usual though, in the lighted cafés and restaurants, and beat music boomed from an amusement arcade.

The drizzle was becoming a deluge. A coach hissed past, throwing scythes of water from its fat wheels, late-season tourists jammed behind steamed-up windows. I came to the Café Raco de Valls, among the sleazier of the town's dives, and peered inside. Miguel was there all right, discoursing to a bored-looking bartender. A squat old man in a beret unstuck himself from the bar and shambled towards the door. I moved into shadow as the door opened to spill yellow light on the sidewalk. Gauloise fumes eddied past me.

'*Sale temps!*' Dirty weather. Oblivious of me, the old man tugged his beret down to his ears before stepping out from under the recess and splashing across the road. I shifted my position to avoid a persistent drip that had discovered the delights of my neck. I wondered if this was the same Andorra I had involuntarily left six weeks ago.

The door opened again to drunken laughter and farewells, and more customers jostled past. Miguel wasn't among them. They had no sooner dispersed into the murk when two more boozers floated out, belching in chorus. The taller of the duo reeled away across the road. The other stood swaying on the edge of the curtain of rain.

'*Salut*, Miguel,' I said, close to his ear.

The swarthy features of Gravemaker's sometime acquaintance, slack with drink, registered only puzzlement. I flourished a fifty euro note. His dark moist eyes caressed it.

'For information,' I said. 'Let's go where we can talk in private.'

Then recognition crowded out money-hunger. He took a pace backwards.

'It is you ... the Englishman.'

My hand made a bracelet around his bicep; he was so skinny my fingertips almost met.

'Come on, Miguel, don't make it difficult.'

He offered no resistance. As if mesmerized, he let me bundle him up the hill, away from the downtown area. The rain by now was intense. It streamed from my hair, over my face, and dribbled down inside my shirt. Two soakings in the same evening. Miguel was worse off, being dressed only in a coarse-knit jersey plus the much-mended jeans. He began to whine.

Only when I thrust him down a narrow space between the windowless walls of two old houses did he make a serious effort to escape, twisting free of my grip and dashing towards the street. I caught him by his sodden jersey, pulled him up with a jerk, and swung him hard against the rough stone wall. Head and masonry connected with a crack that wrung a squeal from his lips. For a few horrible moments I thought his skull must be fractured. But, no, he stayed upright, cringing, clutching his bruised temple. The soft radiance of the street lamp opposite reflected the fear in his eyes. I pinned him against the wall, my knee in his groin.

'Where did they take the girl?' I demanded.

He whimpered. I ground my knee in his crotch, slammed a fist in his ribs. He screeched and would have doubled up had I not held him hard against the stonework. His feet drummed.

'*Where?*' I snarled.

'Holland,' he groaned. 'They go to Holland.'

'Where in Holland?'

A headshake, ignorance or defiance, it was hard to say. I

belted him in the ribs, again and again, but he only screeched and pleaded for mercy. Bones bent, fractured, and still I hit him. When he sagged, became a dead weight, I supported him. He scrabbled at me, coughed weakly; a dark bauble dribbled from his lip.

'*Where* in Holland?' I raged, shaking him so hard his teeth chattered.

But he was beyond speech, and as reason disintegrated into unreason I clubbed him about head and body, smashing him to the ground. There he slumped, a sodden, pulped mass, jaw slack, drooling, a black thread linking mouth to jaw. Unrecognizable.

Spent, panting, frustrated, I stood back and massaged knuckles that were on fire. A guy like Miguel doesn't soak up that much punishment if he has the means of ending it. He truly hadn't known.

'You little shit.' I kicked him, very deliberately, in the head, and watched without emotion as he rolled over into a puddle. Maybe dead, maybe not.

I couldn't have cared less.

Twenty-Five

Egmond aan Zee. In the north of the Netherlands, just another coastal community, white beaches, grassy dunes, an outlook across the grey North Sea towards England. A flat, bleak, seaside community of straight roads and neat yards, typically Dutch.

Also, my only lead to Rik de Bruin. A name recalled from the visiting card he handed me on the evening of our chance meeting in the bar at the Rif Hotel.

An anaemic sun was settling on the watery horizon when I piloted my rented Merc into the town's main street, Voorstraat, with its awninged stores, bare trees, and paved sidewalks, presided over by a church with an undersized spire and a white finger of a lighthouse. In the summer it was probably picturesque, with the colourful awnings extended, outdoor cafés and street stalls laden with tourist trash. Now, in bleak November, it was short on appeal. It also surprised me that de Bruin would have chosen such a secluded and cutesy location for his business or his home, whichever or both. Unless the address on the card had been a phoney.

It was too late in the day to start serious enquiries. Hotels were scarce, but I eventually tracked one down in a back street: Hotel De Graaf, a bed-and-breakfast establishment. They gave me a room facing seaward. By then it was dark. I crashed down on the firm double bed and slept for an hour.

At a little after seven, showered and refreshed, I ventured

downstairs to the lobby. No meals available, just machine-dispensed coffee and snacks. The old guy behind the desk spoke only Dutch and German. When I ran the name de Bruin past him, he shook his head. '*Nee*,' Dutch for "No", was the only part of his answer I understood. He loaned me a local telephone directory. It was unforthcoming on the subject of either de Bruin the individual, or DeB Publications. Maybe he was unlisted.

Restaurants were no thicker on the ground than hotels. The place I settled on was a diner-type eaterie, with booths and a nice-looking blonde waitress of about thirty, who spoke English better than me. The only other customers were a woman with a small boy, tucking into multi-storey burgers.

As the waitress jotted down my order for fillet steak and fries, I tried de Bruin's name on her.

'There used to be a sex shop of that name,' she mused. 'In Voorstraat, by the supermarket. But they went away, oh, years ago.' She smiled cheekily at me, her very blue eyes crinkling. There was a seen-it-all air about her. 'Something special you wanted there?'

An invitation of a certain kind, if ever I heard one.

'What've you got?' I said with a shade less subtlety.

Her smile broadened and the tip of her tongue slid across her upper lip.

'Are you staying at Le Graaf?' she asked.

I nodded. 'Good guess.'

'Not really. It's about the only place that's open out of season.'

She swayed away with my order. My gaze went with her, appraising the roll of her hips. Inside me, the devil of old was awakening from a long sleep. I slapped him down, knowing he would rise again.

The information the waitress had provided was depressing. I didn't see Rik de Bruin dispensing dildos and penis extenders behind the counter of a sex shop. Small-time, he was not. So if the sex shop had been his, it would have to be part of a chain or a franchise set-up, or maybe a front for the real money making operation. The supermarket, or other retail stores on Voorstraat, might be able to point me towards DeB's current trading address. All I had to do was find a single store under the name DeB-something. From there to the DeB nerve centre should be a fast straight run. Still hope then.

I stared through the plate glass window at my reflection overlaying the empty street. It was raining now, the asphalt slick and black. The waitress was behind the counter, resting on her elbows. Her reflected features were in shadow but I sensed she was looking at me.

The meal was nothing to enthuse about. It filled a hollow. Afterwards I skimmed through a Dutch magazine before heading for my room and an early crashdown.

It was while I was rinsing toothpaste foam from my mouth that a knock came at my door. Too tired to wonder who, I went to answer it topless and in my shorts.

On my doorstep was the blonde waitress. It didn't exactly surprise me. The signals had all been there, including the enquiry about my hotel. Her face was made up a shade too heavily. Her smile was the same though.

'Er ... hello,' I said, torn between falling upon her with frothing mouth and slamming the door in her face.

She was wearing a blue coat, just above knee-length, held together by a knotted belt, and very high heels with ankle straps. White stockings. So far, so commonplace. Then unknotted the belt and let the coat fall open. Underneath she had on a bra, bikini briefs, and a garter belt, all in a black lacy material. A black rose tattoo adorned her stomach, its spiny stalk plunging behind the waistband of her briefs and re-emerging on her thigh. Very artistic. Her navel was adorned with a ring that glittered in the light of the corridor. Her figure was good and her timing, if she had but realized, was impeccable. My last sexual adventure was so long ago I couldn't even recall who it was with, let alone when. Now here was an offer, on my doorstep, on a plate. I retreated a couple of steps. Reasonably enough, she took this as an invitation. When I stopped she bumped into me.

'What is the matter?' she said, a frown creasing the bridge of her nose.

'Look ... I can't,' I said lamely. 'You see, I'm ... I'm married.'

So what? her expression said.

I spread my hands, half-embarrassment, half-regret. 'Sorry. I don't screw around.'

Her frown became a scowl. Mine wasn't the standard reaction, I guessed. Chances were she was the town hooker, supplementing her table waiting wages with "presents" from passing businessmen.

Voices travelled down the corridor. She hesitated. For a moment I thought she was going to force her way past me, but no, she flailed me with a few words of Dutch – abuse presumably – and stomped off. No sway, just frustrated hormones.

Refusing sex with a desirable woman, hooker or no, was not the sexually predatory André Warner of old. The lust generated by the waitress exposing herself had been fleeting, routed by my commitment to Clair and Lizzy. The twin reasons why I was here, in Egmond aan See. To go tomcatting with a waitress-cum-hooker would somehow degrade that mission and Clair's and Lizzy's memories. I went to bed feeling almost proud.

Next morning the sun was back. It lifted my spirits and sent me about my business with a shade more bounce in my step than yesterday. First the supermarket. Sexworld, as the DeB business was known, was well, even fondly, remembered, chiefly because its closure left Egmond bereft of such outlets. How did they manage? As to where they were now, shaking heads were universal. 'Amsterdam?' several suggested, but it was only conjecture.

Same story at all the other adjacent, smaller stores. Only one guy, the young manager of a bookstore, was able to offer any info.

'They change their name,' he told me, in reasonable English.

My ears pricked up. This was new.

'What are they called now?'

His shrug sent my hopes plummeting.

'No idea. I just know they changed because the day they move I am talking to the manager, and he tell me.'

I slipped him a card bearing my cell phone no. Asked him to call me if the changed name came to him. He promised he would, but I didn't expect much. Even as he spoke his attention was wandering towards a couple of mini-skirted girls perusing the magazine rack.

So much for Egmond aan Zee. My goodbye was not regretful.

Amsterdam was my next port of call. The helpful official at the Amsterdam Chamber of Commerce was unable to trace DeB Publications, or DeB anything else. Many privately-owned enterprises are never registered, he informed me apologetically, notably those in the more, ahem, dubious business sectors.

From there I was reduced to haphazard ferreting in the red

light district and other sleazy parts of the city down by the docks. Brown cafés, sex emporiums, night clubs, strip clubs (yes, even in these days of free on-line porn, they still exist), private booth operators, brothels, you name it. Anyplace I might spot or bump into de Bruin or a member of his coterie. It was a tour only the dedicated sex fiend would have found stimulating. For me, it was a reminder of the cesspool Lizzy was by now probably immersed in. As the days passed, then weeks with zero progress, I was coming to accept that she and her mother were beyond my reach. Clair, the unintended victim, was almost sure to be dead; Lizzy too, maybe, but even if alive she could be anyplace in the world. De Bruin was still my only lead.

With the approach of Christmas I hired a private detective called Frederik Berkhuisen, whose office on Scharbeekstraat was just outside the red light district. He was a lanky individual of about forty, with receding black hair, very unDutch in appearance. His glasses resembled the ones Himmler used to wear. But he had been recommended as an expert in tracing missing people.

'Henrik de Bruin,' he mused, after I regaled him with a few basic facts.

'You know him?'

He contemplated me across his black Ikea desk. 'The name, not the man. Why are you searching for this man?' Yet another Dutch fluent English-speaker.

He owed me money, I told him. Berkhuisen jotted a few words on a notepad. The Himmler glasses glinted at me.

'Tell me all you know and I will see what I can do.'

So I told him all I knew, which took about five seconds, and left him to see what he could do.

I stuck around for a week or so, mostly hoping from news from Berkhuisen. At a cost to me of eight hundred euros he produced a big zilch. Oh, yes, I received a written report of his enquiries and investigations to justify the outlay. I chucked it in the trash can.

For now though he was all I had. Admitting failure came hard. Even so I was at that point and, instructing Berkhuisen to continue digging, I went home to Andorra. Not without misgivings, running the gauntlet of a charge for my assault or even homicide of Miguel. Learning with relief that he, though still in hospital, had survived. The police didn't pay a call, meaning he hadn't pointed the finger at me.

On the debit side, Lucien and Madeleine were away, and Simone had gone off to winter in her native Grenoble, which made my splendid isolation even more complete. Would I have bedded her if she were available? After some searching self-analysis, I concluded that I wouldn't. Until I knew Lizzy's fate I was committed to her. You can't cheat on someone you don't and probably never will have a relationship with. But that's what it would have felt like.

Spending Christmas alone would have been unthinkable, not to mention unbearable, so the day before Christmas Eve I took off to a fogbound England, turning up unannounced at Julie's, bearing a car trunkful of gifts from Harrods. Just like Santa Claus.

The ball zinged past my ear as if rocket-propelled and I hadn't a hope of playing it.

'Five – two,' my opponent sang out smugly. I gritted my teeth and went to retrieve the object of my humiliation from its resting place. It was almost too hot to hold, a testimony to the pace of the game. Until recently I hadn't played squash for nigh on six months, and had never been more than a keen dabbler. Now, even in my state of relative fitness, I was feeling the strain.

'Ready when you are,' my opponent called with a fine touch of malice. Willie Scott, my brother-in-law, medium height and build, craggily masculine, was four years my junior and revelling in it. I cursed him under my breath and gave the ball all I had, which at this late stage in the game wasn't much.

Five minutes later we emerged from the court, Willie having thrashed me three games to love. My sister Julie, thirty-five, blonde like me though hers was worn shoulder-length and she was altogether lovelier, came down from the viewing stage to meet us. A consolation peck on the cheek for me, a proper mouth-to-mouth job for Willie. After twelve years of marriage and two kids they still regularly behaved like a honeymoon couple.

'You're rusty as hell, Drew darling,' she observed.

As an appellation I disliked Drew. It was Julie's diminutive for Andrew, which was the name I would have been christened if my father's choice had prevailed.

'Och, leave the man be,' Willie said, grinning, in his refined Edinburgh burr. 'He's getting on a bit, ye know.'

'Bollocks,' I rejoined, slipping the cover over my racket.

Julie feigned disapproval at my use of the vernacular.

'I'll get the drinks in while you two shower.'

Later, we sat around a table in the plasticky club bar and indulged in the easy, undemanding chit-chat of intimates. Yarning, trotting out hackneyed jokes, ragging each other harmlessly.

'The girls keep asking when we're going to visit you,' Julie said. Her daughters, my nieces, Cathy, ten, and Christina, seven, were her recreation but not her vocation. That lay in her career as an advertising executive, in her wine importation business, and in the monthly article entitled "Women at the Helm" that she wrote for a national women's magazine. How she packed it all in as well as managing a substantial home was a mystery to all, Willie included.

'There must be another of her,' he had once mused to me. 'A secret clone.'

Busy, contented people. Lucky them. I was glad for them and any small envy I felt was benign. Two weeks ago, they had taken me in, absorbed me into their small family circle for the festive season, and given me the run of their sprawling Tudor pile. They had kept me on the narrow track of sanity. You might even say they saved me from myself.

'Stay on as long as you like – just don't get under my feet,' Julie had said cheerfully and sincerely.

That night in the "cosy" guest bedroom I lay awake long after lights out. Julie's and Willie's house was of the kind that never sleeps, what with the mice scurrying in the wainscoting, and the creaks and clicks that always seem to be a feature of old buildings. When the wind blew, which it was doing now, the defoliated branches of the giant horse chestnut tree that sat in the centre of the lawn rattled and occasionally tapped at my window. Night talk. I didn't mind it. Ordinarily I found it restful.

But of late my spirit was too busy to rest. It wandered still in search of Lizzy, wherever she was. Christmas had been and gone: vivid decorations, a sparkling tree that was too tall by a foot for the low ceiling, children laughing, adults making merry; food, drink; more food, more drink; still more drink. Drinking the blues away. I was well and truly back on my treadmill. At least I kept up my daily exercise regime, which helped while away the hours.

By New Year's Day Lizzy had been missing for a hundred and sixteen days. A lot could happen to a missing person in a hundred and sixteen days. In Lizzy's particular case none of it would be good.

In between exercising and meals I prowled around stuffy, insipid Royal Windsor, went riding on the downs with Julie, played more squash with Willie and kept getting beaten. I even took Cathy and Christina to Regent's Park Zoo on a brittle-bright late January afternoon. On that occasion I also learned a bit about myself when Christina, who was contemplating an old and extremely bad-tempered baboon, whispered to Cathy, 'That one looks as misbul as Uncle Drew.'

Cathy, older and more tactful, shushed her frantically.

'It does, though,' Christina insisted.

I squatted beside her to put us on a level. 'Am I really a miserable old baboon of an uncle?'

Her stare was unabashed and unwinking.

'You wasn't before,' she said consolingly. 'Mummy says you must be in love. Are you in love? What's in love anyway? Is love a place?'

Cathy, scathingly, 'It's when two people like each other very much, silly.'

'Oh.' Pause for dissection. 'I mustn't be in love with you then.'

'Ooh, you're such a nasty little girl,' Cathy said, pushing her sister.

To avert all-out warfare I proposed ice creams and, with a small gloved hand in each of mine, went in search of a source of supply. A serious challenge in Regent's Park in January.

I also resolved to put on a happy face in future.

By the beginning of February I was meandering further afield. A get-away-from-it-all weekend in the Lake District, for instance. It sleeted down without a break. The following weekend in Dublin, reviving an old flame, only to find the ignition was lacking. A disaster.

Mostly though, having used up all Royal Windsor's attractions, I rambled around London's West End. Aimlessly. Window shopping. Dropping in at pubs. Sometimes theatre-going in the evening. I sought no female company. After the Dublin fiasco, not to mention the fruitless quest to Egmond aan Zee, I couldn't work up the zeal.

Of the pubs I frequented in the West End, I was especially partial to the Hog In The Pound Tavern, just off Oxford Street. It was there in the quaint triangular bar that, thanks to a chance meeting, the stopped clock of my life began to tick again.

I was ordering my third-too-many vodka, fast approaching that numb serenity that had again become the desired condition, when my name – my real name – was called.

'It is you, isn't it? Well, fuck me sideways!'

A curly head atop wide shoulders jutted beyond the row of bar proppers.

'Stephen Bloore, by God!'

We advanced towards each other.

'Look at you. Just like a bloody film star!'

'And look at you. Just like a bookmaker.' Which is what he was.

He guffawed. Hands were clasped, backs slapped.

'Where the hell have you been these five years?' he demanded, almost truculent.

I winked secretively and said. 'Next question?'

'Oh, right. Like that, is it? What are you doing in the Smoke? Not back in the spy business, are you?'

'You must be joking.'

We took our drinks to a table by the door that a middle-aged couple were vacating.

Stephen Bloore was a Londoner by birth and temperament, and owned a chain of betting shops in the east and north of the capital. Our friendship dated from my marriage, when he and his wife had lived in the apartment building next door. His marriage had disintegrated, thanks to his philandering.

'How's the rip-off business?' I said as we drank to mutual health, wealth, etcetera. 'Still getting richer while your customers throw themselves from high places?'

His brown eyes twinkled. The wrinkles were more abundant than I recalled. He would be a year or so older than me.

'And you?' He had a knack of replying by turning a question back on you. Much like me.

'Scraping a living.'

We chatted on until closing time. Reminiscing mostly.

'Where are you staying?' he asked as we were almost thrown out onto the street, last to leave.

'Windsor.'

'Christ. Nowheresville.' He put on a thoughtful expression. 'Tell you what, Andy, my old son, I've got a bit of a do going out in the sticks tonight. Nothing grand, just a buffet party with a some friends and acquaintances. There's bound to be a few unattached scrubbers tossing their keys in the ring.' He nudged my arm. 'Know what I mean, wink-wink.'

Any company was better than my own. Even scrubbers.

'Why not?' I said, and collected a slap across the shoulder blades that gave me the hiccups.

'Good man. Be there at nine, no later.' He scribbled on the back of a business card. 'Here's the address. Your car got GPS?'

'Yes, don't worry, I'll find it.'

'Don't be late,' he said as he tucked the card in my breast pocket.

With that we parted. Until nine o'clock, when, drawn by boredom, by the need to fill another empty evening, I rolled through the imposing, pillar-flanked gateway of Ranwyck House, to the south of the village of Iver Heath and within earshot of Heathrow Airport.

It was a considerable mansion, early Victorian, I guessed, size being its chief virtue. The cars carelessly parked before a terraced frontage like scattered toys were high-income bracket. So was the woman who came to the double-locked door, wearing more war paint than a Cherokee chief and a full-length mauve dress with splits and cut-outs all over.

Well, with keys in the ring on the agenda, what had I expected – a dowager duchess in twin-set and pearls?

'Hell-*oh*,' she said, upper-class to the last vowel. 'And who might you be?'

'André Warner,' I announced and threw in a wide smile to ease her qualms.

'I see.' A slight thaw set in. 'How delightful. But I still don't know you, do I?'

Then Stephen Bloore pitched up, drink in one hand, arm candy clinging, appropriately, to his arm.

'Thought it might be you.' He released the bimbette, a skinny piece with synthetic model-girl looks, to haul me inside. 'Marcia,' he said to the woman in the mauve dress, 'this is my old mate, André.'

Marcia's polar icecap now melted completely, and she reverted to her role of warm, welcoming hostess.

'I should have realized such a lovely man couldn't possibly be a gatecrasher.' She attached her lissom shape to mine. I didn't object. Nor did I feel a thing.

We joined a gathering some twenty-strong in a study of sorts, where the wallpaper consisted of books. Heavy drapes shut out the night, and in front of them was a home cinema TV measuring about five feet by two. A mixture of individual and twin seats, were arranged in rows. A long table against a wall was creaking under a vast buffet. Some of the guests were attacking it.

'Are we going to watch a movie?' I asked.

'And a few,' Stephen quipped. 'You'll enjoy them, mate, I guarantee it.'

His salacious grin was a clue to the kind of movie that would be showing. Not Walt Disney, for sure.

'Come and meet everyone,' Marcia said, and took me on a whistle-stop tour. The guest profile was upper-middle class, well-groomed, well-spoken, with a 6:4 male-female ratio. Most of the women were under-attired *à la* Marcia. All but a handful were smoking the kind of weed you can't buy over the counter.

'Who owns this place?' I asked Marcia, as she offered me a drag on her spliff. I accepted, to be neighbourly.

'I do, dahling,' she said, adding, with an exaggerated flutter of eyelashes, 'I'm a Lady, with a capital "L".'

I refrained from asking 'What's a Lady like you doing at a smut show?' The assumption that the morals of the English aristocracy are higher than those of the proletariat was never valid.

When Stephen, raucous as any fairground barker, announced that the movie was 'ready to roll', I was steered by Lady Marcia to a twin seat. She then disappeared but returned in a matter of minutes to keep me company. She was breathing fast as if she'd just completed a circuit of the estate. A dusting of white around her nostrils told the real story, however. It came as no surprise that the non liquid version of coke was among the refreshments on offer.

The lights went out and the noisy chatter dwindled. A light glowed on the front of the DVD box below the screen. The screen went from black-out to instant full colour. "Sex Spectrum" was the title, sex everywhichway was the theme. "All actors are eighteen and over" a tagline assured us. It might even be true. The plot proved to be negligible, just a parade of permutations: two girls together; two older women and a young girl; four men and a girl; two girls and a man;

and within this shuffling of partners were performed acts of flagellation, bondage, bukkake, sadomasochism, oral sex, anal sex, fisting, bestiality, and so on, and so on. None of it entirely original. New variations, perhaps, of tried and tested formats, all proven marketable, all available and more on the Internet. The only difference between stuff on-line and tonight's offerings was the size of the screen.

Initially mildly arousing, this ninety-minute long procession of close-ups of sexual organs in action ultimately became sexually deadening. Erotic overkill. My eyelids began to droop before we reached the halfway point. The audience was transfixed. Not a catcall was heard from opening to closing credits. The only vocal demonstration of any sort came from a bespectacled woman of about fifty, occupying a couch on my right, who let out a muted squeal whenever the camera feasted on a set of male genitals. Marcia was more reserved. Her shows of emotion were confined to the occasional squeeze of my thigh.

As the closing credits rolled up the screen she deposited a loose, wet kiss on my cheek. 'Wasn't that really something?'

'I'll say!' I stretched, flexed my knees.

'Wait till you see the next,' Marcia said, giving an excited wriggle. Her thigh rubbed mine.

I wasn't sure I could sit through another half-hour of coitus uninterruptus. As it happened I didn't even need an excuse to absent myself.

The title said it all: "Naughty Nymphets". Kiddy porn was where I drew the line. I stood up, startling Marcia, and left the room. Directly opposite was a doorway, beyond it a room fitted out as a bar, with a billiard table occupying centre stage. I marched in. Two grey-haired men were chalking their cues, preparatory to starting a game. Another, middle-aged, was at the bar counter, hunched over a drink. Beside it a bottle with a Dalmore stag's-head label. Whisky, single malt, fifteen years in the ageing.

'Join the club,' he said to me, indicating the empty stool next to him.

I hesitated, then accepted the invitation. From the billiard table came the clack-clack of balls ricocheting as the game got under way.

Across the corridor the movie soundtrack was still audible. Monosyllabic dialogue, a few squeals, bland background music; occasional whoops from the audience. I crossed the room and shut the door.

'I like to see a naked woman as much as any man,' my drinking partner muttered as I rejoined him, 'but that stuff with kids turns my stomach.'

I didn't ask why he was here then. He might ask me the same. He poured me a generous dose of the Dalmore. Scotch wasn't my favourite spirit. I downed it anyway.

'Did nobody warn you what was on the agenda?' I asked.

'No. Some friends brought us.' He jerked a thumb at the open door. 'My wife's still in there. Either pissed or stoned.'

One of the billiard players wandered over, cue resting on his shoulder.

'It's all very well you chaps sitting there with a holier-than-thou attitude. The trouble is, some children are just as immoral as adults.'

Maybe he had a point but I wasn't open to conversion. Kids were precious. My nieces came to mind. Innocent, trusting, inviolable.

'It's obvious you don't have any kids of your own,' I said nastily.

His face closed up. The billiard cue twitched. In case he had ideas about using it on me I got ready to counter attack. Another twitch and he would be kissing carpet.

'And you *do*, I suppose,' he snapped, and stalked off back to his game.

Touché.

The next half an hour passed in desultory conversation with George, my new friend. It was close to midnight. Stephen hadn't mentioned an all-night session, but that didn't mean it wasn't. I decided to slip away without saying goodbye.

The door opened and two women came in giggling.

'This one is really special, folks.' Stephen's voice from the movie room drifted in with them, the words slurred with drink or drugs or both. 'Hot from the darkrooms across the water, only arrived this morning.'

'A world premiere!' some woman whooped.

'Invite the Queen!'

Cheering and whistling. The ever-present background music cranked up. On-screen dialogue, too loud. Coarse laughter. Once more into the sewer. My glass was empty. So was I.

'I'm off,' I announced to George. Well and truly smashed, he waved his glass at me.

As I exited from the bar the screen was visible through the movie room doorway in front of me. I glimpsed a girl in a woolly red hat with a yellow pom-pom on top, arching and writhing like a speared fish, as several guys manhandled her to a parked car.

Some inner compulsion fixed my eyes to the screen, made me linger. As the girl was thrust through the rear door the red hat fell off, releasing a streamer of long pale-blond hair. Inside the car another camera took over, dwelling on her face.

It was a youthful face, of course, if heavily made-up. It was, even in its simulated terror, sensationally lovely.

It was also familiar. Heart-stoppingly familiar.

'Oh– my– God,' I whispered. 'Lizzy.'

Twenty-Six

Every fibre in me strained to leave. What had so far been revealed – flashes of pale thigh and white underwear – was only an appetite-whetter, designed to warm up the punters. All too soon titillation would degenerate into total exposure, and from there to hardcore action, sickeningly explicit, lingeringly recorded by the camera.

The detachment with which I had viewed the earlier showing was gone, superseded by a hollow, gut-churning dread.

A yell, meaningless, incoherent, escaped me. I rushed at the TV unit like a crazy man. Over it went with a crash, to howls of outrage on all sides. I whirled around hurling curses. The TV was on the floor, screen upwards. The movie was still running, the dialogue, Lizzy's squeals, manufactured or real, the hooting of the male participants now unnaturally loud.

I kicked out at the DVD box. It fell off its shelf, still running, seemingly built to take punishment. I stamped on the toppled screen. It went black, and the room with it. Arms reached for me out of the darkness. I struck out, connected with bone. A shout, a curse. Fingers clawed at my face. I swatted them away and two-fistedly cleared a space. Then somebody tackled me rugby-style and I was dragged, still swinging, to the floor.

All this happened faster than the telling, and ended when

the room diffused with light. I was on the floor, winded, pinned there by Stephen Bloore.

'Andy, for God's sake, man!'

'Get the hell off me,' I snarled, and as if in a daze he complied at once.

We both stood up. A circle had formed around us and the mood was ugly: the men glowering, the women shrilly resentful. Two men were examining the TV.

'It's fucked,' one of them growled.

'Who do you think you are?' some female demanded.

More ominously and male: 'Let's sort the bastard.'

Too maddened to be scared, I rounded on Stephen. 'Give me that DVD.'

'You gone bonkers, Andy?' He was genuinely upset. 'I invited you here as a friend . . .'

'And I'm asking you as a friend. *Give me that DVD.*'

A collective growl arose. Several of the men closed in on me, but I elbowed them aside and went for Stephen.

'The disc ...' I took him by the lapels and shook him. 'I want it.'

'Well, you can go and fuck yourself, mate.' Our friendship was gone beyond recall. He wrenched free. 'Let's have him out,' he said to those nearest to him. The circle around me contracted, forcing me back into the window recess.

It was all very businesslike. They manhandled me out of the room and down a corridor, past the banquet hall. I went unresistingly to the inevitable eviction, since I couldn't hope to prevent it. No violence was offered. Unless you count the culminating boot up the backside that drove me down the terrace steps to an all-fours touchdown at the bottom. A woman laughed jeeringly.

'Don't come back, will you?'

I got up painfully, both knees bruised, my pants ripped. 'If I do, you'd better not be here.'

Derision accompanied me as I hobbled over to the Merc. I

reversed out of the line. The crowd began to stream back into the house for further helpings from the carnal feast. I drove away, stifling the urge to work off my fury and humiliation on the car. Once out of sight of the house, I stopped and waited, with the engine running and the heater blasting.

Minutes crawled by. I did a three-point turn and chugged cautiously back towards the house on sidelights, until the terrace, which was flanked by several outside lamps, came into view. Nobody around. About fifty yards on a clump of evergreen bushes grew, twice the height of a man. I reversed in beside it. Through gaps in the foliage the entrance to the house was visible, as I had hoped it would be. I settled down for a long wait, serenaded by Radio 2's hits from those swinging sixties.

People began to leave at around two in the morning. The departures were very orderly. Cars drove past my hiding place at regular intervals until only a yellow Chrysler Viper and a DB7 were left, and still Stephen Bloore remained inside. It was close to three o'clock when he finally emerged, his scrawny girlfriend clinging to his arm and staggering a little. Lady Marcia was with them, also shaky on her feet, a champagne glass in her hand. Kisses to the cheek were exchanged all round.

'Sorry about all that shit with my friend,' I heard Stephen say. 'My ex-friend, I mean. Send me a bill for the damage.'

'Wouldn't dream of it, dahling,' Lady Marcia retorted.

As I secured my seat belt, the yellow Viper trundled past. I let it get as far as the road before starting the engine. A car like that would be easy to follow, provided Stephen didn't play boy racer.

Luckily for me, he drove responsibly, even sedately. When you have that many horses on tap you don't need to flaunt it. We headed along the A412 and in due course joined

Western Avenue in the direction of the city. At this hour, even London's traffic sleeps. Keeping the Viper in view without being spotted called for some nifty acceleration at stop lights, but I managed to stick with it as far as the West End, and only once jumped a red.

Stephen's destination was a mews off the Fulham Road, coming into Chelsea. I left the Merc on a meter space just around the corner. Moving smartly and staying in the shadows, I loped down the short access drive. Just in time I came to where the drive opened out into a courtyard, to see him unlocking his front door. His girl friend was being sick by his feet and he was cursing her without much consideration for sleeping neighbours.

Now I knew where he lived. I left without hurrying. I would be back.

The gun I needed was of a rather special genre. Illegal in the UK and consequently unobtainable over the counter. Anyone without connections would have more chance of tracking down the Lost Treasure of the Incas than of getting hold of such a weapon. It so happened that I had such connections.

In the bleak, wind-seared dawn, with daylight still below the skyline, I packed my bags. Breakfasted alone on coffee. Wrote a brief note of thanks and farewell to Julie and Willie and the girls. I couldn't have faced them this morning. Their cheerful, busy, bustling, so-very-normal company would have served only to underscore Lizzy's plight. And what a plight. At the mercy of people without moral or scruple: used, abused, debased. Who knows what physical and psychological damage she might have sustained. Some of it might be irreversible.

The thought of it was a jagged edge sawing at my nerves. So I shut my mind to all but my immediate, urgent mission.

Slipped out, making less commotion than a dormouse having a bad dream.

On the edge of the village of Nuper's Hatch, just inside the M25 between exits 27 and 28, stands a dairy farm. It is a working farm, with cattle, a herdsman, a milkmaid, and a dog. And a very special owner. The farm makes no profit from its livestock. Mad cow disease and the collapse of market prices killed all that years ago. Even so, it will continue to trade for the foreseeable future because its real income is derived not from its farming activities, authentic though they were, but from what goes on in a purpose-built cellar below the barn.

Here reposed an Aladdin's Cave of firepower. I doubt whether even a hundred people had ever seen the inside of it. Visitors were allowed entry only by appointment and recommendation.

The Genie of the Lamp was a Catholic Ulsterman , one Tagd Corry. A human scarecrow, stooped, gaunt and blood-less of complexion, with hands that arthritis had made into talons and fingernails that were perennially dirty, notwith-standing his millionaire status. He greeted me with a cheerful hail in expectation that I was about to spend some money. For why else would I be here?

'Top o' the morning, Tagd,' I said with a grin.

The basement was a good seventy feet long, and divided into two unequal sections: a firing range occupied nine-tenths of the floor space. Windowless and soundproofed to the ultimate degree. The other tenth was given over to a small stockroom-cum-office. It was there we went first, for what Tagd termed the "professional consultation".

'It's been a while, Mr A,' he observed, from the opposite side of his scarred desk, squinting at me through glasses with round lenses and skinny black frames. "Mr A" was the only name he knew me by.

'I've been working abroad a lot lately. No reflection on you or your merchandise, I can assure you.'

'It's to be hoped not. As far as I'm aware I've never lost a client other than through natural causes. Or ...' The rogue-ish grin almost made him look human, 'is it *un*natural causes I'm meaning?'

I chuckled politely at his black humour.

'I need two items, Tagd. A shotgun and a handgun, plus ammunition for both.'

Tagd fingered his Adam's apple. It was so pronounced it sagged over the knot of his tie.

'Is that it?' He rocked back on his chair and hoisted furry black eyebrows towards his hairline. The distance was not great.

'Not quite. I'll be taking the handgun with me when I leave, but I'll be returning it possibly later today or tomorrow, for shipment to the Continent along with the shotgun. To Holland.'

The eyebrows seemed to have set at mid-forehead level.

'Holland, is it? That won't come cheap, I'm thinking.'

'I couldn't care a flying fart. Just do it and bill me. I'll give you the usual on account.' The usual being £1000 on top of the price of the hardware.

Tagd made no notes. Behind the Neanderthal brow there pulsed a brain of Mensa proportions and a memory to match.

'The shotgun,' he said. 'Any preference? I can't recall selling you a shotgun before and that's a fact. Handguns only, I'm thinking.'

'You think right. This is a one-off.'

'Unique, is it? So what's your particular pepper pot: Smith? Franchi? Beretta? They're all in stock.'

I made a negative sound. 'You wouldn't have a Stakeout, by any chance?'

His eyes narrowed. 'Tis clairvoyant y'are, to be sure. 'Twas only yesterday I picked up a pair of the beauties. Not many of my clients ask for Ithacas. If they want a pumper with a pistol grip they usually go for the Smith.'

'Just shows how ignorant they are.'

Tagd produced a bunch of keys and took them to the stockroom, which was separated from the office by a heavy gauge wire mesh partition. He disappeared behind the ceiling-high racks and I heard the clink of metal against metal and the rattle of chain.

The Ithaca he returned with was second-hand. Nowadays Tagd rarely trafficked in new weapons, largely because the cost of smuggling them in had risen beyond the willingness of customers to pay, whereas a used firearm, being already in circulation, carried no such penalty. He bought selectively, personally reconditioning every gun. He even gave a guarantee, albeit of the unwritten variety. His reputation was that solid.

While I played with the Ithaca, testing the smoothness of the magazine pump and getting a feel for the trigger pull, Tagd rustled up more goodies. A trio of handguns whose only common denominator was that they were all revolvers, plus a variety of cartridges to fit. Disregarding them for now, I loaded three no. 8 Birdshot into the magazine tube of the shotgun.

'Let's go,' I said, and Tagd did his stuff with the keys again to admit us to the firing range.

In contrast to the down-at-heel office the range was lavishly, you might almost say lovingly, equipped, with static and moving-figure targets, all illuminated. A computerized scoreboard and headphone ear mufflers were suspended over each of the three shooting stalls. Tagd spent his money where it counted.

Accuracy tests aren't necessary for a shotgun, and I wished only to satisfy myself that it functioned as a gun should function. Not that I really had any doubts. Tagd's own trials would have been infinitely more exhaustive.

Tagd indicated that I should fire into the bank of sand at the base of the target zone. I clunked a shell into the firing chamber, set the safety catch and ascertained that the trigger was now locked solid. Messy accidents I could do without.

Safety off, I held the gun at the hip. Having no butt stock the Ithaca Stakeout can't be aimed. You just thrust in the general direction of the target, and let the spread of shot do the rest. But you can't intimidate unless you (a) have full confidence in your weapon, and (b) are prepared to use it with lethal intent.

Inside the headphones the first shot was no louder than a carpet beater in action. The recoil, on the other hand, was savage. A stockless shotgun calls for the firmest of grips. The sand convulsed, and that was all. That was fine, all I had expected. The only evidence that I had fired at all was the gun smoke pricking in my nostrils, and even this was swiftly drawn away through some unseen extractor vent.

Tagd, lounging in the next stall, headphones in place, nodded his satisfaction. I loosed off the second and third cartridges close together. God, it could kick! It was years since I had last used a stockless shotgun, and I had forgotten about the backlash.

'Does the other one kick as hard?' I asked, removing the headphones.

'About the same. Are you wanting to try it?'

'No, I can cope. Let's see how these handguns of yours perform.'

Back in the office I played with all three revolvers in turn. Swinging out the cylinders, thumbing the hammers, assessing their pointing qualities, testing the trigger pull. Tagd knew his guns and his customers, and the selection was not arbitrary: a Smith & Wesson Model 28 Magnum, a .357 Korth, identical to the model I already owned, and, lastly and of moderate interest technically-speaking, a chromed Uberti Inspector, a .32, made in Italy. The two magnum pistols had 4-inch barrels, the best compromise between bulk and ballistics; the Uberti was an inch shorter.

We returned to the firing range.

'Roll 'em,' I said to Tagd, who was lighting a cigarette – awkwardly, on account of his arthritic digits. He nodded and set the moving targets in motion. They were representations of comic book gangsters with fedora hats, cigarettes drooping from the corner of the mouth, and Chicago-style Thompson guns.

With my twelve rounds from the Korth pistol I scored alternate head and heart hits, and not a single miss. Tagd stood at the back of the range, ear-muffed and smoking languidly. Once, when I glanced at him while reloading, he made an appreciative circle of forefinger and thumb.

'You can't buy better,' he conceded when I told him to wrap the Korth, 'or pay more.' He left the cigarette in his mouth as he spoke, just like his cardboard gangsters.

'I know it. Let me have fifty rounds with it, will you? And a shoulder kit. And don't forget the slugs for the shotgun. Special Grade, huh?'

He gave me an intent look. 'No problem.'

From a Gordian knot tangle of leather straps and webbing I extracted a Horseshoe shoulder holster. It was the older pattern with the back-welt that pushes the gun forward for the fastest possible draw. Again we removed to the office, where Tagd did sums on a desk calculator.

'That comes to £3,467.28.' He smiled thinly. 'I'll knock the twenty-eight pence off as it's yourself.'

No Value Added Tax, naturally. This was not the kind of transaction you record. Without comment on the amount, I made out a cheque drawn on a Swiss account for SwF5000, which, depending on the rate of exchange on the day, would convert to something approaching £3500. My name on the cheque was a pseudonym.

Tagd scrutinized it. ''Tis indeed an honour to do business with you, Mr A.'

'I'll bet you say that to all your customers.'

Tagd laid a plain brown box, the size of a large book, down on his desk.

'Let me load it before you pack it,' I said.

Again that intent look.

'Would you be taking the shoulder rig?'

'No. Send it to Holland.'

The Korth fitted the box exactly. A few strips of parcel tape to keep the lid on, and I was ready to sally forth.

'If all goes well I may be back later today or sometime tomorrow.'

'I'll be looking after the shotgun for you meanwhile, don't you worry.'

'So long, Tagd.'

He saw me off the premises. Up the steps, through a hydraulically operated trapdoor cover, camouflaged with a stuck-on layer of straw. With my purchase locked in the trunk, I drove back towards the city, exceeding no speed limits, jumping no lights. Nothing beats an illicit cargo for converting you into a model motorist.

It was after mid-day when I came to the mews off Fulham Road. Wispy snowflakes were curling down from a darkening sky as I rolled into the courtyard. The Viper was there. As far as I could tell it hadn't been moved since last night.

As I got out, the windows of the cottages stared blindly at

me from all sides, reflecting that dirty-looking sky. I opened the trunk and ripped apart the box and filled my hand with the meaty grip of the Korth. A snowflake settled on my nose, melting instantly. Others tumbled around me, thicker, faster, as plump as goose down.

I thrust the gun down inside my waistband, buttoned my jacket, and crossed the few yards of cobblestone to the door of Stephen's cottage. It wasn't locked, so I barged in and was getting my bearings when Stephen erupted from the woodwork, his face suffused with outrage.

'What do ...?' was the full extent of his expostulations before the sight of the Korth shut his mouth.

'Where's the girl?' I demanded.

'Who?' The outrage was receding fast. 'You mean Emilia? She's in bed ... upstairs. What the fuck is this all about, Andy?'

'Shall we find someplace more comfortable to talk?'

He became sullen. 'If you say so.' He led the way into a long, L-shaped room; a dining area occupied about a third of the floor space.

'Sit down,' I said, and wagged the Korth at him. He sat on a dining chair and glared. 'I've come for that DVD.'

He groaned. 'For fuck's sake, not *that* again!'

' And I want the name of your supplier.'

'You must be round the bleeding twist.' He was recovering fast now. Maybe he reckoned the gun was just a prop.

I eased the safety catch off. It sounded loud in these still surroundings. Though a busy thoroughfare was less than twenty yards away, no traffic noise penetrated.

A stair creaked. I spun round as Stephen's bedmate walked unsteadily into the room, using the wall for support. Wan of complexion, brown hair bedraggled, last night's make-up still clinging on. A Kate Moss clone. Wearing Stephen's bathrobe, by the look of it; the sleeves hung below her fingertips.

'Give him what he wants, Stephen.' Her voice was listless.

'Keep out of this, Emilia,' he said, a warning glint in his eyes.

'It's good advice,' I said. 'I'd take it if I were you.'

The girl, Emilia, subsided inelegantly to the floor, letting her head flop against the wall, as if the strain of holding it erect was too much for her.

'The DVD,' I said easily to Stephen. 'And a name – or I amputate a toe without anaesthetic.'

Perhaps it was the offhandedness of the threat that gave it impact. Truculence faded and uncertainty took over.

'You wouldn't.'

'Yes, he would,' Emilia whispered. 'Look at his face.' She was a better judge of character than him.

'You can hardly complain to the police,' I pointed out mildly. 'Unless you want your slimy little racket blown, that is.'

Still he wasn't convinced. I took a pace towards him, aimed the gun barrel at a Gucci-shod foot. He flinched. He wasn't without guts. What a pity his cause wasn't worthy of the sacrifice. I had no sympathy for him. I had no feelings for him at all. This was strictly business. Personal business.

'Fuck you,' he said, his lip curling. Maybe he thought this was a Dirty Harry movie, and my gun and I were full of blanks.

Pulling triggers was second nature to me, and never was the cause so just. Trouble was, a mews cottage like this was no place to be letting off guns. So, before he had chance to react, I reversed the Korth and brought it down on his kneecap with all the force of my loathing behind it. The crack and his shriek blended. He rolled off the chair, clutching his shattered knee, still squealing. As Emilia rushed forward to succour him, I sat down in an armchair with flowered upholstery, a dispassionate spectator. It would be a while before he got the screaming out of his system and was ready to talk.

And if he still proved reluctant, it would cost him his remaining kneecap. It was all the same to me. If I hadn't needed him, I would have killed him already.

III

Annika

Twenty-Seven

It was three o'clock in the afternoon and dark as night. I drove in a state of dangerous abstraction, in the outer lane of the M25, other vehicles in front and behind and beside. The snow had turned to rain and trucks lashed my windscreen with slush as I overtook them. On the opposite side of the barrier headlights flared past in a dazzling, unbroken daisy chain.

The DVD reposed in the Merc's glove locker. Though it would be no more than a gesture, a ritual Viking funeral, it was destined for cremation. For sure I had no wish to view it, to remind myself anew of Lizzy's degradation. Those images were branded on my brain for eternity. Though they might soften with age, they would never be banished. But, thanks to Stephen Bloore, I was a step closer to paying back the instigator. I now had a name – Bernard Petit, a Frenchman. And an address in Paris.

I glanced at the girl, curled up on the front passenger seat, her head resting against the window, her eyes vacant. My hostage Emilia. My guarantee that Stephen was telling the truth. His only hope of staying alive and getting his knee fixed.

'Do you love him?' I had asked her, before deciding on the next step.

She had nodded, her mouth turned down. 'Stephen? Yeh, I love the shit.'

It had the ring of sincerity. With both of them taped hand,

foot, mouth and eyes, I had driven out into the Kent country-side and deposited him, still taped, still whimpering, still bleeding, in a place where no one would find him unless they knew where to look. In near-zero night-time temperatures I reckoned he was good for a couple of days. By then Emilia should be back in the UK, armed with directions how to find his temporary prison. Unless I had been given a bum steer. In that case she wouldn't be going back at all, and he would die of exposure or thirst or who cared what.

Leaving him, we had detoured to Emilia's flat in Green-wich, to collect her passport, which necessitated removing her bonds. She made no attempt to slip away, made malleable by the knowledge that if she didn't co-operate her lover was a dead man.

Back in the car, she asked where we were going, sounding as though she didn't care one way or the other.

'It's a mystery tour,' I said.

A bleary-eyed shrug was her only comment.

Our next port of call was Nuper's Hatch. En route, I pulled over into a lonely turn-out, and re-blindfolded, gagged, and bound her with some more of that versatile parcel tape. No resistance. Her skinny limbs were slack, flaccid. She was either spaced out or apathetic. Either suited me just fine.

Tagd was openly surprised to hear me over the intercom.

'I thought you were having me on, so I did, when you said you might be back today.'

When I handed over the box his nostrils twitched like a rabbit's. He didn't need to open it to know the Korth had been fired.

'Been hunting out of season, have we, Mr A?'

'For some vermin there's no such thing as out of season,' I returned.

He nodded musingly. 'I've been in touch with Spijk ...'

'Hang fire on that, Tagd,' I cut in. 'I have to go to France first. Get it all parcelled up, and wait until I phone you.'

Pointless, I reasoned, to ship my armoury off to Holland until I established that Lizzy was there. If I needed a shotgun in France I had a local source.

'Is the fire going upstairs?' I asked, referring to the anti-quated coke-fired stove in the farmhouse.

'Feeling the cold, is it?'

I partially withdrew the DVD in its plastic box from inside my coat. 'Some garbage to dispose of.'

Burning a single DVD would be at best no more than a symbol of my desire to immolate the whole lousy, filthy, stinking industry that produced it. Until I achieved that goal it would have to suffice.

We ascended by a second secret staircase, and I lobbed that innocuous-looking plastic disc into the mouth of the stove. It threw up a tongue of purple-laced flame and a stench of burning chemicals that caught in my lungs. I turned away, coughing.

'What the feck was on it?' Tagd asked, flapping frantically.

'Nothing much. Just a kid's life ruined.'

A little after midnight we were at Terminal 4, Heathrow Airport. No chance of a seat on a flight to Paris until 9.45am. We passed the night at the terminal. Emilia soon fell asleep, sprawled across three seats. Weary as I was, I stayed awake.

The hours crawled. Emilia slept like Rip Van Winkle. Reckoning she was safe to be left awhile, I browsed the book and gift stalls. In between I drank coffee until I was sick of the stuff.

When the time came to board, Emilia had to be woken up. Passing through passport control, she behaved impeccably, yawning and saying little, cooperating with the horrendous security procedures.

'Aren't you the smallest bit curious about all this?' I asked her, as we settled in our business-class seats.

'If you want to take me to gay Paree at your expense,' she mumbled, showing a tiny spark of animation, 'who am I to quibble?'

That was the extent of our conversation. She slept the short flight away, while I spent it ruminating over the Petit connection. It was a bit of a mystery, as I had assumed all along that Rik de Bruin was holding Lizzy. Furthermore, unless I was not as well-informed about Dutch topography and architecture as I thought, the movie had been shot in Holland, or at least in Belgium. So where did a Paris-based Frenchman fit in?

We hit central Paris at eleven. Finding rooms took several phone calls. I finally tracked down two doubles at the Mercure, in the Montmartre. I parked Emilia in her room untrussed and still in a zombie-like state, and relieved her of cash and credit cards. If she decided to run for it, she would have to use her thumb.

The address Stephen had given me was the Club Concorde. The guy on the hotel front desk was sniffy when I enquired about it. It was patently not a place for decent people. Nevertheless, I donned the only suit I had brought with me, a dark grey worsted with a vertical silver thread running through it, and a plain maroon silk tie with a matching maroon shirt, to complement it. That way at least they wouldn't have an excuse to throw me out for being improperly dressed.

The capital city of France is renowned above all for its culture and elegance, and the delights of being there in April as once extolled on disc by the late Maurice Chevalier. Among its less appealing features is the great concentration of low life it gives asylum to. Like vampires, these denizens of the back streets hibernate by day, emerging only with the fall of darkness to infest the sidewalks and gutters, and beg or steal or extort their daily crusts. Nowhere in Paris are they more prolific, more pestilent than in the 9e *arrondissement*. If a city can be said to possess an asshole, this is it.

My taxi got stuck in a traffic snarl-up at the Place Pigalle, and looked like taking root for the night, so I paid off the driver and set off on foot. It was raining, a fine freezing rain, and the temperature was noticeably lower than in London.

The Boulevard du Clichy is the 9e *arrondissement's* main artery, a stretch of concrete teeming with vice and lice, relieved by a double line of plane trees down the middle. I was no stranger to its offerings. Segments of my early twenties had been mis-spent in the more celebrated but less ostentatious Rue Pigalle, which abuts onto it.

The boulevard and its adjoining streets are truly the Mecca of the legions of the lost. Represented, perhaps most of all, by the sad, ageing prostitutes who ply for custom from passing cars and tourist buses.

Yet who was I to condemn? I, with my ill-gotten millions, my villa and my yacht, my expensive cars and my decadent taste in women.

Multi-coloured, flashing neon signs lined the street. Their message was consistent and always in English: BEAUTIFUL GIRLS beckoned one throbbing script, SUNNY GIRLS another. GIRLS-GIRLS-GIRLS a third. Girls were what the Boulevard du Clichy was all about. Other messages were blunter: SUPER-SEX – EROTIC – PORN – SEXY – EXTREME. Endless permutations of a common theme.

'*Venez chez moi, chérie,*' a tart murmured in my passing ear. Her face, grotesquely over-painted, lips purple and exaggerated to twice their natural outline, registered like a slide flashed on a screen – there one minute, gone the next. A sex show tout caught at my arm, thrust a ticket at me.

'*Pas cher,*' he mouthed. '*Pas cher.*'

Scarcely breaking my stride, I flung him aside with force enough to send him reeling against a wall-mounted collage of soft-porn photographs. I would have liked to kill him. To make an example of him as representative of the whole festering sump to which Lizzy was now an unwilling contributor. To think that I had once paid money to enjoy and therefore perpetuate this rottenness. How these anachronistic sleaze shows survived in this age of the Internet was beyond my ken.

Then I was there. A sign – LINGERIE CUIR (it sounds so much more exotic than "Leather Underwear") and above it CLUB CONCORDE, in *tricolore*. How patriotic. I entered a dingy passageway lit by a single glow-worm of a bulb. If the boulevard represented the sight and sound of squalor, here behind the neon façade was to be found its odour. Bad drains, stale cooking, staler perfume, piss and vomit. Even a rat would think twice before foraging in these sewers.

A tuxedoed sentry held the door open for me, expecting and receiving a generous *pourboire* for his troubles. I aimed to rock no boats, upset no protocols tonight. I was entering the kingdom of the profane, where nothing is sacred except money, and where outsiders are tolerated so long as they spend freely and keep their profiles invisible.

Inside, a second sentry, bigger, burlier, and with eyes like holes in a Halloween pumpkin, awaited me. Not exactly barring my path, merely causing me to divert around him. The pumpkin eyes stripped me every step of the way, but not because he had designs on me. I was glad now I hadn't come heeled. Bringing a gun into the likes of the Concorde Club would rate as a declaration of war.

The lighting in the main bar was subdued red, apart from the spotlight over a circular stage where a topless bottomless girl pirouetted around a pole. I watched idly for a minute. It was tame stuff by French nightlife standards, mere *hors d'oeuvres* on the menu of erotica that would cater for every last perverted taste. Public buggery not excluded.

Trade was still slack. In a place like this it wouldn't take off until well past the midnight hour. The underemployed trio of bartenders in their wine-coloured waistcoats and bow-ties fairly rushed to serve me. The honour fell to the most nimble-footed, a runt of an Arab sporting a lonely earring and a phoney grin.

'*Un* Tchaikovsky,' I ordered. Vodka with Calvados, a mix that Willie had introduced me to over the festive season. It made a change from Vodka without Calvados.

'*Volontiers, m'sieu.*'

The drink came in a fancy square glass, together with a bill. The size of it explained why the club had no need to charge an entrance fee. It was built in.

'I want to see the boss,' I said to the Arab as he was about to rejoin his chums.

'*Ah, bon? Vous voulez parler à* Monsieur Gabrio?'

'No, whoever he might be. It's Petit I want.'

He hunched his shoulders, what little there was to hunch. '*Il n'est pas ici, m'sieu.*'

I slid a 50-euro note across the counter. 'Keep the change and get him *ici.*'

Before reaching for the note he did a fast east-west recce. Apart from the other barman the only living beings within observing range were an ill-matched couple (male, sixty; female, Lizzy's age, give-or-take) a couple of stools along. The man was engrossed in his pert companion, she in her finger-nails: a fishnet clad leg swung like a metronome to the music's trudging beat. It was a long, shapely leg. For all the impact it had on my libido it might as well have been a leg of mutton.

The banknote meanwhile did a vanishing trick.

'Who shall I say wants him?'

'Warner,' I pronounced it the French way, "Varnair".

'Varnair,' he repeated. A grunt. Not impressed then. 'D'accord.'

A whisper to his workmates, who flashed identical startled looks at me, and he was off. I tasted my Tchaikovsky, letting it trickle unhurriedly down my throat, savouring the fiery edge the Calvados lent to the vodka. The pole dancer, still pounding away on the circular stage, began to rotate her siliconed boobs in opposite directions, flouting the laws of physics and drawing applause from the thinly-spread audience.

'Quels tétons, hein?' a voice murmured close by my ear. Some tits.

I didn't turn. This would be the advance guard, checking me out. I made a suitably coarse remark about the girl's "tétons", provoking a snigger.

'Are you armed?'

Now I looked at him. I had to tilt my head back to meet his eyes. He was the Incredible Hulk in a midnight blue tuxedo instead of green skin.

'Want to frisk me?'

A toothless grin split the battered face. It was the face of a man who had launched a thousand gatecrashers – head first, into the gutter.

'Not here,' he demurred. 'Come.'

Under the wide-eyed scrutiny of the other barmen we crossed the bar diagonally, me leading, the Hulk breathing down my neck, to a distant corner. PASSAGE INTERDIT warned the door ahead. We passaged anyway. On the other side was a corridor with real lights that you could see by, and a reception committee of three: the little Arab, quivering like a cornered mouse, and a pair of meatballs in lounge suits, either of whom would have made two of him.

'This him?' my escort barked at the Arab.

His head bobbed like a puppet's.

'Okay. Get back to work.'

The relieved Arab scuttled off to the sanctuary of the bar.

'As for you, Monsieur Varnair,' my escort grinned, 'hands on the wall and legs apart. *S'il vous plait.*'

A sidekick did the frisking. That he didn't find anything wasn't for lack of diligence.

'Is Petit here?' I asked, when it was all over. I made a performance of smoothing lapels and dusting off sleeves, affecting indifference.

'Come,' the Hulk said again, and beckoned. Now he led and I followed and the lesser goons brought up the rear. We tramped down a corridor to a T-junction, turned left into a dead end with three doors branching off. *DIRECTION* proclaimed the last door, and below, an uncompromising *FRAPPEZ!* In between, a peephole. The Hulk rat-a-tatted with a bent forefinger.

'*Oui?*' came faintly from within.

'*C'est* Tom-Tom, *patron. J'amène le type qui voulait vous voir.*' I've brought the guy who wanted to see you.

'*Fais-le entrer.*'

Tom-Tom the Hulk nudged me in ahead of him into a spacious, well-lit office, soullessly and antiseptically furnished in metal and plastic with black and white carpet tiles underfoot, laid out like a chessboard.

From the inevitable desk a man beheld me without expression. A second man, standing by the desk, did likewise.

'*Vous êtes* Warner?' the man behind the desk enquired civilly enough. 'André Warner?

'*Lui-même.*'

He didn't seem any more impressed than the barman.

'*Je m'appele* Petit.'

In keeping with his name, he was slight of build, with narrow sloping shoulders. The slicked down hair showed strata of grey, and the mouth was lipless; it might have been drawn with a scalpel. A dapper dresser. In an earlier era he would have worn spats and sported a cane.

Tom-Tom had melted back into the corridor, which improved the odds in my favour. Petit wasn't alone though, and was bound to have a gun within grabbing distance. The right hand out of sight behind the desk wasn't there for the purpose of self-abuse.

'Am I allowed to sit?' I said.

'Please do.' From a semi-circle of three lounge chairs before the desk I chose the middle one.

'You will not mind if my associate remains with us.' Petit was telling, not asking. 'Gilles Gabrio, *je te présente* Monsieur André Warner. *Un anglais, bien entendu.*'

Nods passed between Gabrio and me.

'Anglo-Canadian, actually.' I said pedantically.

Gabrio was a stereotype Frenchman. A near-black pelt of hair, sallow Mediterranean complexion. Tough looking. Good physique.

'We have heard about you,' Gabrio said. 'A contract man, *hein*?'

Petit stroked the tip of his nose with a forefinger. 'What do you want from me?'

'Co-operation.'

Gabrio paused in the process of lighting a cigarette, the lighter flame wavering an inch short of the tip, his dark eyes fathomless under projecting brows.

'*Vous avez du toupet*,' he remarked without heat.

330

It was fair comment, I did have a lot of cheek, barging in here expecting a big wheel racketeer to help me out.

'I'm not looking for trouble,' I responded.

'No, but you're looking for a favour. It's the same thing.'

I gave Petit a quizzical look. 'Does he do all your talking? I came here to see the top man, not his lap dog. Still, if you're not willing to help ...' I made to rise.

'Wait a minute.' His tongue passed lightly over his lips, leaving a sheen on them like the trail of a slug. 'Allow me to give you some advice, Warner. Make no threats, or you will not leave here alive.'

'I come in peace,' I rejoined, sinking back into the well-upholstered chair. 'All I want is a little knowledge. For a little knowledge, I will be forever in your debt.'

'Ah, yes ... knowledge. A dangerous thing, knowledge. Too much knowledge can get a man killed.'

'And too little leads to misunderstandings. Between us, Monsieur Petit, there should be no misunderstandings.'

'I agree.' Without bringing his right hand out of hiding, he rotated his chair a few compass points in each direction. It squeaked. He stopped with a frown. 'Tell me why you come to me for this ... knowledge.'

'Obviously because you have it.'

I was gambling on Petit's amenability to reason. Like any gang boss, his every move would be guided by the abacus of profit and loss. In this case he would quickly learn the immediate gains were not gains at all, only losses to be avoided. Loss through strife, loss through damage, possibly loss of lives, including his own.

Not unimportant losses, then. On the plus side, I would owe him a favour, to be called in at his pleasure. A favour owed by a hit man is hard currency in underworld circles.

'Explain your needs,' he said finally, 'and I will help you if it is within my competence.' His smile was twisted. Never-theless, it *was* a smile. Prospects were improving.

Surprise had spread across Gabrio's face, as if he were seeing a new side to his master.

'Quite recently,' I said, 'you supplied a certain sex movie, possibly one of a batch, to a Stephen Bloore, of Chelsea, London. The movie was entitled ...' I tried to repel the evocation of a naked Lizzy, prancing under the camera's pitiless eye, ' "Five-to-One." I have reason to believe it was produced in Holland within the last few months.'

Petit made tapping sounds with his tongue. 'Bloore is my exclusive distributor in England.'

'I know. He sent me to you. He happens to be an old friend of mine. Can I take it that you know the origin of the movie?'

'Not so fast.' Petit made a pacifying motion with his free hand. 'Monsieur Bloore makes a lot of business for me in England. I will not disturb my relationship with him. Not even for someone like you, Warner.'

'Forget Bloore. I'm not interested in him.' I leaned forward to slap my hand on the desk top. 'It's the *producer* I want.'

'Might I ask why?'

'It's personal.'

'Listen, Warner, I know about you. I know your history. If you are pursuing some kind of vendetta against my, ah, associates, this is not good business.'

'We're talking about a supplier, not a customer. Suppliers are ten a penny.'

'Not so. The supplier you speak of could not easily be replaced. His material is highly specialized.'

That word again – "specialized." Only now was I begin-ning to grasp its meaning.

'Oh, sure,' I said with a sneer. 'Like porn is scarce, huh? Look, Petit, I don't give a fuck for the morals of your business. My private opinion is that you and your kind represent the human race in its lowest form, but I'm not on a crusade. Just give me the works on the people who supplied the movie, and I'll get out of your hair for good. Deal?'

He didn't answer at once. His temples contracted as he toyed with his dilemma. To play ball with me was to lose a valuable and possibly irreplaceable source of supply. The alternative was to eliminate me, or at least to try. Yet even here in the 9e *arrondissement*, murder is not taken lightly, is still avoided if less drastic solutions can be found.

When Petit spoke again it was to Gabrio.

'Can the source survive without our friend?'

'In my opinion, it would survive, yes.' Gabrio wasn't going to stick his neck out too far. 'Even if not, there are others making movies in the exact same category, as you know, but they are unknown quantities.' He gesticulated, smoke from the cigarette between his fingers describing whorls. 'But, yes ... supplies would not necessarily be interrupted.'

Another period of absolute quiet ensued. The room was well insulated, not so much as a murmur of the thumping bar music penetrated.

Petit's sigh was long and spelled resignation.

'So be it. But I expect something from you in return. I have business to transact with some, er ... business associates from Marseilles tomorrow. We meet in Fontainebleau. Regrettably these people are of dubious goodwill and certain precautions will be required.'

'You must take great care, *patron*,' Gabrio cautioned, looking troubled. 'You will need a couple of torpedoes at least. Those Midi *escrocs* are no respecters of general rank unless it's backed up by a division of artillery.'

'You are right, my dear Gilles.' Petit's eyes swivelled to me. 'But I am not concerned. I shall have my division of artillery, Warner, shall I not?'

I was dumbfounded. 'Will you? Do you mean you're looking to me for *protection*?'

'Why not?' He sounded almost hurt. 'Protection is a small price to pay for the considerable sacrifice I am about to make.'

It had a certain perverse appeal, I had to say.

'All right, Petit, you just hired yourself a guard dog. So long as you don't expect me to stick around holding your hand beyond tomorrow.'

'Understood.' With a moistened fingertip he smoothed his eyebrows, an effeminate gesture that made me wonder about him. 'You may leave on Saturday and your debt will be discharged.'

He stubbed out his cigarette and stood up, tugging the wrinkles from his dinner jacket. I stood with him.

'Come with me,' he said.

He led the way out. Tom-Tom was standing opposite the door. As I appeared behind Petit, he took a step forward, fists balled.

'Take it easy, Tom-Tom,' Petit said, patting him on the shoulder. He almost had to stand on tiptoe to reach.

'Everything okay, chief?' Tom-Tom said, eyes like agate chips travelling over me.

'*Ça va, mon brave*,' Petit said softly, and his tone was affectionate. Tom-Tom was clearly more than mere employee. 'He is a friend. In a manner of speaking.'

We left Tom-Tom with his wall-to-wall shoulders glowering in our wake, and mounted a staircase to the second floor. Here a short corridor and another bouncer, very black, smaller than Tom-Tom but still with the silhouette of an American footballer, protective padding and all. Only on him the padding was built in.

The black bouncer was guarding a door, which he flung open as we approached. Petit nodded to him. On the other side of this door, instead of the expected office, was a nightclub in miniature, complete with bar, fancy crimson drapes, concealed and dimmed lighting, and a stage just about big enough to hold a couple of performers and their props. The furniture was over-stuffed imitation hide, and all black. The late Michael Jackson whined from some hidden speaker, "I am the one ..." On our side of the bar sat a man in shirtsleeves: a man with a hook nose and a hairless cranium that gleamed snow-white under the concealed lighting. He was plinking away at a laptop keyboard, his face creased in concentration. Our entry had gone unheard, and when Petit called a greeting the man started, instinctive annoyance at the interruption at once converting to bland servility.

'Ah, c'est vous-même, patron.' He slid off the stool for the hand hugging rites. 'I was not expecting you.' He spoke the "pure" French of the Parisian, lightly drawled, the enunciation clear and precise so that even I could follow it without straining.

'Jean-Guy,' Petit said, 'shake hands with André Warner. Warner , this is Jean Guy Magnol, *mon comptable.*'

His accountant. Magnol wore an inscribed gold bracelet on his right wrist. His hand was small and damp, and his grip loose. I was glad to return it.

'*Enchanté, monsieur,*' he murmured, his grin as fake as a Chinese Rolex.

'Glad to know you.' Leaving aside my distaste for bracelets on male wrists, there was an oiliness about him that I didn't take to. He also had a tic in his right eye that I found disconcerting.

'Monsieur Warner will be accompanying me tomorrow,' Petit elaborated. 'In return, he requires a little information from us.'

Magnol lit a cigarette and left it in the corner of his mouth, as the French are wont to do.

'Anything to oblige, *hein*?' Magnol reached behind the bar and faded the music to a drone. 'How can we help the gentleman?'

'He seeks information on DeB.'

'Ah, *bon*?' Unbidden, Magnol rounded the bar to organize drinks. While he clinked bottles and glasses, I absorbed more of my surroundings. The wallpaper in particular was in a class of its own, a frieze of black-and-white photographs, the sickest of sick porn, all subjects and objects portrayed in graphic close-up. Pure overkill.

The drink Magnol brought me was dark amber. The whiff of malt hit my nostrils long before the glass hit my mouth. I had spotted the label on the bottle: Balvenie. Whatever else he may have been, Petit was no cheapskate.

'DeB, you said, patron.' Magnol removed the cigarette to create space for his glass. He made short work of the contents. 'They are our best suppliers. They could double their output, and it still wouldn't satisfy the market demand.'

'I am not unaware of this.' Petit spoke with some acidity. 'Other arrangements will be made.'

'If we are to give him what he asks, we must know why.'

Petit fixed me with a questioning look.

'Jean Guy's experience in the pornography market goes back twenty years. His advice will be of inestimable value to you.'

I hesitated. The request was not unreasonable, but merely to talk of it was painful.

'Good enough,' I conceded at last, and proceeded to relay

the gist of my relationship with Lizzy and her abduction by de Bruin.

When I had finished, the man who had wallowed in filth for twenty years regarded me through streamers of smoke.

'The girl has been in de Bruin's hands for five months, you say?'

I nodded.

'And she has ... performed in movies?'

Muscles in my body knotted.

'All I've seen so far is one movie. It was more than enough.'

Magnol laughed without mirth. 'This I do not doubt. Also ...' He glanced at Petit, as if seeking permission to go on.

'Also?' I said, wanting yet not wanting to hear.

'They get them hooked, you know, to keep them dependent. Cocaine mostly: it helps relax the body and induces well-being and sexual awareness, removes inhibitions. Sometimes crack cocaine or Ecstasy. Only last week I watched a movie featuring this very young girl, ten or eleven, I should think. Her performance was something to see.' He shook his eggshell head in a kind of wonderment. I was arguably more sexually adventurous than most. But the act Magnol went on to describe would have been outlandish between consenting adults, let alone with a child, who was unlikely to have consented.

Mentally, I switched off. Magnol's voice blurred to a meaningless rumble.

Cocaine. Was that what de Bruin had pumped into Lizzy that night in Andorra, when they took her away? If Magnol was right, if she was being fed the drug on a continuous basis, what would be the extent of her dependence after five months?

Total, was my guess.

Magnol was still extolling the high spots of his celluloid masterpiece.

'... then they wheeled on a second *mec* .. .'

'Leave it!' I said, in a voice that to my ears sounded like a rock crusher at work.

'I do leave it,' Magnol assured me, showing no offence. 'We have a house rule not to use such young girls in our organization.' He said this with a perverse pride. 'Never under the age of twelve.'

Never under twelve. Sweet Jesus.

'Is it feasible,' I asked Petit and Magnol jointly, trying to get the conversation back on track, 'that de Bruin would kidnap a girl simply to put her in a sex movie? Would he really commit a major crime just for that?'

'In the ordinary way, probably not,' Magnol said. 'It would depend on the girl. I have heard rumours that de Bruin supplies girls to the Middle East, oil sheikhs and the like, and that he is paid fabulous sums for this service.'

Maybe Petit made warning signs behind my back, because Magnol switched abruptly to another topic, namely the practical difficulties of my mission.

'It will take a commando-style operation to break into the DeB building, if this is what you intend. It is in the Zeedijk district of Amsterdam – a very tough part of town, I can tell you. Have you ever been there?'

I hadn't. 'It's a thrill I'm looking forward to.'

'It's not as bad as it was, but the police are greased to stay clear of it. Last year some eager-beaver *flic* got it into his head to arrest every junkie in sight, which makes for a lot of arrests. He was found floating in the Oosterdok next morning. Bodies are found floating in the Oosterdok most mornings.'

'Skip the tourist pitch,' I growled. 'Tell me how I get in without using a battering ram.'

Magnol chain-lit another cigarette. 'A battering ram may be what is needed. At DeB the doors are thick as a tank's armour. The only way to get in, as I see it, is to wait around until someone arrives and go in on their coat tails. You will need a gun.'

It seemed incredible to me that such an operation could exist and conduct its sordid business in a well-policed city like Amsterdam. I said as much.

Petit explained, 'Apart from the payoffs, the Dutch attitude towards pornography of all kinds has always been very liberal. Officially it is banned, yet you can buy it at any sex shop. It's even a major foreign currency earner for the Dutch.'

'You don't say. Is child porn itself really so lucrative it's worth breaking the law in just about every country in Europe? Ordinary porn, yes, that I can understand is a money-making racket. It's legal. But this stuff with kids, the demand can't be so great as to be worth risking a prison sentence.'

Petit's slender eyebrows climbed his forehead.

'You think? There is far more money to be made from child porn relative to the volume of output than from conventional porn. For one thing, the supply of material is limited and constantly changing; after all, children become adults. For another, they are under parental control and less accessible, though parents do sometimes connive in their exploitation and even actively participate. The average child, however, will have to be secretly bribed. Her or his parents will usually both be working, and consequently neglectful, allowing their children to watch sex DVDs or play in the streets after dark. You know how it is.'

Not being a parent, I didn't know how it was but I understood what he was saying. I nodded.

'Then there are the risks,' he went on, 'which you yourself have mentioned. In most countries, certainly throughout Western Europe, child pornography is illegal and the penalties are severe. The Internet is being increasingly policed and where once the producers could remain anonymous, Interpol now has the ability to trace the source of a site and introduce a virus to disable it. Shutting down sites is only part of the story, though. What they are really after are the identities of the producers, in order to arrest them. Not so easy, but it's getting tougher and tougher to operate the sites. Soon the producers will have to re-think their strategy, operate from more permissive pastures, such as the Middle East or North Africa. They will need ever more sophisticated antivirus systems, and these do not come cheap.' He smoothed an imaginary stray lock from his forehead. 'Which brings me to your original question – is it lucrative. I can tell you that, despite the rising cost of antivirus protection and avoidance of arrest, a gross profit margin of a thousand per cent would be considered moderate.'

That shook me. Translated into actual money, an Internet video costing, say, £100,000, to produce would be expected to gross a million sterling. Impressive and horrific.

It was Magnol who turned the conversation away from statistics and back towards my private project, saying, 'Would you like me to draw you a floor plan of the DeB building?'

'It would be useful. Thanks.'

While Magnol sketched, Petit went over the timetable for his meeting with the Marseillais.

'We start early in the morning,' he informed me in conclusion. 'Be here at eight. *D'accord*?'

He had played ball with me. Now it was my turn.

'I'll be here,' I said.

'Have you brought a gun into France with you?'

'Not this trip. I'm behaving myself.'

'If you're going to be my bodyguard, you'll need to be armed.' He nodded to himself, not needing my confirmation. 'Leave it to me.'

His goodwill even extended to having me driven back to the Mercure in a black Cadillac with a well-stocked bar. I helped myself to a little hospitality as we wended through the wet streets.

Back at the Mercure, I looked in on Emilia. She was in the shower. I walked in and stood by the bathroom door watching her pale shape behind the obscure glass.

'That you, André?' she called out, no false modesty. Or real modesty.

'It's me. Feeling okay?'

'Wonderful.' She certainly sounded more lively. My guess was her new-found sparkle came out of a hypo, but that could just be the cynic in me.

'Glad to hear it. Meet me for breakfast at seven tomorrow and I'll tell you where to find lover boy.'

'Seven!' The shower door shot back. She stood on the threshold, blinking water out of her eyes. 'Is that seven in the *morning?*'

In the raw she was even skinnier than I had expected. She had no tits whatsoever.

'You figure it out, sweetheart.' I turned to go.

'Bastard!' she yelled after me.

Honouring my side of the bargain was the easy part. Petit supplied the hardware, a huge Ruger Speed Six. It made an impressive bulge under my armpit. All that was required of me was to sit in a corner, visible yet remote, exuding menace. Amazingly, it worked. The representatives of the Marseilles underworld were on their best behaviour.

'Not a single tantrum,' Petit remarked afterwards. 'It's strange, don't you think, how the killer instinct stamps itself on a man? It forms an aura around him that is impossible to camouflage.'

That was worrying. 'Thank God you're not a cop, Petit.'

'I also thank God for that.' He tittered. 'Well, perhaps not God.'

It was after three in the morning when he shoved his papers back in his brief case. We were overnighting in Fontainebleau, at the same hotel where the meetings had been held. The place was asleep as we rode the elevator together to the fifth floor. Our rooms were next door to each other, by chance not out of chumminess.

'Now we're even, Warner,' he said, slotting the keycard in his door. 'Don't come looking for any more favours. In fact, don't come at all. Even better, stay away from Paris.'

Threats, especially needless ones, bring out my mean streak.

'Where I go is my business,' I said pleasantly, 'and you and your cowboys better keep out of my way.'

His mouth set in a lipless slit, and he stepped into his room.

'Wait,' I said, holding the door open. I removed my jacket, wriggled out of the underarm holster and handed it to Petit, complete with gun. 'You might have a use for it. I have been known to walk in my sleep.'

I let myself in my room. To the best of my knowledge, I passed the night without sleepwalking.

Twelve hours later I was in Amsterdam.

Twenty-Eight

No. 2 Korte Hoekssteeg, off Zeedijk. A black steel door, crisscrossed with rivet studs, it might have been cut from the hull of a Cunard liner. A plaque screwed to the wall beside it declared it to be the registered office of AnnRik International. The "Rik" as in de Bruin, presumably.

No door handle, no bell, no letter flap. Just a thin slot in the steel door jamb. Casual callers not encouraged. Jean-Guy Magnol had warned me there would be difficulties, and I couldn't accuse him of overstatement. This was not going to be a routine break-and-enter. The windows were of reflective glass and heavily barred on first and second floor levels. At the very top of the house, in the centre of a semi-circular gable-end, had once been a much smaller window, but this was bricked up.

No entry via the adjoining house either, a brothel, reputedly owned by de Bruin. I couldn't envisage the occupants allowing me free passage for the purpose of sledgehammering a hole through into the house of a neighbour who also happened to be their landlord. Which left only the rear of the building. This was equally inaccessible without blasting materials. Although a shared passageway served the rears of 2 and 4, it was barred by yet another steel door. I was developing a rare old complex about steel doors.

I had spent the whole of Sunday morning casing the block. Down the high bank of the canal, the unpronounceable

Oudezijds Achterburgwal, left into Boomsteeg, a short road running parallel to Korte Hoekssteeg, left again into Zeedijk, where I was solicited by a drug-hazed faggot in a caftan. I shook him off and he crumpled up on the sidewalk, just another piece of human wreckage.

By mid-day I had come to the conclusion that No. 2 Korte Hoekssteeg was unstormable, and that only by subterfuge was I ever going to see the inside of it. It was beginning to snow, and I was feeling thirsty, so I abandoned my research and went to seek sustenance.

In the Nieuw Markt, which is where the Zeedijk starts, I stumbled on a grubby little "brown café", the approximate Dutch equivalent of an English pub, except that these cafés serve drugs with the Government's blessing. The "brown" comes from the preponderance of dark wood and smoke-stained walls. This one also served coffee in lipstick-smeared cups. A specialty of the house most likely. The other customers looked healthy enough, so I drank it anyway. Incredibly, it was delicious.

Thus refreshed, I spread Magnol's rough floor plan of No. 2 Korte Hoekssteeg on the greasy laminated table top. The first floor was unequally sectioned into four: entrance hall with stairs off, a thirty-seat viewing room, a projector cubicle, and a cutting room (the last two both defunct since the advent of video and DVD). Upstairs were a conference room, a secretary's office, and the executive offices.

This left the top floor, which was done up as a luxury apartment, and the basement which Magnol suspected to be a staging post of some kind for girls in transit.

'No movies are produced in Korte Hoekssteeg,' he had gone on to explain. 'For that they use some place in the north of the country, close to Harlingen. I never went there. I was never invited.'

'Would that be their centre of operations?' I had asked. But he replied with a Gallic handspread, unable or unwilling to conjecture.

My scrutiny of the increasingly dog-eared and now grease-stained floor plan brought me no nearer to gaining entry. In any case, I wasn't yet ready. My armoury was tucked away in Spijk & Co's Amsterdam warehouse away on the north side of the Ij, the great river that divides the city. Nothing was doing there until Monday. Even gun runners are entitled to a day of rest, I suppose.

As a change from taxis I went by tram from the Central Station back to my hotel, there to fritter away the hours hunched over a succession of vodkas, fruitlessly planning my offensive. The imponderables were too many and too great for any set piece moves. When the crunch came I would be guided by reflex and driven by instinct. Hit first, hit hard, and keep moving.

Simple. Or simplistic?

It was still snowing and the snow trucks were out spreading grit when I went to bed with half-a-dozen measures of vodka sloshing about in my gut. And never more sober in my life.

On Monday I acquired the tools for the job. I rented a Porsche Boxster, capable, the Avis clerk assured me, of over 250 kph. I hoped I wouldn't need all them.

I was at Spijk & Co's warehouse by eleven o'clock to collect my package. Jannie Spijk, son of Julius, the owner, attended to me, charging an exorbitant "handling fee" of eight hundred euros in any hard currency. I paid, without protest, in pounds sterling, converted at a rate that I wasn't in a position to dispute. Still I made no fuss. Merely stored his name and his physiognomy in my memory box as someone to avoid in future.

In the car, with the heater at full throttle, I unpacked and loaded both guns, and wriggled into the Horseshoe rig. The Ithaca shotgun I consigned to the trunk for now. When the time came I would conceal it inside my parka. Having no buttstock it was only about three feet long, and scarcely bulkier than a rolled umbrella.

The Porsche skating a little in the slush, I headed out of the dock area and crossed back into central Amsterdam by the Ij-Tunnel. Back to my hotel, to await the coming of night. Like all those who walk a lawless path, I was more at ease in darkness.

With nightfall the snow, which had petered out, began again in earnest. I drove to Korte Hoekssteeg and parked the car just around the corner, in Zeedijk itself. It was a risk. Theft, I had been told, was second nature to Zeedijk-dwellers. But I had to have transport on hand.

Opposite No. 2 was a former tenement that appeared to have been converted into offices. Came six o'clock most of the lights in the building had been extinguished, and I felt safe in taking up my vigil in its doorway. By hugging the wall of the shallow recess nearest to the street lamp, I was in shadow. Just as well. I was barely installed when a red Rolls-Royce with a snow-topped roof pulled up outside the de Bruin building and disgorged two men and a blonde woman onto the sidewalk. It was too soon, too sudden, for me to exploit the situation. While I still hesitated, the door opened, creating an oblong of white fluorescent light in the dark wall. I had an impression of white paintwork, then the door swung shut and the sidewalk was empty again, the Roller heading off for pastures new. I drew the Ithaca out through the neck of my parka, pumped a round into the breech, locked the safety catch. Tucked it into my armpit where I could bring it swiftly into action. When the next opportunity came, I would be ready to act.

The snowfall thickened, descending at a slant as the wind rose, moaning softly like a ghost on the prowl. The temperature sank and mine with it. I beat a tattoo with my feet on the doorstep and imagined those unending, hot summer days in Andorra when the earth had seemed to pant for rain, and the sky was a vast parabola of sunlight.

Imagined, too, Lizzy, as she had been then, not as she was now. Lizzy who was joy and sadness, pleasure and pain. Her face, her laughter, her big heart, and most of all her love. And my love for her, whatever its true from, whether or not it be good and right and selfless, burned on as brightly as ever.

Footsteps. High-heeled and accompanied by feminine chatter. I pressed against the wall, turned my face sideways inside the hood of my parka. The heels tapped past, slightly deadened by the snow, the conversation running on without break. Even as it faded, a car, on sidelights only, edged into the street. It came alongside, moving at a walking pace. I braced myself, willing it to stop. But it accelerated and shot past on hissing tyres, leaving wet tracks. Another car entered the opposite end of the street. A taxi, unmistakably diesel powered. Korte Hoekssteeg was certainly popular.

The taxi came to a slithering standstill midway between Nos. 2 and 4. Trade for the brothel? A hatted figure emerged, fumbling money from a hip pocket.

'Bedankt, mynheer,' indistinctly from the cabbie.

His fare stepped back and with cautious tread – he had a stick and a limp – made for No 2. I started out of the doorway as the cab trundled forward, headlights slicing through the whirling snowflakes.

The limping man was at the door. Crossing the road at a trot, I passed through the cab's lingering exhaust smoke. The cab itself swung into the Zeedijk, and the noise of its engine faded. The door of No. 2 was opening, and that oblong of white light fell on the limping man. He reached for the top of the plastic card protruding from the slot in the jamb, but my reach was faster than his.

'*Vat* ... ?' He half-turned, then froze when I screwed the shotgun's muzzle into his ear.

'Keep right on going, friend.' For good measure, in case he didn't understand English, I threw in a healthy shove. He stumbled inside. I followed, pocketing the card.

'If you wanting money, I give ...'

'Shut up.'

Behind us the door whispered shut. The latest in security technology, yet still subject to human fallibility, as I had just proved. The limping man sagged against the wall, his frame slack, his jowly, overstuffed face frozen in terror.

'I don't want to hurt you,' I told him, 'but unless you do exactly as I say, you'll never walk again. With or without a stick. Savvy?'

I was taking his understanding of English for granted. After all, he was presumably Dutch.

'*Ja ... ja.*' He dribbled down his scarf.

'How many people do you think there are in this building?'

'I ... I am not certain.' I rammed the gun tight under the bottom-most of his flabby chins. He almost keeled over in fright. 'Twelve ... I don't know ... fifteen, maybe.' His voice quavered. 'Tonight is a private film showing.'

'Is de Bruin here?'

'De Bruin? I cannot say this. Normally he will be here. And Annika, of course.'

'Annika? Who's she?'

'His wife,' he said, sounding surprised that I needed to ask.

I had no quarrel with her. I had no quarrel with anyone other than Rik de Bruin. Unless they got under my feet.

'I'm going to have to hit you.'

His chins shook. 'No, please ... I can help you.'

'Sorry, friend.' I manoeuvred him round until he was kissing wall, and sapped him behind the ear with the butt of the Korth revolver. As he crumpled up I dealt him a second tap, on the temple. Now he was out twice.

With the floor plan in my mind's eye, I lugged the comatose form into what used to be the cutting room. The light switch was in the usual place. I flicked it in passing, and dumped the unconscious man next to a line of fireproof cabinets. These, a portable movie screen, and a slim steel-topped table were the only pieces of furniture. On the table was a conventional splicing machine and some obsolete VHS equipment, all covered in a healthy layer of dust. I went back out to the hall to retrieve the man's hat and stick. As I gathered them up, I heard a metallic click from the front entrance. More visitors? I flung the hat and stick into the cutting room, and myself after them. Chest heaving, I flattened against the inside of the door while several pairs of feet filed past. A close call.

While waiting for the new arrivals to disperse I took in more detail of the cutting room. The wall to my right was external. Through the barred window I could see the street lamp and the office tenement that had sheltered me. The internal walls behind and opposite were bare, that on the left hung with full-length heavy green drapes, which immediately chimed a wrong note with me. Why conceal, embellish, or what-have-you a presumably blank wall? Answer: because it isn't blank.

Mildly intrigued, I located the drawstring, hauled away at the cord, exposing nine-tenths of the wall which, from waist height upwards was no more than a sheet of plate glass separating the cutting room from what I knew to be the viewing room. And the room was in use, a dozen or so people being draped about the double row of seats before a wide screen set in the wall.

I reared back and ducked below the window level, clawing the Ithaca off the table top where I had left it. My heart was thudding like a bongo drum. Any second the door would burst open, and it would be all up with me.

The expected bursting-in never happened. Yet I had no doubt that I had been seen. Shit, I had looked some of them in the eye.

As the minutes crawled by and the sweat cooled on my skin, it came to me that nobody was going to come gunning for me. Inexplicably, my appearance had not prompted a hue and cry. I chanced a peek over the metal window surround. A blonde woman was pacing up and down the aisle. Apart from that, the attitude and disposition of the occupants was as before. I raised my head warily, then with confidence. No reaction.

Relief wrenched a ragged laugh from me. The "window" was one-way only: from the other side it was a mirror. Unnerving though it was to stand in apparent full view of those people, all they could see was their own reflections.

The purpose of this device wasn't hard to figure. The rich and famous would be invited to a viewing of the latest kiddy porn release, to be filmed ogling it. It was just a clever variation on that tried and tested racket – blackmail. You had to hand it to de Bruin, he had his snout in some profitable troughs. Child porn and blackmail, two of the slimiest pots of gold imaginable. The more I learned about him, the less I grew to love him. And King Scum himself was in attendance sure enough. His back was to me, but the close-cropped woolly hair and the seam-splitting shoulders were unmistakable.

The blonde woman intrigued me. As she walked, hands

mannishly on hips, she talked, her lips moving with rapid-fire speech. I had a feeling she was giving her audience a going over. Was this Annika de Bruin? She was about de Bruin's age, and the only other woman present was a generation older. Glamorous but hard as titanium was my snap assessment of Mrs de Bruin. A wide mouth is supposed to equate with generosity, but hers had the look of a man-swallowing trap door. A flawless figure though: breasts prominent and well-defined by the clinging, high-collared dress; waist sensationally slim, hips curving away from it with just the right degree of convexity. The leg show was modest yet promised much shapely calves that tapered to neat ankles. In different circumstances I might even have fancied her.

The lecture ended abruptly. Annika de Bruin (if that's who she was) parked her very presentable backside across the aisle from hubby, and shot him a grin that I can only describe as predatory. Then the screen came alive.

From behind the window I viewed the opening scenes in a trance-like state. Though the girl playing the lead wasn't Lizzy, thank God, she was younger by several years. Scrawny, somehow shrunken, a child grown old before her time. For her energy, for her passion, be it spurious or otherwise, she deserved admiration. For the rest, only pity.

'You're the worst kind of scum!' a German cop had once snarled at me.

Maybe he had had a point. Certainly I broke laws and commandments, took lives, albeit not without discrimination. But the exhibition now before me, these were the scum of the scum: the male participants, and the faceless people behind them, the cameramen, the director, the distributor, and above all the creators, the moguls who put up the money to make it happen. They deserved to die – slowly and in extreme agony.

Inside me it was as if something broke. The professional rule book that I had followed thus far was tossed away. I backed away from the mirror-window. Emotions too forceful to resist directed my finger on the trigger to put a shot though the expanse of glass. In the tiny room the blast robbed me of hearing for a few moments, so that the window seemed to shatter in absolute silence. Then my ears popped, and the ensuing uproar reached me. Faces, white faces with pink screaming mouths, made ugly by terror. People running, scrambling for safety, or simply prostrate and scrabbling at the floor as if trying to burrow into it.

The lights went out in both rooms. Cursing, I fired again, blindly, and a fang of flame momentarily illuminated the scene. A body crashed to the floor. A pistol cracked in response, the bullet flitting past overhead. In the dark my heavier firepower was no longer a real advantage. Time to leave. Skating on broken glass, I groped my way towards the door. More pot-shots from the viewing room made me twitch but it was haphazard stuff, and nothing came near me.

Into the entrance hall, blundering, hand raised to protect my face. Nobody emerged on my side of the viewing room, not even Rik de Bruin. I felt the wall and groped towards where I thought the door was. The darkness was a real handicap though, since I was unsure how to open the electronic lock from the inside. To my relief it proved to be nothing more intricate than a hand grip with an integral trigger. No cards, no codes. I was out in a beat. Still no pursuit from the denizens of no. 2 Korte Hoeksteeg. It wouldn't be long though, before the sirens began to bray. You can't let off guns in a city downtown, and expect no one to notice. Even if the police are paid to hear no evil.

Conditions outside were near-blizzard, and I immediately slipped on the fluffy new snow that had collected on the older packed stuff, losing my hold on the Ithaca. I was on my knees, grubbing in the snow for it, when the red Rolls I had seen earlier entered the street, sliding a little, headlights swinging, pinning me like ballet dancer under a spotlight. Engine howling at top revs in low gear, it mounted the curb and came straight for me. I launched myself into the middle of the road. Something glanced off my foot and tossed me aside, then I was rolling crazily, snow filling my mouth, my nostrils, my eyes. Eventually I came to rest sitting up. Semi-stunned but with all parts still functioning.

The Rolls had slewed sideways, and was now stationary. The wheels were spinning as they sought purchase in the slush. The face of a man in the front passenger seat was turned towards me – de Bruin!

At this range I could have taken him out with a single bullet. I had the Korth free of the holster and was lining it up when a siren's lament floated over the rooftops. It stayed my hand just long enough for the Rolls' tyres to find purchase. A stiff-fingered goodbye from de Bruin and it shot away, rear end fishtailing from side to side, tyres clawing for grip Leaving me with a gun in my fist and nobody to shoot at.

Twenty-Nine

Without thinking, I was up and running for the Porsche – hobbling actually, since my left ankle had been bruised by that glancing blow from the Rolls. As I ran I scooped up the Ithaca from the snow.

Rolls-Royces are few and far between in Holland, and red ones as rare as cuckoos at Christmas. In daylight it would have stood out like a beacon in the middle of the Atlantic and, given the Porsche's superior pace and roadholding, sticking with it would have been a pushover. But it was night and as I accelerated after it, all I had to sight on was a pair of tail lights, already dwindling fast, flicking past slower vehicles, snaking a little in the slush. De Bruin's chauffeur had either no nerves or no sense.

We scorched across the Nieuw Markt square as if coupled, the speedo hitting the 100 kph mark, and into a ruler-straight stretch alongside a canal. The snow seemed to form an endless, swirling tunnel in the headlights, blotting out the high buildings on the right. The Rolls slowed suddenly. A flickering blue light washed across the windscreen. Police! Even as I braked, gritting my teeth against the shooting pain in my ankle, the oncoming police car ripped past, going too fast and too single-mindedly to heed a pair of speeding motorists.

The Rolls was already leaping away again, nipping through the gap between a bus and a turning car, and crossing a set of lights at amber. The same lights were red when I bored past. A small car emerging from the intersection wasn't prepared to concede *force majeure*. My bumper clipped his and when last seen through my mirror he was facing in the opposite direction.

I hunched over the wheel, eyes only for the fleeing red dots ahead. Nose-to-tail we crossed a minor canal, then it was down through the gears for a sharp right-hander, taking us into a broad and busy thoroughfare. The Porsche's wheels thumped over tramlines. The traffic was much denser here, and the road surface consequently free of snow. Ahead, at barely reduced speed, the Rolls weaved in and out of the stream of vehicles, collecting blasts of indignation, redoubled for me when I followed through. Some drivers made an attempt to cut me up, but their hearts weren't really in it. The trams were the worst: stolid and unyielding, their garish yellow paintwork seeming to shout "you can't shift me!" And they were right, you couldn't.

Then we were clear of the tramlines and into another straight, our speed passing the 120kph mark. Here the Rolls pulled away, the driver taking chances that I, even in my temporary madness, was unwilling to emulate. The Rolls' brake lights didn't glow once. In front of the Central Station more traffic lights, amber changing to red as ever. De Bruin was through, and this time the heavy flow of traffic prevented me from following. I sat and fumed and fretted, glaring past the flip-flopping wipers at the cortège trudging across the intersection.

Red winked to green and I was off, gunning through the gearbox, challenging the maker's acceleration figures. As I swept into a turn, using the horn to clear a path, the rear end slid away, forcing me to decelerate. But all the speed in the world would make no difference now. I had lost my quarry.

A10 ZAANDAM ALKMAAR the overhead sign announced. Freeway ahead; *autosnelweg* in Dutch. Was that where he was headed? Forget the guesswork and apply some logic. I slammed on the brake and dragged the Porsche over into a bus stop bay, earning resentful stares from the waiting passengers huddled under the meagre shelter.

The GPS was focused on Amsterdam centre. I tapped at the minus button and reduced the scale. Now the city appeared as a grey-shaded area. Slicing through the west side of it was the A10, jinking north-west, forking at Zaandam to join up with the A9, which serves Haarlem to the south and Alkmaar to the north. A third freeway, the A7, meandered true north to cross the long dike at the mouth of the Ijsselmeer, the vast lake that was created when they sealed off the North Sea back in the thirties.

Reducing the scale some more, I traced the freeway as far as the north shore of the ljsselmeer, where it veered off east towards Groningen. I swore softly. It was hopeless. Who's to say de Bruin was headed north anyway? Again I bent over the map, looking for inspiration amidst the red and yellow zigzags. The engine throbbed gently. It was warm and snug in the car. An insidious weariness lulled me. The madness was receding. Why bother? Why not just forget de Bruin, go back to Andorra? Re-start my life.

My fingertip still rested at the northern end of the great dike, an inch below the town of Harlingen.

Harlingen? Inside my brain a cell stirred. *Harlingen*. Jean-Guy Magnol's words came hammering back at me: '... they use some place in the north of the country, close to Harlingen ...'

That was enough for me. Foot down, rubber slithering on wet snow then biting on the asphalt beneath, hurling the Porsche forward inches ahead of a passing bus. Now I drove as if possessed, headlights on full beam, daring anyone to block my path. Miraculously I encountered no prowling police vehicles. I clubbed a hole through the traffic as far as the freeway. There I flayed more tread from the tyres with a savage right turn into the on-ramp, bottoming the nearside suspension and momentarily, frighteningly, inducing a front-wheel skid that took some fancy twirling of the wheel to correct.

The freeway was clear of snow if not of users. I bullied my way in and out of the fast-moving cars and the occasional thundering truck girded with spray. I drove by the seat of my pants. Suicidally. A direction sign loomed: ZAANDAM CENTRUM, A7 PURMEREND, HOORN, 1000m. That was my cue. The off-ramp came up. I filtered into it, barely slowing. The snow was falling faster here, assaulting the car as if to push it back.

Onto the A7. Traffic much thinner, more slush on the road. Couldn't be helped. I edged my speed up past the 150kph mark: 160 ... 170 ... 180 ... Plenty in reserve. Roadholding was the problem, not speed. No need to use the wipers now, not with a wedge of displaced air pushing ahead of the car. Tail lights sparkled in the murk. Too slow to be de Bruin. I whipped past a people carrier as if it were parked. The road was whitening, the snow laying its deadly mulch, too few vehicles now passing to disperse it. Once, twice, I experienced the dreaded twitch from the rear that spelled loss of adhesion. Still I pushed on down the cone of tumbling fat flakes. Only death could stop me. It almost did, in the shape of another Porsche, a white 911, entering the freeway in a high speed drift, its rear fog lamps flooding my windscreen red. I was doing over 200 kph. I gasped at its nearness. Too late I hit the brakes, so close our bumpers actually nudged. The other car reeled away, brake lights blooming accusingly, to skitter across the hard shoulder and up the embankment that bordered it. That made two notches on my car. Yet it ran on, smooth as ever, no vital organs harmed.

That was my last clash. Presently I came to the start of the Afsluitdijk, great Barrier Dam, the causeway that crosses twenty miles of sea to connect south and north Holland. The Ijsselmeer, the lake created by the building of the dam, edged into view to my right, inky-black, merging with the night. On the other side of the dike, screened by high protective earthworks, lay the North Sea. I passed the turrets of some sluice gates, spectral in the milling snowflakes. Then it was just me and the car and the long white ribbon unwinding beneath my wheels.

If de Bruin had taken this route he was trapped on the dike for the next twenty miles. I had to catch him before he reached the far shore. If I didn't make visual contact before then, I might lose him for good. The thought made me push the pedal down, the needle soaring again beyond the magic double century. A southbound car went past with a slam of turbulence that was like a physical blow.

Minutes and miles unrolled. So long as the road remained dead straight I could hold the Porsche at two hundred, but I dared go no faster. And still no tail lights broke the monotony of blackness and whiteness.

A bridge spanning the freeway jumped into the headlight beams, and to the right of it a tower of some sort. Lights from this artificial oasis glowed palely through the snow. My foot came off the accelerator pedal as details sharpened. The tower was mostly glass with an internal winding staircase, like a helter-skelter slide. In the parking lot of the narrow forecourt a monster container-truck made toys of the dozen or so private cars. Not much activity. And no red Roller ... No, wait ... last in the line of cars, partly screened by the container truck. Red paintwork at any rate, and big.

I throttled back to cruising speed as the red car came fully into view, tail on, carelessly parked, patently a Rolls.

'Got you, you bastard!' My gamble had come good.

I was coming up to the end of the barrier that separated the highway from the parking zone. I braked to perform a definitely illegal U-turn against the directional arrows painted on the exit road. My luck held out, and I met no oncoming vehicles. On sidelights I crept past the Rolls and the container truck. About halfway down the forecourt I found a slot, and reversed into it, positioned for instant getaway. I hopped out. Snow settled on me, slithered chillingly down inside my collar. I patted the gun under my coat. Now to blood it.

Behind the steamed up windows the first floor of the tower appeared to be a bar or restaurant. At any rate people were sitting at tables, blurry figures eating and drinking. It was the only place de Bruin and his driver could be, apart from the top of the tower which, as far as I could tell, was purely for viewing purposes. I was hobbling to the entrance at my best sprained-ankle pace, heart hammering against my ribs, when half the double door opened and a man in a brown suit with a coat draped over his arm came out, jingling change.

To him I was a man in search of refreshment, nothing more. To me he was a familiar face, last seen lounging in a chair in the viewing room at No 2 Korte Hoekssteeg.

Any confederate of Rik de Bruin's was an enemy of the public. I shot him in both legs without forethought as he held the door for me. The magnum slugs passing clean through him and the glass door, throwing out a fountain of blood and glass behind him and ricocheting off to inflict more damage on shelves of merchandise. He went down as if hit by a bus, arms flung out backstroke-style. Coins spun and tinkled on the concrete.

Behind the steamy windows sudden movement, as people

were drawn by the gunshots to abandon their gastronomic pleasures. A face peeped warily around the door. I let off a single shot, harmlessly into the snow-pocked sky and the face went into instant reverse, as if tugged by hidden strings. Further along the building, an emergency exit door crashed open, and a figure burst out and went at a fast clip down the line of cars.

'De Bruin!' I bawled after him. Not that I expected him to stop just like that. I wasn't even sure I wanted it that easy. I hopped off in his wake on my disapproving ankle, too late and too slow. As I rounded the cab of the container-truck de Bruin was wrenching open the Rolls' door.

'De Bruin!' I yelled again. He glanced over his shoulder. No fear there, only defiance.

'Fuck you, Melville!'

'Don't move!' I stopped to aim two-handedly. Though I'd have preferred him alive, I'd shoot to kill sooner than let him slip away a second time.

He didn't even pause in his scramble to get behind the wheel. Maybe the key fob was with the man I had shot, maybe not. I wasn't prepared to gamble on it, so I fired, while the door was still open, and was rewarded by the smack of lead meeting flesh. De Bruin's yelp of pain was for me orgasmic. He clutched at his arm, cursing me. I was confidently advancing on him when the Rolls' engine coughed into life and, door swinging open, it reversed in a ragged loop, grazing a rear wing against the truck. I fired once, twice, striking metal with both shots. Then the car was streaking away, flinging gouts of slush from its wheels, the open door slammed shut by the wind force from its rapid acceleration. I got off a last round, caving in the rear windscreen, before the car hit the exit road and was out of range.

Venting a series of curses, I hastened lop-sidedly back to

the Porsche. Still warm from its recent exertions the engine was instantly responsive to the accelerator. When I hit the highway, whipping round a trailer tanker, the Rolls was still well in sight. The snow had eased a little, becoming more powdery, and I could make out the lights of the north shore mirrored in the waters of the Ijsselmeer. I hit the gas harder than ever, was rewarded by a significant closing of the gap. Less than a hundred yards now separated us.

220kph registered on the speedometer, yet with the Rolls travelling only slightly more slowly it seemed no more than a crawl. A saving grace was that the road surface here was free of snow. The gap between us closed to a bare car's length. I swung the Porsche out into the overtaking lane, and the Rolls immediately swung with me. Bumpers jostled. I dragged the wheel over to get clear, and squashed the pedal down to the floor. The Porsche gave a little surge, then we were neck and neck. I mashed my front wing into his, held it there in the hope of forcing him off the road. The steering wheel juddered in my hands and metal screeched.

It was a bad tactic. His car was a lot heavier than mine. All he had to do was hold a straight line and all the huffing and puffing in the world wouldn't budge him. Again I swiped the Rolls' wing with mine. Again the jarring impact, the scrunch of steel, a flirt of sparks. We swept on side by side like a pair of grappling galleons. Stalemate. Until de Bruin turned the tables on me by using his car's near-ton weight advantage to bully me inexorably leftwards, towards the central barrier.

But for the motorcyclist it might have been all up with me. He was where he had no right to be, riding the white line, crouched over the handlebars, displaying that all-too-common youthful disdain of danger. His rear light was a joke. I didn't see him until we were almost on top of him, when de Bruin peeled away to avoid a collision, zigzagging, losing co-ordination. I chose to hold my course and rely on my brakes to keep me out of trouble. This meant another pounding for my ankle, but my car ran straight and true, unlike de Bruin's, which struck the central barrier at a tangent and glanced off it into my path. By then my speed was down to around 120, still fast enough to be lethal if I hit a solid object. Missing me by millimetres, the Rolls veered back across the highway to brush the barrier a second time. By now I had dropped back. I glimpsed de Bruin fighting the wheel with his good arm. Fighting to stay alive.

A third bounce and, out of control finally, the Rolls ripped through the barrier like a chain saw through a sapling. Both headlights went out and the car blundered across the south-bound lane and up the great grassy ramp that holds back the North Sea. The incline didn't slow it at all. On reaching the crest, it continued on down the far side, the rear lights wiped abruptly from sight. De Bruin was in for a ducking.

I brought the Porsche to a standstill. Ahead, the motorcyclist buzzed on in ignorance of the havoc he had caused. A big hunk of my gratitude went with him.

I reversed the short distance to the gash in the barrier, switched off the engine, and set the hazard winkers. A car passed, reduced speed, then had second thoughts about playing Samaritan and accelerated away. Close on its tail came the trailer tanker I had overtaken a few miles back. No alteration of pace at all. The sound of its engine faded. I crossed the freeway at a painful hobble, following de Bruin's trail through the torn metal. The grassy slope was slippery with wet snow, and I made hard going of my ascent. From the top it was forty feet or so of 1-in-3 gradient to where the black abyss of the North Sea began. Twin parallel grooves ran straight as railway tracks down to the water's edge. The red Rolls was gone, as utterly and completely as if it had never been. With that broken rear screen it would have sunk faster than a gold brick.

The wind sighed across the sea's oily surface. The snow fell all around with a faint rustling sound, like dead leaves blowing across an empty courtyard. Wavelets, pushed by that sighing wind, lapped at the foreshore. I stood there awhile, getting my breath back. Snow tickled my cheeks, dusted my shoulders. A truck growled past on the road. I listened intently for other noises, of cries for help, of splashing. No sound, no movement. At last I accepted it as fact: Rik de Bruin was dead. Either killed on impact with the barrier, or drowned. Dead anyway. Out of my life, out of this world.

Where did his death leave me? Revenged, yes, but that was the sum total of it. Lizzy was no nearer salvation, notwithstanding that she might be held prisoner less than an hour's drive from this spot. Unless I went in search of that "house near Harlingen". How fruitful was that likely to be? How near was near? Five kilometres? Fifty? What was the house called, who officially owned it, and what did it look like? And even if I found it, which might take weeks, what were the chances of Lizzy still being there?

The professional in me weighed the odds and was not impressed. To remain out here in the open, on a road with only two exits, was not healthy either. The shooting at the service area would have been reported, the police mobilized.

Head won over heart. I would run for cover. Such damage as had been inflicted on Lizzy was done. After all, I would be no use to her in a Dutch jail.

I still felt like a coward and a heel.

The resolution made, I pushed my luck further by fetching the Ithaca and wrapping it and the Korth in my parka – the parka whose description would soon be travelling along the wires to every police station in the country. I dumped this bundle in the ljsselmeer. Not the most thorough of disposal jobs, but the best I could do at short notice. It sank fast, at any rate.

I restarted the Porsche and took off fast, as if de Bruin were still ahead, still running from me. In a way I wished he were. Without him, I felt like a rebel without a cause.

Making it off the dike didn't mean all my troubles were behind me. Crossing the frontier into Germany was out of the question. That's exactly where they expect a fugitive to turn up. I would have to go underground inside Holland.

The Porsche that had served me so well was now a liability and had to go. Abandoning it by the roadside would be as good as sticking up a poster saying WARNER WAS HERE. Much more sensible to lose it in the cavern of some multi-storey car park.

This solution duly applied (in the town of Leeuwarden), I entrained to Amsterdam, to hole up among a hundred thousand illegal immigrants, drop-outs, and ageing hippies. My new base was a sleazy but marvellously nondescript flophouse. The press made much of the killing at the service area – it was even reported on Sky News – until a double killing in Rotterdam replaced it. De Bruin's death was not mentioned. Presumably the submerged Rolls was still undis-covered. Being in Dutch, most of what the newspapers printed was beyond my comprehension, though I did struggle through some of their reports with the aid of a dictionary. An identikit picture of "the killer", presumably built up by eye-witnesses from the restaurant, bore no resemblance to the image I saw in my mirror every morning. I chortled over it. All in all though, my week in Amsterdam was memorable only for its unremitting tedium.

A week later I felt safe enough to move on. I caught a train to Breda in the south of Holland and went from there by bus to Baarle-Nassau, a small town just inside the Dutch-Belgian border. Thence on foot, ultimately to cross an unpatrolled section of the border early on a fine, frosty morning, with the false dawn blanching the eastern sky. Nine o'clock saw me breakfasting ravenously at an hotel in the Belgian town of Turnhout, and noon buying a rail ticket for Brussels at Antwerp's Central Station.

And by noon the following day I was home free in Andorra.

Thirty

White fingers splayed out from the snow capped mountains into the ravines, and the sky was that brittle blue, so fondly reminisced over during my long sojourn in the damp air of England. It was as if I had left Andorra only yesterday. With the winter tourist season approaching its zenith, the towns and the slopes were clogged with members of the skiing fraternity. Some came for the sport, some for the *après*. The hoteliers and the bar-keepers put out the welcome mat and rubbed their hands and counted the euros, the pounds, and the Swiss francs, not forgetting the dollars, and beamed on every foreign accent.

Not that the tourist industry was uppermost in my thoughts as I stood in the doorway to sample the razor-edged air that morning, two days after my return. The lightening of my black mood did not last. The drained swimming pool and the terrace bereft of its gaily coloured furniture served only to bring back, hurtfully, images of those days of summer and sun and Lizzy. Especially Lizzy.

Visitors were not part of the morning's program. I was not ready to resume socializing. They came anyway: Lucien and Madeleine, my friends and saviours. Deep down, beneath the self-pity, I supposed I was glad to see them. Any company had to be healthier than moping in solitary confinement.

'We saw the taxi arrive last night,' Madeleine explained.

I kissed her cheeks. 'I was going to come over later.'

'Is there any ... ?' they began together and broke off together.

Madeleine frowned Lucien into submission. 'Is there news about Elizabeth,' was her predictable enquiry.

I shook my head slowly. The conversation dried up for a minute or so, then Madeleine asked if I needed anything.

'What about food, for instance?'

'Thanks, Madeleine. Señora Sist has kept me well stocked.'

'A treasure, that woman,' Lucien enthused, looking slightly uncomfortable.

'I suppose you've been paying her wages,' I said, and to my ears it rang like an accusation.

He shuffled his feet on the living room rug. 'It is nothing, my dear André.'

'You embarrass me, but I'm grateful. I'll square it with you later, and tomorrow night I'm going to take you both out to dinner at Le 1900.' Le 1900 was Andorra's finest and grandest restaurant.

'It is not necessary ...' Madeleine murmured.

Lucien overruled her with a trenchant 'We accept!'

A Calvados later they went home. I missed their company the instant I closed the door on them.

For only the second time in a decade or more I entered a house of God for reasons other than touristic. The church so honoured was in La Massana. I had visited it once before, not long after setting up home in Andorra. That visit had been a washout in the sense that it made no spiritual impact. No impurities had been purged, nor healing hands laid on me. The outcome had been disillusion.

It was mid-afternoon when I slipped through the door of age-darkened wood that smelled of earth and incense and polish and the many thousand bodies who had passed through it over the centuries. I had the place to myself. I sat, ill-at-ease, in front of the baroque altar. As before, what I sought there was unclear, lacking shape. Was it peace? Comfort? Redemption? Absolution then? No, surely not that. No hypocrisy, above all.

The sun no longer streamed through the slitted windows. It grew cold. I sensed hostility around me. Rejection. I sighed and my breath came out white. Okay, God. You win. Again.

I left. No wiser, no saintlier. An outcast.

That night I got drunk. And not merely merry or tipsy, but blind, stinking legless drunk. Sorrows not so much drowned in alcohol as impregnated with it. It lifted me to that higher plane beyond total intoxication, where the images sharpen, and whispers become shouts, and the sense of smell heightens to a supernatural degree. And the sights and sounds and smells were all of Lizzy.

Lizzy offering me the forbidden gift of all of herself.

Although not conscious of climbing the stairs, I was somehow in my bedroom. My gun, the trusty Colt Python in my hand. It felt at home there. It was loaded, as always. I stroked the blue barrel with my fingertips. My lethal mistress of these past twelve years. We were like a middle-aged couple: no longer lovers but inseparable through habit.

Down the stairs I lurched, each foot meticulously planted. Some inner compulsion drove me from the house onto the terrace, the frost searing my nostrils, my breath condensing. Underdressed in my light sweater I didn't feel the cold; inside, at the core, I was a crackling bonfire. My steps were slow and deliberate, like a mourner in a funeral procession. I stumbled once, twice, then my feet slid from under me and I fell, losing the gun. In panic I grovelled for it in the frost-frizzed grass, located it painfully with my kneecap, sending my breath hissing through my teeth. I hugged my knee until the pain dulled, then staggered upright. Another step forward and I was back down on the hard earth. There to remain.

No need to cock the Python. Just squeeze the trigger and out would pop a bullet. A big, butch 9mm bullet with a round nose. Made of lead, designed to spread. Hey, that rhymed. A neat round hole where it goes in, a cavity big enough to stuff your fist in where it comes out. That didn't rhyme, though it made a macabre kind of prose.

The muzzle rested against my temple. Ice-cold and soothing. A pulse pounded beneath it, anticipating the kiss of death, longing for it even.

The sky above was encrusted with stars. It was a fine night for dying. Too bad about Lizzy. I had done my best. In my ears a ringing started up. I dismissed it as pre-suicide tinnitus. It went on, undermining my resolve, dragging me back from the precipice. Against my thigh a vibration. Couldn't put that down to stress. It stopped abruptly. Fine. To continue then ...

The ringing and the vibration recommenced. My mind cleared, like a fog bank blasted away by a gust of wind. It was my fucking *cell phone*. I groped in my pocket, somehow fumbled the response button, and hauled the phone to my ear. It was a long, exhausting haul. I could have used a rest en route. It was squawking at me before the journey was completed.

'You're not there! Why aren't you there?' The voice was petulant, accusing, instantly recognizable. 'Oh ... *shit!*' A sob, distress but no tears. 'Come for me, Alan...'

'I am here,' I managed to say, my tongue a fat slug in my mouth. 'I *am* here, sweetheart.'

An indrawn 'Oh!' of disbelief. Then, 'You're there, you're really there?'

'Yes,' I mumbled, my brain still firing on only half its cylinders. 'I'm really here. Are you all right? Where are you?'

'I can't believe it, it's really you.' Her voice was breathless, lower and huskier than I remembered it. 'Now, listen, *listen*! I don't have much time. I'm in a basement, under a house. The nearest town or whatever is called Le Maynil. At least that how it sounds. Have you got that? Le May-nil.'

'Le Maynil. Yes, I've got it.' I was sobering, but not fast enough. 'Where is it, I mean ...' What did I mean? 'Which fucking country? That's what I mean, fuck it!'

'I don't know, might be France. It's in a forest, it's got a high brick wall all around, the house is brick too.'

'But how ...?'

'No, *listen*! The wall has revolving spikes on top and there's an iron gate, so come in a tank.' A snigger here, nerves not mirth. 'Something else: the house has a turret thing, you know, like an old castle. That's it, that's all I can tell you. I'd better go before that bastard Christiaan comes back. I used a nail to pick the lock and get to the phone. You'd be proud of me, I've been practicing for days. Alan ... Alan, I miss you. Please come soon. It's horrible, they've done ... things ...' She broke off with a sob of a different kind.

'I'm coming. Just hang in there a bit longer. Tomorrow, or the day after at the latest ...'

'Okay, okay.' A seconds-long silence was ended by an indistinct few words that might have been 'I love you.' Then came the whine of a dead connection.

It took me a while to absorb the fact of Lizzy's call, the confirmation that she was still alive, still the same old spunky kid. Even if they had 'done things'. De Bruin had already paid for that, though if I could I would have resuscitated him and made him pay all over again – slowly and in excruciating agony. If some of his cohorts were still active, I would ensure they received their dues too.

Le Maynil. Maybe in France, maybe not. It certainly had

a French resonance. The Internet would lead me to it. I staggered to my feet lurched off towards the house. It was farther than I thought. The study was my first port of call, to switch on the computer. While it was doing its warm-up thing, I showered, hot-cold, hot-cold, alternating. It was brutal. But I was coming back to life. I brewed coffee. The percolator was too complicated for my booze-addled head, so I settled for reliable old Nescafé Gold Blend. Then, with a cupful in my gut, a refill in my hand, I returned to the study, still bumping into door frames, but at least ready to go to work.

Google it, the solution to all ills. I managed to type the words Le Maynil. A ton of references popped up, none of which was a place. Okay, who said I was going to strike a lode at first go? Le Maynile? Forget it. Le Maynill then. Ditto. Le Maynille, although that would have been pronounced May-neel, not Maynil the way Lizzy said it. What I lacked was a private eye's talent for ferreting. Anyhow, Le Maynille was a bust.

I rocked back precariously in my swivel chair (leather, ergonomic, multi-positional; company executives for the use of). *Sounds like* Maynil, she had said. A click inside my skull. The pronunciation of 'may' in French is closer to the English 'my,' so if Lizzy's rendition of it was true, it would more likely be spelled *Meynil*. Into my faithful search engine went Le Meynil. No go, but indirectly I struck gold with it. '*Did you mean Le Mesnil?*' Google demanded imperiously.

Excitement clutched me. It was short-lived. Le Mesnil existed all right, in spades. At least twenty communities of that name in France. Where to start? In most cases the Mesnil was part of a double- or treble-barrelled name, as in Le Mesnil Gillaume, Le Mesnil-St-Denis, et al. Just two entries were suffix-free – one in France and one in Belgium. Try those first then. Le Mesnil France was a village in open countryside. No forest. So that was ruled out. On to Le Mesnil Belgium. In the Belgian province of Namur, almost on the border with France. Population 155.

In the Ardennes.

The Ardennes. Extensive forested area. Scene of the last great hopeless offensive of the German army in 1945. It wasn't a certainty. It wasn't even a probability. For now, though, it was my only hope.

When I crossed the border from France into Belgium it was long after dark on the "tomorrow" I had predicted for Lizzy's salvation. According to my calculations, the drive to Toulouse airport, the flight to Brussels or Nancy, a rental car to my destination, with the usual delays added, would be no quicker than driving myself the whole way in my brand new Aston, identical replacement for the one I had written off escaping de Bruin's mob. So I did exactly that. Nine hundred and twenty-two kilometres at an average of 130kph plus stops.

Desperate as I was to begin the hunt for Lizzy's prison, I realized that to go blundering about in the forest after dark would just get me lost. So I had advance-booked a room at the two-star La Folie, an *auberge* within sight of the border, and less than a kilometre from Le Mesnil village. The location of the house with the turret was anybody's guess. Again, a private eye would have known what to do. I would only know what to do *after* I found it. Oh, yes, that part of the plan was already cut, dried, and set in concrete.

After a tossing-turning night on a mattress that felt as if it were stuffed with rubble, I kicked off the enquiry process over a breakfast consisting of a hard *baguette* and a soft *croissant*, with honey and jam in little pots. It being well out of season, I shared the salon with only a couple of suits. The manager waited on us in person. I snared him as he was delivering my coffee.

'You know a place around here, in the woods, with a crenellated tower and a wall around it?'

The look he gave me was tinged with suspicion.

'Are you looking to buy such a property, *monsieur*?'

'No, I'm visiting a friend, but I've lost the address and telephone number.'

The suspicion faded somewhat.

'*Alors* ...' Extensive lip-pursing and headnodding, which ultimately became headshaking. 'I regret, it is not familiar to me.'

'I think I know the place, *monsieur*,' one of the suits piped up. 'I was there last week.' A self-effacing smirk. 'I sell insurance.'

As the manager drifted away, buck duly passed, I crossed the room and pulled up a chair at the suit's table.

'Can you describe it?'

'It is as you say, a house with a little tower, *comme ceux d'une forteresse*.'

'Built of brick?'

'Ah ... yes, yes, I believe that is so. The walls also.'

Well, it sounded like a respectable contender for the house I was seeking.

'How do I get there?'

'It's not easy,' he said, with an oblique grin that hinted it was bloody difficult. 'The road is very bad, more like a track really.' He produced a notebook from his hip pocket, and proceeded to sketch a plan. 'Here is La Folie ...'

Ten minutes later I was away from there, cheque paid, overnight bag in the trunk, the friendly suit's sketch on the seat beside me. It took me south, back towards the border. Immediately before the unmanned customs shack a dirt road led off to the right. With the GPS advocating a different route I swung onto it. The Aston's springs protested at the jarring surface. Fortunately there had been an overnight frost, so the famous Belgian mud was set hard. Across an area of scrubland consisting of stunted trees and bushes, to a fork. There I bore right, veering away from the border, towards a line of trees, grey-looking conifers mingling with denuded deciduous. Through the trees, out onto another open stretch, more trees ahead. Trees extended on three sides. This was tree country all right. The sun was out, weak and watery north European sun, with hardly enough wattage to cast shadows. The dirt road cut through yet another double row of trees, pines mostly, planted by man. A few hundred metres later, another double row. Ahead lay solid forest, pretty much all evergreens, planted by nature. God, let it be the right place.

As if to accentuate the dangers lurking there the sun went behind a swathe of cloud, draining away what little colour there had been in the wintry landscape. Into the trees I plunged, bouncing, the track narrower now and potholed. The forest embraced me, sombre and vaguely menacing. I braked and, leaving the engine ticking over, got out. I opened the apology for a trunk and used a crosshead screwdriver from the car toolkit to remove six screws from a panel on the underside of the trunk lid. No vehicles passed in either direction. Silence cloaked me. Not so much as a birdcall, just the steady murmur of the car's engine and my own breathing. The panel fell away from the lid. Inside was a compartment with a number of spring clips. Designed to hold rifle, shotgun, or two or three handguns. The Korth was there, with an underarm holster and twenty four rounds in speed-loaders. I strapped on the holster and distributed the speed-loaders about my upper body. My leather windcheater smoothed out the bulges. Zipping up, I checked the cylinder. Five rounds only, one chamber empty as always. I freed a round from one of the speed-loaders and topped up. Revolvers are more dependable than automatics, which was why I had historically favoured them. Their disadvantage lay in the six-shot capacity compared with twelve to fifteen for most modern autos, and their unsuitability for sound suppressors. These were limitations I lived with when needs must. I spun the cylinder, tested the ejector, dumping the cartridges into the empty trunk. As I reloaded with slow precision, the distant stammer of a helicopter breached the stillness. It was scarcely above treetop height when a minute or so later it passed directly overhead, the downdraft setting the foliage thrashing and pine needles tumbling like rain. I glimpsed a black fuselage and whirling rotor then it was gone. I expected the clamour to fade gradually to nothing. It didn't. As I closed the trunk lid the engine note slowed, as if preparing for touchdown. Unless the wood was smaller than it looked on my GPS the chopper was setting down in the middle of it.

Quiet fell once more. A far off croak, raven or rook, otherwise I might have been a hundred kilometres from civilization. Except for the chopper. Curious that. Dwelling on it wouldn't get me any nearer to Lizzy. Back behind the wheel. A touch on the accelerator, the mufflers crackling, hungry for action. Six litres of raw power on tap. I hoped I wouldn't need it, either for pursuit or escape.

Some two kilometres into the wood I reached my journey's end. Through the trees, as I approached a bend, I saw the road terminate at a wrought iron gate, painted a dark colour. On either side of the gate a wall, about three meters high, maybe two hundred long from corner to corner. In wonderful, beautiful, glorious brick. Behind it, the upper floor of a substantial house, more of a mansion really. Single octagonal tower like a turret. All in brick too. If this wasn't the place described by Lizzy, it was its twin. I pulled over. From here on, I would proceed on foot.

The trees were too densely packed to allow parking the Aston off the trail. I had passed a rough track branching off at right angles, less than a half kilometre back. I reversed cautiously down the trail and swung into it. It wasn't much more than a double line of tyre ruts, but I found just enough space to park without blocking it. From the trail it would be hard to spot.

At a lope I headed back along the dirt road towards the house. It wasn't yet ten o'clock but the clouds that had shut off the sun were darkening the sky early. Raindrops spattered my face. Here in Belgium, rain was part of the scenery.

Behind me the noise of a vehicle. I ducked into the trees, shielding myself behind a trunk, and thanking God I had had the foresight to park the Aston off the trail. Underfoot was springy from shed pine needles. The smell of resin tickled my nostrils. The air was as damp as a sauna and a sight chillier.

The vehicle passed, going at a crawl, bouncing over some serious potholes: a Toyota SUV, metallic grey, with two occupants. The driver was male with sculpted blond hair and the kind of profile calculated to transform a respectable woman into a wanton. Name of Christiaan, alias the beefcake boy. How was that for serendipity? It confirmed I was in the right place. Thinking back to his starring role in Lizzy's abduction, I had a special score to settle with him.

As the Toyota approached the gate I paced it through the trees on a parallel course. Where the tree line ended, only meters short of the wall, I paused, my next step undecided. The gate slid back, operated remotely. I hesitated. If I broke cover, tried to enter by using the Toyota as a shield, I was sure to be spotted. Or maybe not. The gloom would work in my favour, and I was dressed in dark colours. Casting hesitation aside, I quit the protection of the forest and, hoping that

Christiaan wouldn't choose that precise instant to check his door mirror, I tucked in behind the SUV. It was moving at about ten mph. At an awkward running crouch, keeping below the level of the rear window, I went through the gateway in its slipstream. Gravel replaced dirt, the crunch of my footsteps blending with that of the Toyota's tyres. Behind me the gate slid shut, squealing a little.

The sky was beginning to dump rain as if it meant it. As I ran I cast around for a refuge from my enemies. Scraggy lawns, bushes, empty flower beds, met my eyes. I decided to stick with the Toyota, though bent double I was struggling to keep up the pace.

'Hey, Christo!' A hail, English of sorts. The hailer was hidden from me by the bulk of the Toyota. To the relief of my spine it rolled to a halt.

'Are the kids ready?' The question came from inside the SUV. Christiaan's voice. I flopped against the rear hatch, wheezing, keeping my head down.

'Sure. The chopper she arrive ten minutes before. All the kids going, yes?'

'That's right, all of them.'

Doors slammed, gravel squished. More dialogue, a third voice joining in, female, rather shrill.

Footsteps approached the rear of the Toyota. I dragged the Korth from my belt. I was ready in that sense, not in another. In my vaguest of plans I had hoped to remain undercover a while longer. The dilemma now was whether to stay put and blast whoever was coming, leading to open warfare, or nip around the other side of the car.

The decision was taken out of my hands by the woman. An imperious 'Christiaan!' was followed a terse few words in Dutch. The footsteps halted, went into reverse. Christiaan unknowingly gained a few more heartbeats of life.

More talk, more footsteps. A door banged shut, house not car. I peeked around the Toyota. All clear. Before moving into the open I scanned the windows, oblongs of reflected grey cloud. If anyone was looking out it wasn't apparent. I made a dash for the nearest corner of the building, some ten meters and a lifetime away. No shouts, no shots. More windows around the corner, along the side of the building, all with lowered roller blinds. Good. If I couldn't see in, they couldn't see out.

The rain was intensifying, soaking my hair, coursing down my face. It was also freezing cold. I hadn't dressed for it. Plenty of sweat potential in what I was doing though.

A strip of grass ran down the side of the house to the next corner. This deadened my tread as I scuttled along it. I peeped around the corner at a vast yard in sore need of green fingers and a blank cheque. A paved circular area, scrawled with weeds, was linked to the house by a paved isthmus. Squatting there, an ugly fat bug, was the helicopter I had seen earlier. Black paintwork, no fuselage markings except the registration number, F-GH then two more letters that were partly defaced, probably on purpose. All the Perspex surfaces were heavily tinted. A guy in jeans and a leather jacket like mine was bent over the left skid, whistling. I heard the chink of metal against metal.

The expanse of gravel between him and me ruled out a surprise attack. My back against the wall, I considered the options. To shoot him would alert the rest of the gang. The only course was to get up close and lay him out. I was preparing to move when a call came from inside the house.

'You want coffee, Rafe?' The pidgin-English speaker again.

'Coffee, yeah, that'd be good.' The man called Rafe straightened up, wrench in hand, and I ducked back behind the corner. He spoke with a Transatlantic cadence, maybe Canadian. I heard him clumping along the paved pathway to the house, whistling anew.

I allowed a minute or so for him and his colleague to get settled with their coffees while I holstered the Korth and reviewed my plan. So far I had only thought in terms of entering the house, knocking off everyone in sight, and freeing Lizzy. Now an alternative was taking shape inside my head. The chopper was here for a reason. The brief exchange between Christian and the other guy had referred to 'all the kids' being ready. It added up to the imminent removal of Lizzy and, presumably, other juvenile victims. An idea was germinating: stow away on the chopper. If nothing else it would reduce the number of adversaries from at least four to at most two. The machine looked to be a six-seater, so it was unlikely a bunch of kids would be accompanied by more than one guard plus the pilot. The idea firmed up, became an intent.

By detouring through the wilderness of the yard I was able to approach the chopper from the other side, using it to screen me from the house. I opened the little door to the passenger section. Besides the two crew positions there was seating for five: a row of three at the rear, and two facing them, back to back with the crew. Between the rear seats and the bulkhead was a narrow area for storage. Enough room at a pinch for a normal sized person. With my foot poised on the door sill, I was hit by a rush of uncertainty. I froze, half in, half out of the chopper. A shouted 'See you tomorrow' put an end to the wavering. I launched myself into the passenger compartment and dove head first into the storage space. My shoulders jammed leaving me helpless, arms pinned. Panic flared. I wriggled frantically and managed to free one arm, and twist sideways to unjam the rest of me. In an untidy slither I subsided to the floor of my sanctuary.

A few moments later someone – Rafe, I guessed– climbed in, humming. He was a great whistler and hummer. A man who enjoyed his work. No qualms about trafficking kids around the world for sex. Hey, it's just a fucking job. If he didn't do it, somebody else would. I could imagine the self-justification tripping off his scumbag tongue.

'Come on, move it.' A curt command from outside. Christiaan again. Subdued voices, young, frightened, a mixture of tongues, drifted through the open hatchway. Sounds of feet coming aboard. A child's nervous laugh cut into another's weeping.

'It's all right, don't cry, we're going on a holiday.' Female, husky timbre. Lizzy? I began to wonder if my stowaway scheme was really so smart after all. The kids would complicate things. In such a confined space, with nowhere to hide, a single stray bullet might hit more than one small body.

'*Où est-ce que nous allons?*' Where are we going? A boy, voice tremulous. A reminder that the de Bruin organization catered for both sides of the perversion spectrum.

'Someplace sunny,' from Rafe, in familiar French-Quebecois.

'Shut up,' from Christiaan, still outside the chopper.

I hoped the Dutch Adonis was booked to ride with us. A bullet would be too easy an exit for him, though even a bullet can be placed where it will guarantee a lingering, agonizing death.

The kids sorted out their seats. A girl with long black hair, very straight, tied back with a blue ribbon, chose the one on the far right of the row of three. Then a boy with blond hair plunked down in the middle seat. I could see the backs of their heads and the sides of their faces. The girl had an uptilted nose with a diamond stud.

Cramp was beginning to attack my left calf. I tried to stretch my leg and gently exercise it. The general bustle as the kids got settled drowned any grunts of pain.

'Don't be late for the rendezvous.' The woman again. 'They won't wait.'

'Quit worrying,' Rafe said, and Christiaan pitched in with a few lines of Dutch.

'See you both on the yacht,' the woman said.

Doors closed on both sides. Desultory chatter among the youngsters was overlaid by the whirr of the main rotor winding up.

'You got the coordinates?' I heard Rafe say.

'Right here.' So Christian was riding co-pilot. Good. 'We're cleared as far as Lille Airport, the rendezvous is about thirty Ks north east of the airport. You want the figures now?'

'It'll wait. Strap yourself in.' On a louder note: 'You kids, fasten your seat belts, if you've got one.'

Some scuffling and clinking ensued. More kids than belts by the sound of it.

'Let me help you.' The girl with the husky voice, playing mother hen. I was sure it was Lizzy. She was likely to be the oldest of the bunch.

Above me the blond head twisted round and an inquisitive young face peered down. A mouth dropped open. I nipped his exclamation in the bud by crossing my lips with a finger. He caught on fast, especially when I followed up with a wink and a raised thumb that were meant to reassure him that I was here with the cavalry. Correction, I *was* the cavalry.

He nodded vigorously. His face withdrew. The rotor was wop-wopping at speed now, the fuselage vibrating. Christiaan and Rafe were talking, but their words were inaudible. A momentary shudder and we unstuck from the ground. This was it. The pilot would be at maximum preoccupation with the take-off, leaving only Christiaan to deal with. I heaved myself out of my hiding place like a missile leaving the launching pad. I did the finger-crossing-lips thing again for the benefit of the seven youngsters in the cabin that was made for five. Lizzy was opposite, in a rear-facing seat with a small girl on her lap, a lanky boy of about twelve beside her. Their expressions, and those of the four who were squashed into the other three seats as they twisted round to goggle at me, were mixtures of shock, disbelief, and – in Lizzy's case – pure joy. Her smile, wide and white, was like a homecoming. Something about her face was different. It was almost haggard. Most of all she looked years older. I very much wanted to hug her. Nothing sexual, just a giving of comfort. But she was out of reach and this wasn't the time.

The chopper was hovering at rooftop height, pivoting on its axis to point away from the house. The rain had developed into a steady drizzle, easily cleared from the screen by the big wipers flopping back and forth. I signalled the black-haired girl and the blond boy to vacate their seats. They responded with alacrity, and I did a sort of flop over the seat backs to finish up on the floor, with my fellow passengers stifling their giggles. I felt like the hired entertainer at a kids' birthday bash.

The helicopter was starting to accelerate, throwing me off balance as I struggled to my feet. Then Christiaan's head turned.

'Hey!' he yelled, and his hand reached into his parka.

His reactions were fast, but he was no gunslinger. I had the Korth lined up on him while he was still groping in the folds of his clothing. The pilot, Rafe, glanced at his companion, then over his shoulder at me. When he saw the gun he was visibly jolted, and momentarily forgot he was piloting a helicopter which suddenly swooped, prompting squeals from some of the kids. Rafe recovered at once and orderly flight was resumed.

'You can't do anything up here,' Christiaan snarled, teeth bared. 'Shoot us, and who flies the chopper?'

'Suppose I just shoot *you*?'

Lizzy tugged at my sleeve. 'Kill him, Alan!'

Kill? Was that really Lizzy talking? It didn't bear thinking about what had been done to her to transform the girl who literally wouldn't hurt a fly into an advocate of murder.

'Yes, kill him!' the lanky boy echoed. Christiaan wasn't popular.

I had a better idea than killing him.

To the pilot, I said, 'You, circle around the house.' To Christian: 'Open the door.' I gestured with the gun in case he didn't feel like co-operating.

He was no pussy. 'Fuck you!'

I sighed and shot him in the shoulder. The magnum round flung him against his door, where he slumped, groaning and clutching his upper arm. Blood oozed between his figures. Rafe flicked another glance at me, his expression scared. He hadn't signed up for gunplay. For now he was behaving himself. The helicopter was circling the house. Down on the makeshift landing pad two people, a blonde woman and a burly guy in a red baseball cap, were watching us. Though the woman's features were indistinct, I could guess her identity. With de Bruin gone, who else but his grieving widow would be holding the organization together?

'Now, Christian,' I said. 'Unfasten the belt, open the door, and take a jump, or the next bullet will be in your head.'

'Aren't you going to count to three?' he sneered. The guy had balls, it has to be said.

Lizzy was clutching at my arm. 'Don't let him go, Alan, shoot him.'

Was this the same Lizzy who believed all life was precious, even low life?

To Christiaan I said, 'No, you fuck, you don't deserve three seconds.'

Maybe the look in my eyes made him a believer. In less time than it would have taken me to put another bullet in him, he unbuckled the belt, flung open the door, and with a last insult to my mother, the beefcake boy was airborne. Taking his chances with the trees rather than the certainty of a bullet. I didn't see him fall. If he got lucky the trees might have let him down lightly. I'd prefer to think the Gods of Justice directed his tumbling body straight into the good frozen earth of Belgium.

'Okay, kids,' I said. The blond boy who had spotted me first was crying, probably as scared of me as he was of his captors. 'Don't worry, I'm one of the good guys. Our friend here -' I indicated Rafe, '- is going to put us down someplace safe and you can all go home.'

At this point Rafe ceased behaving. A thrown wrench glanced off my left temple, sending me staggering back into the rear seats, on top of the blond boy, who protested volubly. I lost my grip on the Korth. Semi-stunned, I tried to rise. The boy helped by pushing me. Lizzy meanwhile had wrapped her arms around the pilot's neck, and was doing a good job of throttling him. In his struggles his legs thrashed about in the vicinity of the control stick. The chopper lurched and tilted sharply to the right. Those of us who weren't strapped to seats were thrown across the cabin. The engine was howling. Lizzy's arms stayed locked around the pilot's neck; strapped in he was unable to get at her. Dials spun crazily on the control panel.

'Let him go!' I shouted at her. 'We're going to crash!'

By then though it was too late.

Thirty-One

The chopper was heading earthwards on its side, the treetops coming at us fast like a green wall. Rafe finally succeed in detaching Lizzy, shoving her into the lap of the black-haired girl. Even as he grasped the stick the chopper's rotor chewed into the treetops and stalled the engine. A loud bang sent a convulsion through the fuselage. We plunged into the greenery to a fusillade of cracking and snapping, accompanied by shrieks of terror from most of the kids. I was yelling a bit myself. The right hand door flew open and the older boy toppled through it. I grabbed his ankle. He was no lightweight, and almost took me with him, but happily my frame was too large for the aperture and by getting wedged I saved both of us. The chopper came to a precarious rest, still on its side, forming a bridge between two fir trees. The wipers quit wiping. All went quiet as the squeals subsided. I felt blood trickling down my cheek. I was still hanging on to the upside-down boy, who was smart enough not to wriggle.

'Steady me, sweetheart,' I called over to Lizzy, and she crawled across and hooked on to my belt to counterbalance the weight of the boy while I hauled him back inside.

'You okay?' I asked as I set him down, and he jiggled his head, grinning the exaggerated grin of a circus clown in his relief.

'Everybody all right?' I yelled at the kids. '*Tout le monde ça va?*'

A scattering of 'yesses' and 'ouis' from the ones who understood reassured me. No response from Rafe. His head was lolling against the window, and he appeared to be out cold. The chopper gave an almost human groan and slipped sidelong. The branches that were supporting us snapped and our descent continued. Luckily for all of us the surrounding foliage continued to act as a brake. We sank to earth in a succession of jolts, the airframe distorting, setting up a creaking and a screeching as it carved a swathe through the foliage. A window on the underside popped out of its socket and Lizzy almost followed it, only saving herself by catching hold of a stray seat belt. Her back thudded into the cabin floor wrenching a yell from her lips. A final complaint of twisted metalwork before we hit the ground with a teeth-rattling crunch in the company of sundry amputated branches and a deluge of pine needles.

The biggest risk now was fire. Cirrus of smoke were already tricking into the cabin from apertures in the roof.

'Get out – quick!' I chucked the smaller boy out through the popped window. Lizzy, the black-haired girl, the skinny boy and two girls of about ten, scrambled out under their own steam. This left only the smallest girl, five or six maybe, big brown tearful eyes and streaks of snot under her nose. I lifted her and passed her through the window to Lizzy. The smoke was spreading. A last look round. The Korth was lying on what now served as the floor. I gathered it up and shoved it in the holster. It might yet be needed. I hauled myself through the popped window, and slid down the roof to the bliss of terra firma.

'The pilot's still in there,' the skinny boy pointed out.

He almost but not quite made me feel bad. I still went back and tried to drag him out, until I realized he was dead. By then the smoke was as thick as a London fog. Coughing my lungs out, I scrambled through the same open window.

Through the curdling smoke flames were licking. If the fuel tank went up we could get caught in the blast.

'Come on, kids,' I gasped between splutters. 'Let's move it.'

With me backpacking the youngest girl for speed, we put distance between ourselves and the wrecked chopper. We had covered about fifty meters when a double boom ripped through the forest behind us. A shockwave of heat propelled me forward to squeals from my terrified passenger. Everyone gave up running and turned to view the spectacle. The ugly black bug was blazing nicely, flames licking at the trees around it. It was going to be a job for the local fire brigade.

'Hey look!' the skinny boy called, pointing. 'There's a car.'

We all looked away from the wrecked chopper. Through the trees a glint of pale blue metal. By chance we had come down a stone's throw from where I had parked the Aston. Never was a sight more welcome.

'That's your car, isn't it?' Lizzy said to me.

'How do you think I got here?' I urged on my little band of escapees. 'Come on. We're going to travel in style.'

With the rising crackle of flames in our ears we trotted over to the car. I unloaded my human cargo.

'*Grazie, signor,*' she said with a shy smile as I set her down, and it was almost the last thing she ever said. A whipcrack report preceded a bullet that passed over her head to gouge a hole in a tree trunk two feet away. Startled, she staggered backwards and went down with a bump. I belly flopped beside her, hollering to the other kids to do likewise. The Korth was already in my fist.

A baseball-capped man of ursine build was weaving through the trees towards us, a machine pistol in hand. He fired again while still on the move, a wild, unaimed burst. Not used to guns then. But with a machine pistol even novices can hit people by accident, and I had seven kids to worry about. Still I held my fire. He was an elusive target, appearing and disappearing between tree trunks . I was as likely to hit timber as flesh. More shots chewed up the ground by my foot, causing a minor eruption of pine needles. I double-gripped the Korth, picked a space between two trees and as he filled it, I let go the five rounds that were left in the chamber. Really fast. I couldn't tell how many struck flesh, but one at least ripped open his neck. Blood burst from the wound like water from a hose. Still he came on, a dead man running, until his legs wobbled and he went down, suddenly like a struck tenpin. A couple of the girls squealed, a token reaction to the blood and the violence of it. What with their time in captivity and today's events, these kids were getting an education in nastiness to remember.

'Open the car, Alan,' Lizzy urged, quicker thinking than me as usual. I fumbled for the key fob and she pulled the passenger door open. The kids needed no invitation to pile in. The rear of an Aston DBS is not exactly spacious but somehow five of them squeezed into it, with Lizzy up front and the little Italian girl on her knee.

Away to my left the blaze was taking serious hold of the forest, casting a lurid orange light between the trees. I reversed the Aston to the main trail. Nobody else showed up looking for a fight. Not even Mrs Annika de Bruin.

As we approached a sign marking the boundary line of the town of Couvin, a fire engine blundered by in the other direction, siren ululating. I steered on the roadside verge and screwed my neck round to scan across seven wide-eyed faces. 'Who understands English?' I asked. Three hands went up including Lizzy's. 'Et francais?' Two hands, one of which was the skinny boy.

'What's your name?'

'Raoul.'

'Okay, Raoul. You may not appreciate it but I've just saved you from a nasty fate. Now I need a favour from you?'

He shrugged, nodded, grinned. He had a bruise on his cheekbone and a gashed lip, legacies of the crash.

'D'accord, monsieur.'

'This is the deal: I drop you off at the police, you explain to them what happened. The only thing is ... I don't want you to mention me, not in detail.'

Again the shrug and the grin.

'You can tell them exactly what happened, just give them a fake description. Tell them I had brown hair with a beard and was wearing a blue suit. Oh, and my car was a Mercedes. Can you manage that?'

'No problem,' he said. Then, curiosity piqued, 'Are you a gangster?'

'No, mon petit, I'm with the good guys. It's just that I have to go someplace, and I don't want to get mixed up in a lot of police merde.'

'I bet you're a spy,' the other boy said, eyes sparkling.

I laughed, ruffled his hair. 'You could say that. Used to be, anyhow.' I pointed at Lizzy. 'And she's with me. She's the reason I came.'

All eyes now swivelled to Lizzy. Being in cahoots with the likes of me automatically boosted her status, and possibly made me more respectable. If anything could.

The pact made, we drove on in search of a police station. In small towns in Belgium they're usually easy to locate. This one was just off a square in the town centre, Belgian flag languishing on a pole over the entrance. On the other side of the square, out of sight of the police station, I stopped again.

'Journey over,' I announced. 'This is where we say goodbye.'

Lizzy dismounted and tilted her seat forward to let the others out. She had a hug and a kiss for them all, the little Italian girl clinging to her hand throughout.

I raised my hand in farewell. 'Be good.'

The Italian girl broke away from Lizzy and came crawling over the passenger seat towards me. She embraced me around the neck, and attached her puckered lips to my cheek. I was so moved I didn't immediately notice the transference of snot.

'*Ciao, signor,*' she whispered, and her shy smile meant almost as much to me as Lizzy's.

Lizzy retrieved her, handed her over to the black-haired girl, and got in beside me. The six of them stood along the curb in a forlorn line, ready to wave us off. A dumpy woman with two loaded shopping bags trundled past, giving them a curious stare.

'Bye-bye, *au revoir.*' Lizzy's farewell gestures involved both arms, bunched fingers, and blown kisses.

The return drive to Andorra was as quick as the outward journey. Not much of it stuck in my memory. Desultory conversation between us, mostly trite stuff about the weather, this and that passing scenery, the idiocies of other road users. No mention of her ordeal. That was reserved for later. Periodically we quit the highway to relieve ourselves, or to eat, or to stretch our legs; on one occasion to sleep. I drove like an automaton. It rained most of the way, even snowed a bit near Reims.

Only when we entered the driveway of my house in Andorra in the small hours did my semi-trancelike state dissipate, and reality intrude: the reality of being home, with Lizzy restored to me, a job well done. Fatigue hit me. With a mumbled 'Good night,' to Lizzy I took off to my bed.

It was mid-afternoon and raining hard when I awoke. I

hadn't drawn the drapes. The sky was a vista of gloom weighing on the countryside, the landscape reminiscent of Belgium but more mountainous. Lizzy was already up. She had lit the fire in the living room, and when I descended, showered but still in my bathrobe, it was a place of warmth and flickering flames and shadows that gave life to inanimate walls. It had also, incredibly, become home again.

'You're up,' she greeted me, a note of censure in the words. She was in an armchair, legs tucked under her, a book open in her lap.

'As you see.'

She made a humph in her throat and returned to her book. Or pretended to.

I brewed coffee and cranked up the iPod. With Bach's Violinkonzerte No. 1 wafting through the house, I went to sprawl on the long couch, coffee cup in hand. Some of it slopped on my white bathrobe. Lizzy abandoned her reading and came to curl at my feet like a cat. We talked. Night settled on the house. We talked some more. By a roundabout route we eventually came to her experiences in the verminous clutches of Rik de Bruin.

'Thank God you showed up when you did,' she said. 'We would have been out in the Bay of Biscay by now.'

'Biscay? How come?'

'That helicopter was supposed to transfer us to somewhere on the coast to be picked up by a boat.'

'I see.' I considered this. Decided it wasn't to my liking. 'So my giving Rik the kiss of death didn't put them out of business.'

'Oh, that was *you*, was it?' A wan smile flickered, on-off. 'It upset the applecart right enough. First we knew about it was when she came to the house a couple of days ago and told Christiaan to organize the transfer. "It's finished here," she said. "Rik's dead." She didn't seem upset at all.'

I grunted. 'You mean de Bruin's wife?'

'Yeah. Annika. I hated her. We all hated her.'

Her jean-sheathed legs became restless. Inside her, a mess of conflict. I waited for it to ebb. Pushing her wouldn't help.

'Alan ... I do want to tell you about it. Every bit of it.'

'No need, sweetheart. Better to wipe it from your memory, hey? Treat it like a bad dream.'

Her laugh was wistful.

'If only people's memories were like computers.' She toyed with my hand; her fingers were trembling.

'I want to tell you,' she repeated. 'I *must.*'

No secrets. The pact still held good. I stroked the tawny tumble of hair. In the background the orchestra was bringing Violinkonzerte No. I to a soulful climax. For a moment I was lulled into believing we could go on from here together. Inseparable.

Moments by definition pass quickly. Castles fall to earth. The cocoon of make-believe goes pop.

I smiled at her from inches away, but the smile that bounced back was not quite Lizzy as was. Traces of sorrow and cynicism had replaced the destroyed innocence. Her looks had not escaped unimpaired. Lines like cobwebs under her eyes and nose, and bracketing the corners of her mouth. Lines that had no right to be there, in a sixteen-year old face. It said much for her strength of character that she could smile at all.

A log collapsed in the grate with a puff of sparks. The music was finished and but for the spitting of the fire all was quiet.

Lizzy began her story, commencing with her abduction. I listened without interruption, carried on stroking her hair, a gesture that was supposed to say I'm here and you're safe and nothing has changed between us. Would that it were true.

By any yardstick her story was horrific. The blood in my

veins turned to liquid ice as the full extent of her debasement was unveiled. Although partly conditioned in advance by that movie at Lady Marcia's, hearing it from Lizzy's own lips was a greater obscenity by far. I tried not to visualize the number and variety of men (and beasts) who had used her body, let alone the atrocities, human and mechanical, practiced on her. Not, it transpired, by Rik de Bruin, but by his wife, Annika. I had to be dispassionate. Act, indeed think, as if the entire episode had never taken place. Just as I had advised her to do.

It was long in the telling and when it was done she wept for almost as long again. Sobbed out her misery and her suffering into my bathrobe, and with such intensity that my own eyes prickled in empathy. By and by I gave her my handkerchief, and she mopped and blew, and reduced her distress to a snuffle.

'I've made you all soggy,' she said, patting the damp patch on my robe.

'I'll never wash it again.'

She laughed shakily. 'I do so love you.'

My mouth opened, closed again. I hugged her, letting my actions speak for my emotions.

'Lizzy, my sweet, I want to ask you a few questions. About ... what you just told me. Do you mind?'

'Not now, not any more. It's all out of my system. Well, apart from ...' Her voice tailed off.

It wasn't hard to guess what wasn't out of her system.

'The drugs?' I hazarded. Her eyes widened. 'I know all about it. We'll get you cured, no matter how much it costs.'

She looked worried, as if I were about to withhold her supplies. 'I have to have it, you know. Every day.'

I nodded and kept the distaste battened down.

'More than once a day,' she persisted.

'Have you, er ... got some with you?'

Now she avoided my eyes. She wasn't so far hooked as to feel no shame. Her 'yes' was barely audible.

It explained her vitality. She was on a high. Later, when the drug's effects wore off, her behaviour might change for the worse. She might become irrational, even violent. In that eventuality, I supposed she would stoke up with more of the stuff. Tomorrow I would seek medical advice.

But that was tomorrow. Today I had a need which over-rode all other considerations.

'About Rik de Bruin's wife ... Annika. You say she was responsible for most of what was done to you.'

'Yeah. She's bisexual. And she likes hurting people. I've still got the scars.' She shuddered violently.

'Did you ever try to escape?'

She became pensive. 'I was going to. One girl did. They brought her back and ... and punished her. We heard her screaming. We never saw her again. Supposed to be an object lesson to the rest of us. It sure put me off the idea.'

I swallowed. 'Where did the other kids come from?'

'All over. Annika preferred blonde girls, but they came in all shapes and colours.'

The picture was still unclear.

'Let me get this straight; are you saying de Bruin had girls kidnapped just because ... well, because Annika had the hots for them?'

'Oh no, it wasn't just that.'

It couldn't have been just that. It was beyond credible that Rik de Bruin had done it for his wife's personal gratification.

'Tell me.' I rose from the couch and chucked a couple of logs on the fire, gave the bellows a few strokes. Lizzy stayed on the floor, legs drawn up, chin resting on knees. Her gaze was far away. I flopped down beside her.

'She and Rik are really just pimps, I supposed you'd call

them. They procure young girls and boys for customers overseas, rich Arabs mostly. The girls who were there with me were all abducted for the Middle East meat market. That was Rik's name for it. I was in a different category, you might even say I was privileged.'

'How so?'

'It seems that the Arab I told you about, you remember, the big shot in Abu Dhabi who offered to pay Mummy for me? Mummy gave him the heave-ho, as you know. So he contacted Rik and Annika and hired them to abduct me.'

'No *shit*? So how come you weren't sent to Abu Dhabi?'

She hugged herself, rocking back and forth.

'That's how the business works. They exploit you for the Internet and DVD market before shipping you off to Arabland. Often for months. You get to become a movie star. When they decide you've served your purpose, earned your keep, whatever, they ... they clean you up and off you go. I was lucky. Annika took a particular shine to me, so I got her personal attention. And I do *not* mean she showered me with love.'

'Did Rik know about that, you and Annika, I mean?'

'Did he *know*?' Her laugh was shrill. 'Jesus, Alan, he was in on it. I've lost count of the times we made up a threesome.'

What I had so far learned from Lizzy did not best please me. She had just blown apart my assumption that in removing Rik de Bruin I had removed the supremo of the organization. If she had read the situation correctly, he and his wife were very much a team.

And she, rot her, was still alive.

It was all making sense now. For all the huge profits of the child porn market I had never been able to rationalize Rik de Bruin's actions in kidnapping Lizzy. For a start, she wasn't a young enough child to appeal to the average paedo. Selling girls and boys as sex-slaves was a proposition of a different hue. Tales abound of fabulous sums forked out by oil-rich Arab princes and sheiks for European youngsters of both sexes, blondes especially. It was without doubt a profitable industry in its own right.

Lizzy's gaze was on me and it was troubled.

'Alan, do you hate me now? Now that I've told you everything.'

I hated all right, but none of it was directed at Lizzy.

'I couldn't hate you, Freckles, even if you'd done it of your own free will. If anything, I hate myself for letting it happen. You were in my care, under my roof. If I hadn't been so fucking complacent – '

She silenced me with fingertips on my mouth. 'Shush. None of it's your fault. You've only ever tried to help. First Mummy, now me, all we brought you is a lot of aggro. And that reminds me – you haven't even told me yet what happened when Rik brought you back to the house. You know, after the crash.'

'Later,' I said curtly. 'It's history.'

She yawned gracelessly. 'If you say so. Right now, I'm too shagged to care. All I want to do is sleep.'

I crouched on my haunches before her. 'Sorry, honey, but there's a couple more things I have to know.' She nodded, and I went on, 'I'm still confused about Annika de Bruin. Was she *directly* involved in the business side?'

'Involved?' Her laugh was humourless. 'Maybe I didn't explain it right. Rik was the front man, but Annika wasn't just *involved* – she was the fucking boss!'

Hearing from your doctor that you're going to die must take a little while to adjust to. When Lizzy shattered my satisfaction at a job well done, I took a little while to adjust to that.

No loose ends, I had deluded myself. Now I found I had left the biggest loose end imaginable. I had killed the monkey instead of the organ grinder.

A full minute passed before I came to terms with it. Still crouching, I gripped Lizzy by her shoulders.

'Are you absolutely sure about that, honey?'

'Absolutely. She was the boss and the brains. Rik did as he was told. I got the impression she started the business with her own money, before they were married even.' Her mouth twisted. 'She's fucking evil, that woman. Evil and sadistic. You've no idea.'

Perhaps I hadn't. Perhaps even among the sewer rats with whom I came into contact in my line of work she would rank as a pariah. Unique in her rottenness.

'I don't suppose anybody ever mentioned your mother?'

'No. I did ask, often. I even asked Annika. All that got me was a beating.'

'Okay, honey. Interrogation over. I'm going to put some more music on, something soothing.' I rummaged through the rack of compact discs. 'Mozart, I think.'

'You're such a dinosaur about music. Anyone would think you were an old man. How about Taylor Swift? Tons of her stuff on my iPod if old Sistitis hasn't thrown it out with the garbage.'

'Down here,' I said firmly, 'we play my kind of music. Why don't you go and lie down for a while. I'll cook dinner.'

As the opening bars trickled from the speakers she said, 'What happens next, Alan?'

'Next, my love? Fetch me my crystal ball.'

Her grin was unsteady.

'Seriously, though, what happens? About you and me.'

'Seriously? It's my turn to tell you things. Clear the air a bit.'

She stiffened, instantly apprehensive. 'Clear what air?'

'About me, about my background.'

'Oh.' A frown, a narrowing of eyes. 'Is it different from what you told Mummy?'

'Look, you're tired,' I said. 'Let's do it tomorrow. Okay?'

'No, let's do it now. Okay?'

'It's no big deal, Lizzy.'

The big deal was not the truths I was going to tell her, the big deal was the lies.

I sat on the couch, and patted the space beside me. She came eagerly, as if she were a little girl and I was Father Christmas, dangling a brightly-wrapped package before her. I put an arm around her shoulders. Made a drama of clearing my throat. Breathed in deeply. That exhausted all stalling tactics.

What could I, what *dare* I tell her? My real name and origins would be only a start. Hints of my past profession as an MI6 agent would make my skills more explicable, and account for my access to guns and a lifestyle from which violence never seemed far removed. Beyond that all would be smoke and mirrors. Lies, and more lies.

'First of all,' I said, tongue stuck in cheek, 'my name isn't really Alan Melville ...'

My alarm clock was bleeping, which was strange as I hadn't set it. I rolled over, fumbled for the stop button, pressed it. The bleeping went on. Bonehead. Now try the cell phone.

Outside it was dark. The clock's digital face tripped on to 6:51 as I reached for the cell.

'*Oui?*' I mumbled into it. At this hour it could only be the kind of joker who gets off on making heavy-breathing phone calls.

I was wrong.

'Varnair? *Bonjour.*'

I sat up fast. '*Petit?*'

'*Lui-même.* Are you well?'

'Enough. Except some French prick just woke me up in the middle of the night.'

'Unavoidable, I'm afraid. I am due at the airport at 7.30.'

I yawned loudly for his benefit. 'Let me be the first to wish you *bon voyage* . . .'

'Don't be a fool.' Sharply. 'Do you imagine I am telephoning you at this hour for a joke?'

Now I'd made him cross.

'Who gave you my number, Petit?'

'Someone who knows us both.'

'Name of du Poletti, by any chance?' I said sourly.

'*Aucune importance.* The grapevine tells me you have taken care of de Bruin. Congratulations on that. But why didn't you do the job properly? It's not like you. His wife is still alive, and it is she who controls the organization. Rik was never more than a ... a marionette.'

'*Now* he tells me. Pity you didn't come clean about his wife when you were being so obliging with your floor plans and suchlike.'

'Your complaint is justified. We had our reasons. However, circumstances have changed and I am about to make amends.'

A second, wider yawn froze on my face.

'Listen carefully, *mon cher ami*,' Petit lisped on. 'I am flying to Tangier to meet Annika de Bruin and certain other interested parties.'

Tangier! I screwed my ear into the receiver while he miraculously gave me all I needed to finish the job. A time, a date, a place, and the pitfalls. And of the last there were plenty.

I committed it all to memory. Notes were incriminating, and I had long since learned to do without them.

'Is all that clear?' Petit demanded, on winding up.

'If it wasn't I'd tell you.' Apart from his motives. 'Why, Petit? Why the about-turn? Why this rush of goodwill?'

The chuckle was mellifluous.

'Can't you guess?'

I stared into the darkness. Dawn was seeping through the shutters and objects in the room were beginning to take shape.

Then I grinned. 'You scheming bastard! You want the DeB organization for yourself, don't you? You want the whole bloody set up!'

'Ah, so there are brains behind the gun after all. But let us conclude matters.' Tone hardening now, becoming business-like. 'Before I leave I will be posting you a cheque ...'

'No!' The refusal came from gut level. 'No, Petit. No cheques. I'm not doing this for money. In fact, I refuse to do it for money.'

He adjusted fast to my apparent altruism.

'I understand. If you change your mind, before or after, I can be reached on my cell phone.' He rattled off a string of digits that I didn't have the means to write down. 'Except on the day itself,' he added. 'I must also re-emphasize that the day and the time are critical.'

I said, 'The twelfth, at 3pm precisely. No earlier, no later.'

'*Bien*,' he said and hung up.

The twelfth was five days hence. Not long in which to make preparations and resolve a jumbo-size problem, namely where to leave Lizzy the best part of a week. Lucien and Madeleine? They'd take her like a shot, but as long as Annika de Bruin was footloose I daren't leave her in such an obvious sanctuary. Unlikely though it was that Annika still had any designs on her, I would never again take Lizzy's security and welfare for granted. With or without the de Bruins, the Arab Prince was still out there, waving a fat cheque.

Which left only my sister Julie. Windsor was remote enough from the de Bruins' hunting grounds, which took care of the chief criterion. Whether she and Willie would agree to have her, I now proposed to find out.

Over breakfast I steered away from sensitive topics. Afterwards, while Lizzy took care of the dishes, I telephoned from the study. Julie and Willie were both at work, but I got my sister's business number from her cleaning woman. My call to the office was ill-timed: Julie was chairing a meeting. She took the call in front of her colleagues and her irritation was unconcealed.

'How was I to know?' I grumbled.

'You weren't,' was the crisp response, 'but that doesn't make it any more convenient. There are five expensive people sitting around this table, apart from myself.'

'Stop prattling then and listen!' I gave it to her in a few terse sentences and, unusually, she didn't interrupt.

The expected objections never arose. Maybe she just wanted me off her back.

'How the hell did you get embroiled in all this? You must be keeping some weird company.'

'You'll have to take it on trust for now. I'll explain more when I see you.'

Fortunately, thanks to those five expensive executives, she was inclined to co-operate.

'A week, you say? H'mm. Is she clean? Not covered in tattoos with pink hair, is she?'

'Christ, Julie! I'll get her de-loused and disinfected if it'll make you happy.' Lizzy's nose ring had gone so I didn't have to mention that.

Sounds of amusement. The sale was made.

401

'Elizabeth ... Powell, did you say?'

'Power. She answers to Lizzy.'

Sigh. 'Do we meet her off the plane or what?'

Lizzy had just finished the dishes when I breezed into the kitchen and gave her the news. She was less than enthusiastic.

'You just *dare* dump me with your sister!' she yelled, waving a bread knife at me. 'I'm not a parcel. You can't send me ...'

'*Shut up!*' I easily out-decibelled her, and she flinched, shocked speechless. 'You'll do as you're told!' I couldn't remember ever shouting at her before. I lowered my voice. 'I have some urgent, unfinished business. It means going away for a few days, a week at the outside. Is that too much to ask – a lousy week?'

'But I've only just come back!' Now would come the Lizzy wheedle. It was her specialty. 'If you really really must go away, why can't I come with you, or just stay here?'

I got the wheedle and more. Threats, tears, tantrums, and, naturally, bad language. I was unmoved and unmoving. For my sake I had to do what I had to do. For her sake, she had to be in a safe, secure place while I did it.

In the little Peugeot we drove to Barcelona. A flight to Gatwick was due to leave at 16.30, arriving there at 17.00 UK time. Julie, Willie, and the girls were to meet Lizzy, *en famille*. How they would cope once they got her home, what with Julie's commitments and Lizzy's heroin addiction, couldn't have interested me less. These were petty details. Keeping Lizzy safe from harm was my sole motive and my sole concern.

'I'll be counting the minutes,' Lizzy breathed as we said our farewells.

'Me too,' I said, running a finger down the side of her jaw. She imprisoned it and kissed the tip.

We hugged. Then, not satisfied with that, she tried for a mouth-to-mouth job. I deflected it onto my cheek.

'When I come back,' she murmured in my ear, nibbling at the lobe, 'can we live together, I mean properly?'

For Lizzy, it was the whole hog or nothing. Any lesser relationship was becoming increasingly difficult for me to contemplate too, though I was resolved to keep her at a distance. To be a parent not a partner. It didn't help my resolution that, for better or worse, she had added a year or more for every month she had spent in the clutches of the de Bruins. She used to look younger than her age. Now, facially, she could pass for mid-twenties.

The moral angle was not the daunting obstacle it had once been either. I was learning to accommodate it, like a boxer rolling with a punch to lessen the concussive effect. Even the generation gap was narrowing in my mind. My real reservations were intangible. It simply "felt wrong". Indecent. Pervy. Outlaw though I was, my conduct and attitudes were in some respects conventional bordering on priggish. No matter how strong the temptation I would do what was best for Lizzy.

'*Can* we?' she demanded, tugging at my coat lapels, when she felt my deliberations had gone on long enough.

'We'll talk about it,' I stalled.

'Coward. Do you know girls can marry at fifteen in France?'

'Been studying French marital law, have you?'

Her eyes sparkled, momentarily eclipsing the drug-glaze.

'Stop being evasive ... André.'

'I will, when you stop being whatever it is you're being.'

The take-off of her plane was delayed. I stayed on as I had promised, to wave goodbye from the viewing platform. A sentimental fool, that was me. Other kinds of fool, too.

It was raining as I drove out of the airport parking lot, a mist of drizzle blanking out the evening sky, darkening it ahead of schedule. I followed an airport bus out along the on-ramp onto the four-lane highway to Sitges.

Towards *Seaspray*.

Thirty-Two

ANNRIK it read, in bold black across the square stern, and below that, *AMSTERDAM*. Close enough in the zoom lens of the binoculars to reach out and touch. Proof of the rewards of the flesh-peddling business. Proof that some crimes pay more than others.

She was quite a size. A hundred and twenty feet or more, flush-decked, and a look of speed about her. Vestal white from waterline to the tip of the mast, except for the blue tinted windows and the drooping red-white-blue Dutch flag. A radar scanner spun lazily above the bridge.

Beside her *Seaspray* was an insignificant tub.

'Never mind, old girl.' I patted the cabin roof. 'I still love you.'

'*Que?*' Alfredo looked up from applying the finishing lick of varnish to the slatted seats in the cockpit.

'Never you mind, young Alf. Finish your chores, then I want you to go ashore and do some shopping.'

'Okay, Señor André.'

Seaspray was at anchor in Tangier Bay, bobbing in a docile swell about a mile offshore. *AnnRik* was closer to the shore, and several small craft were tied up alongside her accommodation ladder. On deck nothing was moving. I wished I had X-ray vision.

A man in a white T-shirt with *AnnRik* printed across the front appeared at the rail. He hefted a bucket, tipped its contents into the sea, repeated the exercise with a second bucket. From nowhere a multitude of screeching seabirds converged on the yacht. The patch of sea where the garbage floated was converted into a battle zone.

It was 11 February, late afternoon. Pallid sunshine, a zephyr of wind conveying the spicy, earthy smell of Africa off the land. We had dropped anchor less than an hour before, after a non-stop sail down the east coast of Spain. Over five hundred nautical miles in eighty-two hours. It had been no joy ride, but using *Seaspray* was the only way for me to enter Moroccan waters without inviting the attentions of Commissaire Ramouz. And even at that I was taking a sizeable gamble. Alfredo was on a generous bonus for crewing for me at zero notice. He remained ignorant of the reason for our haste, and I had no plans to enlighten or involve him.

A patch of royal blue popped up on *AnnRik*'s deck. I focused the glasses on it, and the gross frame of Tom-Tom leapt at me. So Petit had brought his favourite gorilla along. And gorilla he was, in every sense. The long swinging arms, the coarse hair sprouting from the vee of his shirt collar, black crew-cut head tapering towards the crown, and the flashy suit that was as shapeless as the man. I was still focused on him when he cleared his nasal passages: thumb shutting off one nostril, ejecting mucus along the palm of his hand and into the sea. Repeat the process with the other nostril. Disgustingly efficient.

The hands of my watch pointed to a quarter past four. In less than twenty-four hours it would be all over. During the calmer periods of the voyage down the east side of Spain, I had reflected long and corrosively on Annika de Bruin. The sac of venom I had expended on her husband was once more topped up, especially for her. More objectively, I had also mulled over the manner of her demise. If I stuck to Petit's dictum, I would hit her on her boat, which also suited me in view of Ramouz's ban. Yet the numerical odds were daunting. I rated Petit and Tom-Tom as non-combatants rather than allies, so it was me on my own against Annika and four leading lights of the porn world, plus a flock of shotgun riders, whose numbers and quality were uncertain. Not forgetting the skeleton crew of two – the rest were expected to be ashore. Quite a line-up. The watchdog contingent alone represented a formidable obstacle. Even more so if they were all in the Tom-Tom class.

Such arithmetic was profitless. I retired to my cabin to prepare my weapons inventory out of sight of Alfredo. I would be placing a heavy reliance on the Ithaca shotgun from my personal collection, smuggled from Andorra into Spain under the crude law-of-averages rule that hardly any vehicles are inspected by the border police. A hell of a gamble. But in the event, the averages had not let me down.

I broke open a carton of solid shot cartridges. The shotgun solid is the most lethal small-arm round in the world. A cylinder of lead, ¾" diameter, 1" long. The ultimate man-stopper. Only to be used when you mean business. I meant business.

The Ithaca magazine holds five rounds– four in the magazine, one up the spout. I alternated each solid with an SG, short for Special Grade. This cartridge, which is mostly used for boar, deer, and other medium game, contains nine balls of a third of an inch in diameter. Visualize a gun capable of firing nine rounds all together and you have some idea of the destructive potential of an SG cartridge.

Having stuffed the magazine to capacity, I tested the action by jacking all four cartridges out through the ejector port, scattering them across the duvet. Then I oiled the mechanism: pump, ejector, firing chamber, trigger, a couple of droplets apiece. Worked the action and tested the trigger pull. Checked the integrity of the safety button. As satisfied as any perfectionist would ever be, I recharged the magazine. A score of reload cartridges went into the waist gun belt.

The Korth was less demanding, my check more perfunctory. There is precious little to malfunction on a top quality revolver, and the Korth is as close as they come to fault-free. Even so I went through the motions as laid down in the maker's manual and my own unwritten safety code. A misfire at a critical moment could be the literal death of me.

And tomorrow, from 3pm on, critical moments were likely to blend together into a long, unbroken crisis.

Alfredo's wizened monkey-face creased into something approaching curiosity when I told him I was going visiting.

'Who you visit?' The question was idly put, belying the shrewd glint of his eyes.

'See the white diesel job over there.' I pointed.

Ash fell from the tip of his cheroot as he followed my finger.

'The boat you watching?'

He didn't miss much. I grinned wryly.

'That's her.'

His eyes wandered to the polythene-wrapped package I had placed on the cockpit seat.

'If you got trouble,' he said earnestly, 'I want come with you.'

'Not a chance.'

'Alone, maybe you fail.'

I was touched. 'Then I fail, old son.'

Neither the load nor the pay-off were for sharing. Besides, this expedition was a million fathoms out of his depth.

'Get the dinghy ready,' I said curtly. 'I want to be on my way by quarter to three.'

Palpably smarting at the rebuff, he scuttled about his business. I buckled on the cartridge belt. No concealing from him what was in the polythene bundle. Not that I feared Alfredo would take fright. But for his own protection and my peace of mind I wanted him uninvolved.

I was simply and practically dressed for the forthcoming fray. Denim jeans, turtle-neck cotton sweater, sneakers. Huge dark glasses and my battered sun hat would make me unrecognizable until I was safely aboard. A skin-diver's knife was taped to my ankle, the last line of defence. May its services not be required.

At 2.40pm I lowered package and posterior into the inflatable dinghy.

'Good luck,' Alfredo whispered reverently and crossed himself.

'Never mind that nonsense.' My mission hardly merited divine approval. 'Just be ready to up anchor the minute I get back.'

He touched forefinger to forelock. 'Señor.'

The dinghy's Evinrude outboard fired at a touch and settled into a contented rumble.

'Expect me back in an hour,' I said. Or not at all, I didn't say.

Setting out in bright sunshine didn't feel right. But 3pm was what Petit had stipulated, and I had to assume that, for whatever reason, this was the most favourable hour. Safe to assume also that he meant to be out of harm's way when the shooting started. If he wasn't ... well, I wasn't fussy about who got caught in the crossfire.

The distance between *Seaspray* and *AnnRik* was not great, even if it did seem like half an ocean. No means of telling if I was under scrutiny from behind those blank tinted windows, but the sitting-duck feeling was profound. My course was at a tangent to *AnnRik*, making it look as if I was heading for the harbour mouth. This was simply Warner being devious. I had to get as close as I could to the yacht without creating suspicion. Only when I came astern of her, and therefore out of sight of most of the yacht's deck area, would I turn towards her. An awful lot hinged on the hope that nobody would go promenading on that remaining ten per cent of deck in the interim.

Nobody did. The statistics continued to favour me as I made my dogleg turn and came in under the overhang of the counter, outboard dribbling on reduced throttle. Now to put to use the grapnel Alfredo had obtained for me from a ships' chandlery in Tangier. The noise it made when it struck the rail, even swathed in reams of duct tape, was an unwanted calling card. I secured the loose end of the rope to the inflatable, then drew the Ithaca from its polythene wrapping and fed my arm and shoulder through the strap. The Korth was in a clip-on holster. I clipped it to the cartridge belt, dispensed with hat and sunspecs, and shinned up the knotted rope.

As I was cocking my leg over the stem rail a small launch chugged by and I glanced towards it, straight into the gaping faces of a young, fair-haired couple. I waved cheerily to them, as if I habitually boarded boats armed to the teeth, like a marauding pirate. The girl, wearing shorts and a T-shirt several sizes too small, waved back uncertainly. Her companion, less readily assuaged, carried on goggling. Unfortunate, that. The only saving grace being that they were bound for the open sea, and showed no immediate tendency to turn back and report to someone in authority. Minding their own business admirably. Must be Brits then.

Beneath my feet the deck shifted ever so slightly in the launch's wash. I remained still, all senses on full alert. A ship's siren tooted dismally in the port. Here on the yacht the only activity was the sweep of the radar scanner, the only disturbance the slap of water against the hull. A gull took off from the rail of the sun deck above me. I unslung the Ithaca and disengaged the safety.

Whereas at No. 2 Korte Hoekssteeg I had had a floor plan to guide me, here I was in the dark about the internal layout. I checked my watch: five to three. Five minutes to Petit's deadline. If it mattered. From now on events would largely acquire a momentum of their own. The hours and the minutes of no consequence.

'Tom-Tom! *Vous êtes en haut?*' The hail came from up forward. Instinctively, I flattened myself against the superstructure.

'*Ouais.*' The drawled "yes" from the sun deck, directly above me.

'*D'accord. C'est bon. Restes-là, mon vieux.*'

To anyone up there I was invisible, screened by the overhanging lip. I had no wish for a chance encounter with Tom-Tom, non-combatant or not. He might be trained to strike first and ask 'friend-or-foe?' afterwards.

I edged around the corner of the superstructure into a narrow walkway, in search of access to the interior. I had covered only a few feet when a door flew open, almost in my face. Stumbling over the raised lower lip of the doorway, out popped a mountain of flesh – unmistakably a watchdog. Not quite in the Tom-Tom league, but still large enough to demolish me unaided. He gawked at me, his reflexes slower than they should have been for a man of his calling.

Letting off guns in the open air was to be avoided. Tangier and Ramouz were too close. The gorilla didn't seem to share my worry. Having gotten over his shock, he dived a hand inside the loose-fitting sport coat. Oversize he may have been, but he was no sluggard. As the gun came free of his armpit, I stabbed him in the belly button with the Ithaca. Breath exploded from his slack mouth, and he reeled against the open door, retching. I shifted my grip on the gun, lashed him across the side of the skull with the blunt end. It made a noise like a branch snapping. The gorilla fell, eyes rolling up, the drawn revolver striking the deck a fraction of a second before its owner. His downfall sent a tremor through the hull.

'*Qui ça?*' came from above, accompanied by stirrings, as of a great beast awakening. 'Who's that?'

'*Ne te déranges pas,* Tom-Tom,' I called back softly. '*C'est Varnair.*'

My name was my password. The stirrings ceased. I darted through the open door and down a companionway, the Ithaca in a one-handed grip. I dropped the last few steps, landing soundlessly on the carpeted deck. I stood perfectly still, listening. From the bowels of the hull came a faint throb, air conditioner, probably. Doors lined the corridor, all closed and all too close together to be anything more than cabins or store-rooms. Which left only the doors at each extremity worthy of attention. That to my right, towards the stern, was ajar. Through the gap came the mutter of voices. Promising. I crept noiselessly towards it, put an ear to the gap.

'What can be keeping Bernard?' It was a woman, speaking accented but adequate French. 'How long does it take a man to piss, Heinrich?'

'You mean you don't know?' Also in French with Teutonic origins, the tone incredulous. Male laughter erupted.

'I have never actually timed the operation, no.'

'Maybe he's taken one of his own dirty books with him,' someone else suggested, 'in which case he will need a little longer.' The laughter coarsened.

The absent Bernard was obviously Petit. Now I understood

why the timing was so precise. He meant to be out of the firing line while I eliminated Annika de Bruin, and, of necessity, the rest of the opposition. Canny of him.

'While we are waiting for him I would like to recap on the move to Africa, which, after all, is the lynchpin of the new operation.' This from a natural French speaker. Male.

'Go on.' The woman again. Clearly in charge. It could only be Annika de Bruin. My finger closed on the trigger of its own accord.

'I want to be assured that we will have continuity. That any changes in officialdom or government will not mean changes in policy. I would hate to spend all this money only to find the door closed after a few months, or, equally catastrophic, the price of turning a blind eye suddenly hyper-inflates.'

'You're a fool, Jules. Is there anywhere in the world where we can operate with *à la fois* freedom and absolute security? Better, I say, to risk a change of heart or extortionate demands by the officials concerned than a term in a Dutch prison.'

'Not to mention an English prison.' A new voice, Bow Bells English, but obviously with a good understanding of French. 'It's getting bleeding chancy on my patch, I don't mind telling you.'

'Exactly so, Trevor.' Annika made the language switch smoothly. That made her trilingual so far. An impatient click of the tongue, then, 'Where *has* Bernard got to?'

It was five minutes after three. No reason to delay longer.

Behind the door a chair creaked. 'I will fetch him.' The German, Heinrich.

I backed away from the door, which opened seconds later on a short football of a man, aglow with prosperity, an obese cigar growing from cupid's bow lips. His jaw dropped with an audible click and the cigar slid free, tumbling down the slope of his stomach.

'Hello, Heinrich,' I said, and let him have it in the equatorial belt. The first slug was spreadshot. As far as Heinrich was concerned it was well-named. Heavy grain spreadshot rips, mangles, and the results are usually fatal. What was left of Heinrich was whirled away, spraying blood in a crimson vapour. The world was already a cleaner place.

Then I was inside the room, in among them, kicking the door shut behind me. Annika stood at the head of a long conference table, flanked by two men, strangers to me: one youngish, a black African, the other, greying of thatch, wearing rimless glasses. The greyhair was rising and pulling a gun as he rose. My second shot, a solid cartridge, took his gun arm off at the shoulder, a neat piece of surgery. Quantities of flesh spattered the African, who dropped flat as his injured companion, screaming a high thin scream, was hurled against a mini-bar. I worked the slide and – in CIA parlance – terminated the remnants of the grey-haired man with extreme prejudice. I slid across the table on my backside, scattering note pads and coffee cups, and came to land on top of the cringing, wailing African. His reaction was to tuck his head under his arms and coil up like a hedgehog. He died fast with little disturbance.

Which left only Annika, who had gone to ground under the head of the table and, at its foot another man, flattened against the wall, more as a precaution against accidental damage than out of fright. Giorgio du Poletti, my self-styled only true friend.

We faced each other across the gore-smeared table top. Between us the smoking muzzle. One shot left.

'Giorgy...' I said at last, helplessly. 'So you're in on this.'

He was amazingly cool. You could almost admire him.

'We have a stake in it.' Shrugging. 'It is a business proposition. We had nothing to do with that girl of yours. Nothing at all.'

'Against my better judgement, I'm going to believe you. Now fuck off. I just hope you can swim.'

He frowned. 'Why?'

'You'll see. Look out for Petit. He has a plan.'

'Listen, André,' he said, his tone urgent. 'Don't make the biggest mistake of your life. 'Killing de Bruin has already put you in bad with the Family. It is Annika who runs the show, so Rik was no great loss. But you kill her and you're a dead man. I promise you.'

'Get lost, Giorgy, before I change my mind about you.'

He took the hint. Out the door, closing it behind him. He didn't realise how lucky he was.

With one eye on the door, I stuffed four cartridges into the magazine port, still punctiliously alternating SG with solid. Not hurrying. I was calm and detached. I had no thought for my own safety, only of execution, of doing good works for mankind.

'Come out, Annika.' I couldn't see her, but she had to be under the table. It was the only place to hide.

Absorbed in the task at hand, I had all but forgotten about the remaining contingent of gorillas. Sensibly, not knowing whether I was on my own or a team, they had kept their heads down. Contrary to their public persona, most bodyguards have a strong sense of self-preservation. A reminder that they were still an active force came with the kicking open of the door, instantly followed by a gun's boom and a sensation of heat on my upper arm. I dived behind the bar for cover as second and third bullets flitted by and smashed into the wall opposite.

I crouched by the bar, nursing my wounded left bicep. It was only a crease, but it burned like a brand from a hot iron. I was losing blood too. A minor leak, it would soon congeal. In all essentials I was still an effective combat unit.

'It's finished, Warner.' It came from the corridor, an

American drawl. 'Throw down the gun. We'll let you leave.'

Sure they would – on a bier.

'Why fight?' the voice seduced. Now I put a name to it: Baker, Giorgy's sidekick.

I allowed myself a soft chuckle. Baker would want payment with interest for that winged shoulder I had dealt him. Grudges endure in the criminal world. Unlikely he would let me walk away, even if I was willing.

'Let me think about it … Baker.'

Now the mirth came from him.

'Okay, wise guy, but think fast.'

The only thinking I planned to do was on my feet. I squat-walked across the room and was firing as I came opposite the open door. A young guy with glasses was crouching in the centre of the corridor, a revolver in each hand. Tucked in behind him, as if urging him to greater feats of daring, was a second, older goon. Fire spurted from the young guy's guns, but he had aimed high, expecting me to be upright. Neither of them got off any more shots. My first cartridge was SG and they shared its contents between them. They went down, squealing, all tangled up with each other like lovers having a frenetic fuck.

Baker, wiser, had taken refuge behind an outward opening store-room door at the far end. Our shots must have crossed in flight. His sang past my ear. Mine was better aimed. The solid cartridge went clean through the door as if it were cardboard, leaving a hole as big as a screaming mouth. Baker was out of sight behind the door, but I was familiar with the sound of a slug entering flesh. The untidy thump and crash of a heavy body falling was also unmistakeable.

The pair I had shot first were still alive, groaning and writhing. I stepped up to them and finished them off dispassionately, a bullet apiece from the Korth. Euthanasia, sort of.

They hardly bled, which was considerate of them as the carpet was the same light colour as the décor.

So who was left? Annika, Petit, Tom-Tom ... the skeleton crew ... I checked them off mentally. Theoretically Petit and Tom-Tom were on my side. But only theoretically.

As the tension seeped from my body, I topped up the Ithaca again and walked slowly forward down the corridor, towards Baker. As I came to each door I opened it, staying clear of the doorway. Nobody took pot shots at me. Baker was where I expected him to be, his blood smearing the wall and soaking into the carpet. All the cabins were empty. If the crew were around they weren't joining in the fun.

My arm hurt. My head throbbed. I couldn't think straight any more, could hardly think at all. Why was I here? To kill Annika de Bruin, of course. That was straightforward enough. But why – why did I want to kill Annika de Bruin? The reason had gotten lost someplace in the din and the stench of slaughter. All I could be sure about, even in my confusion, was that she still lived and breathed.

Overhead the deck creaked. Sounds of a scuffle, a cry of pain. Tom-Tom taking care of business on my behalf? I faced the stairs, got ready to shoot. No rush of feet or sounds suggesting a counterstrike. Things settled down, all noise ceased. Only the hum of the air-conditioning was to be heard as I returned to the conference room to finish the job I came to do.

Thirty-Three

Annika de Bruin was expecting me. No more skulking under tables for her. Now she was out in the open and in the pink. Pink shoulders, pink breasts, need I go on? Total exposure, in other words. And, by God, in the raw she was exquisite: a waist you could hand-span, pneumatic breasts that were almost too perfectly-proportioned to be true. Below the flat plain of her stomach, the sculpted nest of her pubic hairs proved she was a real blonde who scorned the depilated look. Indeed her entire body was swathed in fine down. In the sunlight that cascaded through the tinted windows she appeared to be coated in spun-gold cobwebs.

My eyes travelled down, over legs that were long and lean, the swell of the calves exaggerated by the high-heeled sling-backs. It was at the other extremity that the perfection was marred. Though lovely, her face had none of that essential womanly softness. The wide mouth that ought to have spelled generosity and kind-heartedness, spelled only calculation and duplicity. Her beauty was the beauty of stainless steel, hardened and tempered and polished to a mirror finish. For all her physical purity there was nothing feminine about Annika de Bruin.

But neither the shape of her mouth nor her armour plating spoiled her allure nearly as much as the automatic pistol she sheltered behind. The gun I understood and should have anticipated; the nakedness was mystifying.

'Do you find me desirable, Mr Warner?' she said, and her voice was husky. Her English was also flawless and accentless.

I laid the Ithaca on the table top. I doubted I could have used it on her anyway, not looking as she did now. It would have been an act of vandalism.

She smiled, interpreting the gesture as surrender. A triumph of the female form over pathetic male weakness.

'More than desirable,' I said, and it wasn't flattery. As ever when confronted with the unclothed female form, my prick was sending urgent messages. Such as, here it is, on a plate, so what are you waiting for, schmuck?

'For a man like you there is a place in my organization,' she said. 'An important place.'

'I don't make deals from the wrong end of a gun barrel.' I was no longer looking at her face. The things she was doing to herself with her free hand were bringing out the beast in me. 'And I already turned down an offer from your husband.'

'Ah, but he had less to offer.'

No disputing that. The hand movements grew more frenzied. Her fingers and the insides of the tops of her thighs glistened.

'How right you are,' I croaked. I was starting to sweat. 'But I'm still not interested. In a job, I mean.'

'This is not a *job* I am talking about, you fool!' She was panting now. And I was right there with her. 'I am offering you a partnership, more money than you could earn in ten lifetimes.' Her eyelids flickered, her mouth parted, she was close to orgasm. The gun slipped from slack fingers, thumped on the carpet.

'Come.' She reached for me. 'Love me.'

The magnet of her superb body was irresistible, and I was too weak to resist it. It drew me into her arms. She was flushed, her body throbbing as if from some mechanism deep inside, and the smell of sex that rose from her was miasmal. My belt was suddenly undone, my fly unzipped, and no sooner had my jeans descended below my thighs, my underpants in close attendance, when my prick was enveloped in a slippery, clinging heat. All I had to do was stand there. Annika was in control. Annika would always be in control. To her men were just studs, sexual adjuncts. I ought to have cared, but I didn't. I ought to have hated her but I loved her instead. And hated myself.

Some women are subdued in their lovemaking, others exuberant. Annika may have been a robot-woman in some ways but her commitment to the sex act owed nothing to robotics. She revelled in it. Every jerk of my pelvis pushed a squeal of delight from the wide, scarlet lips, the squeals growing in volume and intensity as we bumped along towards a climax. She signalled her readiness by lifting her feet off the deck and scissoring my waist with her legs. I staggered briefly as I took her weight – she was no sylph. I cupped the cheeks of her backside, and at that precise instant we both climaxed, as near simultaneously as made no odds.

It was an orgasm to end all orgasms, long-lasting, noisy, and excessively seminal. Gradually though, the screams quietened to groans and ultimately tapered off to a protracted sigh. Hands still interlaced behind my neck, Annika unlocked her legs slowly and let them slide to the deck. The internal muscles of her vagina still clamped me, no less fiercely than during the act. Her sex odour was stronger than ever. To inhale it was to be drugged by it.

Drugged. The word roared in my ears.

Now I remembered why I was here.

I was here for Lizzy.

Lizzy, now a drug addict because of this woman.

420

Lizzy, forced by her into unnatural sex acts. Brutalized. Beaten. Corrupted. Contaminated.

I felt dirty.

We were still coupled when I squeezed the trigger. The punch of the bullet ripped her away from me and drove her backwards to slam into the wall. Incredibly she remained standing. Staring, aghast, at me, at the still-pointing, still-smoking gun. Not downwards at the once-pristine plain of her stomach, now marred by a purple-edged puncture with a halo of flash burns, so close had been the muzzle when I fired. Blood was welling, thick as oil, and a scarlet runnel descended into her pubic hairs, meandering through them as a stream through a forest.

'You ... shot me.' Her legs began to crumple. She slid a few inches down the wall. 'How ... could you l-love me like that ... then ... sh-shoot me?' She was genuinely incredulous. Maybe she had a right to be.

She slid further and faster, until her bottom bumped on the deck, wrenching a gasp of pain from the mouth that was like a slot. In the wall, just above her head, was a hole and around it, dark as burgundy, a splash of blood from the exit wound. Strands of her blonde hair were stuck to it, drawn up from her scalp.

Her mouth squirmed. Her teeth were stained pink, a shade lighter than her lipstick. She mumbled something in an unfamiliar language, her native Dutch I guessed.

'Are you talking to me or clearing your throat?' I said coldly as I stowed the Korth in its holster.

'Why d-did you ...?' she slurred, then her words tapered off in a groan.

'Shoot you?' My jeans and pants were still around my ankles. I hoisted them to more dignified levels.

She was panting now, her eyes all but closed, the colour wiped from her complexion.

'In the ... name of ... God– *why?*' she whispered, as if it mattered any more.

I shrugged as I buckled my belt.

'In the name of God, why not?'

The air on deck was pure and clean after the stink of carnage and gunpowder fumes and the juices of Annika de Bruin. I had spent ten fruitless minutes in search of Petit, calling his name and going from cabin to cabin. Maybe the bastard didn't trust me not to give him the same treatment as his late colleagues. Perceptive of him. I was in the mood for a clean sweep.

At the head of the companionway I came across the spread-eagled form of a man in sailor togs. The epaulettes suggested an officer. No external injuries, but he was dead all right. Tom-Tom's work, I didn't doubt. In the wheelhouse was a second stiff, also a crew member. Again no obvious cause of death.

I propped the Ithaca in a corner of the wheelhouse, and gave the controls a once-over. As you'd expect, the ship lacked no modern navigational aid. She could be sailed by computer. The crew were almost supernumerary. Providentially, since I was disinclined to spend hours reading the instruction handbook, manual controls had not been dispensed with altogether. I was tinkering with the Cetrek auto-pilot when a shadow fell across me. I glanced up. Tom-Tom peered balefully through the open doorway, his bulk blotting out the sun and a good part of the sky. The man was a walking eclipse.

'*Que fais-tu?*' he growled.

If I answered truthfully, I'd have to kill him. Or he me.

So I said, 'Just looking around.'

I edged towards the Ithaca while making a pretence of studying the control panel.

'No, you don't.' He dived for the gun, beating me by a nose.

'You're forgetting something, Tom-Tom,' I said pleasantly, tossing him a comradely grin. 'I'm working for your boss.' I tapped him on the chest. It was like tapping on a stone plinth. 'You and me, we're on the same side. Where is Petit anyway?'

'Waiting for you to leave.' Tom Tom's pebble eyes were bright with suspicion.

'I thought as much. He doesn't trust me, does he?'

He moved in a sidle to the door and, with a notable lack of effort, flung the Ithaca high and far into the Mediterranean. It flew a long, long way before plunging into the pale blue waters. Now I was annoyed. That was an expensive piece of hardware.

'Now, Tom-Tom, that wasn't friendly.' I promptly covered him with the Korth in case he had ambitions towards evicting me by the same method.

'*Dehors*.' Meaning I was to beat it. 'You're leaving, Varnair.'

'Okay, so I'm leaving.' A brawl with Tom-Tom was not on my agenda. I'd had a good run. I was content to settle for what I'd got. In the end it was Tom-Tom who chose war when he could have had peace. As I detoured around him he grabbed for the Korth. Like many outsize blokes he could be cobra-fast when it suited. The only shot I got off before the gun was wrenched away, almost taking my arm with it, definitely hit meat. For all its disabling effect on Tom-Tom I might as well have said 'Bang, you're dead,' and saved the price of a bullet.

Subsequent developments were mostly to my disadvantage. Tom-Tom lifted me bodily and gave me a big squeeze to show how much he loved me. My rib cage buckled. Quite by chance my knee, while flailing about like the rest of my joints, got wedged in his crotch. I drove upwards with my kneecap. Surely in that area Tom-Tom was just as tender as any normal-sized male.

I was only partly-right. The only reaction was a hissing of garlic-fumed breath past toothless gums, and enough of a slackening of the bear hug for me to disengage my arms and deliver a clubbing blow to the side of that pineapple-shaped head. This induced a roar of pain – from me, not him. A cannonball would have been softer. In retaliation he projected me aloft, cracking my skull against the roof. I saw not just stars, but a whole galaxy. This, however, was only the run-up to the short trip Tom-Tom was planning for me: from one side of the wheelhouse to the other without ever touching the deck.

I came to rest in a corner, draped over a fire extinguisher. Dazed, but damage still superficial. Icicles of fear transfixed my heart as the extent of Tom-Tom's physical superiority sank in. More than that, he had a touch of madness about him. His jaw was working in a loose, unhinged fashion, his hands opening and closing in spasms, like mechanical grabs. He advanced on me, mouthing gibberish. My only salvation lay in staying out of grabbing range. I needed room to manoeuvre. Room, bluntly, to get the hell out of there, and off the ship while I was still in a fit condition.

In theory Tom-Tom's ponderous lumber was easy to dodge. I demonstrated how easy by nipping under the out-stretched arms, which brought me within bolting distance of the door, only to be caught by a chop to the back of my neck that lifted me off my feet and out of the wheelhouse altogether. Well, wasn't that what I wanted? My already sore midriff fetched up against the rail, deflecting me back towards the wheelhouse where, kinetic forces expended, I was mercifully permitted to crumple to the deck. Bruised, stunned, weakened. The wound in my arm had opened, bright baubles of blood dribbling through the tear in my sleeve. No respite was forthcoming though. This wasn't a punch-up out of the pages of a Superman comic. Tom-Tom burst from the doorway like a rampaging bull. His grin as he lit upon me was a gummy half-moon of rapture.

'Say your prayers, Varnair,' he said, a thread of saliva dangling from his chin. 'I am going to break you into very small pieces.'

I believed him.

'Now, wait a minute, Tom-Tom, let's discuss this rationally.'

I was in a dead end. Rails to the right and behind, the wheelhouse to the left. Tom-Tom in front and the most impenetrable of the lot.

He shuffled towards me, not hurrying, drawing out the kill. I had only seconds left to put up some kind of defence. The smallest move was agony, but I straightened my leg and tore the skin-diver's knife from the tapes that bound it to my ankle. Its appearance had no deterrent effect on Tom-Tom. It didn't prevent the grab-like hands from locking onto me, nor from hauling me upright, not yet from crushing my shoulders together until my collar bones creaked.

In a despairing last act of self-preservation, I lunged with the knife at his lower gut. So sharp was the blade that it went in all the way to the hilt. The pressure on my shoulders continued unabated. I jerked the knife free. It came with a squelch and a gush of blood that dyed my hands instant red. Again I lunged, twisting, working the blade from side to side. A reaction at last, the grip on my shoulders easing, my weight pulling me free. Still I worked the knife, the blood now spurting, great gouts of it, darkening Tom-Tom's royal blue pants and spraying over me. A half-hearted cuff flung me against the rail. Temporarily Tom-Tom lost interest in me to attend to his hurts.

Such wounds as I had inflicted would have immobilized if not killed most men. But Tom-Tom was to most men as a dinosaur is to a lizard. A strip of band-aid and he would be good as new. I had gained at best a few precious moments, life-giving as a drop of moisture to a man dying of thirst though they were. As Tom-Tom slumped against the rail to get his second wind, I ducked down and took a handful of his trouser bottoms. A startled grunt escaped him. He clutched at my head, probably with the intention of removing it from my body. I rose, yanking at his trouser bottoms, lifting his legs clear of the deck so that he was balanced on the rail, which acted as a fulcrum. He swore, he kicked, he tried to unscrew my head from my neck but the loss of several pints of blood had affected even him. Almost casually, I tipped him over the rail.

A shout exploded from the cavern of his toothless mouth. It wasn't far to fall, seven feet at the most to the main deck, but twenty-plus stone is a lot of deadweight to drop from any height. I swear the ship heeled over when he landed.

I flopped against the rail, puffing harder than a steam loco on an uphill gradient. The Incredible Hulk was splattered on the deck below like a giant spilled jelly. It was quite still, and if the fall hadn't killed it, chances were it would bleed to death.

Back into the wheelhouse then, at a weak-kneed stagger. Find the starter; thankfully, *AnnRik* could be started from the bridge. A turn of the key and engines below broke into a lazy rumble. Needles came alive on dials, illuminated digits and computerized images glowed from the Navstar navigation displays. This plethora of electronic data was just a jumble of hieroglyphics to a traditionalist sea dog like me. Besides, I could manage without it. I looked out across the peaceful bay, its waters winking under the fading sun. Inshore a scattering of boats and skiffs, all at anchor and lifeless. In the opposite direction, out to sea, *Seaspray* was the only craft in sight, her mast a lonely silver lance.

Now for the anchor. It was raised by a motor on the foredeck, controlled remotely from here, which was just as well since I could never have managed the trek to the bow and back in my depleted condition. I located the appropriate button. The anchor came clattering up, the motor cutting out automatically as the flukes entered the hawse-hole. As I moved across to the wheel my toe stubbed against the Korth. I slipped it into its holster. Might need it yet. Tom-Tom might revive.

The beat of the diesels was steady, the revolution counters showing 250 rpm. I folded my fingers around the twin T-bar throttle levers and pushed. Response was instantaneous: a tremble underfoot, a forward surge that rocked me on my heels, and we were on the move, ten knots coming up fast. A touch of negative throttle, and she settled at ten, cleaving the water cleanly. I felt like the master of an ocean liner.

A twitch of the wheel to port, the electronic compass flickering, 265 degrees ... 266,267,268 ... I kept her swinging until 305 flashed up, then straightened up as the reading stabilized on 310, the bows now pointing towards the Atlantic. *AnnRik* was on course for several thousand miles of ocean waste.

Setting the auto-pilot I went below, limping and groaning and feeling sorry for myself. It stank down there. Blood and cordite mostly, smells that stuck to my palate, making the gorge rise and my stomach lurch.

'Petit!' I bellowed. 'It's safe to come out. They're all dead.'

Only the drumming of the engines answered me. *AnnRik* was a ship of ghosts, a floating abattoir. I stepped over the corpses in the corridor.

'Petit!'

The swirl of water along the hull was transmitted through the soles of my feet. Eerie, somehow, to think of that empty wheelhouse and the helm making microscopic adjustments, as if under the direction of some invisible agency. Angrily I shook off the spooks, disregarded my hurts, and went about my business.

On a vessel of *AnnRik*'s tonnage there is no obvious location for the sea cocks. I had to hunt hard to find just two. These were amidships, below the main staterooms, and the flow rate when I opened them was only moderate. It would be some hours before the hull became waterlogged. Long before that, however, the cocks would be inaccessible to anyone other than an experienced underwater swimmer. I doubted whether Petit qualified, or Giorgy, if either of them were still on board. Tom-Tom, if he lived, certainly didn't, although the other two might be able to use him as a life raft when the yacht sank.

A last fruitless hail to Petit before I went up top. A sea breeze had arisen as *AnnRik* passed beyond the shelter of Cap Malabata, with its ugly squat lighthouse. *Seaspray* was far astern, just a speck of white on blue. I made sure Tom-Tom was still comatose, then went aft. The Dutch flag on its short pole agitated about my head. To starboard, in the direction of Spain, two oil tankers were heading towards me in echelon. By my estimation they would cut *AnnRik*'s wake. If they didn't and by some freak chance collided with *AnnRik*, well, that would just hasten the process I had already set in motion.

Seaspray's inflatable was wagging crazily in the propeller wash. Hugging my bent rib cage with one arm, I unhooked the grapnel, flung it well clear. That done, the longer I hung about, the longer the swim, so I went in off the stern rail in a clean shallow dive. When I broke surface *AnnRik* was already a hundred yards away, the square stern rising from the white commotion of her wake, cruising majestically to her doom.

Now it really was over.

To a silent outcry from bruised and mangled limbs I struck out for the dinghy.

Thirty-Four

My sister's pleasure at finding me on her doorstep was not obvious. The cheek I kissed was frigid, the look searching and rimed with frost, the armful of red carnations accepted without thanks or comment.

'Are my flies undone?' I cracked, looking pointedly down.

'Oh no, you're quite immaculate,' she replied, adding, as we went through the hall towards the living room, a sardonic 'As usual.'

What was that supposed to mean? I wondered. To create a solid, respectable presence for the promised explanations I was soberly suited under a tweed overcoat. Maybe she saw through this for the window-dressing it was.

'Is it that time of the month then?' I said spitefully as I chucked my coat over an armchair back, only to have it whisked huffily away. I folded my frame into a second armchair, Willie's favourite TV-goggling perch. Willie himself wasn't home, no doubt still slaving over a hot desk someplace in the City.

Julie had chosen to ignore my last question. Rightly so.

'Sorry,' I muttered to her resentful back.

She stepped away from the carnations, now gracefully arranged in a fat vase fashioned in the shape of a woman's torso. She was in her pearls and twin-set mode, her hair drawn back into a severe bun. Her appearance alone spelled hard times to come.

'Do you want some coffee?' she asked, an unbending of sorts. 'It's freshly perked.'

'Not for now. Are the girls home?'

'Which ones?' A quick, false smile. 'Cathy and Christina are at school. Lizzy is ... upstairs.' Her look was now decidedly hostile. 'Waiting for you to take her away.'

The message was beginning to seep through. My bad odour was connected with Lizzy.

'How is Lizzy?'

'As well as can be expected,' she said stiffly.

'Good.'

'Drew ...' she began, then made a little noise in the back of her throat and put her fingers over her mouth as if she were about to burp. Now she was avoiding my eyes.

I guessed she would find it easier addressing my back, so I got up and sauntered over to the French window that accessed a terrace and a wilderness of back yard. The bare branches of the horse-chestnut tree were like a fracture in the surly February sky. Near the top a solitary leaf bobbed from the very tip of a branch, dead but refusing to let go. The lawn was an anaemic grey-green, dormant pending the arrival of spring; in the centre was a stone pedestal with a sundial on top. The tip of the gnomon was broken off.

'Drew ...' Julie began again, dubious, tentative. 'Look ... this is very difficult for me, your being my brother, but there are some things I have to know.'

'Such as?'

A few seconds of silence.

'Are you ...' An audible swallow. 'Are you aware that Lizzy ... oh my God ... is on drugs ... heroin? I mean ...' I visualized Julie behind me, twisting the pearls into knots as she was wont to do under stress. 'I mean she's addicted to the stuff.'

'Yes.' My voice was strained.

'And not only that, she's ... in love with you.'

My shoulders slumped. My 'yes' was lower, subdued.

'Did she tell you that?' I said a moment later.

'Yes, but don't be angry with her, please. She's so unhappy. She had to talk to someone.'

'I'm not angry with her, Jules,' I said tiredly, turning. She was, as expected, abstractedly knotting her pearls. Later, Christina would be given the job of unravelling them. She was rather proficient at it, exploiting her prowess by charging for the service.

'Anyway,' Julie went on miserably, 'I just wondered how far it had gone. She's an extremely attractive girl. Looks older than she is too, which doesn't help.'

Attractive? Didn't I know it. I who had held out against her teasing allure for months.

'She behaves and talks as if you and she ...' Being something of a moralist-traditionalist, she couldn't bring herself to accuse me of having sexual relations with a girl of sixteen.

'Forget it!' I said, and it came out harsh. Julie's indrawn breath told me she interpreted my brusque dismissal as an admission of guilt.

A barrier reared between us. I glowered down at her, breathing hard through my nostrils, technically innocent of the charge, morally culpable. Julie wasn't cowed. Now the subject was out in the open, she would pursue it, terrier-like, to a conclusion. She took a cigarette from the carved ebony case on the coffee table. A reformed smoker, it was unusual for her to partake of the weed nowadays.

'It's not you I'm concerned about so much as Lizzy. You can fight your own battles. But she's alone in the world, and needs some stability in her life, whatever she's done or had done to her.' Creases of anxiety forked from the bridge of

Julie's nose. 'Tell me the truth, Drew, something *has* been going on, hasn't it?'

'You silly bitch! She's a drug addict. Of *course* something's been going on!'

'You know very well what I mean,' came the stiff retort, and any further pretence on my part was pointless. 'I mean between Lizzy and you.'

'I screwed her, you mean? Why don't you come out and say it?'

It was as if I'd slapped her. She shrank from me, horrified. 'You ... you *admit* it?'

'Like hell I do!' I roared, my self-control shattering. Under her harassed gaze I began to stalk the room. 'The things that have been "going on", as you put it, were not my doing. And the creatures responsible have paid for it. That's all I'm prepared to say.'

'That's not good enough. I want to hear to hear the full story.'

'No, Jules.' This story was not for telling. Ever. 'I couldn't talk about it, not even to you. Better to stay ignorant. You might ... over-react. I wouldn't want you to, well, start erecting electrified fences around the yard and confining Cathy and Christina indoors on account of what I might tell you.'

'It's as bad as that?'

It's worse than that, I could have said.

'These, er ...creatures you mention. How, specifically, did they pay for what they did to Lizzy? Were they arrested?'

'They paid,' I said without melodrama, 'in the only way that was acceptable to me.'

She stubbed out her cigarette, and picked at the snarled-up pearls. 'I see,' she said, fortunately not seeing at all.

Visions of *AnnRik* forging through the waters of the Straits of Gibraltar with her consignment of corpses shut out the oak beams and the rustic decor and the crackling fire. Yes, they had paid all right, the highest price of all.

Rain pattered on the window. The battleship grey of the sky had dimmed to charcoal; night was falling early. Dismal weather for a depressing topic. I went to join Julie on the couch, and placed my arm around her shoulders. Such intimate displays, despite our mutual fondness, were rare, and her instinct was to stiffen, to resist my overtures. Then, with a tiny sigh, she relaxed against me. Runaway wisps of golden hair tickled my cheek. I blew them away.

'Sorry ... about the hair, I mean.' Her hand touched my cheek tentatively. 'About my suspicions too, I suppose. But we really must decide what to do about Lizzy. She's expecting you to take her back with you to Andorra. To live together.' The hand was removed as some of her lingering doubts staged a comeback.

'So? She's well over the age of consent.'

'Is that what you want – to marry her?'

Reproof was woven into the words.

'Now that you mention it, yes, I could bear to shack up with her ...'

'André!' She jerked free of my arm. Her calling me by my full name was a sure mark of displeasure. The pearls were back in action. 'You're over twice her age!'

'If I might finish? I was about to say, I could bear to shack up with her, but I'm not going to. At a practical level, it wouldn't work. The age difference, chiefly. I don't kid myself that when I'm sixty and she's thirty-six or seven, that she'll still feel the same about me. Secondly, more importantly, I made a promise. I owe her a different kind of care and protection.' I hesitated, feeling that once I said it, I would be committed. My sigh was visceral. 'The parental kind.'

'You made a promise? To whom?'

'To myself, dear sister. That means it's sacred.'

'I see.' Julie rested an elbow on the back of the couch, speared me with the brilliant blue eyes that matched mine so exactly it was like looking into a mirror. 'Well, I have a better solution. Willie and I have discussed it, and we'd be willing for her to stay with us, for a few months at least, and maybe, if it works out, for longer.'

'Sounds great,' I said without enthusiasm.

'On one condition ...'

'With you, Jules, there's always a catch.'

'You can visit her here as often as you like, but I'm not having any goings-on in the house.'

I couldn't help laughing.

'You're not listening to me, Jules. Whatever Lizzy's aspirations, she and I will not be having conjugal rights.'

Her expression reflected her scepticism.

'You don't trust me?' I said, not really blaming her.

'Trust you or not, the point is she'll be better off as part of a family. We're prepared to provide a home, to feed her, clothe her, love her too, I suppose. Even with the drugs and things, she's a likeable girl. Perhaps even adopt her, if that seems the wisest course. We'll get her the best medical treatment, get her cured. Whatever's necessary, we'll do it.'

As homes go I couldn't do better for Lizzy. What it might do for me if I were leave her here was best put aside. There would be opportunity and to spare to brood over it in the long, lonely days ahead.

And in the longer, lonelier nights.

Julie agreed to my seeing Lizzy alone to break the news.

'You're allowed half-an-hour. Then I'm coming in, whether you've finished crying on each other's shoulders or not. Understood?'

'You're a hard woman, Jules,' I said.

'I'd prefer strong to hard.'

'I love you, little sis.' If I'd ever told her so before it was beyond remembrance.

Her stern manner softened.

'It's mutual, big brother. I just wish ...'

'Wish what?'

Regret shadowed her handsome features.

'It sounds silly, but I just wish I knew who you really are.'

Then she left me, to ponder in solitude that parting remark and the other things that had passed between us.

The pondering only lasted until Lizzy came. Crashing in like a bracing wind to shred the sombre atmosphere. Alive and aglow and achingly lovely. I had forgotten how lovely. The living reminder was exquisite pain.

'Oh, Alan, Alan ... I've missed you so. Sorry, I mean André.'

She was all over me, demonstrative as ever, her slender body hot through the rather dowdy woollen dress I hadn't seen on her before (Julie's influence?). She looked well enough. Slightly pinched around the cheeks and her pupils were dilated from drugs, but she had put on a bit of weight and her erstwhile zest and sparkle were firmly back *in situ*. The facial alterations were, unfortunately, permanent.

Telling her was going to be tough. I managed to fend off her kisses by swinging her round and round, and hugging her. Only by keeping the contact platonic could I hope to walk out on her.

'How are you?' I asked her.

'Ace. Wonderful. Stupendiferous. Now that *you're* here.' Her arms were around my waist, her lips close to mine. Too close for sanity.

'Have you been all right here?'

'Terrif. Your sister's a real beaut. Ever so kind.'

436

'That's good,' I said abruptly. 'Then you won't mind staying on a while.'

The joy slid from her face like water off sealskin.

'Staying on?'

I came straight, almost brutally, to the point. Told her that whatever there had been between us was over. That I would visit her here at Julie's from time to time and that would be the sum total of our connection. That it should be so was better all round, I assured her, and most of all for her. We were all thinking only of her.

When I had spouted my piece and it had sunk in, she just stared dumbly at me like a kicked puppy.

'Trust me, Freckles,' I said, hating myself and the medicinal compound I was stuffing down her. 'Here you can have a good life, a normal life. You'll go to college, get some professional qualifications, spend vacations with Julie and Willie and the girls. They're going skiing in Austria next month ...' I was selling hard, though my faith in the commodity was tenuous.

'I don't get it,' she said, as if she hadn't heard a word of it. 'Don't you want me anymore?'

Deep inside me, a lacerating.

'Don't be silly. This has nothing to do with what I want. It's to do with what's right for you, for both of us. You can't wish a twenty year age gap away.'

Her face turned to stone.

'*You* can't maybe.' Her eyes searched mine for a chink to prise apart. 'I've only got you. Do you want me to beg? I will, if that's what you want. I will beg.' To my horror she fell to her knees and clung to me. 'It's not fair. Please take me with you. Please!'

I lifted her forcibly, held her at arm's length. 'Lizzy, believe me, I hate doing this. It's just common sense.' It was meant to sound firm and final, but she scented underlying indecision.

'Please, Alan, sorry, André. I couldn't bear it if you went away.'

I cast around helplessly, but nobody was about to come to my rescue. The floor didn't swallow me up either.

'Oh, I know about the risks of marrying outside your age group and all that shit,' she said with scorn. 'Perhaps that's right, perhaps it can't work. But what's the harm in giving it a whirl. All I know is I love you like crazy, and if it all falls apart some day in the future what's the difference between that and it all falling apart today. If we're still both going to be miserable I'd rather put it off as long as I can.'

It made a weird kind of sense. It still didn't move me.

'No, honey. Leave it be.' I took her hands, squeezed them. 'Stay with Julie. I'll come to visit you. We'll have days out together.'

Her mouth had the stubborn set I recognized so well.

'Days out together,' she mimicked. 'What will we do – go to the zoo? Have picnics in the country? Oh, how *lovely*! You know, sometimes you talk to me as if I'm a kid.'

'Give me a break here. I'm trying to do the right thing.'

She looked as if she wanted to hit me.

'Fuck you! And fuck the right thing! You know what I think?' She didn't wait for an answer. 'I don't believe I'll ever see you again. I think you're going away and not coming back.' Her eyes were fierce, her hands made into fists. The temptation to embrace her, to comfort her, to take back every last hurtful utterance was unbearable. The house of cards of my good intentions was in danger of collapse.

Then she took a step back. 'I'm right, aren't I? You're going to leave me and never come back.'

'I have to come back,' I stalled. 'Julie's my sister . . .'

'You can get round that. You could make sure I'm out, or arrange to meet her away from the house, or ... or, oh, anything at all.'

'Sweetheart ...'

'Tell the *truth*, André !' She began to beat at me with her fists. 'Don't be a coward. Tell the truth!'

'All right, all right! You're right, I'm not coming back. Seeing you now and again would be worse than never seeing you at all. Are you bloody satisfied?'

Although she had prophesied it accurately, her hand flew to her mouth. Ashen, the grey eyes wide, believing yet disbelieving, she backed away as if I were a dangerous animal about to pounce.

I stretched my arms towards her, inviting her inside, my need to have her close to me this one last time probably even greater than hers. But she warded me off, making little mewing noises. When I took a step towards her, she whirled round and ran to the door.

'Lizzy, wait!' I shouted, but she had the door open and was gone. Her heels clattered across the hall, another door slammed.

I started after her and cannoned into Julie.

'What on earth's going on?' she demanded as we clutched at each other, tottering. 'Was that Lizzy I just heard?'

'Yes,' I snarled. 'She doesn't agree with the decision we made about her future.'

She held on to me, restraining me from pursuit. 'Oh André, André, what did you expect? Calm acceptance? She's bound to be upset. She'll get over it. A month from now she'll wonder what all the fuss was about.' She shook me gently. 'Believe me.'

Oh, I believed her all right. The trouble was, Lizzy learning to live without me was what I feared most. Doing the right thing, I decided, was a painful business. It was, nevertheless, the right thing. About that I had not the slightest doubt.

I left without seeing Lizzy again. No goodbyes, no parting

hugs. I simply had to get out of there. It was dark. It was raining. I walked, wandered rather, through suburban streets. Hoping to burn off the torture and the torment. First Clair, now Lizzy. How many blows can a man absorb before becoming punch-drunk?

Cars scurried past, the rain highlighted in the flare of their headlights. People came towards me beneath tilted umbrellas, intent only on getting out of the rain, getting home. To live their cosy suburban lives, wrestle with their petty, suburban problems. To ogle TV, to decorate the bathroom, to plan vacations, build castles in Spain, pay the electricity account, make out shopping lists; eat, sleep, make love. Had my life ever been as ordered as that? If so it was gone for good, never to return.

Then all was noise and light: a white glare, intense, dispersing the darkness. Locked wheels rasping on asphalt, air brakes hissing, the blast of a horn.

A shout. 'Oi! What the fuck are you playin' at?'

What I was playing at was standing in the road, lit up by a pair of rectangular headlights. Through the glare I distinguished a head, thrust out of the side window of a high sided truck.

'Tryin' to get yerself killed, are yer?'

I tendered a placatory flap of my hand. 'No such luck,' I muttered, and backed onto the sidewalk.

The truck drove on to an angry clash of gears, revving hard all the way to the STOP sign, some couple of hundred yards ahead.

No death wish had guided my feet into the truck's path. I had strayed unaware. Deep as my depression was, I no longer had any taste for oblivion as a purgative. What I needed right now was a stiff drink, followed by a beautiful woman, expert in the process of arousal. Placebos both, but they would help me cross a personal Rubicon, commit me to go on, to return to the highway I was so used to travelling. To regard the last few months as a mere detour. Or better still, as if they never happened.

I was getting soaked. I turned up my collar and headed for the station.

IV

Nobody

Thirty-Five

My inclination, on unlocking the door of my house late on a Wednesday evening, was to make for the bar. To pour a vodka and toss it down my throat. To relish its warmth in the pit of my stomach and be comforted by it. Then to pour another, and another, and another.

And so on, down that old easy familiar route. Instead, I opened my mail. Two weeks of it, neatly stacked on the hall table by Señora Sist. I sat in the kitchen and sifted through bills and circulars and a couple of airmailed *Sunday Times* newspapers. It wasn't until I had worked down to the bottom of the heap that I came upon an actual letter. Not just any old letter, but a letter with a Nigerian stamp, postmarked Port Harcourt, three weeks earlier give or take. The handwritten address was incomplete: Mr Alan Melvill without the 'e', La Messana, Andorra. A miracle it had found me at all. Especially addressed to my alias. I slit it with my ornate Moroccan paperknife. Inside a single sheet of lined notepaper, a creamy colour, grubby and stained. I glanced at the signature.

It was from Clair.

I stared at that signature for long while before starting on the letter itself. Unable to accept that it wasn't simply an illusion. Half afraid to read what she had written. Why? Was it because I had failed to keep Lizzy safe from harm? Because, thanks to my incompetence, the carefree, happy girl Clair had involuntarily left in my care was now a drug addict? Now superficially aged ten years and almost certain to be damaged psychologically.

It was true I had much to castigate myself for and that telling Clair would come hard. Yet that wasn't the real fear, the big fear. As I sat there in my house of memories, Clair's letter under my outspread hand, little by little that other, bigger fear crystallized: I was afraid because of my feelings for her daughter, and hers for me.

Yet the content of the letter, when I nerved myself to read it, blew away my guilt.

Dear Alan

Excuse my handwriting, I'm working by candle-light with a pencil stub. I hope this letter gets to you. I'm giving my last $20 to Mostafa to put a stamp on it and mail it. He's always treated me OK so I'll have to trust him.

I'm being kept on an island off the African coast. Some sort of staging post for kidnappees I think. All young girls, some very young. Lot of crying, you can imagine. Last night I overheard the three men who guard us talking about killing me. Writing it cold like that makes it seem unreal but it's real enough and I'm so afraid. They speak a kind of pidgin English but I think I understood what they were saying. Somebody called Hassan has been given the job. Oh God I can't believe this.

I must stay focused. Reason for writing you is Lizzy. After they grabbed me and Lizzy got away I assume you took her under your wing. If you didn't that makes me a bad judge of human nature. I sincerely believe you're a good man. (Here I winced.) If you're in a position to do anything for her please contact my old friend Suzanne Rissmeyer who lives in Brighton in the UK. Can't remember her exact address. Her husband Stephen is something big at the US Embassy. Do it for me please please please. Don't let me down, I beg you.

That's all I guess. Thanks for everything. Funny thing is I'm worrying about Lizzy not myself. Tell her the insurance papers and will are in the desk top drawer. Give her all my love and a big hug and be kind to her. I can't believe I'm really writing this. My best to you. Clair X

The letter was six months old give or take. So Commissaire Ramouz had only been wrong by a couple of months when he surmised she was dead, way back in June. It wasn't the same anyhow as this in-your-face confirmation that they had killed her. Even the letter wasn't a hundred per cent conclusive, but if "Hassan" hadn't followed through, if the order had been rescinded and Clair had been spared, she would have found a way to write again, even without twenty dollars to bribe her guard.

A life ended then, a door closed. It saddened me, not so much on my own account as for Lizzy. Her hopes had dwindled, but never quite to vanishing point. Her acceptance never quite absolute. Now this, the quietus. Kinder perhaps not to tell her? Let the half-healed wounds scar over naturally. Certainly it would be easier for me if I mailed the letter to

Julie, and let her decide. Better that such devastating news came from the mouth of a woman, a mother with daughters of her own. More empathy there.

Yeah, right. Nice cop-out, Warner.

'André?' Very few people called me by my given name these days, but I would have known her anyway.

'Who else?' I said into my cell phone. 'Hello, Lizzy. How are you? Are you still with Julie?'

'André ... my mum's dead, you know that, don't you? I mean really dead, like for-sure dead. That letter you sent Julie ...' Her voice cracked. Seconds crawled by. I didn't speak. Couldn't. 'Anyhow, I want to come back. I want to come home.' Straight to the point, as ever.

I glanced involuntarily at the half-packed suitcase on the bed. I was booked on a night flight from Toulouse to Rome, thence to Florence. The "home" Lizzy wanted to come back to would be unoccupied an hour from now.

'Does Julie know you're calling?'

'It's nothing to do with Julie. It's to do with you and me and us. I miss you so terribly.'

'Freckles ...'

An angry hiss travelled along the waves. 'Don't say it! Don't fob me off with your tired old bullshit.'

'I was going to say this isn't your home. Your home is ... is ... well, not here, that's for sure.'

'You're doing it,' she groaned. 'You're talking as if you were my father. I'm coming just the same, whether you agree or not. I belong with you.'

'I won't be here,' I said coldly, ducking for cover behind an uncaring front. 'I have to go to Italy.'

That threw her, but only for a couple of seconds.

'Italy? What for, on vacation?'

'Business.'

She demanded to know what kind. I declined to say. My secretiveness didn't go down well. I was reminded of our pact. Avowals of love came down the line, battering at my *sang-froid*.

'Tell me why you have to go, André. *Please!*'

Dare I tell her? Would it be enough to destroy her love? Half of me would have been glad, the other half desolate.

While I still vacillated, she blurted, 'You're going to kill somebody, aren't you? Don't deny it! Is it because of me, or my mother, or what? Tell me, tell me, *tell* me!'

'No, Lizzy, it's not because of you or your mother,' I said, and even to my ears I sounded tired and defeated. 'That's all done with. But yes, I am going to kill someone. For money. A lot of money.' A long pause, then I went on, 'That's what I do. That's my job, killing for money. Do you understand what I'm saying? I *kill*.'

The reaction I expected – a cry of horror, revulsion, maybe a rebuttal – never came. On the contrary what I heard sounded very much like a chuckle.

'I know you do, my love,' she said, and in a tone so tender and full of loving that my sense of shock was instantly dissipated. 'I know *all* about you.'

My silence was longer this time as I came to terms with her declaration. Finally, though, all that remained was to say goodbye.

So I said 'Goodbye, Lizzy,' and tapped the red bar to terminate the call.

Back to my packing, only now my actions were no longer precise and leisurely. I tossed items of clothing into the suitcase any old how. I had to leave, and fast, before my heart overruled my head.

The cell phone summoned me again, and in my mind there was an imperative in its tone.

I couldn't bring myself to switch it off, so I left it on the bed and walked out and down the stairs, away from its summons. I went out onto the terrace, to sit by the pool and try to restore order to my emotions. Water has always been good therapy for me. The sun was peeping from behind clouds that resembled scraps of torn cloth. Daffodils were pushing through, spring's advance guard, making no concessions to the snow that still carpeted tracts of hillside.

This would be my premier visit to Florence. I was even looking forward to it. A city stuffed with Renaissance works of art, birthplace of Dante and Machiavelli. An opportunity to improve my mind, no matter that the purpose was to kill a man. The contract had been offered as an olive branch, in atonement for the death of the de Bruins. No pay, despite what I had told Lizzy. Just peace of mind. Just life instead of death. To refuse would be to take on the dogs of retribution. And they were large fierce dogs, many to my one.

In time I returned to my packing. No more calls came. Only an accusing silence and the sense of an unseen presence that I was sure would be still be here, waiting for me, when I came home.

END

Read the next volume of the André Warner series

ANDRÉ WARNER, MANHUNTER– VOLUME III

THE MAN
WHO
HUNTED
HIMSELF

**will be published later this year
as an eBook on
amazon.co.uk, amazon.com, and amazon.ca
and smashwords
at £3.99 – $4.99 – C$5.99
And in paperback B-format at £7.99**

READ ON ...

Andre Warner is a former operative of the British Secret Service, turned contract killer. He kills bad guys and only bad guys. His next victim will be his forty-fifth.

An approach by Robert Heider, an American racketeer, whose elder brother, Jeff, was assassinated two years previously, seems routine enough at first sight. Heider is resolved to avenge his brother's death, as are Jeff Heider's son, Nick, and his nephew, Robert, who together with Robert Heider, control a Houston and Las Vegas-based business empire. Despite exhaustive enquiries, Heider Sr. has been unable to identify the assassin and is willing to pay Warner a $1 million fee to find and execute the man responsible.

This kind of assignment is Warner's meat and drink. Killing one of his own kind doesn't trouble him. On the contrary, he welcomes the challenge of pitting his skills against another professional. Unfortunately it's not as straightforward as that. A complication arises that he can see no way around. Nor is walking away from the contract the answer.

Reluctantly, he agrees to go ahead. The customary fifty per cent of the fee is paid over, and he flies to Las Vegas, ostensibly to glean information from Jeff Heider's stunning widow, Maura. If seduction is required to win her over, he will take this hardship in his stride too. However, making enquiries will only be going through the motions, putting on an act to keep the Heider's satisfied. In reality he must find a fall guy for the killing, which itself presents a further problem: to meet Warner's moral code of conduct the fall guy must himself be on the wrong side of the law, ideally a killer.

In Las Vegas, with Maura Heider proving receptive to his advances and unexpectedly falling for him, the enormity of the challenge becomes apparent. As his relationship with

Maura arouses the suspicions of the Heider family, and the net tightens around him, he has only two choices - fight or run. Or maybe there's a third option ...

This is how it begins ...

The girl was alone and the four guys had backed her into a corner. The way it was shaping up they were hell bent on rape.

Standing in the forecourt of the filling station, I watched the scenario unfold behind the glass front of the brightly-lit office. The guys were too preoccupied with their intentions to notice me. The girl was gutsy all right. No yelling her head off, no cringing at their feet. In her right hand a large pair of scissors, wielded dagger fashion. She wasn't going to surrender her virtue without a fight.

The guys were young and uniformly dressed in jeans and windbreakers. Their taunts came to me through the glass, though my Spanish wasn't good enough to translate them all. One, possibly the ringleader, was wearing an olive green baseball cap back to front; fists on hips, his whole stance reflecting his arrogance. Even as I took an uncertain step forward, another of the group produced a switchblade knife, taunting the girl with it. She subsided against the wall, her bravado tested to its limit.

Noble dragon slayer I was not. For starters, could I take on four young thugs and come through without serious injury? For seconds, however this ended up it was likely the Guardia Civil would be dragged in, and I had good reason to stay clear of the law and all its works.

Consequently I hesitated. Until the girl did finally cry out when they wrested the scissors from her, and the ringleader flicked a slap at her face that was audible from the forecourt. A sense of ignominy thrust me forward. When I opened the door to the sound of ripping of clothing, nobody heard me. By then the girl was down on the floor, making sobbing noises, and they were stooping over her, pumped up and cawing with excitement, egging each other on.

So I announced myself.

'Buenos tardes, señora, señores!'

ANDRÉ WARNER, MANHUNTER –
Volume IV

SHE KILLS

To be published in 2017